BLOOD
OF
EDEN

Also by Tami Dane:

"Werewolves in Chic Clothing"
In
The Real Werewives of Vampire County

BLOOD
OF
EDEN

TAMI DANE

KENSINGTON PUBLISHING CORP.
http://www.kensingtonbooks.com

KENSINGTON BOOKS are published by

Kensington Publishing Corp.
119 West 40th Street
New York, NY 10018

ISBN-13: 978-0-7582-6709-2
ISBN-10: 0-7582-6709-6

First Mass Market Printing: December 2011

10 9 8 7 6 5 4 3 2 1

Printed in the United States of America

Acknowledgments

I owe a sincere thank-you to a great many people for the help and support they gave me while writing this book. First I'd like to thank my wonderful agent, Natasha Kern, for her enthusiasm and dedication. I'd also like to thank my editor, Audrey, for seeing the potential in this story and giving me the opportunity to experience the joy of writing it. I'd also like to thank the many people who read and critiqued the opening chapters, as well as my wonderful beta readers, April and KB. And finally I'd like to thank my husband and children for the encouragement and enthusiasm they've shown for this story, as well as their patience, as I sat at my desk hour, upon hour, staring at my computer screen and lost in my head.

Thank you all.

Man can believe the impossible, but can never believe the improbable.

—Oscar Wilde

I

Rotten eggs and sulphur. Oh, the sweet stench of home.

The gray cloud of *parfum d'sewer* rolled out of my apartment door as I juggled my keys, two mocha lattes—heavy on the whipped cream—and bagels. Standing in the hallway, I shouted, "Is it safe to come in, or do I need my gas mask?"

That was not a rhetorical question. My roommate, Katie Lewis, was playing with chemicals again. And I was guessing this morning's experiment was an epic failure.

She'd converted our kitchen into a chem lab last year. Made sense, since neither of us cooked food. Since then, I've learned to live with safety gear at the ready, at all times. Splash goggles. Gas mask. Fire extinguisher. Fabric deodorizer. It goes without saying, *Casa* Skye/Lewis isn't the average home of a couple of grad students. But every now and then, having a chemist at my beck and call, 24-7, came in handy. Especially now that Mrs. Heckel in 2B has stopped reporting us to the DEA. We've been raided twice.

"Sloan?" Katie was sporting her everyday wear—apron, goggles, heavy rubber gloves . . . and slippers with stuffed Albert Einstein heads on the tops. It wasn't a look every girl could pull off, but she did—and still managed to look cute. If she wasn't such a sweetheart, I might have hated her for it. "Did you happen to get cream cheese? We're out."

"Sure did." Taking my cue from Katie, who wasn't wearing her gas mask, I hurried inside and shut the door. "Whew, whatever you just blew up reeks. Do you have the exhaust fan going?"

Grimacing, Katie waved a hand in front of my face. "Yeah. The smoke should clear up in a few minutes. Sorry." She slid her goggles to the top of her head and swiped one of the coffees from the cardboard tray.

"Did you figure out what went wrong this time?"

"Not a thing. It was supposed to do that." Katie took a slurp and smacked her lips. "Mmm, good coffee. They used just the right amount of chocolate this time. Not too little, not too much."

"Good." After I set my coffee and the bag of bagels on the coffee table, which served double duty as our dining table, I headed straight back to my room. I checked the clock on my nightstand. It was a twenty-eight-minute drive to the FBI Academy. That left me exactly four minutes to finish getting ready.

"Are you geeked about your big day?" Katie hung back, standing just outside my bedroom as I rushed around, digging out my laptop case and tossing the essentials into it. Pens, notebook, spare change, cell phone, Netbook.

"I can't tell you how nervous I am." I sighed. "I gotta pee again. This is the third time in an hour. I swear, I have the bladder of a sixty-year-old mother of twelve."

"I'm so excited for you!" As I shuffled past her, toward the bathroom, Katie caught my shoulders and gave them a quick shake. "My best friend's working for the freaking FBI. You'll tell me absolutely everything, right?"

"Sure, I'll tell you everything that isn't classified." I dashed into the bathroom and took care of my personal issue, hoping I wouldn't get the urge to go again in the next three minutes.

"Call me later," Katie yelled through the door.

"Will do." I dropped a throwaway toothbrush into my

purse, zipped it shut, and, heading out into the hall, scooped up the laptop bag I'd left next to the door. Racewalking across the living room, I slung my bag over my shoulder and grabbed my lukewarm mocha latte and a dry bagel while on the way to the exit. "Don't burn the place down while I'm gone." Before heading out, I doused myself in Febreze.

Katie pushed her goggles in place and headed toward the kitchen. "You have nothing to worry about."

I'd heard that before, exactly one minute before the last explosion. And the one before that. What can I say? We both like to live a little dangerously.

With not even a second to spare, I yanked open the door and almost crashed into my mother, her hand raised to knock. She was wearing her threadbare hot pink bathrobe—and God only knew what underneath. Two different shoes poked out from beneath the ratty hem, and her hair—today it was the shade of a new penny—looked like it had been styled with an eggbeater. A huge suitcase sat next to her feet, and an unlit joint as thick as my thumb was protruding from the corner of her mouth.

Nothing new there.

I grinned, plucked the joint out of her mouth, and dropped it into my purse. "Hi, Mom. What a pleasant surprise."

"Honey, I need your help. The power's out in my building again and the landlord says it's my fault. He's exaggerating, of course."

"Of course," I echoed.

"It's not my fault the building's wiring is outdated. I was just trying—"

"It's okay, Mom. You can stay with us until it comes back on." I gave her a peck on the cheek and handed her my coffee as I hurried past. "I'm sorry, I've gotta go. It's my first day with the FBI. There's bagels inside. Your favorite. I'll call you later." After ditching the contraband in the scraggly shrubs next to the building's main entry, I sprinted out to my car, my laptop case bruising my hip and my empty stomach rumbling. I hit my mom's landlord's phone number on my cell, programmed on speed dial, prepared to give the usual "it'll never happen again" speech.

I'd already handled my mother's little problem and was in the middle of an emergency handbag repair—making creative use of a couple of paper clips and a broken pencil—when my new boss, Special Agent Murphy, finally emerged from his office. "There's been a mistake," he informed me. "We won't be able to use you this summer. . . ."

Of course, there's a problem. There always is. The question is, what can I do—

"We've selected another intern. . . ."

Another intern?

"I'm sorry." Murphy scowled and glanced down at his cell phone. "Excuse me for just a moment."

I should have known it was too good to be true. But after two decades of dreaming and studying and hoping, I—Sloan Skye, the only offspring of a schizophrenic philosopher-self-proclaimed inventor and delusional biology professor—wanted to believe I'd landed the internship of my dreams. I didn't expect it to blow up in my face my first day on the job.

As I struggled to recover from the bomb that Agent Murphy had just lobbed my way, Gabe Wagner—who should have been doing grunt work for some senator in DC, not anywhere near the FBI Academy in Quantico, Virginia—came strolling by.

That was it; I knew exactly what had happened. His internship had fallen through, so somebody had pulled a fast one on me.

Again.

As a few choice expressions played through my mind—all of them involving specific anatomical parts and physically impossible actions—I gave Gabe, my frenemy since freshman year, a blindingly bright smile. "Hey, Gabe, does this mean the dream job with the Waste Management Department is still open?"

"No, I'm pretty sure that one's been filled. Sorry." Looking as evil as ever, Gabe sauntered within reach, but I resisted the urge to snap his neck like a toothpick. "Why? Were you interested in applying?" Lucky for him, I possessed an iron will, an allergy to prison air, and—I'd never admit this to Gabe—I secretly enjoyed our little verbal tussles. They made life interesting. "If you're really hard up, I could ask my dad to pull a few strings, get you an interview at the meatpacking plant in Baltimore."

Argh! Animal guts gives me hives.

"Gee, thanks. I'd love to spend my summer elbow deep in pig intestines, but I'd hate to impose. I'm sure Senator Wagner has more important things to do, like slip his pet pork barrel projects into the latest bill the Senate's debating. You never know, that nineteen-million-dollar study on cow flatulence might solve the energy crisis someday."

Murphy returned, giving each of us a bland look. "Good morning, Mr. Wagner. I'll be with you in just a moment, if you'll wait over there." He motioned toward a grouping of chairs a few feet away, next to a table with a coffeepot, cups, and a mug full of primary-colored swizzle sticks. Once Gabe was out of my reach, Murphy turned to me. "Miss Skye, I tried to call you this morning, after I discovered the administrative error, but it was too late. We're looking into something else for you. I'll give you a call as soon as I know something."

Translation: Don't call us. We'll call you.

"Thanks, Agent Murphy." I fought to look cheery, but I knew I wouldn't fool anyone, especially Gabe. I was, without a doubt, the world's worst actress. In my defense, I don't think even Reese Witherspoon could have pulled this one off.

Feeling a little defeated, I slumped into a nearby chair. It rocked back, almost dumping me on the floor. Not to sound like a pathetic whiner or anything, but this was unbelievably unfair. It's not that I expect life to be one big wonderful world full of happiness and justice for all, but I'd been preparing for this job my entire life. And when I say "entire life," I'm not exaggerating. As I lay in my crib, my mom fed my brain a steady diet of everything from analytic philosophy to quantum physics, a thick joint tucked between her lips and a cloud of pot smoke circling her head like a halo. As a result, not only had I memorized the work of just about every major player in the world of psychology by the time I'd graduated from elementary school—Freud, Jung, Adler, just to name a few—but I could square eighteen digit numbers faster than most people could add two. And I could recite the *Divine Comedy* . . . in Italian. "I'll just mosey on home and wait for your call. Thanks again."

"Good luck with the job hunt." Gabe waved from the coffee stand. "Call me if you want me to hook you up." He had the nerve to actually waggle his eyebrows.

I threw up a little in my mouth.

What a day. Thanks to Gabe, I was not only out of a dream internship but out of a steady paycheck as well. I received an annuity payment every fall, which kept us afloat for the year and helped pay my tuition. I had my dad to thank for that. But I'd promised to pay my mom's landlord a thousand dollars to cover the damage she'd caused. My bank account was on the brink of imploding. How would I pay next month's rent? Electric bill? And, more important, how would I take care of Mom? SSI barely kept a roof over her head, even when she wasn't causing minor catastrophic damage. If I didn't subsidize her pathetic income, she'd end up living under a bridge, smoking marijuana and talking to invisible zombies . . . again.

Damn it!

All of my dreams for the summer—kicking ass and taking

down bad guys, anyone?—were slipping from my grasp. But I have never been the kind to stand in stunned silence and let everything fall apart. I had to do *something*.

But what?

I looked down at my hands, and just like that, I had an idea.

Lucky for me, Gabe was called away to handle some super-important, top-secret intern stuff before I had to throw myself at Murphy's feet and beg for a job. Quickly, before I lost my nerve, I muttered, "In case the other thing doesn't work out, I'm pretty handy with a broom." Sweeping the Behavioral Analysis Unit's offices was better than the alternative.

"Oh?" Murphy glanced at the paper clips in my hands, then at my cheap Prada knockoff purse, its broken strap dangling off a nearby desk like a dead eel.

"And a vacuum," I added, hoping I was making my point clear. For a guy who puzzled together clues on a daily basis, Murphy seemed to be having a hard time getting my drift.

"Yeah." He nodded, glanced at his phone again, and lifted a finger. "Just a minute."

"Sure." I beamed a silent thank-you, hoping I'd soon be the recipient of some good news. Anything, and I mean *a-n-y-t-h-i-n-g,* would be better than last year's summer job, cleaning behind a pack of greasy, belching, middle-aged mechanics who thought the word "wash" had a letter *r* in it and a high-school diploma constituted an advanced degree. I have never been an intellectual snob—it's a lot more fun laughing at people who think they know everything—but come on. There was only so much a girl could take.

I'd been lucky to get that job last year, even with two bachelor's degrees and a master's in the works. And this year, things were even worse. The guy who was sweeping my uncle's garage this summer had a master's degree in mechanical engineering.

I finished up my handbag repair, and was about to tackle the broken chair, which posed a genuine threat to national security, when Murphy returned with a woman who looked like an older version of myself. The agent's dull brown hair, the same shade as mine, had been scraped back from her face and tied into a tight knot at her nape. Her nondescript polyester suit had fashion disaster written all over it, just like mine. And little-to-no makeup enhanced her unextraordinary features—also, sadly, just like mine.

"I think we've found a solution to our problem." Murphy motioned to the woman. "This is Special Agent Alice Peyton. She's chief of a new unit in the FBI, and she could use your help."

Yes, yes, yes, the angels were singing! And I was ready to join them in a lively round of Handel's "Hallelujah Chorus."

I had no idea what kind of work Chief Peyton's unit was involved in; I didn't care. All that mattered was I had a job, and it was within the hallowed halls of the FBI Academy. Gabe hadn't ruined my summer, after all. And dear old mom wouldn't be sharing the overpass with Crazy Connie, the bag lady—who wasn't crazy at all, if you ask me.

Sane has always been a relative term in my world.

I cranked up the wattage of my smile and offered a hand to my soon-to-be boss for the summer. "Sloan Skye."

"Alice Peyton. It's good to have you with us."

"Glad to be here." That was no lie.

Murphy turned my way. "Special Agent Peyton will take care of transferring your paperwork. I hope you have a good summer, Miss Skye."

"I will now. Thank you." I shook his hand.

Chief Peyton motioned toward the elevators. "Let me show you where you'll be working. We're one floor up."

"That would be great. I'll get my things." As I snatched up my purse and laptop case, I caught Gabe's openmouthed gawk. I couldn't help noticing he held a coffee cup in both hands.

Within Gabe's earshot, Chief Peyton said, "I'm hoping you can do more than fetch coffee. Do you have a valid passport?"

Karma was my new best friend.

I tossed Gabe a little smirk. "You mean I'll be traveling with the unit?"

"Of course, Skye. Wherever we go, you go too." Chief Peyton stopped in front of a bank of elevators. "Speaking of which, Skye is an unusual name."

"Yes, I suppose it is, statistically speaking. According to GenealogyToday-dot-com, it was the sixty thousand one hundred eighty-fifth most popular surname in the . . ." *I'm doing it again.* ". . . Sorry, I get a little carried away with statistics sometimes. . . . Um, I was told my father was Scottish."

"I thought he might be. What does he do?" Chief Peyton pushed the elevator's up button.

"Well, my father's dead. He was a professor at the University of Richmond."

"I'm very sorry." When the elevator door opened, Chief Peyton motioned me in first, then followed.

I stepped toward the back of the car. "It's okay. He died when I was young."

She hit the button for the third floor. "I see. He was a professor of . . . ?"

I wondered for a second or two why Chief Peyton seemed to be taking such an interest in a man who'd been dead for more than twenty years. But I quickly shrugged it off as small talk, her way of making me feel more comfortable. "Natural science—specifically, biology." I left out the part about how he'd been shamed into giving up his position at the university after publishing an article arguing for the existence of fictional creatures—vampires, werewolves, ghosts, and goblins, that sort of thing. I was fairly certain that would be low on Chief Peyton's need-to-know list.

"That's very interesting." As the elevator slowly rumbled up to the third floor, Chief Peyton began explaining, "The PBAU is a brand-new unit within the FBI. We'll be handling our first case this week, and we're very fortunate to have you on our team." When the car bounced to a stop, she motioned for me to exit first, then followed me out.

Wondering what the acronym PBAU stood for, I headed straight for the open area where the unit members' desks sat in tidy rows. It was exactly as I'd imagined the Behavioral Analysis Unit, aka BAU, would look. Semitransparent half walls separated a half-dozen identical cubicles from each other. And around the back ran a raised walk, which led to a couple of rooms closed off from the main space. But this wasn't the home of the BAU; it was the *PBAU*. And instead of a bustling room full of busy agents, it was eerily silent.

"I'm very happy to be a part of the team. I'm eager to get started," I said.

"We'll be meeting for our first case review in a few minutes. I want you to join us."

Join them? I almost giggled like a little girl, I got so excited. I never giggled, not even when I was five and I'd built my first robot, using Legos and a few electronic bits I'd "borrowed" from various sources around the house. Mom didn't need that old drill, anyway. Or the toaster. We never ate toast. And the computer . . . it had been useless, outdated, and begging to become spare parts for Heathcliff, my new best friend. "Sure."

My new boss tapped the back of a chair, tucked under a nearby cubicle desk. "This'll be your work space. We'll get you a computer, supplies, and phone by the end of the week."

"I get a desk of my own?" I peered at the inhabitants of the adjoining cubicles, thinking I'd introduce myself, but both had their backs to me.

"Sure. Of course you get a desk," Chief Peyton answered.

"Well, thanks. Don't worry about the computer. I brought my own." I lifted my computer case.

"We'll need to have it checked for security before you can log into our system."

"No problem." I set my case on my desk and unzipped it. "This is great. It's like I'm a permanent part of the team." Trying not to think about the fact that this whole thing sounded too good to be true, I tried the chair out for size. It was a perfect fit.

"Perhaps you will be someday." Chief Peyton patted my shoulder, then announced, loud enough for everyone to hear, "Case review in five minutes. Let's take it up in the conference room."

Scuffling and chatter followed; in less than five, I was introduced to the three other members of the PBAU.

Of course, there was Chief Peyton. Also on the team were Special Agent Jordan Thomas, Special Agent Chad Fischer, the media liaison, and Special Agent Brittany Hough, the computer specialist/techie geek. They had all transferred to the PBAU from other units. That meant I was the only clueless newbie. Each greeted me with a friendly smile and a handshake.

Finally, with the introductions over, we all took our seats. Standing in front of a whiteboard, Fischer taped up a color photograph of a dead body. Fischer launched into his presentation. "The Baltimore PD is asking for our help solving a suspected murder case. At this point, all indicators are pointing to a nonmortal suspect. . . ."

Did he just say "nonmortal"? No way.

". . . Bite wounds on the victim's neck suggest we may be looking for a vampiric predator. . . ."

Vampiric?

". . . It's too early to say what the cause of death is, but local law enforcement doesn't want to wait. The media's hot to cover the story, and they can't be held off for long."

Had Chief Peyton known all along who my father was and what he'd researched?

No. Okay, maybe. Crazier things have happened.

". . . It appears to be a single vampire killing, blitz attack. We don't know much, but one thing is certain. This unknown subject—unsub—won't stop until we catch him."

They all looked at me.

What were they expecting? Should I have whipped out a wooden stake and led the charge, yelling, "Die, you blood-sucking bastard"?

My phone, set on vibrate, started buzzing.

"Skye, what are your thoughts?" Chief Peyton asked.

"Well . . ." Lucky me, not only was my mother calling, asking me to solve another crisis, no doubt, but it also seemed I'd just been dubbed the FBI's Buffy the Vampire Slayer. There was only one problem. My mother had taught me plenty—Latin, vector integral calculus, quantum physics. For some silly reason, though, she'd eschewed vampire psychology and comparative biology of shape-shifters.

I didn't know a Sasquatch from a yeti.

When no coherent response came from my direction, Chief Peyton turned back to Fischer. "I agree. If the unsub is a young vampire on a feeding frenzy, there will be more. And soon."

Vampire. They were actually thinking this crime was the act of a vampire?

Again, I should've known it was too good to be true. This had to be some kind of joke. A freaking brilliant, absolutely hilarious one. Gabe Wagner was behind this. It had his name written all over it.

"Not only must we profile our killer's personality, but also his species," Chief Peyton said.

Species? God, this was good. Anytime now, one of Gabe's

friends was going to pop out of a corner and shout, "You've been punked!" Then everyone was going to laugh, including me. And then I'd be escorted to my real boss, and I'd find out I don't get a nice desk and my own computer and phone, but rather a rusty old file cabinet, a yellow legal pad, and that crappy broken chair, shoved into a supply closet.

"Excellent point," Fischer said. "The being's physical characteristics will influence his behavior as much as psychological factors."

Yep, any minute now . . .

My phone, sitting in my lap, started vibrating against my leg.

Gabe?

No. Mom again.

I ignored the call and played along with Peyton's game, nodding at the appropriate moments, raising eyebrows, and scribbling notes on the pad of paper that I'd dug out of my laptop case.

Very interesting. The body had bite marks on the neck.

Oh, yes. Fang marks were most definitely a sign of a vampire attack.

It appeared blood was missing from the victim's body, but if so, the body hadn't been completely drained.

Hmm. "Perhaps the unsub had been interrupted midfeeding. *Cena interruptus,*" I offered.

Everyone concurred with a nod.

Okay, this practical joke was stretching on too long. I leaned back and tried to peer around the corner. I didn't see any sign of Gabe or his posse. Where was he? This had to be a joke. It couldn't be real.

I checked my phone, thinking maybe I'd missed his call. Nope. Nobody had called but my mother.

At the end of Fischer's presentation, the team members stood, each one giving me a look as they filed out of the room. Finally Chief Peyton walked to my side of the table, pulled the chair out next to me, and sat down. "We'd like you to come with us."

"You would."

"To Baltimore. We'll be leaving in just over an hour."

"Oh. Um, I don't know." I am so rarely struck completely mute, but this situation had done just that. There were so many questions clogging my brain, I couldn't think.

"This case is local, but I should mention, every member of my team has to keep a 'go bag' with them at all times, stocked with the basics—a couple changes of clothes, toothbrush, makeup, hairbrush—"

"Excuse me, but what exactly does PBAU stand for?" I asked.

"Paranormal Behavioral Analysis Unit. Like the BAU, the mission of the PBAU is to provide behavioral-based investigative support to local FBI field offices. Unlike the BAU, the cases we are called to assist with all involve acts of violence that have some tie to the unknown, the paranormal, or the occult."

Seriously?

I couldn't help asking, "You don't really believe there are Edward Cullens running around, chomping people in the neck. Do you?"

"Not the kind of vampires you see in movies, no. Of course not." Finally this very sensible-looking woman was saying something reasonable. I pulled in a lungful of air and let it out slowly. "I have yet to see a vampire that sparkles," she added, looking dead serious. "Now, come on, I'll tell you more in the car. I thought we'd all drive together. It'll give us a chance to discuss the case." She checked her wristwatch. "Time's tight. We need to get going. Sunset's a few minutes after nine tonight." Not waiting for me, she headed for the conference room door.

I followed her. "Is it too dangerous to be outside after dark?"

"We'd like to get as much time as possible at the crime scene during daylight hours. It's hard to see after sunset."

Why did I feel like I'd just said something totally stupid? "Gotcha."

She waved Jordan Thomas over. As I'd noticed earlier, he was the closest to my age. Fischer and Chief Peyton were older, thirties, maybe early forties. I'd noticed another thing about him too—he wasn't hard on the eyes. He had nice . . . glasses. "JT, I need you to give Skye a rundown of our policies and procedures before we leave."

"Sure, Chief."

Chief Peyton tapped my arm and looked me straight in the eyes. "Are you with us, Skye?"

That was the fifty-thousand-dollar question, wasn't it?

The way I saw it, I had two options: either forget about an internship with the FBI, and let my mom down; or chase imaginary monsters.

When I looked at it that way, spending three months profiling vampires and werewolves couldn't be any worse than emptying Porta-Potties in the county parks. And that I'd done, for more summers than I cared to remember.

I shrugged. "Sure. I'm in."

I would rather live in a world where my life is surrounded by mystery than live in a world so small that my mind could comprehend it.

—Harry Emerson Fosdick

2

"According to Wikipedia, a vampire feeds on a mortal being's life essence, which is most often defined as blood," Fischer recited as Chief Peyton navigated her black government-issue Suburban through thick Baltimore traffic.

Chief Peyton flipped on her turn signal and changed lanes, somehow defying the rules of geometry by wedging the huge vehicle into a space the size of a Chevy Volt. "I think we all know this. But I suppose I'd better ask, since this is the team's first case, does anyone *not* have a rudimentary grasp of vampire legend?"

Riding shotgun, I raised my hand, hoping I wouldn't be the only one. About a half minute later, I learned I was. And I couldn't help laughing at the irony. Throughout all my years in school, *that* had never happened. Not even after skipping one grade in elementary school, one in middle school, another in high school, and starting college at the age of fifteen. For the first time in my life, I didn't know something that everyone else did.

I was both amused and mortified.

If Chief Peyton was disappointed in my lack of knowledge of supernatural beings, she hid it well. "I guess we'll start from the top, then." She pointed at the file sitting on my lap. "Skye, you'll need to review everything in that file. I hope you're a fast reader."

"I am," I assured her.

"Excellent. Fischer, continue."

Sitting directly behind Chief Peyton, Fischer read from a book. "'While ancient cultures all had some form of vampire-like creatures within their legend systems, the being most commonly associated with the word vampire has roots in eighteenth century Eastern European lore. This being is commonly described as ruddy or purple-ish in color, bloated—'"

"Not skeletal and pale, like Bram Stoker's Dracula? Sorry for interrupting," I interjected, somewhat confused by the difference between the vampire I was vaguely familiar with and the one Fischer was describing. I'd caught maybe twenty minutes of *Dracula* playing on television one Halloween. To say my exposure to vampire legend was limited was a gross understatement.

"Don't apologize. You're a part of this team for a reason, and I want you to keep asking questions. Questions lead to answers. Or, in some cases, more important questions." After a beat, Chief Peyton continued as she cut across three lanes of traffic to exit onto I-295. "The type of creature you're describing is what we'd call the contemporary vampire. It's an adaptation of older vampire legend. Fischer, could you please give Skye the book you're reading?"

"Sure." Fischer handed the heavy hardcover to me.

"I understand. But I have to ask, aren't there living, breathing, *mortal* people who think they're vampires? Or pretend to be vampires? And if so, couldn't this murder have been committed by a human being with an unusual fetish?"

Chief Peyton nodded. "Sure. Our job is to develop a profile that local agents and police personnel can use to eliminate suspects. While we're talking as if it's a given the unsub is a vampire, until we have enough information to make a clear determination, we will not set our minds on any one possibility."

"Got it." I set the case file on top of the book and flipped it open. The very first thing I found was a photograph of the victim, a woman, lying with arms and legs askew, on a sidewalk. Like every dead person I'd ever had the misfortune of seeing, she looked like a mannequin. It was hard to guess her age, but I estimated her at about thirty-five. Judging from her clothes, hairstyle, and level of skin wrinkling, she appeared to be older than me but younger than my mother. Her mouth was slightly open, eyes staring blindly. Her clothing was still in place, shoes on her feet, hair slightly mussed. Overall, she looked like she'd simply collapsed and died of natural causes.

Except there were those puncture marks on her neck.

"The wounds were made before she died." JT, who'd been inhabiting the seat directly behind mine, leaned over my shoulder. He indicated the redness around the injury. "See here, she bled. Dead people don't bleed."

"Yeah. No heartbeat, no circulation." I leaned to the side, a smidge uneasy by how close he was. With his shaggy brown hair, dark eyes, razor-sharp cheekbones, and adorable dimples, he was a little too good-looking for my comfort. He also smelled really nice. Normally, this wouldn't be a problem. But I was an intern. He was an agent. That made him strictly off-limits to me, and me to him.

Reading my body language, he sat back. "Didn't mean to crowd you."

"It's okay." I shifted in my seat and stared down at the file on my lap. My cheeks were burning, which wasn't good. But I knew he couldn't see them, since he was still sitting behind me. When I was almost positive my cheeks weren't the color of the traffic light we were stopped at, I twisted, facing the back of the vehicle. "I'm a little overwhelmed. I didn't expect to be hitting the road my first day, profiling a murderer. I mean, I'm just an intern. I assumed I'd be filing paperwork and fetching coffee."

Fischer, busy reading the rest of the documents in the case file, responded to my confession with a quick smile.

JT leaned forward, elbows resting on his knees. The seat was big and cushiony, but he was bulky enough to make it look small. The guy obviously spent some serious time in the gym. "Since this is our first case, we're all a little overwhelmed. And excited. We have a lot to prove."

"Are you new to the FBI?" I asked him.

"To the FBI, sort of. I was a field agent, low on the food chain. I've only been out of the academy a year, not long enough to apply to the BAU. When I heard about the PBAU, though, I knew it was the place for me. Luckily, the qualifications aren't as strict." He motioned for me to come closer and whispered, "I think they're having a hard time staffing the unit. Most of the agents in the bureau—the ones that know about it—think it's a joke."

"I did too . . . kind of."

JT nodded, his expression clear of any anger or defensiveness. "None of us would have taken it personally if you'd said, 'Thanks, but no thanks' to Peyton's offer. We know we're neck deep in *The X-Files* territory, risking ridicule. But we're all determined to do our best and hopefully save lives by helping local authorities get killers off their streets, whether they end up being homicidal vampires, psychotic werewolves, or sociopathic mortals."

I liked this guy. "A noble cause, for sure," I said.

"The cases we'll be taking are the ones no other units want to touch. For the victims of these crimes, we are their voice." After a moment, he pointed at the photograph on his lap. "Notice anything else?"

"No. Did I miss something?" I opened my file and stared at the picture.

"Look again. A good profiler will pay attention to every minute detail."

Slightly bothered by the fact that I wasn't catching everything I should, I concentrated, starting at the upper left corner of the image and moving across the photo slowly enough to give my mind time to register everything I saw. I scrutinized the woman's hair, eyes, face, neck, shoulders, the patch of cement sidewalk beneath her. "There's no blood on the sidewalk."

JT lifted the photo and pointed at the dry area just under her neck. "She stopped bleeding before she collapsed."

"Did that mean she was already dead when she was placed here?"

"Good question." He handed me a pencil and pocket-sized notebook. "You'll want to make some notes for yourself, so you'll remember to ask the right questions when we're at the crime scene."

"Thanks."

He set his hand on my headrest. "We're in this together. We all want the same thing—to do our jobs and do them well. And I know, once you get your feet beneath you, you're going to be a valuable member of this team."

"Thanks."

JT's words echoed in my head during the rest of the drive as I read *The Vampire Encyclopedia* and then scoured each document in the file, looking for clues. By the time we'd made it to the crime scene, I knew the basics about every vampire legend in the world, from the West African Asasabonsam to the Greek Vrykolakas. I was ready to prove to my new coworkers, and myself, that criminal profiling was the perfect job for me.

This was *not* the job for me.

I swallowed. At least a dozen times. I breathed through my

mouth and closed my eyes. I concentrated on taking slow, deep breaths. And still, I couldn't stop it. I puked. In front of Chief Peyton, as well as the other members of the PBAU, and the local FBI contact, and a whole passel of Baltimore's finest men in blue.

Little had I known, but getting up close and personal with a recently deceased person was not the same as seeing one that had its hair done, makeup on, and was posed in an appropriately peaceful manner, snug in a coffin.

I was ready to crawl back in the Suburban and die of embarrassment.

Chief Peyton was nice enough to compliment me for not contaminating the crime scene. Then, kind soul that she was, she suggested I accompany JT in interviewing a witness who claimed to have seen the victim collapse. The witness was standing at least twenty feet away.

After doing what I could to eliminate all signs of my shamefully weak moment, I headed in the direction Chief Peyton had indicated, quickly locating the pair.

JT greeted me with a nod before turning back to the witness. "This is Sloan Skye."

The witness, a woman wearing a dress at least four decades old, turned bloodshot eyes my way, giving me a quick assessing glance before looking back at JT.

"Can you tell us what you saw, Mrs. Zumwalt?" JT asked.

"*Miss* Zumwalt," the witness corrected, her wispy gray hair whipping into disarray as an almost imperceptible breeze blew through it. "I saw a woman walking from that direction." She pointed a shaking hand toward a tall redbrick building hidden by a small grouping of trees. "I was going this way, toward Centre Street. I collect the cans and bottles people throw into the street. You know, just doing my part, keeping the city clean. . . ." Her words trailed off, and her eyelids slid over her eyes.

"Miss Zumwalt," I asked, "what happened next?"

Miss Zumwalt's eyes snapped open. Looking a little confused, she glanced around. "Oh. Yes. Where was I?" Her hands disappeared into her pockets.

"You saw a woman. Coming this way." JT pointed toward the redbrick building.

Miss Zumwalt fingered her mouth. "Yeah. She came from that way. We passed each other here, at the intersection. A few seconds later, after I turned the corner, I heard something behind me. A dull thump like a heavy sack being dropped. When I turned around, she was lying on the ground, just like she is now."

JT scratched some notes in his notebook. "Then you didn't see the victim fall?"

"No, I guess I didn't." The witness swayed slightly. She blinked in slow motion.

Swaying. Slow reflexes. Bloodshot eyes. Shaking hands. Was this witness credible? Regardless of my doubts, I took notes on both what the woman said and what she did.

I asked, "Did you happen to notice if the woman was bleeding as she walked toward you?"

Miss Zumwalt's forehead crinkled into deep grooves. "Bleeding? No. But . . . now that I think about it, she didn't look right."

"In what way?" JT asked.

"She was kinda pale. And I think she was sweating. With this cold snap—it was downright chilly this morning, for June—and dressed the way she was, she should have been cold, not hot."

I jotted, *sweating, pale.* "Did you see her carrying anything? A purse?" I asked, recalling the one useful detail I'd retained from the crime scene.

"No." The woman paused. Nodded. "I take that back. Yes. She had a purse."

"What did it look like?" JT scribbled more notes.

"Brown." Miss Zumwalt tapped her chin, then shook her

head. "I'm sorry. That's all I remember. The bag couldn't have been big. That would have stood out. But it was big enough for me to see it. So, I'm guessing medium and brown. Or maybe it was black." The witness sighed. "I don't remember. I looked at her face, not her purse."

"It's okay. You're doing fine," I reassured her. The details the woman had been able to give us were remarkable, especially considering her state. I had a sneaking suspicion she existed on a primarily liquid diet, and it wasn't coming from the local soup kitchen. I'd seen my share of hard lifetime alcoholics to recognize one when I saw it. "Did you hear anything? Gunfire? A struggle?"

Miss Zumwalt shook her head again. "No gunfire. I would've ducked for cover if I'd heard a gun."

"Okay. Thank you for answering our questions." JT flipped to a fresh page in his notebook. "Do you have a phone number where we can reach you if we have any more questions?"

Miss Zumwalt's eyes brightened. She ran a hand over her mussed hair, catching a thin tendril and curling it around her finger. "No, but you can always find me at St. Edith's during lunchtime. They serve the best soup. Maybe you'd like to join me sometime?" She gave poor JT a coquettish smile.

"Thank you for the invitation, but I'm afraid I can't. It's against agency rules." JT glanced at me. "Do you have any other questions, Skye?" I shrugged. I couldn't think of any. "Thank you again, Miss Zumwalt. You've been very helpful."

"I hope you catch whoever killed that nice woman. It's terrible of me to say this, but I'm grateful it wasn't me. You never know if you'll be in the wrong place at the wrong time. I'm thinking I almost was today, just like my friend Lulu." She made the sign of the cross over her chest. "God rest her soul." The fear in Miss Zumwalt's eyes couldn't be missed. "Lulu was buying some cigarettes in a 7-Eleven when it was robbed. Bastards shot her. For no reason."

Again, I could relate. Once, years ago, I was almost mugged on campus. A man came out of nowhere and grabbed me. I had no idea what he was going to do. Luckily, a campus security officer saw it. He dashed to my rescue, and the man ran off. I'd never felt so helpless, vulnerable, or terrified before.

"We're going to do our best to help the police catch whoever did this. I promise." I wrote down St. Edith's, and JT and I started back toward the rest of the team. I saw Chief Peyton talking to the local FBI field office liaison. Agent Fischer was talking to a couple of Baltimore police officers.

"I wasn't sure about that witness when we started," I admitted before we were within earshot of the other agents. I didn't mention Miss Zumwalt's obvious flirting, figuring JT probably dealt with that kind of thing all the time. He clearly knew how to handle it.

JT nodded. "It's probably alcohol. But she gave us some good details. I wish she'd seen the victim collapse."

I chewed on my pencil eraser as I reread my notes. "The purse was a good catch. I don't remember seeing the victim's handbag. Maybe it was a robbery. Or she could have collapsed. Miss Zumwalt thought she might have been ill." I took a quick glance around. "This doesn't look like the best neighborhood. Someone could have stolen her handbag after she passed out."

"The witness saw no blood. That would suggest the bite was an old wound."

I stood next to a parked police car, intentionally positioning myself so I couldn't see the body. "Not necessarily. Puncture wounds don't always bleed, or if they do, they don't bleed for long."

"Sure, but a puncture striking the jugular?"

I shrugged. "Could have missed the major blood vessels."

"I guess it's possible." JT stared over my shoulder, in the general direction of the dead body.

I cleared my throat. "I think I'll go find Chief Peyton, ask her what she'd like me to do next."

"Sure." JT gave me a knowing smile. "It gets easier, Skye. I promise. The first body's the worst."

"Thanks." I swear, I was so embarrassed my cheeks were hot enough to melt lead. I'd hoped he hadn't seen me throw up. So much for that.

JT, bless him, didn't say another word about my weak stomach. "The ME's here. Before I talk to him, I want to double-check and see if a purse has been found. We need to identify our victim."

"Has her car been located?" I asked.

"Probably not, but we can check the meters and run the plates of any cars parked at the ones that are expired."

"What about a bus?"

"Looks like there's a stop back there, so that's a possibility. I'll be looking at maps of the area later, once we've finished up here."

I took one sweeping look around, at the old brick and concrete multistory structures crowded together. There had to be hundreds of people in the neighboring buildings. Which one had the victim been headed for when she'd died? And why had the killer chosen this location for the crime?

The traffic wasn't heavy, but it wasn't light either. And there were pedestrians walking around, people gathering at the bus stop, businesspeople walking to and from cars. It was a busy intersection, the meeting of not two but three roads. Behind me sat a homeless shelter; in front, some kind of large, sprawling building. To the left and right were a deli, beauty salon, and church. To me, it seemed like a very risky place to jump someone.

As I approached Chief Peyton, I overheard part of the conversation she was having with Agent Nelson from the Baltimore FBI field office.

Nelson was saying, "There haven't been any similar deaths

reported, that I'm aware of. That's why we couldn't get the BAU in here. The locals don't think it's an FBI case."

"You don't agree?" Chief Peyton asked as she gave me a slight nod, signaling for me to stay put and listen.

Nelson added, "Something just doesn't sit right with me. I'm hoping you'll get to the bottom of it."

"We're going to do our best." Chief Peyton's phone rang, and she glanced down at it, smiling. "Just a minute." When Nelson acknowledged her with a nod, she stepped aside, out of both his earshot and mine, and flipped open the phone to answer.

That left me standing next to an agent I didn't know, an agent who had seen me throw up. I might as well have been wearing a big scarlet letter *N* for "Newbie" on my chest.

I had no idea what to say. I tried to push aside my discomfort by focusing on the case.

Our job wasn't necessarily to gather evidence; that was the work of the local detectives and agents. We were there to interpret the evidence they uncovered, to determine if a paranormal element was involved in the crime. If there was one, we were to provide a profile of the creature responsible. It was all very *X-Files*.

But, of course, we didn't have a profile yet. So, instead of standing there feeling out of place, I turned to look back in the direction the victim would have come from.

That's when I noticed the sign. The blue rectangle with a capital *H* in white.

"Excuse me, Agent Nelson, but is that a hospital?" I indicated the building on the opposite side of the street.

"Yep. That's Good Samaritan."

Could that be a coincidence? My mother didn't believe in coincidences.

The victim had looked as if she might be sick.

She'd collapsed within eyesight of a hospital.

Seemed like the hospital might be a clue.

I asked, "Has anyone checked to see if our victim was a patient?"

Nelson nodded. "We checked both the ER and the cashier. Nobody fitting the victim's description was seen in the emergency room or clinic. Nor was anyone fitting her description discharged this morning. However, visiting hours start at nine. She could have been visiting a patient."

"I see." I took a few more notes.

Chief Peyton gave my arm a tap, letting me know she was back. "There may not have been another death like this in Baltimore, but there has been one in a town close by. Agent Nelson, the rest of my team will stay here with you and follow up. I'm going to take Skye and see what we can learn from the first victim." She didn't wait for Nelson to respond before she started toward her Suburban. "Hurry up, Skye, we need to pay a visit to the hospital before the victim's body is released to the family."

"Another death?" I echoed, trying to keep up. For a woman who needed three-inch heels to stand eye to eye with me, Chief Peyton sure could move fast. "Do you think we're looking for a serial killer?"

"I don't know yet, but I'm hoping the pathologist can tell us something useful. Let's go."

Many have puzzled themselves about the origin of evil. I am content to observe that there is evil, and that there is a way to escape from it, and with this I begin and end.

—John Newton

3

Hospitals aren't my favorite places. I hate the smell, that cloying combination of antiseptic and blood. The sounds of moaning patients, squeaking shoes, and chirping monitors. Certainly, the sight of fresh blood isn't high on my list of favorite things either.

So, of course, because hospitals make me uneasy, I had to be dragged to the very bowels of one on my first day on the job.

Down in the basement, where patients never tread.

Who would ever think that something surrounded by sand, silt, and clay could be so white? The floors, the walls, and the ceiling of the basement were stark white. The only color breaking the blinding glare were the little signs pointing the way through the maze of identical hallways to such thrilling locations as records. Accounting. And, of course, the morgue. We, however, had no need for the signs. We had a personal escort, a security guard who said very little as he led us to our destination.

I'm guessing I looked a little pale by the time we reached the morgue. Chief Peyton took one look at me and said, "If you'd rather stay outside, I understand."

Bless her.

"However," she continued, "I brought you along for a reason, and I'd like you to at least try to come in."

Urgh.

I'd had one unfortunate episode with a recently deceased person today. Did I really need another one so soon? The answer, of course, was no. But there was this little problem. A job with the FBI, particularly the BAU, was going to involve regular exposure to dead people. Sooner or later, I was going to have to get over the wooziness.

Sooner was definitely better than later.

It was decided; I would go in.

Pulling my lips back in what I hoped was a passing attempt at a smile, I said, "Of course, I'll come in."

"Excellent."

In we went.

The pathologist who had conducted the autopsy was waiting for us, with the body laid out on the metal table, lights fully illuminated. Thankfully, a sheet covered the body from head to toe.

"Thank you for meeting with us." Chief Peyton offered the doctor a hand.

The doctor gave it a shake. "Not a problem. Bob Davis." Dr. Davis looked at me.

"Sloan Skye." Standing as far back as possible, I gave a little wave. "The room's kind of small. I think I'd better stay out of the way."

Dr. Davis nodded and turned his attention back to my boss. I surmised he was used to people reacting the way I had. "I have a Caucasian female, thirty-one years old. This was an interesting case, unique. I don't know exactly what you're looking for, or how it might be tied to your case in Baltimore, but I'm more than happy to share my findings."

Chief Peyton moved a little closer to the table. "Thank you. I'm anxious to see what you discovered."

The doctor uncovered the victim's head, neck, and chest. Even from a distance, the rash covering the woman's upper body was still visible. "This patient died of—"

"Typhoid?" I asked.

"Yes, this patient consumed food or water tainted with the bacterium *Salmonella enterica typhi* and later died from complications," Dr. Davis explained. "Intestinal perforation and encephalitis."

"But what about the puncture wounds on the neck you told me about?" Chief Peyton leaned over the table.

The doctor pointed to the side of the patient's neck farthest from Chief Peyton. "They're located here, just under the right ear. They are odd. Deep and fairly large. Bite wounds, not clean punctures. The skin is torn. But it doesn't appear they played a role in the patient's death. Whatever made them missed the major blood vessels."

"Just like our victim in Baltimore." Feeling okay at the moment, I moved a little closer, to get a look at the wound.

"Had the patient recently traveled out of the country?" Chief Peyton asked.

Dr. Davis picked up a clipboard and skimmed the chart. "The family said she hasn't."

Peyton inspected the rash closer. "And that didn't strike you as odd?"

"Roughly four hundred Americans contract typhoid fever every year," I commented, reciting a statistic I'd read a few years ago.

The doctor gave me a raised-brow look. "That's correct. So, no, it didn't. But what did strike me as odd is why this generally healthy patient, with no underlying health conditions, died from a disease with a relatively low fatality rate. I also question why she wouldn't have seen a doctor before it got to this stage. Treatment is generally successful. It isn't invasive or expensive."

"Did you mention your concerns to her family?" Chief Peyton asked.

Dr. Davis set down the clipboard. "No. I felt it was better to let things be. I know it's difficult accepting loss. Why make it worse by giving the family a reason to wonder if the death might have been prevented?"

Whatever the reason for the woman not seeking medical care, the way I saw it, her death was obviously caused by a pathogen. Not a vampire.

Case closed.

"One more question," Chief Peyton said. "What about blood volume? Was it low?"

Dr. Davis took a look at the chart again. "On the low side of average, no lower than if she'd donated blood the day before."

"Okay. I guess that's it for now. Thank you, Doctor."

He pulled the cover over the body and shook Chief Peyton's hand again. Within a handful of minutes—thank God—we were on our way back to the team's temporary home away from home, a conference room in Baltimore's Central District PD.

We'd just pulled up in front of the building when Chief Peyton's phone rang, pulling me out of the book she'd handed me when we left the hospital, *The Element Encyclopedia of Magical Creatures,* by John and Caitlin Matthews. Fascinating reading, but her phone conversation was more interesting. From her end, I figured something major had happened. I hoped it didn't mean we'd be making another trip to a morgue tonight.

"There's been another death," she told me as she maneuvered the car into a parking spot. My hollow stomach slid to my toes. "The victim has the same wounds on the neck. Another woman. She collapsed in front of a fabric store in Arlington, Virginia."

"A third death?" This couldn't be a coincidence . . . or

could it? Three people dying suddenly, and all displaying what looked like bite marks on the same area of the neck. The odds were incredibly remote, considering the population in the city of Baltimore alone.

The chief didn't cut off the engine. She shifted in her seat, facing me. "You're doing a good job, Skye. You were thrown in the deep end of the pool, but I knew you'd swim okay. You're intelligent and, more important, you have good instincts." She poked an index finger at my forehead. "Trust yourself."

As long as I could remember, I'd been told I was smart, but somehow this was different. This meant more. "Thanks, Chief. I will." My stomach rumbled loudly. Embarrassed, I jerked my arms around my waist.

"I want you to get JT up to speed on what we've learned." Chief Peyton poked at the number pad on her cell phone. "I'm going to call him now and have him take you to get something to eat."

"I am a little hungry." I checked my watch. Eight hours had flown by since I'd walked into the FBI Academy this morning. I hadn't eaten lunch yet, and it was dinnertime. It was no wonder my eyelids felt like they were weighted down with sandbags.

"I need to get going." Chief Peyton lifted her phone to her ear and waved me out. "JT leased a car for the day so the team could split up and get more accomplished. After dinner, he'll drive you back to Quantico, Sloan."

"Great, thanks."

As I scrambled out of the car, she reminded me, "Don't forget your bag."

"Oh, yeah. Thanks." A smidge unsteady on my feet—low blood sugar—I opened the back door and dragged my laptop bag off the backseat. Once I'd set it on the ground, I pulled the telescoping handle out and shut the door. And before Chief Peyton had maneuvered the car out of the parking spot,

I headed toward the police department's entry, my bag's handle in one hand and Chief's book in the other.

When I stepped inside, I found JT standing at the front desk, chatting with the officer on desk duty. I gave him a wilted smile as I dragged my weary self toward him.

He hurried across the lobby. "You look tired."

"I'm okay. Hungry."

"Me too." Proving himself a gentleman, he took my laptop case and together we headed outside. "The car's around the corner." He pointed at a blue Chrysler. "Would you rather eat before heading back to Quantico, or wait?"

"If I wait, I may pass out."

"Not a problem. The boys said the café down the street has good food. Would you rather drive or walk? It's only a block away."

"We can walk. That's fine."

JT reached for my laptop case. "I can throw this in the car—"

"If you don't mind, I'd rather not." I smiled, hoping he wouldn't think I'm crazy for insisting on dragging it around. "Call me paranoid, but I don't like to keep valuables in a car."

"Actually, that's very smart. Can I carry it for you?"

"Only if you insist."

"I insist." JT fell into step beside me, dragging my laptop case behind him.

"Thank you."

We headed into the cute little restaurant. The hostess escorted us to a table tucked in a cozy corner. We ordered sandwiches and drinks. As she scampered off to fill our orders, I rubbed my neck. It was stiff, sore. Thanks to JT, a few other bits of my anatomy were sort of achy too, but in a good way.

"What a weird and fascinating day," I said. "Outside of making an ass out of myself at my first crime scene, I think it went pretty well."

"You didn't make an ass out of yourself."

Despite JT's sincere expression, I wasn't buying that. "Well, I don't think I made a good first impression with the detective," I said, hiding my embarrassment under a chuckle. "Or the rest of the PBAU. Or the Baltimore PD. . . ."

"Hey, every one of them, including Peyton, probably hurled at their first murder scene too."

"Probably." Wondering why I'd even brought that up, I redirected the conversation into safer territory, tried to lighten the mood. "Judging from today, I think this is definitely going to be a summer I'll never forget. Probably more exciting, and disturbing, than the year I worked for a traveling carnival. Let me tell you, I saw some freaky stuff that summer."

"You were a carny?" JT laughed. I liked his laugh. And I liked the way his eyes twinkled when he was laughing. "Hopefully, you didn't see any dead bodies . . ."

". . . with bite marks on their necks?" I finished for him. "No, no dead bodies. Or vampires. Thank God. It wasn't a bad job. Except for the food. And the scary clowns."

"Speaking of shitty summer jobs, one year I was a mascot for a restaurant. I had to wear this ugly dog outfit and stand outside for hours, waving at cars as they drove by. I think I scared more people away than anything. And yes, before you ask, it's hotter than hell in there." JT gave me a funny look, the kind a guy might give a girl on a first date.

I swallowed hard.

As our eyes met, I reminded myself this man was off-limits. Period. It sucked, since I was already beginning to see that JT was not only very good-looking, but also intelligent, easy to talk to, and he seemed to *get* me. There weren't a lot of JTs in the world.

"So," we said in unison. We shared a laugh as the waitress brought our Cokes. Then we apologized, once again, in unison. Finally JT motioned with a wave of his hand for me to speak, and he took a healthy gulp of his cola.

"I guess we should get to work." I pulled my notebook from my back pocket and flipped to the last page. I normally wouldn't have needed to skim my notes; I always remember everything I write down. But my gray matter was a little mushy tonight. "The lady at the hospital died from typhoid fever. The bite played no role in her death." I pointed at him. "Your turn. What did you get?"

"The Baltimore victim's COD, complications from malaria."

"Seriously, malaria? Is the ME sure?"

JT nodded. "We received the initial report just before you rolled in with the chief. It was caught by RDT—rapid diagnostic test. It'll be confirmed with a blood smear later."

The waitress brought our food and hurried away.

I read over my notes as I ate a few bites of my sandwich. "So we have two victims, dead from two different infectious diseases. And so far, the only thing they share in common is a pair of puncture wounds on their necks." That sure didn't sound like a vampire on a rampage to me. But that didn't mean it wasn't weird or suspicious either. "Could this be a bizarre coincidence? Statistically, it seems so improbable, but . . ." But what?

"How many people have you seen today with a pair of puncture wounds on their necks?" JT took another bite of his sandwich. He had a little smear of mustard on his lip. I kept staring at it.

"Two. And they were both dead."

He pointed a fry at me. "Doesn't sound like a coincidence to me."

"Okay, but what are we dealing with then?"

"I don't know. Hopefully, by tomorrow morning, we'll have more information." JT dabbed his face with a napkin. No more smear. But I still kept staring at his mouth.

"That doesn't leave us with much to do tonight," I said, a little sorry the day was coming to an end.

JT pushed his plate away. There wasn't much left on it. "I'm going to head into the office for a while, do some more reading. And I need to take a look at some maps. But I'll probably call it a night before ten."

"Sounds like a plan. Tomorrow's going to be another long day." Sensing that JT was ready to go, I waved at the waitress, who happened to be at a nearby table, and asked her for a box. "Ready to hit the road?"

"Yeah." After I packed what was left of my food into a foam box, JT gave me another one of those looks, the kind both of us had to know he shouldn't be giving me. "It's good having you on the team, Skye."

"It's good being here."

I tried not to think too much about that I-like-you look. Not as we drove home in silence, and I pretended to read *The Element Encyclopedia of Magical Creatures*. Or when I ate the rest of my lunch/dinner at my new desk, my Netbook's screen glaring at my tired eyes. Or when I leaned back in my chair, closed my eyes, and slowly sank into a shallow slumber.

It was in the room with her again. She always knew it was there. The air turned cold and dead, like everything had been sucked out of it. She squeezed her closed eyes harder and silently prayed for it to leave her alone this time.

Why her? What did it want?

A frigid gust drifted over her, making the hairs on her nape stand on end. Goose bumps prickled the skin of her arms, back, and shoulders. The feeling of death was growing stronger. The scent of rotting flesh filled her nostrils and her eyes teared.

Please leave me alone. Please.

Something hard, sharp, scraped down her arm and she shivered.

Please go away. Not again. Oh, God, not again.

Beethoven's Fifth was playing. Somewhere close by.

My phone.

I lurched upright. My eyelids snapped open.

I shook off the memory of that creepy dream. Clearly, this vampire stuff was getting to me.

Hands trembling, heart pounding, and eyes squinting against the light, I rocked forward, shoved my hand in my purse, and dug for my cell phone. After I'd rescued it from the deepest corner, I checked the number and hit the button, answering, "Hey."

"You scared me to death!" Katie yelled into my ear. "Why didn't you call me? Where are you?"

I glanced at the clock on the wall. It was just after eleven, but it felt like it was three in the morning. "It's been a long, long day. You have no idea."

"Well, I hate to break it to you, but it's about to get longer." I couldn't miss the laughter in Katie's voice. "Your mother was disassembling small appliances again."

My stomach twisted into a knot. "What did she do now?"

Nothing is permanent in this wicked world. Not even our troubles.

—Charlie Chaplin

4

I smelled the smoke before I'd reached my apartment door. But that was nothing new. Katie was always burning something. However, as I stumbled inside and shut the door, I was surprised to learn the lights in the living room didn't work. *That* was new.

I dropped my bag by the door and picked my way across the room, toward the kitchen. I successfully maneuvered around a chair and the coffee table, and a basket full of unread magazines. Just when I thought the coast was clear, I slammed into something big and hard, and down I went. Like a bag of rocks. I cracked my head just before I went totally horizontal.

"Shit, that hurt." I lay prostrate on the floor, cradling my pounding head, pretty stars twinkling in the blackness. I blinked a few times, waiting for my head to clear.

Something—sharp—poked my belly.

"Don't move or I'll skewer you like a shish kebab," a voice said. I knew that voice.

Oh, no. Not again.

"Mom, it's me, Sloan." I didn't budge, didn't flex a muscle. Didn't even blink. If my mother was in the throes of a full-on psychotic episode, she could very well live up to her promise. Then I'd end up with an unwanted piercing. A very deep one, at that. When the sharp thing jabbing me in the belly didn't move, I repeated, "Mom, it's Sloan. Why don't you turn on a light and you'll see it's me."

"The lights aren't working." Her hand found my head, ran down my face, fingering my nose. Her sigh of relief was echoed by one of my own. "You have your father's nose. I would know it anywhere." At last, she removed the weapon, and I breathed freely, without worrying a deep inhalation might cause a fatal injury.

"What happened to the lights?" I asked, slowly and carefully sitting up.

"I tried to warn you," Katie called from somewhere to my right.

I turned toward my roommate's voice. "You said she was disassembling a few small appliances."

"Yeah, well, that was before she decided to use the parts to build some crazy contraption, and *plug it in*. She fried the wiring. The power isn't just out in our unit. It's out in the whole building, Sloan."

"How was I to know the transformer from your microwave oven was defective?" my mother snapped, sounding insulted. "It could've caused a fire, you know."

I could imagine her features twisted into her trademark injured look, the one she'd used so many times before with great success. She really did know how to push my buttons. But now that I couldn't see her face, I was slightly immune to her manipulation.

I emphasize, *slightly*.

"I'm going to bed. I have an early class tomorrow," Katie grumbled.

"Good night," I said, fingering the sore lump forming on my forehead. Katie was normally a roll-with-the-punches type of girl. Lately it seemed her patience with Mom was wearing thin.

Shifting onto my hands and knees, I felt around me. I

found the big thing I'd tripped over. The thing beside it, the one I'd smashed my head into, was the wood side table, which usually sat in the room's corner. "Mom, we've talked about this before. You promised you wouldn't plug in your inventions before I've had a chance to check them out."

"But I kept my word . . . for a long time."

I sent some seriously mean eyes at the dark blob standing about five feet away. "In the past twelve hours, you've broken your promise twice. And you've fried the electrical systems in two buildings. I've all but emptied my bank account, paying your landlord off so he won't evict you. And now this!" My voice was rising, and I didn't like that. But the pain drilling through my head and the exhaustion weighing upon my shoulders was getting the better of me. I was furious, frustrated, and slightly panic-stricken. I wouldn't be getting a paycheck from the FBI for a couple of weeks. If our landlord was going to come knocking, looking for compensation for this catastrophe, we were all going on a crash diet, whether we wanted to lose weight or not.

Truth be told, I could stand to lose a few pounds, anyway. But not my mother. And definitely not Katie.

"I'm sorry, Sloan. I was only trying to help."

I'd heard that line once, twice . . . okay, a million times. Many eons ago, I quit asking my mom why she felt she needed to "help" with anything (or more importantly how her inventions would help). My mother's logic never made sense to me. I assumed it was more a failing of my nonschizophrenic mind than a deficiency in her reasoning. When I reached the hallway, I drummed up the nerve to stand. For safety's sake, though, I leaned back against the wall for support. "Mom, are there any surprises in the hallway?"

"No. But about the sleeping arrangements . . ."

"Yes, of course, you can take my bed, and I'll sleep on the couch." My room was at the end of the hall. I curled the fingers of my left hand around the door frame and waved my right arm in front of my body as I blindly picked my way across the room to the dresser. I pulled the first garments I found out of my pajama drawer, a T-shirt and a pair of cotton shorts.

The mattress creaked. "I'm sorry about the power," Mom said from the general vicinity of the bed.

I wanted to scold her again, but I knew it was useless. My mother did what she felt she needed to do, regardless of any warnings, dangers, or laws. Nothing I said would ever change that. The truth was, in her twisted logic, her actions made sense because she believed she was protecting me. From what, I suspected, I'd never figure out.

Schizophrenia was a real bitch.

"Did you take your medicine today?" I asked as I rolled off my panty hose and threw them, wadded up, onto the top of my dresser.

"Yes, Sloan. I took every pill. I always do."

That was the frustrating part. She did take her medication, exactly as prescribed. Her doctor had changed her prescriptions so many times, I'd lost count. And each time, she'd be better for a little while—the voices and delusions easing for a few months—but then they'd come back as strong as ever. This time, the quiet had only lasted a little over two months. I had more than a sneaking suspicion things were going to head downhill from here. The doctor had already warned me that they'd exhausted all drugs currently approved for treating my mother's disease. However, because I was an optimist at heart, I decided to put in a call to his office in the morning. Maybe there'd been a new drug approved by the FDA since our last visit? Unlikely, sure. But I could dream.

I shrugged out of my outdated polyester suit jacket and laid it flat on the dresser. Off came my skirt, my blouse. It felt like heaven getting into the comfy shorts. "Okay, Mom. We'll talk about it tomorrow. I need to get some sleep. I had a big day."

"All right. Good night, Sloan."

"G'night, Mom."

This time, I had some idea where the danger zone was as I staggered and groped my way across our living room. I managed to get to the couch without seriously maiming myself. I only added a single painful bruise on my shin to my list of injuries. I set the alarm on my cell phone, after checking the battery to make sure it wouldn't die before morning; then I settled on the couch, hoping I wouldn't have another one of those bizarre nightmares.

I didn't have any nightmares, thank God. But I couldn't shake the uneasy feeling that somebody was watching me all night long. I must've woken at least a dozen times. Each time, I glanced into the deep shadows clinging to the room's corners. I peered out the window. Eventually I fell back into a dreamless slumber.

When my alarm went off at six-thirty, my eyelids felt like they were swollen. My eyeballs were scratchy, like they'd been plucked out, rolled in sand, and stuffed back into my sockets. My head was foggy. I needed another hour of sleep, and after that, caffeine. Lots of it.

Katie had already left for class by the time I dragged my weary self off the couch at seven-thirty. I put the side table back where it belonged and hauled Mom's invention to the coat closet—it weighed a freaking ton. I shoved it as far back as I could so she'd be less likely to mess with it. I rubbed my eyes as I padded barefoot into the kitchen, rummaged in the back of the cabinet for the instant coffee, and lit the gas stove to boil some water.

Mom joined me just as I was guzzling my second cup. I set a clean mug on the counter and motioned to the hot kettle. "Water's hot. Help yourself. I need to get going." Over my shoulder, I motioned to the cupboard. "For lunch, you can cook some noodles. Add boiling water, let them sit for three minutes, and you're good to go. I'll call the office a little later and find out how long we'll be living like Neanderthals."

"Thanks, honey. Again, I'm sorry about the accident."

Twisting, I gave my mother a wilted semismile over my shoulder. I swear, if I didn't love that woman as much as I did, I'd have gone ballistic on her ages ago. But I did love her, and I couldn't be cruel to her. No matter how much trouble she caused. "Promise me, you'll keep your word from now on. No powering up your inventions until I've tested them."

Mom smacked her right hand over her heart. "I swear I won't get anywhere near a wall outlet until you tell me it's safe."

I headed into the shower, wondering how long she'd keep her word this time.

The big red numbers on the digital clock hanging on the conference room wall read twenty-five hours, fifty-nine minutes, and thirty-three seconds, and it was counting backward. To what deadline, I had no clue yet. But it was safe to assume it wasn't counting down the hours till the season finale of *The Bachelor* or the premiere of the next *Twilight* movie.

I wasn't the last to hurry into the conference room for our morning meeting. That made me feel a little better. Chief Peyton, the only member of the team who wasn't waiting in the conference room, was in her office, on her phone. But I knew I had to have been the last to arrive at the unit, thanks to a side trip to my apartment complex's office.

Good news: the official "cause" was faulty wiring—I wasn't about to argue, especially with my bank account balance approaching zero.

The bad news: no power for another day or two.

JT gave me a half grin as I settled into a chair. His dark, come-hither eyes said something I didn't want to try to interpret right now. So, to avoid thinking too much about how charming he looked this morning, I busied myself, setting up my Netbook, gathering a pen and notebook to jot notes, and sneaking bits of a stale granola bar into my mouth. I'd forgotten about putting that in my purse a couple of months ago, thank goodness.

The chief rushed in just as I swallowed the last mouthful of chocolate and granola. She pointed at the clock and announced, "This is how much time we have until the next victim dies."

It was all very Hollywood.

Absolutely, I was extremely skeptical about this whole thing. Who wouldn't be?

Granted, because I'd dragged in much later than everyone else, I had to assume I didn't know everything the other members of the team did. In my book, the deaths were strange, perhaps a little fishy, but hardly clear-cut murders.

"This is what we have so far." Chief Peyton clicked her laptop's mouse and an image displayed on the white wall behind her.

Nifty. PowerPoint.

The chief pointed at the picture of the Baltimore victim. "Jane Doe Two. Approximate age, thirty-five. She collapsed a few minutes before ten yesterday morning in Baltimore, within walking distance of a hospital. Cause of death, complications of malaria." She clicked the mouse again, and this time, an image of the woman from the morgue we'd visited yesterday displayed. "Hannah Grant. Collapsed and died outside of a coffee shop in Frederick, exactly forty-eight hours before Jane Doe Two. Age, thirty-one. COD, complications of typhoid fever." She clicked the mouse a third time, and another photo appeared. It was of a dead woman who looked a great deal like the first two. "And this is the unsub's first victim, Jane Doe One. Age, early thirties. Collapsed and died outside of a fabric store in Arlington, exactly forty-eight hours before Hannah Grant. COD, complications of dengue hemorrhagic fever. That's three women, very close in age and appearance, all with identical bite marks on their necks. Each died within forty-eight hours of the previous from an infectious tropical disease. The one victim who has been identified has not traveled outside of the United States, and thus the mode of infection is unknown. Also, she didn't seek medical care because, according to family members and coworkers, she didn't show any symptoms prior to her collapse."

Okay, when Chief Peyton put it like that, I had to admit there did seem to be something going on here. But I still felt we weren't the right team to solve this case. It sounded more like some kind of epidemic.

I raised my hand, gaining the chief's attention. At her nod, I asked, "Wouldn't it be wise to turn this case over to the Centers for Disease Control, since the victims died from infectious diseases?"

Chief Peyton nodded. "I've sent the case files, including each victim's full medical reports, to my contact at the CDC. But at this point, I'm not ready to drop our investigation. The CDC will tackle it from its angle, and we'll continue from ours."

Having two federal agencies investigating the same case seemed like a waste of resources to me, but who was I to judge? I was, after all, nothing but a lowly summer intern. I supposed the chief wasn't too eager to hand off the unit's first case, because that might prove the unit wasn't really necessary.

And where would that leave us?

Out of a job, that was where.

"Sounds good to me." I glanced down at my notes, trying to figure out what we might do next. I had no idea. Since learning I'd be working for the FBI this summer, I'd watched every cop/FBI/PI show on TV. Those television cops/agents/private investigators made it look so freaking easy.

"We're going to work this case like it's a serial murder.

Which means we need to find the connection between the three victims," Chief Peyton said. "We'll start with victimology. Why did these three women die? I'm going to split up the team." She pointed at me and JT. "Skye, JT, I want you to take the Arlington victim."

I glanced at JT. His gaze met mine, and something sparkled in his eyes. I felt my cheeks warm. I hoped they weren't Day-Glo red. "Yes, Chief."

"Fischer, I know you have your hands full, reviewing other cases for the unit. But we need your help with this. I'd like you to take the Baltimore victim. I'll take the second, Hannah Grant. Hough'll stay here and lend support." Chief Peyton stood. "I want to know everything about those three women. Where they work and live, what they eat for breakfast. Who their friends and enemies are. Everything." After a beat, she smiled. "Good luck."

Orders assigned. Of course, I was paired off with the one man I shouldn't be left alone with.

"So . . ." I fell into step beside JT as we strolled out of the room. When he stepped around a trash can, my shoulder bumped his arm. Another rush of heat blasted to my face. It was pathetic. I was pathetic. I hoped he didn't notice. "Where do we start? We have a corpse with no identification on it. How will we figure out who she is, let alone what she eats for breakfast?"

"By now, she must have been reported missing. We'll begin by looking into new missing persons reports." Instead of going to his desk, JT turned toward a doorway I hadn't noticed before.

Inside. Nirvana! The IT nerd jackpot. The unit's analyst Brittany had a wall full of monitors, all displaying something different. Being something of a computer geek myself, I was in awe.

"Hey, Hough," JT said. "Can you give me a list of all new missing persons reports in Maryland, Virginia, and DC?"

"Sure. On it." Fingers flew across the keyboard to the sound of snapping gum. Several screens flickered and pictures blinked across the screen. Done with her rapid-fire commands, she spun around and smiled at JT, pushing a pair of hot pink framed glasses up a pert nose. "Couldn't you give me something a little more challenging?"

Not as young as I'd first thought she was, Brittany looked to be more my age than a teenager. It was her funky Forever 21 style that had thrown me off. I could take a few hints from her.

"How about female, ages twenty-five to forty?" JT asked.

"Done." A couple of taps and the printer behind us whirred as it powered up to print out the report. "You're in luck. There's only five."

JT glanced over his shoulder at the printer. "Great. Now we just need photographs."

"Let me see what I can do." Brittany's fingers danced over the keyboard. A Facebook page popped up. "Here's one of them, a Maryanne Levinstein."

Standing behind Brittany, I squinted at the screen. The crime scene photograph in the file wasn't the best, so I had no idea if Maryanne Levinstein was our victim or not. I shook my head. "What do you think, JT?"

"Hmm. Not sure yet. Can you check the profile for more pictures, Hough?"

Brittany clicked the tab, but the photo section was blocked. "You have to be a friend to view them. Let me see what I can do. . . ." A second later, the folder opened, revealing over twenty images of the woman, smiling in every one of them. In some, she was posing with other women; in a few, with a man; and in a lot, she was with a couple of kids. It really hit home then that this woman, who might be dead now, had once been a mother, a wife, a sister, someone important to somebody. And those somebodies would hurt like I had when my father died.

If she was our victim.

This morning, I'd been skeptical and hadn't taken the case as seriously as I should have. But these pictures made it more real to me.

Unfortunately, even though I was taking the case much more seriously now, I felt useless. I wasn't a hotshot FBI agent. My ridiculous IQ, my knowledge of foreign languages, psychology, mathematics, and science wasn't doing me a damn thing. My head was full of useless facts like the incubation period of the GBV-C virus and how to speak in Ket. While Brittany and JT were actually working, I was standing there like a dork, being useless.

"I don't think Maryanne Levinstein's our victim. But I'll give the name to the lead detective and let him check it out." JT swiped the printout off the printer's tray and starred the name. Frowning, he read through the list. "We have Hannah Grant's address. Hough, can you run these addresses, see if any of them are in the same area as Grant's?"

Brittany nodded. "Sure. Give me a minute." A few more taps, and she had all five addresses plotted on the map, along with Grant's, whose address was indicated by a little red virtual pushpin.

JT pointed. "We should start with that one." He pointed at the little yellow pointer closest to the red one. "Deborah Richardson." He handed the list to me. "Let's start by faxing this to the BPD."

"I'll do it." Heading for the door, I asked, "Are we going to wait until someone verifies the victim's identity before we get in touch with the family?"

"We have to wait." JT nodded. "Unless we find something more concrete. But it won't take long for the detective to check it out. In the meantime, we can do some work on this end."

"You'd be surprised how much dirt I can dig up on a person," Brittany boasted, her smile stretching from ear to ear, her eyes flicking over to me. It made me wonder if she wasn't talking about me, instead of our victims.

Feeling slightly violated—and I wasn't even sure if I should—I headed out of Brittany's computer cave to fax the list of potential victims to the Baltimore detective. That menial task done, I headed back toward Brittany's office. At the sound of her giggle, though, I stopped and peered in.

JT was standing very close to Brittany, looking over her shoulder. Brittany was looking up, into his eyes; the smile that had been devious was now dazzling.

It felt like somebody had kicked me in the gut.

"Shit," I muttered under my breath as I backed slowly from the door. There was no way I was walking in on that . . . whatever it was.

Instead, I went back to my desk. My Netbook had been cleared to use on the network, so I flipped it open and Google Mapped Deborah Richardson's address, using Street View to get a good look at the house. While I knew Google Maps wasn't always 100 percent correct in identifying the exact address, it was still worth checking. It wasn't usually off by much. The building looked very ordinary: a typical middle-class vinyl-sided Colonial on a typical street. The backyard was adjacent to a large park. Nothing suspicious there. Next I mapped Hannah Grant's residence, also   assuming Google was correct—a suburban home. The brick-and-vinyl Colonial was also located very close to a park—this one with a play-ground, outdoor skating rink, and nature trails.

Could I have found something?

When JT finally emerged from Brittany's office, I waved him over.

"I was wondering what happened to you," he said, leaning a hip against my cubicle wall. He dropped his notebook on my desk.

Hoping I was hiding my uneasiness, I motioned toward my

computer screen. "I was making myself useful while you were busy. . . . Er . . . I found something."

"Yeah? So did we. You first." He set a flattened hand on my desktop and leaned over my shoulder, just like he had with Brittany. I decided it was annoying.

I shifted slightly to the left, away from him, even though there were a few bits of my anatomy that liked being in close proximity to some of his. Those parts weren't the most intelligent. "If Deborah Richardson is one of our victims, and Google mapped their homes correctly, two out of three victims live in homes with lots that are adjacent to a park," I told him, pointing at the map displayed on my computer's eight-inch screen.

"Really?" His brows rose as a look of surprise spread over the face I was trying hard not to admire. Evidently, he hadn't uncovered the same fact I had. "We found out Deborah Richardson works less than half a block from where our Jane Doe collapsed. She's a secretary for a church. I'm confident enough that she's our victim. I'm not waiting for confirmation. Let's head out."

There can be no good without evil.

—Russian Proverb

5

Have you ever been really bothered by something, and then been disturbed by the fact that it bothered you in the first place? This wasn't a first for me, but it was the most frustrating time. And annoying. And irritating.

When I closed my eyes, I saw in my head Brittany's big, girly grin. It made me grit my teeth. The fact that it bothered me so much made me even madder. Thus, I probably wasn't the best company during the drive to Deborah Richardson's hometown. I had no idea if JT noticed or not. He didn't say anything.

By the time JT's car rolled up the Richardsons' driveway, I didn't need to know the lead detective had called JT to confirm her identity. The cars parked out in front of the house told the whole story.

JT parked. We hurried up to the house.

Inside, we found a tired man in his midthirties with a pale face, made paler by bloodshot eyes. He was talking to a detective, arms crossed over his chest.

"Agent Jordan Thomas and Sloan Skye," JT said to the detective.

The detective nodded. "Agent?"

"FBI," JT explained.

"Agent Thomas, this is Trey Chapman," the detective said. "And I'm Detective McRoy."

JT offered a hand to McRoy first, then Chapman. "Sir, we're very sorry for your loss."

The man blinked. His lips quirked. Not in a smile, but in a grimace. He sniffled. "Thank you. This is all such a shock."

"I'm sure it is." I offered him my hand next, and he accepted it, giving it a firm shake.

JT pulled his notebook from his pocket. "We're going to do our best to find out what happened to your . . . ?"

"Fiancée," Chapman finished. "We've been engaged for over two years." He sighed, shoved his hands through his hair, and mumbled something under his breath.

I didn't catch what he'd said. Sure wish I had.

McRoy checked his phone. "I've gotta take this call. I'll be in touch, Mr. Chapman, as soon as I have any more information."

"Thank you, Detective." Chapman turned to JT. "I don't understand. Why all the fuss? FBI? Debbie got sick and she . . . and she died. There's no crime to solve. . . . Is there?"

"We're not saying there is, sir. We're just checking out some information that may or may not be related to your fiancée's death."

"What information?" Chapman crossed his arms over his chest.

"I'm sorry, but I can't tell you that." JT flipped to a fresh page in his notebook. "Would you mind answering a few questions for us?"

"I . . . don't know. Do I need a lawyer?" He looked at me, as if I would tell him whether he was under any kind of suspicion or not. What was I supposed to say?

"You don't have to answer any question you're not comfortable with," I told him. That, I figured, was a safe answer.

Chapman gave me another look, then nodded. "Okay."

I glanced around the living room. "Do you mind if I take a look around the house while you're talking to Agent

Thomas? See if I can find anything that might tell us how your fiancée became ill?"

He scowled. "I—I guess that would be okay."

I gave him a reassuring smile. "Thank you."

Now what? I had permission to search the house, and I had no freaking idea what I was looking for. Because my time was limited—I couldn't wander around all day—I headed upstairs to the victim's bedroom first, thinking I'd start in one of the most private parts of her home.

Her bedroom was tidy, the bed made. There were no medicine bottles on the nightstand.

This room looked nothing like mine when I was sick.

I wandered into the bathroom, still not sure what I was looking for. It was spotless too, nothing out of place. I felt kind of creepy taking a peek in her medicine cabinet, but I needed to see if she had any medications that might indicate she was treating symptoms of dengue hemorrhagic fever. I knew the symptoms could appear anywhere from three to fourteen days after infection, but they were severe. Chills, fever, rash, vomiting—eventually leading to a shocklike state. I don't know how anyone could ignore those kinds of symptoms.

I found a bottle of expired over-the-counter pain reliever and a brand-new, unopened box of cold tablets. No antibiotics. Not even a bottle of Pepto.

Was it possible she'd felt no symptoms until immediately before she'd died?

I wandered out into the hallway, checked the second bedroom, which looked nothing like the rest of the house, from what I'd seen. With the dark walls, clutter, and clothes strewn about, I surmised it was the habitat of a teenager. I confirmed it with a quick look at the desk. Buried under a mountain of books and papers, CDs and DVDs, was a photograph of a blond girl with braces; her arms were flung over the shoulders of two girlfriends.

Not wholly convinced a person couldn't catch a disease in that room, I headed down the hall to the third bedroom, which had been converted into a cozy home office. The desk's top was clear of clutter, the laptop shut off, the cover shut. Behind the desk, the window's shades were up. The house sat so close to its neighbor, I could make out the details of the Justin Bieber poster hanging on the hot pink wall in what must've been a kid's bedroom next door. I moved closer to the window to get a better look.

Was this bedroom, with its bed piled high with stuffed animals and its desk cluttered with the trappings of a child—a bug house, the Potato Head family, and a plush unicorn—the average room of a kid?

When I was younger, I'd been anything but average. And now I assume, my room had been as unusual as myself. My walls hadn't been papered with pages ripped out of teen magazines, like this one. The yellow walls—painted that shade because my mother had read yellow stimulated brain cells—had been completely obscured by prints by Renoir, Gauguin, and Monet, long before I'd graduated from elementary school. My desk had been buried under a mountain of inventions—gadgets and gizmos I'd erected from disassembled small appliances.

There'd been a very noticeable lack of stuffed critters on my bed.

Allergies. Polyester-filled plushies were dust mite magnets.

Something thumped downstairs, and I tugged the string, lowering the blinds, turning back to the task at hand. Hoping our victim might keep a journal on her computer, I opened it and powered it up. Luck was on my side—she hadn't set up a password.

I was in.

The wallpaper was a photograph of Deborah Richardson and the blond-haired teenager from the photograph in the messy room. First thing I checked was her Web browser.

My fave Web sites—the ones I visited every day—launched automatically when my browser opened. If my luck continued, Deborah Richardson's would do the same thing.

Bingo.

Deborah was an eBay shopper. Her Yahoo! mail page loaded. I skimmed the messages in her in-box. Spam. She'd left nothing unread before she died. That told me she'd signed on and opened her e-mail that morning before leaving for work. I heard footsteps coming up the stairs, so I shut down the computer. There didn't seem to be anything useful on it.

Out in the hallway, I met JT.

"Find anything?" he asked, chewing on the end of his pen.

"Nothing. It's like she woke up that morning and everything was normal. She checked her e-mail, made her bed, got dressed, and headed for work, just like any other day. I don't see any sign that she was sick, not even some aspirin. I don't know what we're looking for."

He smacked his notebook with his pen. "The fiancé didn't give me much to work with either."

"There is a teenager living here too, though. Maybe we could talk to her, ask if she noticed her mother being sick."

"Yes, Chapman told me. She's a counselor at a summer camp. She had to go up a couple of weeks before camp starts for training." He motioned toward the stairs with a tip of his head. "Ready to head out?"

"Yeah, I guess so." I clomped down the stairs after him, trying not to notice how broad his shoulders looked from that angle. "You said she died from complications of dengue hemorrhagic fever. What exactly killed her?"

"The ME hadn't completed a full autopsy yet, of course, but liver damage was the early diagnosis." Pausing midway down the staircase, he turned to look up at me. "I think I saw a neighbor at home. Maybe she noticed something. Let's go talk to her."

"Okay." I followed him down the remaining stairs, sort of

glancing this way and that. I was hoping if there was something out of the ordinary in the house, it would catch my eye. In the foyer, we said good-bye to Trey Chapman, after having verified that the daughter, Julia, had been away since the beginning of last week and wouldn't be returning until late tomorrow. Then I officially gave up; my first search for clues had been an utter failure.

So far, I was about as useful to the FBI as a freezer to an Eskimo.

Outside, JT pointed at the house on the east side of the Richardsons' home, the one I'd been peeping into earlier. "The neighbor was working on the flower beds. I saw her from the window."

We followed a stone path around the side of the neighbor's house. JT stopped at the wooden gate closing off the backyard. He called out, "Excuse me, ma'am?"

After a little bit of rustling, a woman shuffled around the corner. She tipped her head and pushed back the brim of her straw gardening hat to wipe her forehead with a gloved hand. "Yes?"

JT flashed his credentials. "Agent Thomas, with the FBI. We'd like to ask you a couple of questions, if you don't mind."

"Sure." The woman wandered toward us. She looked puzzled as she stopped at the gate and draped a hand over its top. "How can I help you? This won't take long, will it? I have to go to work in a while."

"Not more than five minutes, tops. Did you happen to notice anything unusual about your neighbor in the past couple of days?" He pointed at Deborah Richardson's house.

She thought for a moment, shook her head, then glanced at the victim's home, as if it might tell her something. "No. Not that I can think of. Her daughter, Julia, has been gone. She's a summer camp counselor. With her away, the house has been quieter than normal. Though Debbie keeps to herself, anyway. Why?"

He toyed with his spiral notebook as he asked, "Did you know she died yesterday?"

The woman's eyes widened. Her gloved hand smacked over her mouth. "Died?" After a beat, she added, "That poor child, losing her mother. Was she . . . murdered?"

"There's nothing to suggest it was murder, ma'am," JT said.

"Then why is the FBI investigating?" She glanced at me.

"We're just following up on some information that may or may not be related to her death," I said, repeating what JT had told Chapman earlier.

"This is very surprising." The woman chewed her lower lip. "Did you talk to the boyfriend? If you're looking for someone suspicious, I'd check him out first."

"What makes you say that?" I asked, slanting a glance at JT.

Chances were, our victim hadn't been murdered, but had simply ignored her symptoms—how and why?—and had died when she started bleeding internally. But Chief Peyton had decided we were treating this case like a murder investigation. So, that was what I was going to do. If nothing else, it could prove to be good practice for when I got my job with the BAU.

A suspicious boyfriend could be a good lead in a murder investigation.

"Well"—the woman tapped her chin with an index finger—"on those police shows, isn't it always the husband or boyfriend who kills the victim?"

I nodded. "Generally, yes—"

"I think they were having troubles," the neighbor said. "It was strange. He seemed to be living with her. But only for a month or so. I believe he moved out only last week."

"Moved out?" I repeated, giving JT a pointed look.

JT's lips thinned. His neck turned red. He swung around and glared at Debbie Richardson's house.

Trey Chapman's car was gone.

The neighbor continued talking. "Yes, I heard some fighting. And then I saw him packing up his car. As far as I can tell, he hasn't been back since."

"He was in the house today," I told her.

She grimaced. "Really? That surprises me. I don't think the breakup was a friendly one."

Now I was confused. Trey hadn't mentioned that he was an *ex*-fiancé. I kicked myself for not looking in the bedroom closet. That would've told us if he was living there or not. I could say 100 percent for certain that I hadn't noticed any man gear in the master bathroom. No shavers, shaving cream, aftershave, hair products. No toilet seat left up. That should've raised some red flags.

I was the world's worst detective.

All of this raised one vital question: if he'd broken up with Debbie Richardson, what was he doing at the house today?

"Did you notice if your neighbor was sick recently?" I asked. "Did she have the flu in the past couple of weeks? Did she miss work at all?"

"No. I don't think so."

JT, who was visibly gritting his teeth, handed the woman a card. "Thank you for your help. If you think of anything else, please feel free to call me."

We both looked back at Deborah Richardson's house.

"Damn it!" JT mumbled as he stomped toward the home once more.

We weren't going to get back in the house now. Nor were we going to get the chance to ask Trey Chapman if he was a fiancé or an ex-fiancé.

Walking alongside a visibly frustrated JT, I asked, "Do you think the neighbor's right about the breakup?"

JT paused in front of the house. "If she is, Trey Chapman should go to the top of the persons-of-interest list." He rammed his fingers through his hair. "I'm going to make a call, let the lead detective know what we found out. We need to verify whether they were broken up or not, ASAP." He went to his car.

"What do you think? Workplace next?" I suggested over his car's roof. "Maybe someone there will know if they broke up."

"Good thinking." JT jerked the door open and slumped into the seat.

After having a quick chat with Debbie Richardson's most recent employer, we were stumped. She hadn't called in sick, not once in over a year. She'd shown no signs of illness prior to her death, and she'd said nothing about any troubles with her fiancé. I spent the car ride back to the FBI Academy staring at the notes I'd scrawled in my notebook. There'd been no mention today of vampires; I decided to ask JT, "Have we given up on the notion that some kind of paranormal activity played a role in this death?"

Navigating his car onto a freeway that looked more like a parking lot than a highway, JT shook his head. "Absolutely not."

"So, do you really believe there are paranormal creatures out there, committing crimes—assault, rape, murder?" When he didn't answer right away, I added, "I promise, I won't tell the chief if you don't believe in ghosts and goblins." Still nothing. "Please tell me I'm not the only one who thinks the whole paranormal angle is a joke."

"Okay." He sighed. The car rolled to a stop behind a school bus packed full of kids. They were making funny faces at us through the back windows. He made one back at them. "You're not the only one. I have a few doubts." He inched the car forward when the bus moved up. "I took the job because I felt it would be good experience. I knew Peyton was having a hard time getting applicants. I knew every member of the team would be valued. And so, I saw it as a shortcut to getting out from behind a desk and into the field. I requested a transfer."

"You were right about that," I said, chuckling. "I haven't spent any quality time in my cubicle, and I'm an intern."

"No matter what, if we do our jobs well, we'll both benefit." He glanced over his shoulder and eased the car into the right lane. Our exit was up ahead. "If the unit is eventually disbanded, I'll leave with a hell of a lot more in-field experience than I would have if I hadn't transferred. So will you. Assuming you apply for a full-time position after graduating."

"Sounds like a good career move on your part."

"Would've been nice, though, if Peyton had been able to attract at least one more senior agent. Fischer's been around a while. The rest of us are relatively new. Don't have the experience to do the job."

"All you can do is your best."

"Yeah. But if I'd had some experience under my belt, maybe I wouldn't have fucked up with Trey Chapman."

"You didn't 'fuck up.' How were you supposed to know they might have broken up?" When JT didn't respond, I asked, "What's next?"

"We dig up all we can on Chapman."

The "Clock of Doom" read twenty hours, twenty-eight minutes, and thirty-six seconds when I strolled into the unit a little while later. I had a white paper bag full of greasy burgers and fries in one hand, a half-empty cola in the other. JT had left, saying he had a personal matter to take care of. He asked if I'd do some digging on Chapman.

Feeling slightly guilty for sitting in an office, munching fries while somebody out there, somewhere, was living the final twenty hours of her life, I headed to my desk and flipped on my Netbook as I fought to consume the messy burger without slopping ketchup and mayo on the keyboard.

I wasn't "Miss Hacker-chick," like Brittany Hough. Nor did I have open access to all the systems she did, so I accepted the fact that I would need to ask for her help. It was painful, but necessary.

I put on my big-girl panties and prepared to talk to her.

After making sure I wasn't wearing condiments on my face, I headed into her office to ask her to do some digging for skeletons in Chapman's closet. That task done, I headed back to my desk.

A certain someone, who happened to have stolen *my* internship, came strolling into the unit just as I sat. Gabe gave me a casual wave as he sauntered by. "Hey, Skye. What's up?"

I spun my chair around to watch him go to the cubicle behind me and flop into the chair like he owned it. Adding insult to injury, he kicked his feet up on the desktop and grinned.

I knew that grin.

My gut twisted. "What are you doing here?"

He picked at his fingernails. "Kicking back and chillin' for a few."

Nothing like stating the obvious.

I gave him a mean scowl. "Yeah, but shouldn't you be doing that down in the BAU?"

"No. Why would I do that?" He looked confused. Perplexed. Mystified. It was a convincing performance. The boy—I emphasize *boy*—was one hell of an actor. Sadly, this wasn't the first time I'd seen his thespian skills at work.

It had been my senior year in high school, when he'd pretended to like me so I'd help him with physics. I'd just turned fifteen. He was two years older. And much more experienced. He'd charmed me through hours of tutoring every afternoon and—eventually—out of my clothes.

Thanks to all my hard work, he pulled what would've been

a B- up to an A, which led to him being accepted into the National Honor Society. And thanks to his hard you-know-what, and the bone-melting kisses that had preceded the loss of my virginity, I'd had nothing but trouble for years to come.

You see, no sooner had he gotten what he'd wanted from me than he was lobbing my shattered heart back at me and turning his smoldering dark eyes on his next victim, Lisa Flemming.

It was my first, my only, heartbreak. I was so devastated, I failed my AP chemistry final exam. And I blew the interview with the Naval Academy recruiter, which ultimately cost me a promising career as a naval officer.

Truth be told, that part was probably a blessing in disguise.

I scoffed. "Bravo. You just might get an Oscar for that performance."

"I'm not acting, Sloany. Why would I be chillin' in the BAU when I'm working for the *PBAU*?"

Working for the . . . ? No. Effing. Way!

A rage like none I'd ever felt before burned through my body like a surge of magma, threatening to blast off the top of my head. I had to clamp my mouth shut to cut off the stream of profanities that surged up my throat.

Gabe was working for the PBAU now, after causing me to lose the internship of my dreams?

"Why?" I managed to mumble through gritted teeth as I searched the room for a way to cause his *accidental* death. I wondered if there were security cameras in the room; and if there were, how might I pull this off?

"Come on. It's obvious they need my help. Why would I stick with doing grunt work for the BAU? It was a terrible waste of resources."

"Resources?" I spat, rummaging through my desk drawers. Death by . . . stapler? Nah. I'd never convince anyone he was stupid enough to staple himself to death accidentally.

"My brilliant mind, of course." He cupped the back of his head and rocked the chair back.

I bit my tongue. Someday, hopefully soon, someone else would poke a hole in his overinflated ego. It wouldn't be me. But if I was lucky, I'd be there to watch him deflate.

Maybe I could knock into the chair, causing him to fall backward, striking his head on a . . . on a . . . ?

No, that would be too gruesome and painful. Even a job-stealing, virgin-despoiling jerk didn't deserve to have his skull cracked open like an egg.

"I requested a transfer," he continued explaining, oblivious to my thoughts of vengeance, "and Chief Peyton was all too happy to welcome me aboard." He winked. "I'm gonna kick some vampire ass."

All is a riddle, and the key to a riddle . . . is another riddle.

—Ralph Waldo Emerson

6

My cell phone rarely rang. And when it did, it was generally bad news. But I answered it, anyway, with a cheery "Hellooooo?!" because I'm strange that way.

"Your mother's run away!" Katie's screech just about perforated my eardrum.

After switching the phone to the other ear, the one with all vital bits intact, I reasoned, "I'm sure she didn't run away. She just went out . . . to get some food . . . or something." I checked the clock on my computer's desktop. It was almost five already. Where was JT? Had he forgotten about me? Or had he decided I was useless and continued the investigation without me?

"She left a note. But it's in some kind of crazy code, and I can't read it. Someone who's gone out for bagels and coffee doesn't leave an encoded note behind."

I couldn't help chuckling. "I thought you knew my mother by now."

"I do." After a beat, Katie said, "Please come home and take a look. I'm worried."

Argh!

I glanced at the Clock of Doom, then at Gabe, who was still parked in the cubicle behind me. Shortly after dropping the bomb about having joined the team, he'd run home to get his laptop, and he was now gleefully *tap-tap-tapping* on his keyboard. As much as I wanted to believe he was playing some stupid online game, I had a feeling he was doing something else. Something that would make me look even more pathetic to the rest of the team than I already did.

"Okay. I'll be there in a few." I shoved my Netbook into its case, looped the strap over my shoulder, and trudged to the elevators. On the way home, I reminded myself that my mom's brain worked very differently from mine and Katie's. She wasn't missing, hadn't run away, and would most likely be safe and sound in my cozy-but-electricity-free apartment by the time I got home.

She wasn't.

Katie met me at the door, waving a piece of paper like it was a ransom note. "I just know she's in trouble. Can you read it? What's it say?"

"No, I can't read it. Not when you're flinging it around like that." After several failed attempts, I finally caught my melodramatic roommate's wrist, halting its frantic motion. "Thank you for worrying about my mother. I'm sure she's okay." I gently plucked the paper from Katie's hand and wandered into the living room, staring at the bizarre characters on the page:

BEWARE THE LIGHT THAT FLICKERS IN THE NIGHT.

I recognized the script right away. Theban—aka the Witches' Alphabet.

I flopped onto the couch, set the paper on the coffee table, and pulled out my Netbook. "I thought I'd told you, when I was a kid, my mom and I used to play this game, writing everything—even the grocery list—in code. We tried to stump each other. But it's been ages since either of us has done that."

"No, you never said anything about codes." Standing with

one foot in the kitchen and one foot in the living room, Katie chomped into a peanut butter and banana sandwich. "If you had, I wouldn't have freaked out. You know how I get with your mother."

"Sorry." I swear, Katie worried about Mom more than I did sometimes. It was both a good and bad thing.

"So, can you read it?" She washed down the mouthful of bread, peanut butter, and banana with a chug of diet soda.

"My mother only used Theban once before, when I was about seven or eight. I remember the script well enough to recognize it, but I can't read it. Not without a little help." I powered up my Netbook. "Luckily, it's common enough that I should be able to find it on the Net." I connected to my fave search engine, and within seconds, I had the key to unlock my mom's note. "'Beware the light that flickers in the night'?" I read aloud. I sighed. My heart sank to my toes.

"What the hell does that mean?" Katie took another bite of her sandwich.

I sighed again. "It means it's definitely time to make another visit to Mom's doctor. When—*if*—she comes back."

Katie gave my shoulder a pat. "Sorry, hon."

"I guess you were right, after all. There is reason to worry. Damn it, I was hoping this medication was going to work." I dropped my face into my hands, indulging in a mini pity party. This had been going on for so long. I was tired of it all. Tired of the "accidents," which had, over the years, cost me tens of thousands of dollars. Tired of the periodic disappearances, which cost me hours, days, months of worry—not to mention time, while I tracked her down. Tired of the constant struggle to drag my mother out of the darkness, which was always there, waiting for an opportunity to steal her away.

I loved my mother, but I hated her disease. Despised it.

It was a faceless, formless monster, ruthless and cunning. How I wished it could be slain like the vampires I'd read about in that stupid book Chief Peyton had given me.

Vampires could be killed with a strategically placed wooden stake or a shower of holy water. Real-life monsters weren't so easily defeated.

Katie's arm wrapped around my shoulder. Sitting beside me, she pulled me up against her side. "You know I'll help."

"Yeah. Thanks." After I'd pulled myself together—didn't take too long, thank God—I glanced around the living room. "Did you notice anything else? Did she make another invention? Leave any other notes? Did she take anything with her?"

"I don't know. . . ."

The two of us began a search of our apartment, looking for clues to where my mother might have gone. Katie started in the kitchen; I headed for my bedroom. I discovered Mom had borrowed some changes of clothing, a pair of shoes, and a duffel bag. She'd also taken her toothbrush. Katie found she'd taken a small set of tools and a can of insect repellent.

I decided I'd check out Mom's apartment first. With luck, she'd simply gone back there. Katie rode shotgun. Neither of us said a word. We'd been through this more than enough to know what the next step would be if we didn't find her by morning.

I used the spare key to get into Mom's apartment. It was dark and quiet, the shades drawn, shutting out the gradually fading sunlight. It didn't look like she was here now, but I saw something promising on the couch. My duffel bag. I hurried to it. "She's been here. I'm guessing she's coming back."

"OhthankGod!" Katie said, her breathless exclamation echoing my own. "I wonder why she just up and left, without saying anything?"

"That's Mom for you." I unzipped the bag and searched through the contents. Everything was there, but one set of clothes and the shoes. "She changed out of her pajamas."

"I wonder where she went?" Katie headed down the narrow hallway leading to the small bedroom in the back. Just as I was about to follow Katie, Mom came strolling in, a pair of green canvas grocery bags hanging from her shoulders.

"Sloan? What're you doing here?" Mom headed toward the kitchen with the bags.

Following her, I said, "Looking for you. Why'd you leave? Katie was worried."

"I got a call this afternoon. Power's on." Mom hit the wall switch, and the light hanging over her little dinette set illuminated. "As much as I love staying with you, I'd rather be here where I have a microwave, refrigerator, and television. You know how I hate to miss my shows."

I was so relieved, I could've cried. In fact, I kind of did this little laugh/sob thing. Katie rushed into the room, visibly biting back a rant. Together we helped Mom put away her groceries. Once that was done, my mother pulled a bag of marijuana from her pocket and headed for the couch.

"Mom, before we head out, what did you mean by that message?"

"Which message?" she asked as she dumped a mountain of dried leaves onto a paper plate sitting on her coffee table. I hated watching her smoke illegal drugs, but many, many years ago we'd come to an agreement. As long as she smoked in the privacy of her home, I wouldn't interfere.

I said, "The one you wrote in Theban. 'Beware the light that flickers in the night.'"

Mom shrugged. "I don't recall leaving a message, let alone one written in Theban. I haven't used Theban in years. I'm not even sure I remember it well enough to compose a message. Are you sure it was from me?"

"If it wasn't you, who would it be?"

"I don't know, Sloan. It's very curious. A riddle." She shrugged as she sprinkled a line of crushed leaves onto a piece of cigarette paper. "You'll figure it out, I'm sure. You've always been very good at riddles."

I exchanged a look with Katie. "Okay. I guess we'll head home. Mom, remember our agreement."

Licking the paper to seal her freshly rolled joint, she waved her good-bye.

"Where did you find that note?" I asked Katie as we trotted out to my car.

"In the living room, on the top shelf, you know, under the window." Katie rounded the car, asking over the top, "Are you still worried about your mom? It had to be her, right? She must've forgotten she'd written the note."

"I'm not sure what to think. Like I said before, it's been a long time since she's used Theban. She might be telling the truth."

Katie slipped into the passenger seat, giving me a bug-eyed look. "If she is telling the truth, then what?"

"Then I guess we'd better figure out what the message means."

On the way home, Katie and I generated a list of lights that flicker in the night. By the time we'd walked into our apartment, we'd concluded I needed to beware of everything from fireflies to stars . . . and the neon sign in front of the party store down the street, and the lamp in our living room that sputtered when it was bumped—when we had electricity—and candles, and campfires, and . . . at least fifty more things.

Danger was all around me.

Being the daughter of a paranoid schizophrenic, I knew being afraid of everything was no way to live.

The first thing I did when I got home was to check the window in the living room—the one above the shelf where the note had been found. It was shut, but the lock didn't work; there was also a very suspicious rip in the screen. I wedged a big book in the frame to keep an intruder from opening it, ate a peanut butter and potato chip sandwich—I was running out of ideas for new and exciting peanut butter–based sandwich ideas fast—guzzled my lukewarm caffeine-free cola, brushed my teeth, and settled into bed. Katie slept with a tire iron and a battery-powered soldering iron. I drifted off to dreamland with nary a thought of dangerous flickering things.

It was back, the dark thing. It had sucked the life out of the air in the room, the warmth, the oxygen, leaving it a cold, empty vacuum. Pretending to be asleep, she silently prayed for it to leave her alone this time.

Why did it keep coming back?

An icy gust drifted over her face, neck shoulders. Goose bumps prickled. The stench of death burned her nose; the scent of rotting flesh growing so strong, her throat closed. Fighting the urge to gag, she rolled into a ball, wrapping her arms around her bent legs. Something sharp touched her shoulder, piercing the skin.

No. Not again. Please.

Hootie & the Blowfish's "Only Wanna Be with You" woke me at 5:00 A.M. The snappy tune almost wiped out the lingering images in my mind, of a little girl trembling in her bed, a shadowed form standing over her. It was exactly the same as the nightmare I'd had the other night. Creepy. Unsettling. I'd thought the first nightmare had been caused by all that talk about vampires, and that book, *The Vampire Encyclopedia*. But last night, there'd been no mention of bloodsuckers of any kind.

Very strange.

Sluggish, and needing a hefty dose of caffeine, I went through my morning ritual—minus the blow-drying of the hair. Instead, I gathered it, wet, into what I hoped was a tiny knot on the back of my head and used enough pins to keep it in place in a hurricane. After fluffing on a little blush and slicking some lip gloss on my lips, I put on a bland pair of black pants, a white blouse, and black pumps and stumbled out into the early morning a good two hours before Katie would resume consciousness.

Today I wouldn't be the last one in the office.

After making a quick stop at a 7-Eleven for a coffee, I headed into work.

Gabe was already there. Worse than that, he was having a friendly chitchat with Chief Peyton. Even from a distance, I could see he was using his mojo on her . . . and it seemed to be working. Since I'd started with the PBAU, I hadn't ever seen the chief smile. Not that she'd looked unhappy or mean—she'd just always exuded discipline and authority.

Not now.

Was that an eyelash bat?

I threw up a little in my mouth. This was wrong on so many levels.

I dumped my stuff on my desk, plopped into my chair, and quickly consumed my pathetic excuse for a breakfast while waiting for my computer to power up. I eat fast; my Netbook runs slow. By the time I had my fave sites loaded on my browser, JT was strolling in, looking fresh and scrumptious and ready for work.

The chief paid me a visit while I was reading an article on infectious diseases on ResearchGate.com. "Good morning, Skye. We've had some interesting developments in our case. How did you and JT make out yesterday?"

Interesting wording—"make out"?

Wishing I had something earthshaking to tell her, I shook my head. "We didn't get much. There is an ex-fiance who's—"

"Hold off on the update until we're all together." She lifted a hand, halting me midsentence. "We're all here. Conference room. In ten. For a briefing."

"Okay." The minute the chief had wandered off to talk to someone else, I headed for JT's cubicle. He was on the phone; I pretended I wasn't trying to listen in, and watched the rest of the team going about their morning rituals. I didn't rap on his divider until after he'd ended the call. "Hey," I said.

"Hey." His smile made my insides do cartwheels. Would I ever get over this crush? "Did you get anywhere yesterday?"

"Not really, but Brittany dug up something interesting on Chapman. McRoy also uncovered some information on Deborah Richardson. Which first, Richardson or Chapman?"

"Chapman," I said.

"He has a sealed juvenile record and a more recent conviction for stalking a coworker."

That was interesting, indeed. "Okay. He's no Boy Scout, but we don't have any concrete reason to believe he had anything to do with his ex-fiancée's death . . . yet. Now, what about Richardson?"

"She just wrapped up a very messy divorce a couple of months ago."

I was confused. "Divorce? Didn't Chapman say they'd been engaged for over *two years*?"

"Yep. Evidently, she was engaged to Chapman while she was married."

And my mother wondered why I was in no hurry to get married? Although I wanted to believe two people could fall in love and stay in love for the rest of their lives, I had yet to see it. Was anyone happily married these days? "Okay, so we have a potentially pissed-off ex-husband, an ex-fiancé who wasn't ready to be an ex, a dead woman who hasn't been sick a day in the last several months but died from dengue hemorrhagic fever—"

"And hasn't ever traveled out of the country," JT added.

"About that. This morning, I checked the statistics of dengue hemorrhagic fever infections in the United States. According to CDC data, contact between the Aedes mosquito and U.S. residents is so limited that the vast majority of cases of dengue in the States is acquired elsewhere by travelers and immigrants. The last documented outbreak of dengue in the continental U.S. was in Southern Texas in 2005. A small outbreak occurred in Hawaii in 2001. No other outbreaks have been verified since. However, dengue is a significant problem in parts of South America. Do we know if our victim has traveled to Texas recently? Or Hawaii?"

"We don't, but we can find out. I'm sure the CDC is working the case. They may know the method of transmission already."

Noticing the other team members were moving toward the conference room, I glanced at the clock. "I guess we'd better get in there."

"Yep."

"The chief said there were some interesting developments in the case last night. Do you know anything about that?" I asked.

"Nope." He motioned for me to go first. I led the way to the conference room, checking the Clock of Doom on my way to a seat. Two hours, thirty-eight minutes.

Would somebody else really die when that clock ticked down to the last minute?

Chief Peyton cleared her throat and gave the room a somber-faced sweep with her eyes. She really did have a flair for the dramatic. Despite my cynicism, I found myself sliding to the edge of my seat.

"First, we have identified all three victims. Their names are Debbie Richardson, Hannah Grant, and the most recent victim is Laura Miller. In addition, we have determined in the last few hours that all three deaths are indeed murders," she announced gravely. "We are dealing with a serial killer. There are some issues with the DNA analysis, but the lab found foreign saliva on the victims' necks, and they were able to extract DNA. It matches in all three cases."

Identical DNA. Huh. That was hard to dismiss.

But did it prove inconclusively that the victims were murdered?

"In addition," she continued, "upon further examination of the bodies, proof of a struggle, specifically skin and blood under the fingernails, was discovered. The DNA from that material matched the samples found at the neck."

I glanced at the clock.

If what the chief was saying was true, in exactly two hours, thirty-one minutes, and seventeen seconds, *someone else was going to die.*

Imagination is more important than knowledge.
Knowledge is limited. Imagination encircles the world.

—Albert Einstein

7

Try as I might, I could no longer deny the fact that the three deaths we had been investigating weren't simple cases of virulent diseases. Somehow, someone was using infectious agents to kill women. Brunette women, in their early thirties—two out of three residing near a park.

Debbie Richardson, Hannah Grant, and Laura Miller.

Why those victims? Why that mode of killing?

We were still a long way from answering either of those questions.

I shared my discovery that two of the three victims lived on properties bordering a park. I hadn't known Miller's identity, so I hadn't had a chance to locate her home yet. The chief verified that she lived near the same park that Debbie Richardson did. JT shared the names of Richardson's ex-fiancé and her place of work, hoping we might discover a link tying her to the other victims, besides the park. None of the victims worked together. As a matter of fact, the other two victims, a medical sales rep and a librarian, worked in different towns. However, they lived within a half mile of each other. That, we all agreed, was significant.

When it was Brittany's turn, she gave us the lowdown on Trey Chapman: "The juvenile record includes one conviction

of petty larceny. That's it. Don't ask me how I found that out."
She grinned. "He's currently unemployed. Hasn't kept a job
for more than six months in the last three years. Tends to take
jobs at places frequented by wealthy, single women, like spas,
restaurants, and retail stores. I get the feeling he's a leech, a
pretty boy who hooks up with rich women and lives off them,
but I doubt he's a killer." She punched a few keys on her
laptop. "I also did some digging into Deborah Richardson's
ex-husband. He's squeaky-clean, hasn't even had a traffic
ticket in the past five years. He has his own accounting firm,
which is running in the black. Outside of the messy divorce,
which, on closer examination, wasn't so messy—he voluntar-
ily gave his ex-wife the home and custody of their daughter—
there's no reason to suspect him of any crime."

Chief nodded. "Good work. I'll let you get back to it."

"Thanks, Chief." Brittany excused herself.

Chief Peyton motioned to Fischer. "Fischer, what do you
have on Laura Miller?"

"She was a sales rep for a medical supply firm. She owned
the house she lived in, but shared it with a longtime friend
and her friend's daughter. She lived a relatively quiet lifestyle
when she wasn't traveling for work. She spent her spare time
at home, writing. She was working on a novel. She hadn't
dated anyone recently, hadn't been acting different, and hasn't
traveled anywhere south of the Virginia–North Carolina
border. Her roommate noticed nothing out of the ordinary
before her death. And she hadn't appeared sick."

Just like Debbie Richardson.

Gabe was the only one who didn't have anything to report.
Whatever he'd been doing yesterday, it hadn't been working
on our case.

"All right. Let's take a look at our unsub," Chief Peyton
said, moving to the whiteboard and uncapping a black
dry-erase marker. "What do we know about him or her?"

"Do we know from the DNA his or her gender?" I asked.

"At this point, no." Chief Peyton wrote a capital *G* and a question mark.

"His or her mode of killing is disease," I stated.

"He bites his victims, leaving marks that are not characteristic of a human bite," JT added, pointing to the close up of one of the victim's neck wounds. "We see only canine punctures. No incisors. And no lower-teeth marks."

"He must have some seriously long canines," Gabe said. "Could be wearing fake fangs."

Could be. But why?

"Is he delusional?" I asked.

Chief Peyton shook her head. "I doubt it. The killings don't appear to be that of a disorganized killer. However, we don't have an MO yet. All we have is a victim type—female in her thirties, brunette, and living close to a park or school. But we don't know yet how he approaches or overcomes his victim, what tools he uses in his killing, or the time and place the crimes occurred."

"What about a signature?" I asked. "Are the bites a signature? Could he be killing to bite, rather than biting to kill?"

Chief Peyton nodded. "It's a possibility."

Tapping his pencil against his notebook, Fischer added, "The unsub doesn't kill right away. He relinquishes control after the attack, risking the victim identifying him. That's the action of a confident killer—"

"Or a disorganized one," I added. "Psychotic killers don't fear being caught, because they don't realize what they've done is wrong."

"True. We have a lot of work to do." Chief Peyton pointed at the clock. "And not a lot of time to get it done. We have just over two hours to figure out who the unsub is and stop him, or another woman is going to die." She pointed at Fischer. "Fischer, I want you and Wagner to go through the coroner's reports for all three victims with a fine-tooth comb. Look for any clues that might lead us to a crime scene. Trace evidence, fibers, that kind of thing." She pointed at JT. "JT, I want you and Skye to retrace the steps of all three victims on the day they died. Where did they go? Who did they talk to?"

"But there's no way they could have been infected the same day they died," I piped in. "The diseases were too far progressed. Take Laura Miller, for example. The incubation period for malaria is seven days, minimum, meaning she was infected at least a week *before* she died. . . ." The significance of that fact sent a chill racing up my spine.

The next victim was probably already infected. She just didn't know it yet. There was a ticking time bomb set to go off inside her body.

How could we stop a killer who could be as much as a week ahead of us? And was there any chance we could save his next victim?

"That may be true. They may have been infected days, or weeks, before they died. But what about the fresh bite marks? Not to mention, the foreign DNA sample that was found on all three victims?" the chief asked. "They couldn't have possibly picked that up a week before their death."

Which meant what? The unsub was going back to visit his victims after they collapsed? Why?

Every member looked sober as we gathered our things and headed toward the door. Somebody nudged me as I was leaving the room. I twisted to look over my shoulder. As I suspected, it had been Gabe.

"What?" I snapped, worrying I'd hold up JT. We had important things to do. Now was not the time for silly schoolyard games. When Gabe didn't say anything right away, I motioned toward JT's cubicle. "JT's waiting. We have a lot to do."

"Yeah. I know. This won't take long." He grabbed my elbow—he actually had the nerve to touch me—and pulled me off to one side. I glared at his hand and clamped my lips shut. "Look, I know you're mad about the BAU, but I wanted you to know I had nothing to do with that." He honestly expected me to believe that pile of dog poo?

"Okay, whatever." I jerked my arm out of his grasp and tried to muscle my way past him. He was such a freaking huge ox. Why was he blocking the way? "Gabe."

"You don't believe me."

"No. Of course, I don't. But that doesn't matter. None of this does. Right now, what matters is JT, who's standing over there by the elevators, twiddling his thumbs, wondering why I'm wasting time having a tête-à-tête with you."

Looking almost pathetic, Gabe shrugged. "You're right. Good luck, Sloan." He stepped aside to let me pass, and I scampered to my cubby, crammed my Netbook into the case, slung the strap over my shoulder, and headed for the elevators. I gave JT an I'm-sorry smile and checked the elevator call button to see if he'd already pressed it. Yep, it was glowing red.

"Which victim do you want to check out first?" I asked, catching my breath after the mini sprint I'd done to catch up to him.

"I was thinking about that." The elevator door slid open and JT motioned for me to go in first. "All three fit the same profile, so I don't think it matters. But I think we'll go with Laura Miller."

JT drove, leaving me free to think. Now that the case had taken a sharp left, into Life-or-Deathville, I wanted to do my best to help. Nobody would hear any smart-ass comments about the Clock of Doom from this girl again.

I flipped to the copy of Fischer's notes. He'd made a copy for every member of the team and left them on the table. "This guy's thorough," I said, impressed. "He included a minute-by-minute breakdown of Miller's final day."

"That'll make it easier. I'm assuming we need to start at her house."

"Yup." I reread the itinerary. "Damn, I wore the wrong shoes this morning."

"Why's that? I don't see anything wrong with them."

I glanced down at the butt-ugly, cheap vinyl pumps. The man was no judge of shoe quality. "Our victim ran over five miles that morning."

He sniggered. "Ah, I see."

I stared down at my feet. Five miles in those shoes, and I'd be crippled for weeks. "I have an idea."

"What's that?" He flipped the turn signal and glanced over his shoulder, inching onto the freeway.

"You jog the route, and I'll follow you in the car."

"Sure. We can do that." He pointed at the gearshift. "You do know how to drive a stick, don't you?"

Shit. Why hadn't I noticed that before? "Um, the answer to that would be no."

"I'll let you give it a try when we exit."

"No, that's okay." My toes cramped at just the thought of hiking five miles in pumps with man-made uppers and absolutely no arch support. But there was no way I was going to drive JT's car. I'd tried driving a stick once. It had been a car I'd found on a used-car lot. A fierce little beast, a Mazda something-or-other, red. I wanted to buy that car so bad. It took me at least ten minutes to get it off the lot when I'd tried taking it for a test drive. Then I stalled it in the middle of an intersection as I was trying to make a left turn. There was a Frito-Lay truck barreling at me at about a hundred, or so it seemed. The ending was pretty predictable. The truck won. The Mazda wasn't so fierce after that.

I vowed never again to attempt to drive a car with a standard transmission.

"Are you sure?" he asked.

"Positive." I sighed and wiggled my toes in my shoes, enjoying them while they could still move without causing agony. All too soon, we rolled up to what I assumed was

Laura Miller's house. It was nothing special, a carbon copy of the other Colonials on the street. Vinyl siding. Faux-brick facing. Along the front of the house was a weedy flower garden. The petunias were looking a little neglected.

"I'm hoping the victim's husband will know the exact route his wife took." JT switched off the car and climbed out.

I followed him up the front walk.

I glanced at my cell phone. "It's after nine. What if Mr. Miller left for work already?"

"I called him this morning. He said he'd wait for us." On the porch now, JT rapped on the off-white–painted front door.

"Smart move."

The door swung open and a pleasant-looking man greeted us with a weak smile.

"Good morning, Mr. Miller. I'm Agent Thomas." JT flashed his badge. "This is Miss Skye."

I offered the man my hand. "I'm sorry for your loss."

He shook it. "Thank you."

"Thank you for agreeing to speak with us." When Miller stepped to the side to let us in, JT headed inside. As usual, I followed. We entered into a living room with beige carpet and walls. The house's interior wasn't any different from the exterior. Relatively neat, while at the same time showing a few signs of neglect, including a pretty hefty coat of dust on the bookshelves lining one wall of the living room.

"How can I help you, Agent Thomas?" Miller asked.

"We'd like to confirm the information you gave to Agent Fischer, regarding your wife's activities the day she died."

"Sure. Like I told the other agent, my wife took her morning jog and then went to work. She liked to stop at Einstein Brothers for a bagel and coffee on her way into work. That was probably her last stop before . . . before . . ." He scrubbed his face with his palm, glanced at a family portrait sitting on the fireplace mantel, and sighed.

"I'm sorry, sir," I said after glancing at the photo. "I realize this must be hard for you. We'd like to try to find some answers for you . . . and your daughter. Can you tell me if your wife ran the same route every morning?"

"Yes, she did. She took Trotter up to Clarksville Pike, then came back down to Great Star Drive and back home. It's about six miles, round-trip."

Six miles was worse than five. I wasn't looking forward to this. Maybe JT would can that silly notion of walking it. Really, if we drove, we'd still get some idea of what our victim saw. And I'd avoid getting blisters.

"Did she ever mention someone was following her? Was she uneasy about jogging in the last week or so?" I asked.

Miller didn't hesitate to answer. "No. Not at all. She would've told me if there'd been anything like that going on."

"What about unexplained injuries? Bruises? Scrapes?" JT asked.

This time, Miller took a moment before responding. "No, I don't remember seeing anything like that."

"And you're absolutely certain she ran the exact same route every morning, including the day she collapsed?" I asked.

Miller nodded. "Yes. I'm positive."

That seemed odd to me. If I'd been accosted by some strange man while I was out for my morning jog—not that I had to worry about that happening, because I am so *not* a jogger—you wouldn't see me running down the same street again.

Unless I didn't remember.

"And finally," I asked, noticing JT was staring at his notebook, deep in thought, "were you home the morning she collapsed, when she returned from her jog?"

Miller nodded. "Yes. I leave for work after my wife does—did."

"And again, you noticed no injuries? No scrapes or bruises?" I asked.

"Nothing. I saw her . . . er . . . get dressed after her shower." Miller hesitated, looking a little uneasy. I got a feeling I knew why, and it had nothing to do with our case."Um, I would've noticed anything unusual that morning."

I got his drift.

After thanking Mr. Miller, we headed back to the car. JT tucked his notebook into his pocket. "Okay, let's start walking."

I gave JT a look, the kind that said, "Are you crazy?"

He chuckled and opened the car door. "I'm with you. We'll drive the route first."

"Thank God!" I climbed in, buckled myself up, and watched out the open window as JT followed the victim's jogging route. Once we got outside of the subdivision, the roads were two-lane highways cutting through lightly wooded landscapes. Here and there were sprinkled ranch homes, tucked between patches of forest. The traffic was very light. "It would be easy enough to surprise a jogger out here."

"Sure would." He turned left onto Clarksville Pike, and I pointed at a landmark I recognized. "Take a look, that's the park Richardson lives behind. Oh, it's a school, not just a park."

"Interesting."

We drove past the River Hill Garden Center and the cemetery. I tried to spot Debbie Richardson's house from the road, but I couldn't. "I don't believe for a minute that it's a coincidence Laura Miller was jogging every morning less than a quarter of a mile from Debbie Richardson's house. Do you?"

"Nope."

"The unsub could've stumbled upon her anywhere along her route, infected her with the malaria, and nobody would have heard her cries for help. Then he could have released her. And if he gave her an amnesic, she wouldn't remember being attacked. Thus, she wouldn't be afraid. That must be how it went. It's the only explanation that makes sense."

JT chewed on his lower lip as he steered the car onto Great Star Drive, which took us back into the subdivision. "Maybe. But how do you explain the fact that she showered after she jogged? A shower should've washed away the unsub's DNA."

"Huh. Good point. He must've waited until after she showered." When JT pulled up in front of the Millers' house again, I looked at him. "Now what?"

"We head to Einstein Brothers Bagels."

"Okay. I could use a shot of caffeine . . . and maybe an everything bagel while we're there. Or maybe one of those egg sandwiches, with spinach, mushroom, and Swiss cheese. Ever had one?"

"No." He navigated the car back onto Great Star Drive, heading back to I-95, which would take us into the heart of Baltimore. It was a quick drive, thank God, just under a half hour. I was salivating for egg, spinach, and Swiss cheese already. I'd need a drool bib if it took any longer.

"They're insanely good," I told him. "You have to try one."

He scrunched his nose. "Not a fan of eggs. Nope."

"Your loss."

By the time we rolled up in front of the Einstein Bros. Bagels store, my stomach was making all kinds of embarrassing noises. If not for the radio—JT loved to listen to talk radio—I would have died of embarrassment long before we'd reached our destination.

I hurried inside. The smell of coffee and toasted bagels made my stomach rumble louder. I wrapped my arms around my waist and took my place in line, behind a woman dressed from head to toe in black. In front of her was a man dressed similarly. I checked my watch. It was after eleven. It was no wonder I was starving. I glanced behind me, expecting to find JT. He was nowhere to be found.

I placed my order and agonized over the wait. Finally I had my little bag and paper cup in hand—I'd opted for an iced tea instead of coffee. I strolled outside.

I looked in the general direction of JT's car. No JT. I looked left. I looked right. Still no JT. I went to the car and set the tea on the hood, after taking a slurp. I partially unwrapped my sandwich so I could take a bite. Half of it was gone before I realized I'd eaten any of it. Then it was all nearly gone.

Still no JT.

I tried the door. Unlocked? Where did he go?

After washing down the last bite of sandwich with some tea, I put my cup in the car's cup holder and wandered around one side of the building.

I found JT in back, Dumpster diving. The life of an FBI agent is oh, so glamorous.

"Did you find something?" I asked the only part of his anatomy I could see—his butt.

"No." With one hand flattened over the back of his head, he stood up, turned around, crunched his way to the edge, and climbed out. "I don't know how I got in there. One minute I was checking the back of the building—I thought I saw someone running back here—and the next, I woke up, feeling like my head had been flattened in a sheet metal press, and smelling like month-old meat."

"Oh, my gosh, you're kidding." I took a cautious look around. I wouldn't want to end up getting clobbered on the head and thrown in the trash too.

"Does it look like I'm kidding?" Standing somewhat unsteadily, he picked bits of crumpled napkin, mushy bagel, and unidentifiable ick from his clothes.

Evidently, JT's personality got ugly after a knock on the melon. I didn't hold it against him. Mine would too.

I brushed a piece of bagel off the back of his shirt. "Sorry. Of course, it doesn't look like you're kidding. Are you okay? Is your wallet missing? Your gun?" I reached for him, offering some support if he needed it.

He rejected my offer with a shake of the head. Which led

to a staggering sway. "I'm fine." He patted himself down. "Wallet's there. So is the gun."

"How strange." I circled around his back and tried to get a peek at his head. His hair was matted down and covered in something dark and sticky. Congealed tea? Melted chocolate? Blood? "Maybe we should get you looked at."

"No, I'm okay." He shuffled toward the side of the building. "Shit, my head hurts." He glanced back at the Dumpster. "What did you do?"

"Me? Nothing. What do you mean, what did I do?"

"To my head. It hurts like a son of a bitch." Grimacing, he fingered the place where the sticky stuff was. "Did you hit me with something?"

I was thinking . . . concussion. Definitely. Or . . . had he been doped too?

I gently steered him toward the car. "Let's take a ride. You need to get checked out." I had no idea where the nearest hospital was.

Thank God for GPS.

It wasn't easy convincing JT that he needed to be the passenger, not the driver. He was one stubborn man. But after about ten minutes of him repeating himself, and then vomiting, he finally slumped into the passenger seat and belted himself in. I took the driver's seat. I rummaged through the contents of his trunk and scored a plastic shopping bag. I handed it to him, just in case he felt sick again. It took about five minutes to adjust the mirrors, seat, and steering wheel. In that time, JT tried, and failed, to convince me he wasn't hurt. And while I looked up the location of the closest emergency room, he reminded me that I didn't know how to drive a stick, and that there was a killer running loose, and his next victim didn't have much time left.

There was no need to remind me of any of those things, especially the last one. I was more than aware of how fast time was flying and how little we were accomplishing. Wasting hours upon hours in an emergency room was the last thing we needed to do. But it was necessary. Vomiting after a head injury was a bad sign in an adult.

I handed my phone to JT. "Here, you're the navigator. Tell me when I need to turn. I can't hear the GPS very well. Stupid phone doesn't have a decent speaker."

"Okay." His head bobbed to the side. His eyes rolled around in their sockets. He was going to be as useful as a toddler.

Before he dropped the phone, forcing me to pull over to retrieve it from the floor, I snatched it from him and set it in my lap. "Miss GPS" was my only company as I lurched and sputtered JT's car to the hospital. JT took a nap.

When we pulled up to the emergency entry, I had to more or less drag him out of the vehicle. He put up a fight. A security guard wheeled a cussing JT inside, while I stalled the car twice in the driveway before bouncing it into a parking spot. I called Chief Peyton before I headed inside, asked what she wanted me to do—stay with JT or continue without him. She told me there hadn't been a new victim reported yet, so I should stay with JT, so that's what I did.

JT slept some more.

After JT was taken back to a room, I opened the romance novel Katie had downloaded onto my phone. I wasn't a big novel reader, but what the hell? Katie had been bugging me for months to read it. I couldn't get a signal on my laptop. And I was in the mood to be amused. Surely, *The Viking King and the Maiden* would amuse me.

A nurse came to the waiting room to get me just as I was opening my newly downloaded e-book. She escorted me back to JT's room and asked what the problem was.

Sporting a blue hospital gown, JT looked at her with squinty eyes and snapped, "I told you, nothing's wrong."

I said, "He was hit in the head and is acting weird."

She nodded, Velcroed a blood pressure cuff around his

arm, and squeezed the little bulb at the end of the rubber tube to inflate it. "Do you remember what happened, sir?"

"Yes." JT looked at me. He looked at her. "No." He winced, fingered the back of his head. "Damn, my head hurts. And I feel sick."

"He threw up once already," I mentioned. "You might want to give him a pan."

The nurse finished taking his blood pressure before fetching a pink plastic basin from the cabinet. Lucky for her, he didn't need it before that. He made use of it shortly after she handed it to him, though. I had to look away. It felt wrong watching him lose his breakfast like that. It was a private, shameful moment. Granted, he'd seen me toss my cookies at the crime scene my first day on the job. But he was a man. Men were supposed to be strong. And he was a strong man. But he sure didn't look it when he was vomiting.

A doctor who looked like she was fresh out of junior high came in a few minutes later. I didn't think much about it. I'd graduated a smidge early myself. But I did think something about the timing of her arrival. I read seven words per second. The fact that she came strolling in before I'd finished a single paragraph suggested they were taking JT's injury seriously. This was a good thing. I didn't like what I was seeing either.

She greeted him with a cheery "Hello, sir."

He responded with a mumbled "Hi."

"What happened today? Why are you here?" the doctor asked, skimming his chart.

"I dunno." He closed his eyes. "I'm tired. And I think I might hurl again."

"Hmm." She grabbed the little handheld light from the wall and twisted the top to illuminate the little bulb. "Open your eyes, please." As she checked his pupils, she asked, "Do you know what day it is today?"

"Thursday."

It was Friday.

"Can you tell me who the president is?"

"Obama."

"Good." She turned off her light. "Where does your head hurt?"

"Back here." Grimacing, he touched the lump on the back of his head.

"Can I see it?" she asked.

"You tell me, can you?" he answered.

The doctor gently pried his hand away. "Can you sit up, so I can take a look?"

"Yeah." He slumped forward.

She gently palpated his scalp, stopping when JT let out a yelp. "You have quite a lump there. Do you remember how you got it?"

"No."

She looked at me.

"I found him in a garbage Dumpster, behind an Einstein Brothers Bagels shop. He said somebody clocked him."

She gathered up some supplies—gauze and alcohol to clean the wound. "Was he knocked unconscious?"

JT ouched as she dabbed his scalp with a soaked gauze wad.

I answered, "I can't say for sure, because he was awake when I found him. But it's possible. Or, I worry he might have been drugged. We're working a case. Can't say more. Either way, I don't know what happened. I was inside, getting a sandwich. It took a few minutes."

"Okay." She dropped the bloodstained gauze in his pink pan and took a step back. "He's probably okay, but I'd like to get a CAT scan, just to make sure. And he should probably have a tetanus shot too."

I nodded my agreement. "Better to be safe than sorry." As soon as the doctor headed out, I went back to reading.

JT went back to sleeping.

"Sloan Skye?" he slurred.

"Yeah, JT?" I scooted my chair closer to his bed so he could see me.

"I like your name."

"Thanks. I like it too." Trying not to chuckle—at the moment, it was kind of like talking to a younger JT—I clicked the button on my phone, turning the page in my e-book. So far, I was sort of liking *The Viking King and the Maiden.* The vocabulary posed no challenges. The sentence structure was simple, like second-grade simple. It was super easy to comprehend. I hadn't read a book that easy since kindergarten. But the images the words painted were making me a little warm— in a good way. I had never imagined I'd get into a man with big muscles, small clothes, and a big . . . sword, but there it was.

"Skye makes me think of angels," JT said.

"That's nice, JT. Angels are good things to think about when you're in a hospital."

"You're an angel, Sloan."

Urk. Awkward.

My heart did a little pittery-pattery thing in my chest. Maybe it wasn't such a good thing that I'd been sitting here reading a love story. I clicked the button, closing the file."Um, thanks, JT."

"No, really. I think you're beautiful."

Now, that wasn't awkward. It was funny. Me? Beautiful? No way. Evidently, after the mean phase, JT turned extremely affectionate after a hard knock on the head. This side was definitely more charming. But also more dangerous. "JT, as much as I appreciate the compliment, I think your head must be hurt worse than we both thought. You're seeing things."

"No, I'm not. I thought you were gorgeous, and sexy, and fucking hot, since the first day we met. I just didn't know how to tell you, until now."

I was speechless.

If JT wasn't an FBI agent, and if he wasn't suffering from what I was beginning to suspect was a life-threatening concussion, I might've pursued this. "Gorgeous" was much more applicable to JT than me. And "sexy." And "hot." And it sucked that I didn't know if he genuinely meant what he was saying or not. And it sucked even more that it didn't matter, because I couldn't do anything about it, no matter how much I wanted to.

And, boy, did I want to.

"Skye?"

"What, JT?" I braced myself for another compliment.

"I'm going to hurl."

Uncertainty and mystery are energies of life. Don't let them scare you unduly, for they keep boredom at bay and spark creativity.

—R. I. Fitzhenry

8

Six hours later, I walked a groggy-headed JT out to the car. The diagnosis: a concussion. No surprise there. The treatment: rest, and someone waking him up periodically to make sure he was okay. Again, not a big surprise. As we strolled to the car, JT informed me he lived alone. He didn't have any family close by. Nor did he have any friends.

In other words, he didn't have anyone to handle wake-up duty.

I decided I could volunteer for the job, but only if we stayed somewhere safe. Somewhere public.

Once we were snug and belted in, he dug a hunting knife out of his glove compartment. Before I could stop him, he cut the plastic hospital bracelet off. I thanked "The Big Guy Upstairs" JT's hand didn't slip, and I contemplated where to take him. The FBI Academy was probably my best bet. I could try to get some work done while he slept, and I wouldn't be alone with him for any length of time. It wasn't that I didn't trust him. He'd made it clear, after his heartfelt confession, and after throwing up, that he'd never do anything to compromise our jobs.

The problem: I was not 100 percent sure I could trust myself.

This was new for me. I'd never been attracted to someone I shouldn't be. Not this attracted. And not when so much was at stake. I liked JT. A lot. When our eyes met, little sparks of electricity sizzled through my body. I haven't felt that way about a guy in ages.

Not since Gabe.

When the car jerked and sputtered out of the parking lot, aimed for the freeway, JT said, "Easy on the clutch. Where are we headed?"

"To the office. You're on desk duty. You heard the doctor. You need rest."

"I'm fine. I haven't thrown up in at least a couple of hours."

That was true. He was also looking a lot less shaky. His eyes weren't rolling around in their sockets anymore. His CAT scan had come back clear. He had no bleeding in his brain. Or bruising. But I didn't care. I wasn't going to take any chances. If he was clunked in the head again, he could suffer long-term, irreparable brain damage. Brain damage was nothing to scoff at.

"You're going back to the office, and that's final." It was a little after rush hour, and the traffic on the freeway had eased up. I navigated his car into a spot between a bus and a beer truck. My knuckles turned white.

"Are you nervous, Skye?"

"No, I'm fine," I lied. Truth was, I hated driving this car, on the freeway, especially with trucks. And even more, with trucks going eighty miles per hour. "How about we work on our case while I drive? Organized or disorganized killer?"

"Organized. Definitely," he said.

An organized killer was, basically, a psychopathic killer. Organized killers avoided capture. They planned their kills. They killed strangers. They hid evidence, controlled the crime scene, controlled the victim, and usually followed the media reports of their crimes. They were intelligent, had lovers, friends, spouses, and sometimes children. They were the Ted Bundys and John Wayne Gacys of the world.

I had to agree. So far, what little evidence we had pointed to an organized killer. "If that's the case, then we'll find no personal connection between the unsub and his victims. It's also highly unlikely he lives near them. But I think the Columbia area is his trolling grounds. Maybe he uses a ruse, like Bundy?"

"Maybe."

"Male or female?" I asked next. JT had been referring to the unsub as a male all along, but my gut told me he was a *she*.

"Male," JT stated, sounding very sure of himself.

"Why do you say that? There seems to be no sexual motive to the crimes. No mutilation or torture. Poisoning is used more often by women. I'd consider injections of a lethal infectious agent to be a poisoning."

"Sure, but what about the saliva?" he countered. "The biting and licking could be related to a sexual fetish. And he's killing strangers. Women kill patients in hospitals, people they know, rarely strangers."

He argued his case well, but I wasn't swayed. "Okay, so we've settled upon an organized killer, male—though I'm not convinced you're right there. That leaves motive. Is our killer a visionary, mission-oriented, or hedonistic killer?"

"Hedonistic. Most definitely."

I didn't disagree with that. There was no sign the killer was trying to rid the world of dangerous thirty-year-old brunette women, or was suffering from a psychotic break. "Thrill killer, you think?" I asked.

"Yes."

I had my doubts there too. "Okay, but here's the thing. Thrill killers feed off the victim's fear. If he's using an amnesic to make his victims forget about the attack, what's he getting out of it? The victims are walking time bombs, but they don't know it. What need does that satisfy in the unsub?"

The pieces weren't exactly snapping into place for me. Some of them fit okay. Others, not quite. I decided I'd go on the Internet when we got back to the office and read up on criminal profiling. It had been a while. My memory wasn't hazy, but I wondered if I might have missed something.

While I kept us alive for the rest of the drive—no small feat, considering what I was driving—JT called Chief Peyton to talk about our profile . . . which, I couldn't help noticing, did not include any species but Homo sapiens. This kind of surprised me. That first day, they'd been so quick to jump to conclusions about the nature of our unsub. Specifically deciding he or she was some kind of vampiric creature. What had made them completely dismiss the idea of a nonhuman unsub now?

After a quick trip through a drive-through, we rolled into the FBI Academy's parking lot a little after six. I parked the car and dropped JT's keys into my purse. I didn't want JT to get any stupid ideas about trying to drive tonight. He didn't seem to notice.

He was quiet as we rode the elevator up to our floor. And he didn't say anything as we each headed to our respective cubicles. The unit was dark. Silent. Our footsteps echoed on the gleaming tile floor. *Tap, tap, tap.* For some reason, the hollow sound gave me a case of the shivers. The paper bag in my hand—dinner—crinkled. The cola in the paper cup—caffeine—sloshed. My laptop bag smacked against my hip, the material giving off a soft sloughing sound with every step. While I carted my bagged meal to my desk, JT flipped on the lights. I blinked as my eyes adjusted. They focused on the folded piece of paper sitting on my desk as I sank into my seat.

That handwriting looked familiar.

I unfolded the paper and looked at the last line. No wonder it had looked familiar.

Gabe.
I felt my teeth clench.

*Heading home for a change of clothes. Be back in
less than an hour.*
                                              Gabe

Ugh.
Why was he leaving me notes?

He hadn't left a time on the note, so I had no idea how long
it had been. There was no sign of Fischer, Chief Peyton, or
Brittany. I assumed Fischer and Peyton were working—they
wouldn't call it a day with so little time left. Brittany, on the
other hand, was a big question mark. It was a Friday night.
She might not be back until Monday morning. At any rate, I
was semirelieved we wouldn't be alone in the office for long.

"I'm going to wash up," JT said, his voice echoing
through the stillness, making me jerk. A fry that had been on
its way to my mouth flung from my hand, smacking the
frosted glass pane in my cubicle's wall. It rebounded and
landed with a plop on the desktop. For some reason, it didn't
look so edible after all that.

"Okay." I dug into the paper container for a fresh one and
shoved it into my mouth before I lost it too. Just as I was polishing off my dinner, JT returned from the bathroom, looking freshly showered, his hair damp, his go bag slung over his
shoulder.

He dumped his bag on the floor in his cubicle. I heard it
land with a dull thump. Then I heard the sound of dragging.
I glanced over my shoulder. He was pulling a chair toward
me. I scooted mine over when I realized what he was doing.

He went back to his desk, grabbed an armload of things,
and returned to my cubicle, unloading them on my desk.
Then he flopped into the chair, now in very close proximity
to mine.

Nothing like taking over a girl's space.

"So . . . what's all this?" I asked, motioning to JT's stuff, which was crowding out mine—much like his very sexy scent and very bulky male body was overwhelming me.

"I was sitting there at my desk, thinking two heads are better than one, especially when one isn't exactly functioning at prime operating condition. Rather than make you move to my space, I thought I'd come to yours."

"How thoughtful." I stuffed the wrapper for my sandwich and the little paper cup for my fries in the paper bag and dropped it in the trash can under my desk. That freed up about six square inches of space.

Have I mentioned how small our cubicles are? Or how big JT seems when we're crowded into a space the size of a broom closet?

He grabbed a folder, flipped it open. "Fischer left some things on my desk. He's chasing down a lead in Baltimore."

"Great. What do you have?" I leaned toward him to get a look at the file. But instead of looking down, something made me look at his face. Our eyes met, and something unexpected happened. We had a little moment—you know, a guy/girl moment. An invisible current zapped between us, leaving me a little shivery, in a good way. Some girls might not see JT as the kind of guy that would turn heads if he walked through a crowded room. To me, he was mind-blowingly gorgeous. His hair was a little on the long side, but I liked it. The way his crisp white shirt fit over his thick shoulders and arms made me a little dizzy. And I liked his eyes and his mouth. His lips were a nice shape, indeed.

Were they coming closer to mine?

"Sloan," he whispered.

Oh, my God, he's going to kiss me.

I was frozen. Couldn't move. Not an eyelid. Not a toe. I couldn't breathe. Couldn't speak.

We can't do this. Can't. Shouldn't. Oh, shit.

"Helloooo?" Gabe called from somewhere close by. Too close. Much too close.

I lurched backward.

JT jerked away.

A rush of heat gushed up my neck.

Had Gabe seen . . . ? I looked at Gabe. He looked at me . . . and smiled.

Shit!

"We were just looking over Fischer's notes." I poked a finger at the folder, which should have been in JT's lap. It wasn't. It was on the floor. My finger was pointing at something else.

My cheeks flamed even hotter.

"Yeah, Fischer's notes." Gabe's eyes narrowed ever so slightly.

I curled my fingers into a fist; gritting my teeth, I tried to think of a comeback that wouldn't get me in deeper trouble. "The victim's best friend works at a pharmaceutical lab . . ."

JT calmly scooped up the file, stood, and shoved it into Gabe's hands as he strolled past him. "She's telling the truth. I'm feeling like shit—damn concussion. I think I'd better lie down for a while. Skye, don't let me sleep for more than an hour."

"Okay," I said, my voice a little shaky.

Gabe glanced at the file in his hand, then at JT's retreating back.

I give him credit, he didn't say a word until after JT had closed himself in the conference room.

He began, "Sloan—"

"If you tell anyone about this, I will find a way to get back at you."

"I'm not going to tell anyone." He slumped into the chair JT had abandoned and handed the file back to me. "But I gotta say, I never thought you'd go for a guy like that."

"Like what? Er, I'm not 'going' for him, anyway. Nothing happened. Nothing is ever going to happen." Trying to look busy so he'd drop the subject, I flipped through the papers in the file. "If you don't mind, I'd like to get back to work."

"Sure, Sloan. If that's what you want." After a beat, he sighed. "We've had this love-hate thing going on for years. It's been fun. But I think it's time we set our past problems aside and moved on. High school was a long time ago."

If only he meant that.

I rolled my eyes. "Do you expect me to buy that line of baloney, after everything you did to me this week?"

"Did to you *this week*? What did I do?"

How could he have forgotten? I was beginning to wonder if Gabe had been knocked in the head too. "Where do I start?" I unfurled my right index finger. "You stole my job with the BAU, and then decided it wasn't good enough—"

"Hey, I told you, I had nothing to do with that." Gabe glanced over his shoulders, checking to see if anyone (who?!) was listening. "I don't know what happened here, why they decided you didn't belong in the BAU, but I was called in for an interview weeks after you were hired. When I was waiting to be interviewed that day, I overheard a phone conversation between Murphy and someone else. They were talking about you, about your transfer to another unit."

"What?" I shook my head. It was late. It had been a long day. My brain's circuits were clogged. I wasn't following him. "If they had already decided I was transferring to the PBAU, why would they let me think, for one minute, that I wasn't going to have a job this summer?"

"I don't know."

I squinted my eyes at him. "And why did you play along if you knew the truth?"

He shrugged. "Why not? I figured it was harmless fun. You weren't getting fired, just transferred. I assumed they wouldn't let you sweat it out too long. And I was right."

"This makes no sense."

"Neither does our case," he said, smacking the case file in my hands, "but that's not stopping you from working it, is it?"

"What do you mean by that?"

He glanced around again. I was beginning to think he was a bit paranoid. "I took a look at the DNA results. They're very interesting."

"Yeah? How so? The chief said there was a problem with them." Feeling like we were wasting a lot of time, I skimmed the first page of Fischer's notes.

"Well, for one, there are too many chromosomes for the unsub to be a human being. Like, nineteen too many."

"That must be why Chief Peyton said there was a problem with the results." So far, I wasn't finding anything earthshaking in Fischer's notes. What exactly was he expecting us to do with all this meaningless detail? I guessed this was why he was the media liaison and not a profiler.

"Okay. But if there was a problem with the results, why hasn't she requested another analysis?" Gabe asked.

Without looking up, I dismissed Gabe's speculation with a shrug. "She has, I'm sure."

"No, she hasn't."

"How do you know that?" I flipped another page. Fischer wrote down a lot of stuff, but most of it was useless.

"I have my sources."

"So . . . what are you suggesting? She's lying to all of us? Why?"

"I don't know. Maybe she doesn't trust us yet." He looked over his shoulder and gave me a nudge. Scowling, I gave him a dose of mean eyes. He answered with a tip of his head.

JT was shuffling toward his cubicle. Clearly, Gabe didn't want JT to know what we were talking about.

What was he thinking? That Chief Peyton had hired each of us for some very specific reason, only to hold back information, thereby making it harder for us to solve our first case? What would that accomplish?

And still, I couldn't completely dismiss what he was saying. It wasn't like Gabe to jump to silly conclusions. I'd known him—unfortunately—for years, certainly a lot longer than I'd known Chief Peyton. He was many things—devious, shifty, and downright manipulative. But he'd never been paranoid or prone to jumping to ridiculous conclusions.

Gabe snatched Fischer's notes out of my hands. "How did I miss that? The victim's best friend works at a pharmaceutical lab? She could have access to infectious agents? Where did you read that?"

"Um, the third page." I pointed.

Gabe checked his watch. "It's only a little after six." He looked at the clock in the conference room. "I feel useless. Do you want to go see if she's home?"

"You want me to go with you?" I asked him.

"Sure, why not?"

"Should we? We're not agents; we're interns. We have to take JT. . . ."

Gabe gave me a pointed look and heaved an exaggerated sigh. "Fine. He can come too, if you insist."

"He has a concussion—"

"I know what you're thinking." He jabbed me in the ribs and waggled his eyebrows.

I clamped my lips closed, knowing anything I said could—and would—be used against me. I excused myself from my own cubicle and went to JT's to tell him what we were thinking. He was hunched over his computer as I approached, his fingers flying over the keyboard. I noticed his screen went black the moment I was close enough to see it.

I pretended not to notice the screen. "I thought you were going to rest for a while."

"I couldn't sleep."

"I found something in Fischer's notes and thought we should check it out."

"Yeah? What?" He drummed his fingers on the desk.

"I mentioned this earlier, I guess a friend of Hannah Grant's works in a pharmaceutical lab. Name's Yolanda Vargas. She might have access to infectious agents. Could be the break we need."

"Huh. Could be. But I'm onto something here. Why don't you two go check it out?"

"Can we do that? I mean, we're not agents. We don't have any authority."

"Yeah. Hmm."

"Plus, you shouldn't be left here alone," I reminded him. "You have a concussion."

"I'm fine. The CT scan came back normal."

I gave him a warning glare. "JT."

"There'll be people in and out of here all night. I won't be alone." JT gnawed on his lower lip. "I hate to leave this. . . ." He glanced at the countdown clock, which was now displaying all zeros.

Clearly, we were all very aware that our time had run out.

"Let me see if I can get Peyton or Fischer on the phone. Give me a minute." JT lifted his phone off the cradle and dialed.

"Okay. I'll go get ready." I headed back to my cubicle.

Gabe was waiting for me there. "What's up?"

"I don't know. He's keeping something from me. Says it's important. Doesn't want to leave right now. He blacked out his computer screen just as I got close enough to see it."

"I'm telling you, something's going on here."

"Maybe. Maybe not." I plopped in my chair and Google Mapped the friend's address. "JT said he's going to call the chief or Fischer. In the meantime, we can be productive. The friend lives way over on the other side of Baltimore."

"Traffic should be easing up by now."

I printed the map and hit the power button, shutting down my computer. "You drive."

"Okay." Gabe stuffed his hands into his pants pockets.

"Left my keys on my desk. Be back in a few." He passed JT as he hurried to his cubicle.

JT's expression was serious as he approached me, 100 percent business. I was relieved. Maybe the scare with Gabe had put a chill on things between us, but that was okay. We needed to stay focused now, anyway.

Just to put his mind at ease, I said, "If you're concerned he'll tell anyone—"

"Nope. Not worried."

"Okay. Good." I stood, looped my laptop case's strap over my shoulder. "So what's the verdict? Can we go check out this lead? Or do we need to wait? It's getting late."

"I just got off the phone with the chief. Fischer's going to meet you and Wagner at the friend's house in an hour."

"Oh. Sure. Okay."

JT beamed. "We're good, Skye. Nothing to worry about. I can't tell you what I've found yet, because it might be nothing. But I don't want to drop it now."

"Yeah. Sure." God, I sounded so stupid. "I hope it's something, JT. We've run out of time."

"Exactly." He glanced at Gabe, who was strolling our way. "Good luck. I'll be here when you get back."

"Thanks."

As I left the building, I wondered if Gabe's speculations were making me overly suspicious, or if there really was something up. Either way, I decided I couldn't waste any energy trying to figure it out. All I could do was follow the leads I had and bring back what I'd found to the team. They'd take it from there.

Gabe's car was a brand-new Jaguar. I wasn't big on cars, don't care much about specific models, but I knew an expensive sports car when I saw one. This one was sleek and sexy black. The inside, on the other hand, wasn't sleek or sexy. It was a mess. The entire backseat was piled with books, boxes of stuff, and baskets of clothes. If I didn't know better, I'd swear Gabe was hauling around his entire life's possessions back there. As he cleared off the front passenger seat for me, he mumbled an apology and some kind of explanation about taking some stuff to Goodwill.

As Gabe drove us back down I-95, toward Baltimore, I almost admitted I was glad he'd joined the team. At the moment, I was feeling a little more like an outsider than a member of the PBAU. At least with him here, I wasn't alone. I wasn't the only outcast, the unpopular kid, wanting to be a member of some secret club.

What had made me think things would be different out in the real world? Once an outcast, always an outcast.

"You're quiet," Gabe said. "I've never seen you this quiet before."

Staring out the window at the landscape flying by at roughly eighty miles per hour, I hugged my computer case to my chest. "Just goes to show, you don't know me at all. I'm not always the gabby twit you think I am."

"I never said you were a 'twit.'"

"No, but you've thought it," I replied.

"Never." Gabe accidently bumped my knee as he set his hand on the car's gearshift.

A little something—an odd sensation—buzzed through my body. I shifted in my seat, moving my knees closer to the door and out of his reach.

"The truth is, I've always known you're smarter than me," Gabe remarked.

I didn't say a word. What was there to say? "Thanks" would be so . . . lame. "You're lying" would be closer to the truth, but I didn't feel like getting into a debate right now. Gabe's IQ had mine beat by almost ten points. We both knew that.

For years, we'd been locked in this strange love-hate competitive thing. It probably qualified as a relationship on the most basic level. But it was a difficult thing to label, let alone deal with. Since that terrible time so long ago, we'd been fairly successful at not killing each other by avoiding each other whenever possible. Clearly, that wasn't going to happen this summer. I had no idea at this point what kind of effect the next three months was going to have on our future.

"Do you think there's any chance we're going to identify the killer before someone else dies?" Gabe asked.

"I'm beginning to have my doubts. If you think about it, time already has run out for his next victim. She's out there somewhere, infected. She just isn't showing any symptoms yet. We don't need to know who the killer is. We need to know who the victim is. And we need to know what she's been infected with."

"You sound defeated." Gabe stretched his arm over part of the back of my seat and twisted to look over his shoulder before changing lanes. He didn't move his arm afterward.

"I'm trying not to feel defeated, but it isn't easy." I shoved his arm away. "I don't have a clue what I'm doing—but damn it, I can't just give up." Tired of my pity party already, I tried to turn my mind onto more productive tasks, like solving our case. "We're going about this all wrong. We should be looking for the next victim, not the killer. That's the only way we're going to make a difference. It's the only way we can save her life."

"But how can we find her if we don't know where to look?"

"I don't know. The only connection we've found so far between the three victims is the proximity of their homes to a park or school. Two of the three are located within a half-mile radius, but that hardly helps us. If only we knew how many residents living with homes backing those parks are in their thirties and brunette."

"I have an idea." Gabe shot across three lanes of traffic to get to the exit ramp. I grabbed the dashboard, squeezed my eyelids shut, and said a little prayer. "We could pretend to be taking a survey or something and go door-to-door, asking to speak to the lady of the house."

"Not bad. But what about Fischer?"

"Let him handle the lady at the lab. We'd just be there taking notes. And, based on Fischer's notes on Laura Miller, you and I both know Fischer is a master note taker. Fischer could teach the best court stenographer a thing or two about taking notes. We don't need to be there."

At the end of the exit ramp, Gabe turned left. Almost all four wheels were on the pavement when we took the corner.

"Good point. Where are we headed?"

"The closest spot with Wi-Fi. I hope your laptop battery's charged up."

The farther backward you can look, the farther forward you can see.

—Winston Churchill

9

Twenty minutes after we'd made that dizzying exit off the freeway, we were strolling up to the first house, not far from Debbie Richardson's home, our ruse all figured out, props in hand. It just so happened that Gabe's junk in his trunk had a purpose. My computer had come in handy too. We learned there was a local zoning issue that some folks were trying to get on the next fall's election ballot. They needed signatures. We needed a reason to go door-to-door. It was a perfect excuse. We printed out some fake forms at a nearby library and headed out.

After we'd visited twenty homes, however, we realized we had a big problem. A good two-thirds of the female residents in the area fit the description of our next victim.

After we'd talked to our twenty-first brunette, aged thirty-something, I decided we were wasting time. Precious, irretrievable minutes. I wasn't sure Gabe agreed with me.

"Now what?" At an intersection, I dropped the clipboard on the grass and plopped on my butt on the curb. So what if I looked ridiculous as I sat on the ground? My feet were killing me. I was exhausted. And I was more frustrated than I'd ever been in my life. "I'm going to need foot surgery after today."

"Go ahead and rest for a few. I'll take the next couple of

houses solo." Gabe loped down the sidewalk, with that loose-hipped swagger I hated so much.

A minute later, a little girl wearing a plastic firefighter's hat, rubber boots, and a tutu came rolling up from the opposite direction on a plastic three-wheeled bike. She skidded to a stop at the end of the sidewalk and asked, "Who are you?"

"I'm a stranger," I answered. I've never been a big fan of kids. Right now, I wasn't in the mood to change that. "Didn't your mother tell you not to talk to strangers?"

"Yeah." She shrugged, gave me an up-and-down assessing look. "You don't look so dangerous, though. What are you doing?"

"Working," I answered, not bothering to argue with her about the dangerous thing.

"You couldn't be working too hard. You're sitting down."

"I'm just taking a break for a few minutes."

"Oh." The kid climbed off her bike, pointed at the clipboard sitting on the grass. "Are you selling something? My mom hates it when people come to our door, selling stuff. She pretends we're not home."

"I do that too . . . sometimes." I kicked off my shoes and rubbed my right foot. My toes were numb. That couldn't be good.

"Tutu Girl" pursed her little lips. I tried not to notice how cute she was. "That's lying. My mom tells me lying's bad."

"Yeah, well, there are times when lying isn't such a bad thing." My arch cramped and I gritted my teeth and stretched my foot. "Anyway, don't you have a . . . a play date or something?"

"No. Everyone's at day camp or in day care. I'm bored." She kicked a rock. It skittered down the sidewalk. "I used to go to day care every day, but my mom quit her job. Now we stay home all the time. But next year I'll be in kindergarten." She pointed down the street, in the general direction from which we'd come. "My best friend, Veronica—she's in third grade. She lives in that house, down there. But she's gone. She went to summer camp with Julia even though it doesn't start for two whole weeks. Her mommy's all alone now, and she got mean. So I can't play there." She leaned close. "I think her mommy's sad she's gone."

"I bet she's very sad. I would be," I lied. I'd always told myself I'd have no kids. Kids were a bad idea for me, for so many reasons. For one, I have no patience whatsoever. And two, I was doing the world a favor by not passing down my DNA to future generations.

"I have an idea." My new friend plopped her little tutu-clad butt next to mine. "How about I help you? I know everyone on the street. I know who's at home and who's not. They won't be able to pretend they're not home."

"Thanks for the offer, but I think we're just about done. It's getting late."

Gabe was heading back. He was looking a little defeated now too.

After eyeballing Tutu Girl, Gabe said, "This is getting us nowhere."

"I totally agree. But what do we do next?"

"You could come to my house," my new friend suggested, adjusting her plastic helmet. "I have money. In a soup can. I've been saving for a new bear at Build-A-Bear."

I grabbed my clipboard and slid my feet back into my shoes. "Thanks, kiddo, but we couldn't take your money. We're not selling anything, anyway."

"Running . . . hmm . . ."

Standing next to me, Gabe stared off into the distance. The setting sun created deep shadows across his face, emphasizing the angle of his cheekbones. He looked older. More mature. More dangerous than I'd ever seen him. Nothing like the little punk I'd known since high school.

"You said one of the victims jogged in the morning?"

Begrudgingly, I pushed up to my feet. "Yeah, Laura Miller did and . . . ?"

"My mommy goes jogging sometimes," Tutu Girl said. "She pushes me in a big stroller. But I'm not a baby."

"I wonder if the other two victims were joggers too. Did you find that out?" Gabe asked.

"Victims?" Tutu Girl echoed.

"No. We didn't make it to the other victims' homes today. We were supposed to, but instead, we took a little detour to the hospital." I motioned toward the car, parked a quarter of a mile or so away. "We were following up on Fischer's notes. I hadn't read them all yet. He keeps very . . . detailed notes. If they were joggers, you can bet we'll find it in the file."

"At least that would help us narrow things down a little. Let's go." Gabe took long strides toward the car.

I gave Tutu Girl a little wave and followed Gabe, my heels *click-clacking* on the cement with every step.

And with every step, I gritted my teeth. The agony. I would never wear high heels to work again.

Behind me, I heard the rumble of plastic rolling on cement, the rhythmic *thunk, thunk, thunk* of the big front wheel hitting the cracks in the sidewalk. It seemed we were being followed. By one very curious firefighter/ballerina.

We crossed the street.

The sound stopped.

I glanced back. The kid was sitting on her bike, at the corner. Probably wasn't allowed to cross the street. She looked across the chasm between us, her eyes dark. For just a moment, I thought I was looking at myself as a child. Desperate for companionship. I smiled, and she smiled back. I waved, and she waved back. She dragged her little bike around the other way, climbed aboard and *thunk-thunk-thunked* her way back toward home.

I hurried to the car, dug out Fischer's notes, and sat down to read them. There was no mention of either Debbie

Richardson or Hannah Grant taking a morning jog. To double-check, we called the contact person for each. They verified that neither was a jogger, walker, or cyclist. We had hit a wall.

"Damn it." I glanced at the clock, then at my throbbing feet.

"I was so sure. . . ." Gabe gave my shoulder a little shake.

"We've just wasted . . . how much time? Maybe we should've met up with Fischer, after all."

"We did what we thought was best." Gabe started the car and shifted it into gear.

"We made a mistake." I watched out the window as the car rolled down the street. I watched Tutu Girl pedal her little bike down the sidewalk, and I wondered why she was outside so late. Fireflies were twinkling like little stars in the deepening shadows. This was the hour a preschooler should be safe and cozy, tucked in her bed, in her home, with a storybook and a teddy bear.

Down the street, we continued. Around a corner. Past Debbie Richardson's house. The porch light was on. And another light shined through an upstairs window.

It hit me then. Tutu Girl had been talking about someone named Julia. It could be *the Julia,* Debbie Richardson's daughter. We hadn't talked to her yet. She hadn't made it home from camp when we'd interviewed Trey Chapman. I doubted the teenager would be staying in the house alone, but it looked like somebody was in the house. I tapped Gabe's shoulder. "Go back."

"Huh?" He hit the brakes, stopping the car in the middle of the street.

I opened the car door and scrambled out, heading back toward the house. I had no idea what I'd say to her if she was there. I had no idea what questions I needed to ask. But I wanted to talk to her.

I was on the porch before Gabe had turned the car around. I knocked. No answer. I knocked again. Still nothing. I told myself the lights were probably left on to make the house look occupied. That's what people in the burbs did. But just for the hell of it, I knocked a third time.

Inside, I heard a thump. My heart started to pound. What if I'd caught a burglar? What if . . . ?

The door swung open, and a disheveled teen girl gave me a perplexed look. "Yeah?"

"Hi, are you Julia Richardson?"

"Um . . ." The girl glanced behind her. She combed her fingers through her blond hair. "Maybe."

"My name is Sloan Skye. I work for the FBI. We're working on a case—"

"FBI?" The girl, who I was 99 percent sure was Julia Richardson, gnawed on her thumbnail. "What's the FBI investigating around here?"

"It's a complicated matter." I heard Gabe's footsteps behind me. "This is Gabe Wagner. Can we ask you a few questions?"

"Um. Hang on." Julia shut the door. Behind it, we heard shuffling. The muffled sound of a male's voice. The slam of a door. Then the front door opened again, and Julia, looking a little less nervous—and a little less disheveled—stepped aside and waved us in. She gathered her hair over her shoulder, almost covering the ginormous flaming-red hickey on her neck. "I just came home to grab a few things. I'm staying with my dad now. . . ."

"Thanks for talking to us." I moved toward the staircase, giving Gabe some room to come inside. There was no male in sight. Romeo was probably hiding upstairs somewhere. Naked. "I apologize if this is a bad time. I saw the lights and thought I'd take a chance and see if someone was home."

"I guess it's your lucky day." Julia shrugged.

And some horny boy's—if that love nibble was any indication. "We won't take up much of your time." Trying not to judge the teenager for messing around with a punk so soon after her mother's death, I pulled out my little notebook. People handled grief in strange ways sometimes, especially kids. She was probably trying to hide from the pain. Or numb it. "We were told you were away at camp when your mother became ill."

"Yep."

"When did you leave?"

"A couple of weeks before she . . . died." Julia's eyes reddened. She blinked, sniffled. And the teenager who'd seemed so grown-up and sure of herself suddenly looked small and vulnerable. She fingered the mark on her neck, shifted her weight from one foot to the other, and stared at the floor.

"I'm sorry." I touched her arm. She flinched ever so slightly. "Nothing's going to bring her back, I know. But we're trying very hard to find out what happened to your mother, to give you answers." A tear slipped from Julia's eye as she blinked. "Did you notice anything different or unusual about your mother before you left?"

"No."

"Were you in contact with her after you left?"

"Yeah, she insisted on calling me every other night."

That was good news.

"Had she changed anything? Habits? Hobbies? Interests? Was she acting different in any way?"

After taking a moment to think about my question, Julia shook her head. "No. Nothing."

"What about people close to her? Friends? Coworkers? Family? Did she mention anyone acting strangely?"

"No." Julia grimaced. "I'm sorry. I can't think of anything. It was all so sudden. I didn't see it coming."

"That's okay."

Julia's scarlet-tinted eyes found mine. "Do you really think someone did this to her? That she was killed?"

"At this point, we're not ruling out anything." I scribbled my cell phone number on an empty notebook page and tore it out. I handed it to Julia. "If you think of anything, or notice anything, give me a call. Even if it's something small, even if you're not sure it's anything at all."

"Okay." Julia glanced at the paper before folding it into a tiny square and shoving it into her jeans pocket.

I headed to the door. Gabe stepped out before I did. I said a final thank-you and trotted down the front walk, trying hard to disguise the pain I felt with every step. Julia stood there, at the door, watching us, looking like she wanted to tell us something. I thought about going back, asking her if some stray thought was nagging her. Before I could, she closed the door.

Back at the car, I sank into the passenger seat and gently pried my shoes off my swollen feet. "We have absolutely nothing. Not a single clue. Damn it."

"It was worth a shot." Gabe gave me a little nudge on the shoulder. "You're letting this case get to you."

"Do you think Fischer found anything at the lab?" I asked, ignoring his comment. He was right. I was letting the case get to me.

"I'll call him and find out."

I sat and tried to get the blood flowing to my toes while Gabe called Fischer. Before Fischer had even answered, I watched Julia sprint out of the house, alone, drop a duffel bag in the backseat of the car parked in the street, and drive off.

Where'd she leave the boy? Or had I just imagined she'd had company?

"Was it me, or did you think she had company?" I asked, figuring Gabe hadn't gotten Fischer on the line yet.

"I bet she sneaked him out the back door. Probably guessed we'd be watching the house."

"Hmm, maybe."

"Obviously, you've never sneaked a boy into your house?"

"No comment." It was beyond awkward talking about this

with Gabe. My face felt like I'd been sunbathing on Mercury. "What's going on with Fischer?" I asked, intentionally steering our conversation back to safer territory.

"I'm not getting an answer."

"Damn."

He shoved the key into the ignition and cranked it.

"Where do you want to go next?"

He shrugged as he shifted the car into gear and pulled away from the curb. "I don't know. Anywhere but back to the office."

"Okay." I scooped up the file and started flipping through the pages inside. "It's getting late, but I guess we could try to finish up what JT and I started this morning."

"Okay." Gabe looked my way after stopping the car at a light. "Where to, then?"

"We were tailing Laura Miller's trail. She'd stopped at the Einstein Brothers Bagels a short distance from where she'd collapsed. We've already been there. Our next stop was where she was found."

"Then that's where we'll head next. We'll just keep going all night, until something comes up."

"*If* something comes up." I sighed, knowing it was going to be one long night.

The most beautiful thing we can experience is the mysterious. It is the source of all true art and science.

—Albert Einstein

10

We didn't know her name yet. Didn't know whether she was a mother, or a sister, or a wife. It was safe to assume she was a daughter, and a friend. She was a person with a life, and goals, and dreams. Well, she had been.

Now she was dead.

I was pissed.

We had failed.

And all thoughts about JT hiding evidence from me were shoved aside.

This was not the time.

The son of a bitch had done it again, killed yet another woman. All we needed for proof: those two little puncture wounds on our latest Jane Doe's neck.

I wanted to kick something. I wanted to scream. I wanted to wrap my hands around the killer's neck and wring the life out of him or her. I wondered if I'd ever get the chance to look her in the eye and ask her why she'd done it. Why she'd stolen four women's lives. Try as I might, I couldn't understand it. What had these women done to deserve this? Had they done anything at all? Maybe they'd been at the wrong place at the wrong time and she'd seen her chance and taken it.

As I studied the corpse, I didn't throw up this time. Maybe

I was too furious to get sick. That could be the key. This scene was no less gruesome than the last. The victim had collapsed outside of a hair salon. JT was talking to a witness. Gabe was with Peyton somewhere close by. Fischer was talking to the lead detective.

Thankful I'd taken the time to change into a fresh set of clothes—and, more important, more comfortable shoes—after dragging all over Baltimore last night with Gabe, I squatted down to get a closer look at the body.

Right away, I noticed the bright red pinpoint spots on the woman's legs. The medical term—petechiae. There was also dried blood around her mouth. My guess: this victim had also died from dengue shock syndrome, resulting from an undiagnosed case of dengue hemorrhagic fever. The incubation period for dengue could range from three to fourteen days, but the average was four to seven. I assumed the difference explained the delay in the victim's death, and underscored the fact that nobody could anticipate when any individual would become ill from any infectious disease. Too many factors came into play. I was beginning to believe the first three victims dying within forty-eight hours of each other was a fluke.

But that brought up another question. Why would the killer use a method that was so difficult to control?

"Are you okay?" JT asked behind me.

I stood, turning to face him. "Yes. I think I'm getting the hang of it. Thanks."

"I didn't get a chance to thank you last night. For staying at the hospital with me yesterday."

"Hey, it's okay."

"No. I mean—sure, you were doing what Peyton asked you to do. But maybe if you'd gone on without me . . ." He motioned to the victim.

"Don't go there, JT. There's no sense in making those kinds of assumptions. Besides, Gabe and I went back to Baltimore last night. We were out all night, tracking the movements of all three victims before they died. We found absolutely nothing. I had hoped . . ."

JT's touch on my arm was soft, fleeting, but it was enough to make me meet his gaze. Our eyes locked, and I saw the frustration and anger I could hardly contain mirrored in his expression. "We all feel the way you do."

I blinked, almost certain I was going to cry. It was the exhaustion. The stress. I could normally handle pressure. In fact, I excelled under it. But this was a different kind of stress. It wasn't about test scores or competition. It was about life and death.

I crossed my arms and chewed my lip. "When I applied for this job, I thought it was going to be so different."

"Yeah, you'd be filing, pouring coffee." JT winked.

"No, I thought the clues would be easier to identify, and the cases easier to solve. I feel so stupid, having assumed it would be anything like books, television, or movies. How ridiculous."

"We all think that way in the beginning. I came into the FBI believing I would be the guy who would crack open every case that landed on my desk. So did Fischer. And Peyton."

"Maybe." I glanced around. Everyone was busy, collecting evidence, analyzing it. Except for me. I was staring at a dead woman, feeling helpless, and useless. "I'd better get going, find out what Chief Peyton wants me to do next."

JT set a hand on my arm. "Don't let it get to you, Skye."

"I won't." I hurried to Chief Peyton. The lead detective on the case was just leaving her as I stepped within listening distance. "Chief, it looks like everything here's wrapped up. What would you like me to do next?"

"I'd like you to go home, get a shower, and get some sleep," she said as she motioned toward Fischer.

That wasn't what I'd been expecting. "I'm fine."

"You're exhausted."

"Sure, okay. Maybe I'm a little tired, but I can still work. I want to work."

Peyton shook her head and looked me straight in the eye. "Skye, you need to learn to pace yourself. If you don't, this job is going to take everything from you. Your friends. Your family. Your life."

"But there isn't much time—"

"That's for me to worry about. Not you. Got it?"

Reluctantly, I acquiesced with a nod.

"Be back at"—Peyton checked her watch—"three o'clock."

"Okay."

"And take Wagner with you."

"Will do."

Feeling a little like a scolded kid, I went in search of Gabe. I found him inside the salon, talking to the receptionist. The moment he saw me, his expression darkened. I gave him a little wave, and he excused himself.

"What's up?" he asked.

"We're being sent to our rooms, so to speak."

"What for?"

"For our own good, it seems."

"Bullshit." Gabe clenched his jaw so tightly, his lips turned white.

"I'm not happy about it either, but I'm not going to argue with the chief."

"If you won't, I will." Gabe strode off, looking like a man who was ready to tell his boss what he thought. He returned less than five minutes later, looking like a very different man. He grumbled something I couldn't understand and motioned for me to follow. "I'm parked this way."

He didn't say two words as he drove back to the FBI Academy. He pulled his car up behind mine, parked in the lot, and rammed the gearshift into park.

"See you later." I gave him a weak smile, scooped up my

laptop case, and dragged my exhausted body out of the vehicle. His wheels skidded a little on the pavement as he pulled away.

I returned home to a quiet apartment. A quiet apartment that reeked of chemicals. Thanks to Katie's latest experiments, the smell of burned this and distilled that generally didn't bother me. But this stench did.

And so did the bazillion dead bugs littering every horizontal surface in the place. Floors, tabletops, kitchen counter, shelves . . . my bed.

Urgh.

So much for crashing for a couple of hours before taking a shower and heading back to work. There was no way I was going to sleep in a bed full of dead insects. Blech.

Surely, Katie hadn't slept here last night. Probably taken this . . . infestation . . . as an excuse to spend the night with her boyfriend. I checked her room. I was wrong.

Awakened by the sound of her bedroom door opening, Katie lifted her head and blinked at me. "Sloan?"

"What happened here?"

"Fireflies."

"Fireflies?" I echoed. I'd never heard of a firefly infestation.

"Yeah. I went out for a while yesterday, and when I came home, just after lunchtime, there were hundreds of them in here." Katie sat up. Her hair looked like she'd combed it with a cake beater. "So I set off some bug bombs."

I looked down at the carpet. "Looks like they did the job."

"Yeah, they did. I wanted to make sure I got them all, so I bought some extras." Katie stretched, yawned, and slowly crawled out of bed. She winced as she stood, then rubbed her temples. "Damn it, I have another migraine. I hate PMS." Katie got a two-day migraine every single month, like clockwork. Every month, she suffered. And every month, I suggested she go see a doctor to get something for the pain. The over-the-counter stuff didn't touch it.

"That time already?" I asked.

Katie heaved an exaggerated sigh. "Yes." She padded barefoot toward me. "Gotta pee, then eat, so I can take something for this fricking headache."

"I think I'll start by stripping my bed . . . after I consume a gallon of coffee."

At the bathroom door, Katie paused. "Did you stay up all night?"

"Yeah. This case is pissing me off."

"Sorry, hon." Katie gave me a sympathetic smile, then shut herself in the bathroom to take care of business.

I headed to the kitchen, realized everything—even the sink—was covered with deceased *Photinus pyralis*. I decided a coffee run was much needed and headed out. I returned from Einstein Bros. to find my mother standing in the middle of my living room, her mouth gaping, and Katie frantically vacuuming the couch so Mom could sit before she fainted.

I shuffled in circles for a moment, looking for a clean, flat surface upon which to set the coffee and bag of bagels before using my elbow to rub a clean spot on the sofa table. As soon as I had my hands free, I went to my mother and supported her as she tiptoed across the floor to the now bug-free zone.

"What in heaven's name?" Mom asked when she was safe on the couch.

"We had a little infestation." I handed her a coffee.

"Are they . . . roaches?"

"No, fireflies." While Katie helped herself to a bagel, I went to the kitchen for a paper plate and knife. Thankfully, there weren't any dead insects inside the cupboards, and Katie had taped plastic bags across the front, to protect our dishes and food. I put the bagel I'd intended for myself on the plate and handed it to my mother, along with a package of cream cheese. "Here you go."

"Thank you." Mom pushed the paper cup of coffee away. "That coffee's terrible. Much too sweet. I've told you that before. Why you keep buying it, I'll never know."

I smiled and took a sip. In my book it was perfect, as usual. "Can I get you something else?"

"No, no. That's okay. I didn't come here for breakfast."

"Okay. I'm just going to get started. We have a lot of cleaning to do, and I need to get back to work in a few hours." I took a few healthy swigs of coffee, then went in search of some cleaning gear. "Was there some reason for your visit today, Mom?"

"No, not really. I just hadn't talked to you in a couple of days, and you know how worried I get when you don't call."

Using a dry washcloth, I cleared the bookshelf under the window of all the dead critters. "Sorry about that. I've been a little busy."

"How's the job going?"

"Okay."

"That's it? 'Okay'?"

"I can't say much more. I will say this." I dunked a second washrag in a bucket of Murphy Oil Soap and wrung it out. "The job is a lot harder than I expected."

"Hmm." My mother munched on the bagel. "I think that's a very good thing. You're being challenged." She glopped some more cream cheese on the top of the bagel before taking another bite. "I've been thinking about getting a job myself."

"Really?" My mother hadn't worked in decades. I couldn't remember the last time she'd held down a job. So to say this was a surprise was a bit of an understatement.

"Yes, really. My mind needs stimulation. I need a chal-lenge. Something to make me think." She stuffed the last bit of bagel into her mouth and nodded. "Yes, make me think. That's exactly what I need."

Having finished with the bookshelf, I moved on to the sofa table, using the dry rag to dust the insects into a small trash can before wiping it down with the wet one. "What kind of job would you like to find?" I asked, deciding there was no harm in encouraging her.

"Oh, I don't know. I could check with a few of the local community colleges—see if they're hiring for the fall semester."

"You mean, you want to teach?"

"Sure, why not? I am qualified."

That she was. But she'd always said she would never teach at a college, not even if her life depended upon it. Her reasons had never been clear to me, but it didn't matter much, anyway. Her medical condition had kept her out of the workforce, collecting SSI, since I was a kid.

"Then again," she said, wiping her hands on the paper napkin, "I could put in an application with the FBI."

I was almost 100 percent sure the FBI could not hire someone with a documented case of schizophrenia. But I highly doubted my mother was serious about applying. She couldn't know about the rigorous physical-fitness tests a new FBI applicant needed to pass before being accepted into the academy. The mile-and-a-half run alone would convince her it was a bad idea.

"The FBI, huh?" Finishing up the sofa table, I moved on. "Any other ideas?"

"Yes, I've been watching that show recently, the one about that bounty hunter, Dog. Such a strange name for a man. Anyway, I was thinking his job looks very exciting."

"A bounty hunter? Mom, are you serious?"

"Sure. Why not? You see, he's scary-looking—so, of

course, the fugitives run from him. But I'm not scary-looking at all, so they wouldn't suspect I'm a bounty hunter."

"That much is true. But you do realize those people are criminals—"

"Alleged criminals," Mom corrected. "They haven't gone to court yet."

"Alleged criminals who are trying to skip out on bail. I imagine they're not the friendliest bunch." At the side table now, I dusted some dead insects off the lamp. "Mom, you've always been antiviolence. Antigun. I can't imagine it being safe chasing fugitives without a gun."

"Hmm. Yes, I'd have a problem with the gun."

"You know, FBI agents have to shoot guns too."

"Do they?" Mom grimaced. "I guess that's out too." She heaved a loud sigh. "All the fun jobs require guns."

"Not all, Mom. I'm sure you'll think of something." I gave her a little pat on the shoulder with my elbow and pointed toward the kitchen. "I need to get the kitchen cleaned next."

"That's okay." Mom gingerly rose to her feet, scowling at the carpet, which was still covered with bugs. "I think I'll go home and do some more research."

"Sounds good. Good luck!" On tiptoes, I followed my mother to the door. Before she left, I gave her a quick hug, being careful not to touch her with my icky hands.

"Bye, Sloan." She patted my cheek. "I worry about you. Don't take any dangerous risks."

"I'm just an intern, Mom. I don't take risks."

"Everyone takes risks." She gave my cheek one final pat. "And make sure every single one of those creatures is dead. You wouldn't want a live firefly in your house."

"Sure, Mom," I said. Mom had a longtime aversion to fireflies. I'd never understood why. They didn't carry diseases, like mosquitoes or cockroaches. What harm could a little firefly do? "I don't think it's possible any of them are alive."

"Good-bye, Katie!" Mom yelled.

"Bye, Mrs. Skye!" Katie responded from the back of the apartment.

I went back to work, cleaning the kitchen. Katie came in just as I was finishing up the stove and dug in the cabinet, grumbling about her headache. I felt for her.

"Just shoot me now and put me out of my misery," she said as she pried the top off an aspirin bottle.

"Sorry, I won't be your Dr. Kevorkian."

"Bitch." She stuck her tongue out, like a bratty kid, dumped a couple of aspirin tablets in her mouth, and filled a glass with tap water.

"I can't believe you just called me that." I feigned a mortal wound and clutched my chest. I wasn't, in fact, wounded at all. Not physically or mentally. I knew Katie didn't mean it. But I was a little surprised. Katie had been raised in a very strict household, and although she'd strayed from her conservative Christian roots when she'd first read Darwin's *On the Origin of Species,* she rarely used curse words. Not even when beakers exploded in her face. The worst I've ever heard from her was "freaking."

Katie shrugged and headed back to her room. I switched on the radio and danced around like a dork as I finished cleaning the kitchen. When I went to claim the vacuum cleaner from Katie's room, I found her lying in bed with a blanket thrown over her head. Assuming her headache was the cause of her strange behavior, I closed the door, to help cut down on the noise. I then proceeded to vacuum every inch of the kitchen, living room, and my bedroom. I finished cleaning my room early enough to catch an hour nap before getting ready for work.

I woke up, feeling slightly refreshed. I could have used another hour or two of sleep; but out there, somewhere, was another woman with a time bomb ticking in her body. I wasn't going to let a little thing like lack of sleep stop me from doing whatever I could to help her. I would simply have to consume some extra sugar and caffeine. It just so happened, I liked stuff with sugar and caffeine, anyway.

This afternoon, I was smart. I donned some comfortable pants and a knit top. And I tossed those awful pumps in the trash and slipped my feet into the most comfy flats I owned. When I hurried into the PBAU, I found the place as lively as a mausoleum. I plopped into my chair, powered up the Netbook, and checked my e-mail, hoping Chief Peyton had sent me a message. Nada. I checked my phone messages next. Nothing. And there were no notes on my desk either. Not from the chief, JT, or Gabe. There wasn't even a new batch of notes from Fischer to peruse.

Feeling very lonely, I wandered over to Brittany's office. Her door was closed. I knocked. No answer.

This sucked. I was going to have to find a way to be useful on my own.

I headed back to my computer and started Googling everything and anything I could think of that might be related to our case. Malaria, dengue fever, suspicious puncture wounds, bite marks. While I was reading a Wikipedia article about typhoid, Gabe came strolling in, looking rested and cheery. He gave me an up-and-down look as he passed my cubicle, on the way to his.

"What's up?" he asked.

"Nothing. Nothing's up at all. They're all gone, even the computer girl. And I'm sitting here with nothing to do but stare at the walls. Ever since you joined the team, I've been treated like a leper. I don't get it."

"Don't take it personally." He slugged my arm, then pulled a chair up and sprawled into it. His eyes narrowed. "You look like shit."

"Gee, thanks. That's the way to make me feel better."

"Didn't you get some sleep when you went home?"

"No, there was a little . . . situation . . . I had to handle."

"Your mother again?" he asked.

"No. We had a minor insect infestation. Fireflies. Not anything icky. Katie bombed the place last night, but that left a big mess for me to clean up this morning."

His brows pinched together. "Who ever heard of a firefly infestation?"

"I know. But that's what they were. No doubt about it." I pointed at my computer. "Anyway, I've been sitting here, trying to make myself useful, reading up on anything that has to do with our case."

"Find anything interesting?"

"Not yet."

"Then let's get out of here," he said.

I was all for that, but only if we would be productive. The stakes were too high to be cruising around just for kicks. "Probably we should call the chief and ask her what she wants us to do."

"Probably." He took out his cell phone and dialed.

I eavesdropped on his end of the conversation while I skimmed Google search results.

"She wants us to stay here and wait for the rest of the team. They're on their way back."

Damn. "Okay." I sounded as thrilled as I felt.

He leaned over my shoulder; for a brief moment, I wondered what the hell he was up to. He whispered, "While we're waiting, I have something for you. Meet me outside, at my car."

"Okayyyy." I was 90 percent sure this was a bad idea.

"Don't go out right after me. Wait a few."

Now I was 99 percent sure. "All right."

This was either going to be interesting or dangerous.

I went back to surfing the Net. He headed out to his car. I checked the clock on my computer every minute or so, until it had finally counted off eight minutes. Then I headed out to the parking lot and slid into the passenger seat of his Jag.

He handed me an envelope. "Do you know anyone who can analyze this?"

"What is it?"

"Remember, I told you about the DNA analysis?"

"Yeah?" I opened the envelope and peered in. I found some sheets of paper and a small insulated package. Inside the package was a test tube containing a frozen sample. I knew for a fact this was serious. Serious enough to get both Gabe and me fired. But I was curious to see what the problem was with the testing.

"I have a sample, and the results. So, do you know anyone who has access to a lab?"

"I don't know. Katie's a chemistry major. She doesn't run DNA analyses, but she might know a way to get this sample tested at school." I folded the envelope, taking care not to break the test tube. "What about your friend?"

"Too risky."

"And trying to sneak this sample into the university isn't?"

He pointed at the envelope. "This might be our only lead."

"Or it might be grounds for dismissal. Maybe even grounds for being arrested."

"All the more reason to make sure whoever you get to run the test is trustworthy."

"I don't know if I like this." I left his car, heading straight for mine. I stashed the envelope under the passenger seat of my car.

As I straightened up, somebody said, "What do you have there, Skye?"

The true mystery of the world is the visible, not the invisible.

—Oscar Wilde

II

I whirled around and forced a smile, hoping the person behind me couldn't tell I was absolutely petrified. Considering JT worked for the FBI, profiling criminals—and therefore a pro at reading body language—I doubted I'd be successful pulling it off. "Heya, JT. I was . . . looking for my . . . cell phone. It fell off the seat when I was driving."

"Can I help you look?"

"Oh, no." I dove into the car, shoving my hand under the seat. My fingers hit the envelope. It crinkled. "Wow, there's a lot of trash under here. This might take a few. I'm sure you have more important things to do. You don't need to be wasting time out here with me."

"Well, the sooner you get inside, the better. You're a valuable member of the team too."

If you asked me, that was a bald-faced lie, but I decided calling him on it wasn't the best idea at the moment.

"Thanks." I grimaced as my fingers brushed against something sticky. It had been a long time since I'd cleaned out my car. There was no saying what that might be. "If I don't find it in the next few seconds, I'll head inside, anyway."

"Okay."

I shooed him off with the hand that wasn't elbow deep under the front seat. He loped away. And even though he was beyond my line of sight within thirty seconds, I kept up the looking-for-my-phone act for a while longer, trying to decide where else I could hide the envelope. I'd be stupid to leave it where it was. Granted, I didn't think JT was the kind who'd sneak out to my car and look to see what I'd lied to him about. But I couldn't take the chance.

I glanced around the parking lot.

Where could I hide the envelope? Where?

I popped the trunk but slammed it shut right away. That was too obvious. I considered stashing it in a wheel well, then popped the hood and shoved it into the first crevice I found that was big enough. I took a few minutes to calm myself down before heading back inside.

Everyone was in the conference room, except for Brittany Hough. They all stared at me as I joined them. I slinked to the closest chair. JT was on my right; Gabe was on my left. They both shoved a blank piece of paper and a pen at me.

I muttered, "Thanks."

"And so," Chief Peyton said, continuing a conversation I had missed, "I'm afraid we will be forced to split the team. JT will be lead for the first case. Fischer will take the reins on the second. Skye, you'll continue with JT. Wagner will go with Fischer. I'll be supporting both teams."

A second case. I wondered what it involved.

"The next team meeting will be tomorrow at oh-eight-hundred. Good luck."

Evidently, the PBAU worked a seven-day schedule, including Sundays.

I turned to JT. "I guess you're stuck with me."

He didn't look too put out. "We make a good team."

Gabe and I exchanged a look as he followed Fischer out of the room.

"So what's on our agenda this afternoon?"

"I need to bring you up to date, since you were out today. Then I say we'll call it a night."

"That's it? You're sending me back home? With someone else on the verge of dying?"

"Skye, I'm doing you a favor. You can't let this job take over your life. You won't last long if you do."

I glanced at the countdown clock. It still displayed all zeros. Chief Peyton hadn't reset it. "But women are dying so quickly. I feel guilty—"

"Don't." He shook his head. "There's no reason to. If you push yourself too hard, you'll either get burned-out or sick. The bottom line is, how many people do you think you'll be able to help if you catch the flu or stop caring because you're just too damn tired?"

"I guess I see your point."

"The file's on my desk. Let's get you up to speed and then I want you to go home and get a good night's sleep." JT followed me to my desk, pointed at my phone, which I'd forgotten had been sitting in plain view when I'd gone out to the parking lot. *Stupid, stupid, stupid.* "Well, look at that." JT raised his brows, motioning toward the phone.

"I swear, I don't remember bringing it in." I shoved the dumb thing in the front pocket of my laptop case.

"You didn't sleep today, did you?"

If the phone thing didn't make me look sleep deprived, I supposed the enormous bags under my eyes did. "I slept. For an hour. I had a little problem to handle at home."

"I swear, if you come in tomorrow morning looking like you do today, I'll turn in a recommendation to the chief to put you on sick leave immediately."

"That wouldn't be very nice."

He gave me a squinty-cyed glare. "Don't make me do it, Skye."

He used my last name. He must mean business.

"Fine." I was tempted to do something nasty behind his back when he turned and sauntered toward his desk. Of course, I didn't. Instead, I plunked down in the chair he'd pulled up to his desk and waited for him to give me a run-down of what he'd been up to since we'd parted ways.

"At this point, we don't have much on this unsub. DNA analysis was inconclusive. The samples were all tainted with foreign DNA. About the lead I was following last night, turns out Debbie Richardson's best friend was sleeping with Chapman for the last six months. They got married last night in Vegas." JT handed me a thick file. "I haven't had a chance to dig into the friend's background yet. Been too busy. I'd have Hough do it, but she doesn't work weekends. We spent most of the day collecting information about the latest victim. Name's Patty Yates. She lives in the same subdivision as Debbie Richardson. Age, thirty-four. Married. No kids. A nurse. COD, complications of dengue hemorrhagic fever. Hasn't traveled recently. We're looking into the possibility that she was exposed to dengue at work, though the bite marks suggest she was infected the same way the other victims were. She showed no symptoms prior to collapsing." JT paused for a moment. "So we're up to four victims, most of them living within a one-mile radius of each other, all of them displaying the bite marks, and all of them dying from infectious diseases while showing no symptoms prior to death. Now go home."

"Okay." I tucked the file under my arm and stood. "I guess I'll do some reading tonight. That's allowed, right?"

JT caught my arm as I turned. "Skye . . . Sloan . . . I'm not trying to be a prick. You know that, don't you?"

"Yeah, sure." I pulled my arm out of his grip.

"I haven't been with the Bureau long, and yet I've seen two good agents burn out and walk away from it all. Everyone suffers when that happens. The unit. The agent. The victims. You'll make a damn good agent someday, and you'll save lots of lives, but only if you learn to pace yourself."

I couldn't argue with him. In one respect, what he said made a lot of sense.

I thanked him, packed up my stuff, and headed out to my car.

I popped the hood and fished out the envelope before climbing in. I didn't notice the broken window until I sat. One piece of glass stuck me in the ass. I lifted my laptop case to find the majority of the remains of the passenger-side window lying in the front passenger seat. The rest of it was scattered on the floor, the center console, and, unfortunately for my ass, the driver's seat.

Someone had broken into my car. Who? And why? Had they been looking for the envelope? Or something else?

I'd left the unit before JT had. He couldn't have done this. But if not him, who had? I cleared my seat with a snow brush and sped out of the lot, watching my rearview mirror for a tail. I took a few turns, going out of my way to make sure nobody was following. After the fourth turn, I noticed the car.

I knew that car.

I pulled into a 7-Eleven parking lot and waited for the tail to park next to me. I knocked on the window. "Mom, what are you doing?"

Mom adjusted her very large, very dark sunglasses. If that was her idea of a disguise, she was in for a big surprise. If I made her, anyone could. For one thing, the copper penny hair was a little hard to ignore. "I'm following you."

"I see that." I pointed at the sunglasses. "Nice disguise."

"It was the best I could come up with at the spur of the moment." As if she read my mind, she added, "I didn't think it would work."

She climbed out of the car. She was wearing sneakers, a black T-shirt, and jeans. I can't remember the last time I saw my mother wearing jeans and a T-shirt, let alone tennis shoes. Of course, they all looked very familiar. Ironically enough, I owned a pair of black canvas shoes just like those. And my drawers were full of black cotton T-shirts. And . . . now that I got a better look . . . those jeans were familiar too. I hadn't worn them in ages. Way too tight. Yet, I couldn't make myself part with them. Wishful thinking, I guess. What bothered me more than anything—she looked good in that getup. Decades younger than she had earlier today.

"Mom, did you happen to borrow those clothes from my closet?"

Mom hurried toward the store's entry. "It's a good thing you stopped here. I'm in the mood for a Slurpee. Do you want one too?"

I followed her into the store. "Mom."

She made a beeline for the Slurpee machine in the back, pulled a cup from the stack, and then started filling it. "Yes, Sloan. I did borrow the clothes. I don't have any good PI clothes. I didn't want to take the time to go shopping. It can take hours to find a pair of jeans that fit right, you know." Wasn't that the truth? "Plus, I'm a little short of cash until my next Social Security check comes. You don't mind, do you?"

"No, I guess not." I decided a Slurpee sounded good. Standing next to her, I began dispensing yellow banana–flavored frozen beverage into a paper cup. "So . . . you're a private investigator?"

"Yes, I am. And I'm on my first case."

"You are?" I was confused. And slightly worried. "Who hired you?"

"I can't tell you that. I have to respect my client's privacy."

"Okay. So, can you tell me what I have to do with your case?"

"Sorry. No." Mom snapped the domed lid on her cup and carried it to the cash register. At the counter, she motioned toward me. "My daughter's taking care of this."

"Yes, madam," the clerk said, punching buttons on the cash register. When I strolled up to the counter, he announced, "That'll be two ninety-eight."

I stuffed my hand into my pocket, withdrew my cash, handed him three singles, and headed for the door. "Put the change in the 'Feed the Hungry' jar."

"Thank you," the man mumbled, dropping the two pennies into the jar.

I felt a little guilty and went back to the counter. I shoved a dollar into the jar and headed outside.

Mom and I stood between our parked cars, sucking down ice-cold frozen drinks.

"You can't tell me who you're working for, or what you're investigating. What can you tell me?" I asked.

Mom smacked her lips. "I can tell you . . . this is very delicious."

Argh! "Mom, you know that's not what I meant." Slightly perturbed, I yanked open my car door.

"Where are you heading now, Sloan?"

"Home." I slid into my seat, started the car, and rolled down the window. "Mom, were you watching my car in the FBI parking lot?"

"No, of course not." She strolled around the front of my vehicle. "What happened to your window?"

"Someone broke it."

"Well, that's not very nice. Why would anyone do such a thing?"

"That's what I'd like to know. Unfortunately, I don't have time . . ." A lightbulb blinked in my brain. "Would you like to take on another case?"

"Oh, I don't know. The one I have now is going to keep me pretty busy. . . ."

"I'll pay you."

"How much?"

I didn't have a lot of expendable cash at the moment, thanks to Mom's antics. But I had to wonder if hiring her would keep her away from her so-called experiments, thereby saving me money in the long run. I didn't believe for one minute that she'd been hired by anyone, yet. She was just telling me that, so she could follow me around and make sure I stayed safe . . . and alive. "A hundred dollars."

"I'll think about it." Mom slurped. "My other client's

paying me a lot more. But I might do it for you at that price, as a favor. Since you are my daughter."

"Gee, thanks."

"I'll let you know tomorrow." She got into her car and smiled. "Ready to head home?"

"Yep." I pulled out of the store parking lot, with Mom tailing behind me. She followed me into my apartment's parking lot, parked the car, and met me at my apartment door.

"I thought, since I was here, anyway, I'd join you for dinner."

"Sure, come on in. Everything's all cleaned up now." I followed Mom into the apartment. It was dark, quiet. There was no scent of burned chemicals. No sound of clattering chemistry equipment. No Katie. The kitchen, I noticed, was spotless, just as I'd left it. No spilled liquids of unknown identity stained the counter. No powders collected where the counter met the wall. The kitchen hadn't been used at all. I could actually cook in there, if I wanted. Not that I would. That was plain silly.

I snatched the stack of take-out menus from the closest drawer—the one that most people kept cooking stuff in—and asked, "What're you in the mood for tonight? Chinese? Thai? Italian?"

"How about Mexican?"

"We can do that." I found the menu for the closest Mexican restaurant from the stack, scribbled down her order, and called it in. "It'll be ready in twenty minutes. I'll run out and pick it up in a few." I headed for my room, anxious to change into a pair of sweats and a T-shirt. I halted in my tracks, though, when I saw Katie standing just inside her bedroom, staring at the wall. She was so still—she looked like a mannequin. The light was off. She wasn't moving. It was weird. "Hey, Katie. What's up?" When she didn't respond, I gave her shoulder a little shake.

"Don't touch me," she snapped, her upper lip curled like a snarling dog's.

I jerked my hand away. "O-okay." I half stumbled back out into the hall. "Sorry. Didn't mean to startle you."

Katie didn't move. She didn't speak. She just stood there, staring at the wall.

I headed to my room, changed my clothes. On my way back out to the living room, I checked on Katie. She hadn't budged. "We're getting Mexican for dinner. Do you want anything?"

Katie didn't answer.

"Mom, there's something wrong with Katie." I checked the clock on the microwave. I needed to leave in a couple of minutes to get our food.

"What's wrong with her? Is she sick?" Mom looked concerned. Katie and I had been close for years. Her folks were both dead. Mom had basically adopted her before we'd finished our first year of college.

"I don't know. She's staring at the wall, and I swear she snapped at me like Mrs. Heckel's Chihuahua, Daisy, when I touched her. Her eyes look a little buggy too, like Daisy's."

"She's probably just stressed-out. School did that to you too."

"I don't know." I grabbed my license and debit card, slouched into a hoodie and stuffed the cards in my pocket. "I've been living with Katie for years, and she's been in school since I met her. She's never acted like this."

"We all handle stress differently," Mom said, following me out the door.

Stress could cause some bizarre symptoms. And couple that with PMS, and the effects of whatever medication Katie might have taken for her migraine, and it was no wonder she was acting oddly. "I guess that's possible. Are you going with me?" I asked.

"No, I'm following you. I have a job to do, remember?"

"Mom, I'm just going to the restaurant down the street to pick up our dinner."

"That's okay." She went to her car. I went to mine. She tailed me the half mile to the restaurant, parked a few spaces away from me, and waited as I walked in. Then she followed me as I drove home, parked in the lot, and followed me back into my apartment. It was silly. I wondered who in their right mind would pay someone to follow me 24-7.

Nobody, that was who.

"Mom, don't you get a dinner break or anything? Do you clock out after six?"

"Nope. This is an important client. An important job. If he, or she, wants me to follow you everywhere, then that's what I'm gonna do."

"That's fine and dandy, but the FBI might have a problem with you tailing me while I'm working."

"Not a problem." Mom shrugged. She didn't seem at all concerned. This made me even more curious who she thought her mystery employer was, and what he or she was looking for.

I set us up with glasses of diet cola, napkins, plates, knives, and forks while Mom clicked through the science channels on television, looking for something to watch while we ate. She settled upon *Mystery Diagnosis*. Lately she'd become quite the television watcher. She'd done a complete one-eighty from a few years ago, when she'd vowed TV would lead to the ruin of our culture. Cell phones, social networking, and other portable gadgets had recently taken its place as the bane of her existence.

Mom had the mystery illness solved before the first commercial break.

Katie strolled in just as we were digging into our food. "What's this? Mexican? Smells so good." She inhaled. "Where's mine?"

"I asked you if you wanted some, but you didn't answer."

"Of course, I answered. I told you I wanted a beef-and-bean burrito, with extra sour cream." Katie glared at me. Then her squinty, mean eyes slid south, to my full dinner plate and the beef-and-bean burrito sitting in the middle of it. "Why would you order one for yourself, but not for me?"

"I . . . uh . . ." I looked down at the delicious meal on my plate, cursed under my breath, and vowed to find a way to get my roommate in to see a doctor if she kept acting so strangely. "Mom?"

"I thought I heard her ask for the burrito dinner." Mom chewed, then nodded. "Yes, I'm pretty sure that's what I heard."

Of course, the schizophrenic who regularly heard voices would say that.

With my mouth full of saliva, at the mere thought of digging into that plate full of Mexican heaven, I handed the dish to Katie and stood. "My mistake. You can take mine. I'll dig up a little something in the kitchen."

"Thank you." Katie settled next to Mom and plunged her fork into what should have been my Mexican rice and beans, smothered in sour cream. It was probably for the better. My jeans were getting a little snug in the thighs.

In the kitchen, I found a jar of olives in the refrigerator and a box of stale Cheez-Its in the cupboard. After that piddly dinner, my jeans would be fitting better by morning. I choked down the old crackers and tried to convince myself they were yummy, while Mom and Katie stuffed themselves full of beef, cheese, and rice. A little while later, Mom left, hauling what was left of her meal in a little foam box. Katie wandered off to her room without so much as a "good night." I decided I'd wait until tomorrow to ask her about the DNA sample, and placed it in the freezer for safekeeping. After getting the weather report—we were in for a deluge tonight—I took a trash bag and roll of duct tape out to the car to close up the gaping window. Once that minor task was finished, I decided to go to bed. When I was asleep, I wouldn't feel hungry.

All we know is still infinitely less than all that remains unknown.
—William Harvey

12

"*Don't hide from me. You can't hide anymore. I'll find you.*"

It was back again. She could tell. As always the warmth, the life, had been sucked from the room. Her eyelids squeezed tightly, she concentrated on breathing slowly, evenly, and silently prayed for it to leave.

Don't move. What does it want?

"*Where are you, my little mouse? Come out of your hole. I have a nice treat for you.*"

The stench of death seeped through the blanket covering her face. Her throat constricted. Don't gag. Something poked through the blanket, piercing the skin of her upper arm. She fought the urge to flinch.

"*Ahhh, there you are, little mouse.*"

The blanket slid down her body. Goose bumps prickled over her arms and shoulders. A draft so cold, it burned drifted across her body. She opened her eyes and looked up, toward the voice and—

"Wake up, Sloan!"

I jerked up. My eyes darted around the dark room. My hand smacked against my breastbone, as if it could still my racing heart. "What? What!"

"It's me, Katie."

"Katie." I took a breath. Another one. I still felt shaky and foggy-headed. "Oh."

"Sorry, I didn't mean to startle you."

"It's okay. What's wrong?"

"I don't know. I feel . . . strange. My head. It's not working right. Can't think."

"What do you want me to do? Is it another migraine?" I asked.

"No. I don't think so."

"Were you inhaling fumes today? Did you take too many pills for your migraine?"

"I . . . I don't know. I can't remember." Her voice rose with every word. "I can't remember what I did today, Sloan. Why can't I remember?" Katie grabbed me. She shook me. She squeezed my arms. And I saw stars as my brain splatted against the inside of my skull.

"Katie! Stop!" I broke out of her grip and scuttled out of her reach.

"Everything's a blank," she said. "I don't remember."

I glanced at the clock. It was just after midnight. "I'm going to take you to the hospital, okay?" On hands and knees, I crawled to the opposite side of the bed. Katie mumbled while I tied on a pair of tennis shoes and stumbled into the bathroom. Squinting against the glaring light, I finger-combed my hair. "Let's go."

Katie clung to my arm as we hurried out to my car dodging fat raindrops. I put her in the backseat, afraid there was still some glass on the front, and sped down flooded streets to the closest emergency room.

Hours later, the rain had stopped. And my soggy clothes and hair were dry. I drove Katie home, now doped up on Xanax. The diagnosis: anxiety. The doctors had found nothing medically wrong. I caught a few more hours of sleep before dragging myself to the shower. Katie was still asleep when I headed out to work. Mom's car was in the lot. She waved at me. I waved back and strolled to her car.

"I'm making a coffee stop on the way to Quantico. Do you want something?" I asked.

"Sure. I'll take a bagel and some black coffee." Mom scowled. "You look terrible, Sloan. You need to take better care of yourself."

"I'm trying, Mom. I really am. I have a lot going on right now." Hoping JT wouldn't notice the bags under my eyes were now big enough to hide a small child, I scurried to my car and settled in for the drive. At the bagel shop, I bought our bagels and coffees, delivered Mom's to her car, and chugged half of mine before I pulled out of the lot. I noticed Mom didn't try to follow me all the way to the FBI Academy. Because the building is located on a military base, only people with a military ID were permitted. She did, however, give me a little wave good-bye.

I hurried into the office, my breakfast in my hands, my laptop bag slung over one shoulder. Inside, I headed straight for my desk. JT, I noticed, was already at work, pecking at his laptop's keyboard. I chomped on my bagel as I set up my computer.

"Did you think I was lying?" he asked, standing behind me no more than a minute later.

"I don't know what you're talking about. Lying about what?" Did he think I suspected him of breaking my car window? Or was he referring to turning me in to the chief?

"When I said I'd put in for you to take a medical leave, I meant it."

Aha. "But I'm not sick." I donned my best pity-me look, normally reserved for police officers who've pulled me over, and turned to face him. "And I went to bed early. I swear I did." I didn't mention the fact that I didn't stay in bed. "I believed you. Absolutely."

He squinted at me. His jaw clenched ever so slightly. "You're lying."

"No, I'm not. You can call my mother and ask her. She was at my place last night. I'll give you her number."

"That won't be necessary." He leaned closer, and I panicked just a little, knowing the deep bruiselike circles would be that much more obvious up close and personal. There was only so much the inch-thick layer of concealer I'd caked on could do. "We roll in five minutes."

"Okay." I stuffed a piece of bagel in my mouth and washed it down with the last of my coffee. "I'll be ready."

Thankfully, he said nothing more, just walked stiffly back to his cubicle. I skimmed my e-mails and shut down my computer. I stuffed it back in the case and stood just as JT was heading my way again.

"Ready?" he asked.

"Yep." I fell into step beside him. "Where are we going?"

"To interview a witness who claims she saw Patty Yates get into some kind of altercation the morning of her death."

"Hmm, okay. The morning she died? Couldn't be the killer. He or *she,*" I said, putting intentional emphasis on the feminine, "would've had to inject the pathogen several days earlier."

JT poked the down button, calling the elevator. "Maybe *he* was watching her, waiting for her to collapse, like we talked about. And maybe Patty Yates recognized him and tried to get away? Remember, the saliva samples?"

"I guess I could see that."

The trip to Baltimore was fraught with tension after that point. Ever since the trip to the emergency room, JT had been acting a little differently toward me. It was a subtle difference, but pronounced enough for me to notice. I wasn't convinced he was concerned about my sleep deprivation. "JT, you know

I wasn't the one who clobbered you over the head and threw you in the Dumpster, right?"

"Of course. Why would you ask me that?"

Now I felt a little stupid. "Because you've been acting differently toward me since that day." Then another possibility came to mind. "If you're worried about what you said at the hospital—"

"I'm not." He glanced over his shoulder to check for traffic before changing lanes. His gaze flicked to me for a second, then jerked back.

"What's going on, then? Will you tell me?"

"Nothing's going on." His jaw clenched. He was lying. About what? His gaze zigzagged between me and the road a couple of times."Everything's fine, Sloan."

"If everything's fine, why'd you black out your computer screen when I came to talk to you the other night?"

He shrugged. "I always do that. I hate it when people read over my shoulder."

"I see." I didn't, of course, but there was no use trying to drag the truth out of JT. He wasn't going to spill. At least, not without the help of another bonk on the head.

"What does it matter, anyway? I told you what I'd found."

I didn't say a word the rest of the drive. Neither did JT. It was painful, sitting in that small space, the tension so thick I could taste it. It was a lot like being on a bad date. But I survived. Bad dates are my forte. I just lost myself in my thoughts, and occasionally looked behind us to see if Mom was following. Before I knew it, we were pulling up in front of yet another suburban Colonial. I dug a notebook and pen out of my laptop case and followed JT up to the house.

No sign of Mom. Evidently, she didn't feel the need to follow me when I was riding with an agent.

He knocked. We waited. No answer. He knocked again.

"Are we here too early? It is Sunday." I checked my watch.

It was a little before nine. "Or maybe your witness has gone to church?"

"No, she said she'd be home." He knocked a third time, harder.

We waited some more. I stepped off the porch to get a better angle on the front window. It looked dark inside. A lace curtain fluttered. "I think I see someone." An orange tabby cat walked along the window ledge, tail sticking straight up. "Cancel that, it's only the cat."

A second later, the front door's lock rattled. The door inched open. JT introduced himself through the two-inch crack between the door and the frame. By the time I'd made it back on the porch, he was inside the house.

"Mrs. Ester, this is Sloan Skye."

I offered my hand. "Mrs. Ester."

Mrs. Ester, who could very well be older than God, took my hand in a delicate grip and gave it a little shake. Her hand, heavily wrinkled and veined, was fragile and soft. "Miss Skye." She turned eyes the shade of a winter sky toward JT. "I saw the whole thing. I was on my way to the store to pick up a few things, and I saw her fighting with another woman."

"Where did you see this?"

"Just down the road." The woman pointed a finger toward the west. "On the side of the Dempsters' house. I can show you." The woman took a wobbly step toward a door to the left, which probably led to the garage. "I need to get my scooter, though."

"We can go in a minute." JT jotted a few notes. So did I.

Mrs. Ester opened the door and hit a button, powering up the automatic garage door opener. I peered into the garage and immediately realized there was no car. I hadn't seen one on the street either.

"I don't drive anymore. Failed the eye exam three times. I think the test is rigged so folks like me can't drive." Mrs. Ester took a faltering step down. "My son, the little bastard, took my car so I couldn't drive it after I got caught driving without a license six months ago. I showed him. I wrote him outta my will. Everything I have is going to The Critter Connection. They rescue abandoned guinea pigs." I rushed to her aid, supporting her down the second concrete step and the short walk to her electric cart. "If you'd be so kind as to unplug me." She motioned to the rear of the cart.

"Sure." I yanked the plug.

"I don't need no license to drive this thing, but it's a pain in the ass when it's raining. And snow and ice? It gets stuck in a two-inch drift. I'm going to be housebound from December till March, unless we get a midwinter thaw." Mrs. Ester's little cart hummed as she drove it at a snail's pace out into the morning. JT and I followed. She stopped the cart a couple of houses down and pointed at the area between two identical Colonials. "They were there."

"Between the houses?"

"No, farther back. Almost at the fence."

JT and I looked at each other.

Granted, these properties were hardly sprawling, but if Mrs. Ester was correct, she'd been watching the exchange from a distance of no less than seventy feet. She'd failed the eye exam and lost her driver's license. How reliable could her testimony be?

"What did you see?" I asked.

"I saw the first woman jump over the fence. She cleared it in one leap."

I looked at the fence. Chain link. Taller than the average residential fence. I estimated six feet. Probably because the property on the other side was a school. I didn't know any woman, or man for that matter, who could leap over a six-foot anything.

"Are you certain she *jumped*? Maybe she climbed?" I suggested, growing more skeptical by the second. Did we have another Miss Zumwalt on our hands?

"No, I'm sure." Mrs. Ester nodded. "She just hopped right over it. Never seen anything like it."

"What time was this?" JT asked, hiding his thoughts on the witness's reliability, or lack thereof, very well.

"It was early. A little after seven."

"And you were out that early?"

"I needed some milk for my tea. And cat food. Nibbles gets nasty if he doesn't have his breakfast."

"Don't we all?" I joked. JT didn't laugh. Neither did Mrs. Ester. "So what happened after the woman 'hopped over' the fence?"

"The woman grabbed Mrs. Yates and shook her. And then they started wrestling. I've always thought Mrs. Yates was a strong girl. She liked to jog and ride her bike. And she taught a Zumba class at Bee's Dance Academy. I went to the class once, but it moved too fast for me. But even as strong as she was, she didn't stand a chance against that other beastly woman. That woman tossed Mrs. Yates around like a rag doll. And then, the strange woman did the oddest thing, she kissed Mrs. Yates."

"Kissed her?" I echoed.

"Yes." Mrs. Ester nodded. "I figured they were lesbians, secret lovers. Fighting over . . . well, heaven only knows what. Poor Mr. Yates. He couldn't have known."

"Why do you say that?"

"Well, at our block party just a week before, he was crowing about what a dedicated wife he had. I didn't have the heart to tell him. That's why I called you after those other agents had left. I didn't want him to overhear. He'd be devastated. His whole life is—was—that wife of his. They'd never been able to have children. He'd blamed himself, but now I'm thinking it had nothing to do with him. Them sperms can't do their job if they aren't where they need to be, if you get my drift. Then again, maybe I should tell him. So he won't keep blaming himself anymore . . . what do you think?"

Ah, the intrigues of suburbia. Lesbian affairs, misplaced sperm, and catfights.

"I think you should do what you think is best," I said. "Are you sure the attacker kissed Mrs. Yates? Could she have . . . bitten her?"

"Bitten?" Mrs. Ester grimaced. "Why would anyone bite someone? I suppose it's possible. . . . I don't know."

"So you believe the two women knew each other?" JT asked, redirecting the conversation.

"I didn't at first. But the more I think about it, the more convinced I am."

"Can you describe the woman you saw attacking your neighbor?" I asked.

"I can try. She was more petite than Mrs. Yates. That I can say for certain. Her hair was light and short, shorter than yours." She pointed at my head. "Her skin was very pale. And she was wearing shorts and a sweater."

I scribbled more notes. "And you're absolutely sure the attacker was a woman?"

"Yes."

"What makes you so certain?" I asked. "She was clearly very strong, to be able to 'throw' your neighbor around so easily, not to mention leap over a six-foot fence."

"It does sound strange, doesn't it? I know. But all I can say is she moved like a woman. Not like a man."

"Do you have prescription glasses?" JT asked.

"I do." Mrs. Ester pointed at her eyes. "I only wear them at night. I look better in contacts."

"Why did you fail the eye exam if you have prescription lenses?" I asked.

Mrs. Ester tapped her temple. "Cataracts. I'm afraid to go under the knife, but I know I'm going to have to suck it up and go, sooner or later."

I looked into her eyes, and sure enough, I could see the slightly milky reflection of the cataracts in her pupils.

"I can still see good enough to do most everything else," Mrs. Ester said. "Just not drive."

"I understand." I looked at my notes. She hadn't given us much that was useful. The only piece that fit was the possible bite. As far as the unsub's description went: petite woman with short, light hair? There had to be hundreds of those running around this neighborhood. "Did you notice anything unusual about the attacker? Something that would help us identify her? Did she have any scars? Tattoos? Anything?"

"What a silly question. Even if my eyesight was twenty-twenty, do you think I'd see a little scar?"

I swallowed a chuckle. Mrs. Ester was quite a character. I liked her. "Probably not, but you never know."

"And as far as 'unusual,' don't you think it's *unusual* for a woman to leap over a six-foot fence, toss another grown woman around like she's a doll, and then bite her?" Mrs. Ester asked.

I nodded, exchanging a grin with JT. "I do."

"Then, there you have it." She gave us a look that said she was done with us, if we were done with her.

JT handed her a card. "Thank you, Mrs. Ester. You've been very helpful. I have one last question, if you don't mind, and then we'll get going."

Mrs. Ester nodded. "Shoot away."

"Have you ever seen the attacker before? Did she look familiar?"

"I didn't get a good look at her face. Most of the time, her back was turned to me, or she was moving quickly. But I'd have to say, no, I haven't seen her before."

"Thank you." JT pointed at the card. "If you think of anything else, or see the attacker again, I'd appreciate it if you'd give me a call."

"Will do. Bye-bye." Mrs. Ester stuffed the card down her shirt, hit the button on her scooter, and motored away.

We exchanged another grin.

"What an interesting woman," I said.

"Yes, very interesting," JT said.

"I don't think we can believe her testimony, not a word."

"Hmm. What about the bite? That fits." JT started wandering toward the site of the alleged attack, his gaze focused downward.

"Sure, but we sort of suggested it, didn't we?" Following his lead, I slowly walked between the houses, looking for signs of a struggle. "This was disappointing. She's the only possible eyewitness who's come forward, so far."

"She won't be the last." JT checked the fence, then the area around it.

Not far from him, I checked the grass around a bush, hoping I'd find a piece of torn clothing or something to back up Mrs. Ester's story. "You sound very sure of that."

Still at the fence, JT stooped down and ran his hand over the ground. "I am. Assuming she actually saw the unsub and didn't imagine it all, she walked away alive. She's a witness. The unsub is getting sloppy. Which means, there will be more witnesses."

"What if that wasn't the unsub she saw?"

"Then, there's a mystery woman running around, leaping high fences in a single bound, and kissing women." He stood. Shook his head. "There's nothing here."

"I'm not finding anything either. I wonder if she's delusional. What do you think? Alzheimer's? Diabetic dementia?"

"Could be. Of course, there is another possibility. And we can't eliminate it yet." At the car now, JT pulled open the passenger-side door for me. He stepped aside.

"You mean, the unsub really can jump over fences—and she wasn't kissing the victim, she was biting her." I waited until JT was in the car before asking, "Seriously? You believe that?" Was he actually willing to take a nearly blind woman's testimony at face value? When we hadn't found a single clue to back her story?

He shoved the key into the ignition and cranked it. "Sure. Can you tell me for certain that every myth about every paranormal creature is only that—a myth? Couldn't there be some kernel of truth in them all?"

"I thought you didn't believe in that stuff. That's what you said."

He shrugged. "Maybe I'm starting to change my mind."

"Maybe I'd be more willing to go there if I had the testimony of somebody at least semireliable to back it up. But thus far, we don't." When he didn't respond, I added, "I'm not close-minded, though. Give me proof that vampires, werewolves, whatever exist, and I'll eat my words."

He gnawed on his lower lip for a moment. I liked when he did that. "Okay, how about we have a little bet?"

"I think this is silly, but I'm listening. See how open-minded I am?"

"By the time we solve this case—which I believe we will—I will produce irrefutable proof that paranormal creatures exist. If I don't . . ."

"You'll be my personal assistant, aka slave, for forty-eight continuous hours, handling any personal or professional matter I require without compensation," I finished for him.

"Agreed." JT nodded. Then he leaned closer and gave me a baby-you're-mine look. "And if I succeed, you'll go on a date with me."

"But that's against FBI—"

JT cut me off by laying an index finger on my mouth. "Chief Peyton's policy is, 'what I don't know won't hurt you.'"

"And how do you know this?" I mumbled, every cell in my body aware of his touch.

He removed his finger to cup the gearshift. I had mixed feelings about that. "I asked her."

"You didn't!" I jerked my seat belt over myself, making sure to hide my face. I swear, my cheeks were so hot, they might blister.

"I didn't mention names. It was presented as a general question."

"And you don't think she guessed who you were talking about?"

"Actually, I think she assumed I was interested in Hough." I could see how she'd think that. But I wasn't going to say as much. Immediately, my mind leapt back to that awkward moment, when I'd been standing outside Brittany's computer cave. I recalled how close JT had been standing to her, and how she'd been smiling into his eyes. My stomach felt like it had just gone through a wringer.

JT was a player. I didn't like players. They tended to be selfish, cocky, annoying. Why didn't I find JT any of those things?

He said, "Brittany and I like to flirt. It's a game we've been playing for years. She's the only woman I have ever done that with."

Besides me.

He glanced in the rearview mirror before pulling the car away from the curb. "It's because I know I'm safe flirting with her."

"Safe?" I echoed.

"She's a lesbian."

I'd seen the glimmer in her eyes that day. There was no way she could've been faking it. "She lied to you. She's no more a lesbian than I am."

"No way. She couldn't be lying." He said that like he knew, without a doubt, she was gay.

"How can you be so certain?"

He stopped the car at an intersection and gave me a heart-halting grin. "I gave her away. At her wedding. She married Michelle last summer. It was quite a ceremony. First gay wedding I've ever been to." After a beat, he asked, "So, does this mean you're gay?"

I couldn't argue with that kind of proof. "No, of course I'm not gay."

His smile was smug. "Good."

I decided the view out the window was safer; then I decided to give Katie a call, to check on her.

No answer. Did I need to be worried yet?

JT nudged me. "So, do we have a bet?"

"Fine." I turned my head to find he was holding out a hand. I placed mine in his and gave it a quick shake before yanking it away. Touching that man for any longer than necessary was dangerous.

So was looking at him.

And smelling him.

And thinking about him. . . .

Creativity comes from looking for the unexpected and stepping outside your own experience.

—Masaru Ibuka

13

After touring Patty Yates's neighborhood for a while, JT decided we needed to take a lunch break before heading back to Yates's house to interview her husband later that afternoon. I was glad, because I was starving. But more than that, I was happy because that meant I'd get out of the car for a little while.

I'd never felt so closed-in before. The tension in the air was ridiculous, thick enough to taste. There were parts of my anatomy that appreciated the chemistry sizzling between us. Other parts did not.

But what ruined it for me: I began to wonder if this bet would ultimately end up biting me in the ass. I mean . . . what if JT started flirting more? What if people saw him? What if Chief Peyton found out?

I needed to nip this in the bud now, before I lost all hope of a career with the FBI.

First step: I needed to discourage him from treating me like a girlfriend, and encourage him to treat me like a coworker.

I didn't let him get the chance to open the car door for me. I knew he wanted to. After parking in the restaurant's lot, he cut off the engine and jumped out of the seat. I scrabbled out of the car and slammed the door behind me. Then, anticipating his next move, I racewalked to the restaurant's door and yanked it open before he had a chance to do it for me. Inside, the narrow little restaurant's air smelled like roasted meats and pickles. My mouth flooded with saliva.

Looking like he wasn't fazed by my strange behavior, JT headed for a booth in the back. I decided it would be a good idea to take advantage of the free Wi-Fi, which was advertised on the restaurant's front door, and headed back out to the car.

While I was out there, I tried calling Katie again. Still, no answer. Mom greeted me in the parking lot. I was actually kind of glad to see her.

Probably before I took my first bite, I'd change my mind.

"Mom, how'd you find us? Have you seen or talked to Katie today?"

"I have my ways. I think I'm getting better and better at this PI stuff. And no, I haven't talked to Katie. Why?"

"I had to take her to the hospital last night. The doctors said she had an anxiety attack."

"Oh, dear. Anxiety? I'm sure she'll be okay." Mom studied the sign on the building. "A deli, Sloan? Haven't I told you how bad processed meats are for you?"

"Yes, you have. But I'm not ready to give up my Reuben addiction yet. Come on. I'm sure they offer something you can eat. I'll buy you lunch, if you'll go over and check on Katie for me."

Mom scowled but didn't fight me as I led her inside. "They'd better have at least an edible salad."

JT looked quite surprised to see we had company.

"JT, I'd like you to meet my mother, Beverly. Mom, this is Special Agent Thomas. We call him JT."

"Good to meet you, madam." Beaming, JT stood and offered his hand.

Mom gave him a dose of evil eyes. She wasn't much for boys and their charms. "If you're sleeping with my daughter, I'll make your life a living hell."

So much for making nice. "Mom, that isn't necessary." Then again, maybe it was a good thing.

JT took the threat well. He laughed. "I'm not sleeping with your daughter, but I'll definitely keep that in mind if I decide to take her up on her offer."

"What! My offer?" Now it was my turn to squint at him. "I haven't offered any such thing." Mom turned those evil eyes on me. "I swear to God. I'd never throw myself at a man."

The waitress, whom I hadn't noticed before, said, "I would throw myself at him if I were you. He's one nice-looking man."

I swallowed a retort that wasn't very kind and stared at my menu, trying to come up with a more appropriate response, something that didn't involve a four-letter word.

"Hey, Mel," JT said.

"Heya, JT," the waitress answered. "The usual?"

"You know him?" I asked.

"Sure. We went to school together, grew up in the same neighborhood. Oh, you thought I was saying I'd throw myself at a man I don't know? I'd never do that. JT here is a good guy." She gave him a pat on the shoulder.

If he was such a good guy, why wasn't she dating him?

"I'd throw myself at him shamelessly, if it weren't for the fact that I'm happily married to my high-school sweetheart. We're expecting our first baby." She patted her stomach, which was flatter than mine had ever been.

"Congratulations," I said.

Mom echoed me.

JT jumped to his feet, gave a little whoop, and threw his arms around Mel, the waitress. Afterward, with one arm still looped around her neck, he said, "I tried to steal her away from Kevin, but she had eyes only for him. Didn't help that I weighed less than she did at the time."

Mel laughed. "He was a string bean." She elbowed him in the stomach and he returned to his seat. "If only I'd known how hot he'd be after he filled out." She winked at him and he winked back.

I thought he only flirted with Brittany, the lesbian.

"Now that that's settled, can we order?" I asked, sounding a little snappy.

"I'll take a bottled water," Mom said.

"That's it?" JT asked, turning what I could swear were concerned eyes her way. "Don't you want anything to eat? My treat."

"Well . . ." Mom glanced at the menu. "In that case, I'll take a house salad, no meat or cheese. But please give it a good washing first. All the vegetables. I don't suppose you buy your produce from an organic farmer?" At Mel's shake of the head, Mom added, "Vinegar and oil on the side, please."

"Got it. One well-washed salad." Mel turned to me. "And you?"

"I'll have the Reuben, fries, and a diet cola. And a cup of chicken noodle soup to go, please."

"Okay. I'll be back with your drinks in just a minute." She bounced off, scribbling in her little waitress pad.

An awkward moment stretched between us as I stared at Mom and JT, and they stared back.

"So, Mrs. Skye, what do you think of your daughter working for the FBI?" JT finally asked.

"I was completely against it when she first told me."

JT's eyebrows arched. "Really?"

"My experiences with our government haven't been good. I didn't want my daughter working for a bunch of . . . for the government."

Looking very amused, JT nodded. "I see." He looked at me, as if he expected me to add to Mom's already damning confession.

"Obviously, I didn't let her stop me," I said.

The waitress trotted up, a tray of drinks balanced on her

flattened hand. She handed Mom her bottled water first, then me my diet, and finally JT a tall glass of milk.

Mom took one look at the milk and said, "JT, you really shouldn't drink that stuff. It's loaded with estrogen and progesterone. Haven't you heard? Milk and cheese consumption is linked to testicular cancer."

Ah, the joys of dining with my mother.

I stepped in before Mom could continue with the lecture. "JT, let me explain something to you. Just about anything you eat or drink is going to harm you in some way. Vegetables are bathed in pesticides. Meats are imbued with hormones. So please don't let my mother's food issues ruin your meal." I turned a warning glare on my mother and leaned close to her. "Mom, behave yourself."

"But this comes from a reliable source, Harvard—"

"Please, Mom," I interrupted.

"You like this boy," Mom said.

"He's not a boy. He's clearly a grown man. And no, I don't like him. Not like *that*. But I do need to have a reasonably friendly *working relationship* with him, don't I?"

"Huh." Mom crossed her arms over her chest and snapped her mouth shut. "That's the thanks I get for trying to save the man's testicles."

Just shoot me now.

I knew how to stop Mom from tailing me. "JT, my mother is a private detective. She's on a case right now."

"Really?" He grinned. "What kind of case?"

Mom fiddled with her bottled water. "I can't talk about it, of course. I must respect my client's privacy."

"Of course," he echoed.

"She's following me," I told him.

He nodded and took a long gulp of milk. "I see."

Another uncomfortable silence fell over us. This one lasted until Mel brought our food.

Mom grimaced as the salad was set before her, but—thank God—she didn't complain.

I decided it was wise to just concentrate on what looked like a glorious Reuben, stacked thick with corned beef, sauerkraut, and cheese. The tangy rye bread was toasted to perfection. I just about had an orgasm after my first taste, it was so good. Before I knew it, my plate was empty.

It was then that I realized Mom and JT were chatting away like old friends. That could be a bad thing.

Mom stood, gave JT a warm hug, and thanked him for lunch. She waved at me, the foam cup of soup in her hand. "See you later, Sloan. Off to deliver lunch to Katie." She scurried away.

"Call me if there's a problem," I said to her back.

She responded with an over-the-shoulder wave.

"Your mother's a very interesting woman."

"You could say that."

"Intelligent." JT pulled out his wallet. He set a credit card on the bill, at the edge of our table.

"Yes, she is. Thanks for picking up her lunch." I pulled out my wallet.

"Not a problem."

"I'll pay for mine." I pulled out a ten-dollar bill and set it on top of JT's credit card.

"No, you won't." JT snatched it up and dropped it on the table, in front of me.

"Yes, I will." I put it back on top of the bill.

"This is a working lunch. It's on the bureau's dime." Once again, he grabbed my money and shoved it at me.

"Okay. Fine." I put the ten back in my wallet. "You'd better be telling the truth."

"I would never lie to you." JT waved at Mel.

I thought about explaining my mother's medical condition to JT while we waited for Mel to cash us out, but I quickly decided that wasn't a good idea. People reacted strangely to hearing about my mother's condition. They tended to treat me differently afterward, like I was the sick one.

"Ready?" he asked, after signing the bill and thanking Mel.

"Sure. But I should probably make a trip to the bathroom first."

"I'll wait for you in the car." He headed outside.

I looped the strap of my laptop bag over my shoulder—so much for working during lunch—and headed to the bathroom. I took care of some personal issues first. While I was in there, I also decided my hair needed a touch-up. And my makeup. When I strolled outside a couple of minutes later, I found Mom standing next to JT's car, talking to JT through the open window. She scuttled off before I got close enough to hear what they were talking about. I decided it would be a good idea to keep her away from JT.

"Sorry about my mother," I said as I opened the back door and dropped my laptop bag on the backseat.

He started the car. "No need to apologize."

I slid into the passenger seat and snapped myself in. "I've tried to tell her she can't follow an FBI agent. It's gotta be against the law, isn't it?"

"It's against the law to interfere in an FBI investigation." He maneuvered the car out of the parking spot.

"If you'd explain that to her, it might go better. She's more likely to believe you than me."

"Already did." After waiting for a break in traffic, he pulled the car onto the road.

"Good." Knowing my mom, that wouldn't completely stop her from tailing me. She smoked marijuana, and that was against the law. But it might inspire her to keep a wider distance between her and us.

In ten minutes, we rolled up in front of Patty Yates's home, another typical 1980s construction, with brick facing and vinyl siding. A mound of woodchips graced the perimeter of the foundation. Weeds poked out of the chips, here and there, but otherwise, the outside of the home was tidy.

Inside, we soon learned, was even more pristine. Spotless. Everything was white. Walls. Floors. Window coverings.

Mr. Yates, who was as immaculately groomed as his home, welcomed us, leading us back to the great room in the rear of the first floor. The kitchen was on the left, a sunken family room on the right. "How can I help you, Agent? I've already told the police everything I know, which isn't much."

"Thank you for talking to us, Mr. Yates," JT said in his FBI agent voice. "We know you've already talked to the police. We'll make this as quick as possible."

"Thanks." All knotted up in a black pinstripe suit, white shirt, and tie, Mr. Yates crossed his arms over his chest.

"Let's start with the week before your wife's death. Did you notice her acting differently than normal?"

"No. Differently, how?"

"In any way. Was she ill? Sleeping more? Sleeping less? Eating less? Complaining about any symptoms?"

"Nothing. Patty was training to run a marathon for breast cancer. She ran ten miles the morning she died."

"Can you tell us the route she took?" I asked.

"Patty didn't run outside. She has a treadmill. Or she goes to a local gym."

"Okay. Thank you." I jotted some notes. Another runner. Could it be a coincidence?

"Had she mentioned making any new acquaintances recently?" JT asked.

"No. Nothing's sticking out. I don't get it. When I left for work that morning, everything was normal. A couple of hours later, and everything was wrong. My wife, who never got sick, was dead from some tropical disease I've never heard of. I just don't understand."

For the first time since stepping into the house, I saw a

sign of the grief this man was feeling. His hands shook as he straightened his tie, tugging the knot tighter.

"Can you tell us about your neighbor, Mrs. Ester?"

"That woman's batty. She told me my wife is—was— a lesbian." He wandered over to a cupboard and pulled out a mug. He pointed at us with the cup. "I can tell you, without any doubt, that my wife was *not* gay." He cleared his throat. I think his male pride was a little bruised. "You can't believe a word that woman says. I'm not trying to be mean. She's diabetic. Never takes her medication. Her son comes over once a day at dinnertime to make sure she's eaten, and gives her a shot of insulin. But she's getting worse. Seeing things and hearing things that aren't there. Won't be long before she's in a nursing home."

"Thank you." JT motioned to the stairs. "Would you mind if we took a quick look around?"

"The police searched the house, but sure. Do what you have to do." Mr. Yates went to the coffeemaker. "Coffee?" He filled the cup and offered it to us.

JT and I both said, "No thanks," and headed for the staircase in the foyer. Upstairs, we found the master bedroom and bath first.

"What are we looking for?" I asked. "We know from the previous three victims that we're not going to find any signs of illness. No open aspirin bottles, even."

JT went to the window and peered outside. "They have a nice view of the park from this room."

"Is that significant?"

"I doubt it." He turned around. "We're looking for anything that doesn't fit. I can't be more specific because I don't know either. I won't know until I see it."

"Okay." I opened the closet. The clothes were organized by color, his on the left, hers on the right. "These people are OCD. Look at this closet."

"And yet the front flower bed was weedy."

"Do you think that's significant?"

"Probably not." JT went to one of two dressers in the room and opened the drawer. "The dressers are organized too."

"I'll check the bathroom." I wandered into the attached full bath. It was the picture of luxury with one of those fancy super-deep, jet-action soaker tubs. It was spotless, as was the rest of the room. No medications whatsoever in the medicine cabinet. "Nothing interesting in the bathroom, though I have a serious case of tub envy." I headed back out to the bedroom.

JT was holding a medicine bottle.

"What did you find?" I asked, hoping it would be useful.

"Cialis. It was hidden in Yates's underwear drawer."

"Hidden? Do you think his wife knew he had a little problem?"

"I'm guessing she did. But if she didn't, it doesn't matter." He put the bottle back in the drawer and closed it.

I sighed. "This case is so frustrating."

"We'll get a break sooner or later." JT motioned toward the hallway. "I think we've taken up enough of Mr. Yates's time. Let's head out."

After thanking Mr. Yates, we went back to the car.

I plopped into the passenger seat and rubbed my temples. I didn't have a headache. I was hoping the massage might stimulate the circulation to my head, and thus increase the blood flow to my brain cells. I was desperate. "The unsub's going to kill again. We're running out of time, and we're no closer to having a profile than we were the first day."

"Sure, we are. We know who he's hunting. We just don't know why. I have a plan." He gave me a look. I didn't like it. "You're going undercover."

"Undercover?" I echoed.

"Yeah. I called the agent handling a bank-owned house on the next block. You're going to stay there."

"I'm going to offer myself to a killer?"

"The house will be wired. You will be wired. You'll be

watched twenty-four–seven. Not just by me, but by several agents." JT set a hand on my knee. I looked down at it, then up into his eyes. "I won't let anything happen to you. I promise."

I believed he meant those words.

Still, I wasn't liking this plan. Not at all. Even if he was watching me around the clock, and his intentions were noble, things happened. Even the best-laid plans went wrong.

But on the other hand, it was the opportunity I had been waiting for. I would be doing something, taking action, helping solve the case. I would finally be a productive member of the team. Nobody else could do this, except for maybe Chief Peyton. We both were brunettes, although I was too young and she was too old, if the killer stuck with the same MO.

JT fiddled with his keys. "Do you have a gun, to protect yourself?"

"A gun?" Those two words scared me, almost more than the idea of becoming a killer's target. "No, I've never touched a gun. Unless you count a Super Soaker."

After a tense moment, JT said, "Sloan, if you don't want to do this, you don't have to. I'll be close by. At all times. But it's still dangerous."

"What about your promise not to let anything happen to me?" I challenged. "Reneging already?"

"No way. But legal, and Chief Peyton, told me I have to inform you of all the risks."

I laughed. It was a weird moment for a guffaw, I'll admit. But I couldn't help myself. I guess it was the fear bubbling up inside of me and bursting out.

JT gave me an odd, worried look. "I went to the chief with this plan days ago, before Patty Yates was found. The chief shot it down right away, said there was no way we could use an intern in an undercover operation. Something must've made her change her mind, though. She called me today and gave me the thumbs-up."

Lucky me.

"Give me a minute," I said, holding up an index finger. JT nodded.

I turned and stared sightlessly out the window.

All along, I'd felt like I was failing, like I was letting down the victims who had died, and the ones who were yet to die. Out there, somewhere, was a woman who didn't realize her time was almost up. And out there, somewhere, were God only knew how many more women who might lose their lives if the killer wasn't caught.

Up to this point, following the path of victims, of death, wasn't doing us a damn thing. We needed to anticipate the killer's next move. How else could we do that?

There wasn't any other way.

"I'll do it," I said, sounding less resolved than I wished I did.

JT lunged forward and hauled me into his arms. And I, being a little overwhelmed for a lot of reasons, sank into his embrace. I closed my eyes and simply enjoyed the moment. He smelled so good. And he was so big, so strong. I felt safe in his arms. Protected.

"I wish you could stay with me," I said.

"Me too." His flattened hand skimmed up and down my back, and little waves of tingles swept through my body. Those tingles were nice. Very nice. And bad. Very bad. "But the more time you spend alone, the more likely we are to lure the killer to you."

"I agree."

He loosened his hold and leaned back enough to look me in the eye without either of us going cross-eyed. "I won't let you down, Sloan."

I glanced at his mouth. At his eyes. At his mouth again. I wanted to kiss him. And I think he wanted to kiss me too. But I knew that would be a mistake. An enormous one.

"I believe you," I said.

He eased back. Something changed in his eyes.

The moment was over.

He said, "I need to ask you something. Did you get that sample analyzed yet?"

"What sample?" I knew I was looking guilty as hell, but I couldn't admit the truth.

"The one you stashed in your car."

The hairs on my nape prickled. "Were you the one who broke my window?"

"No. But I did go back to your car later to get the sample. When I got to it, the window was already broken. The sample wasn't under the seat, where I'd seen you put it. I was hoping you'd stashed it somewhere else."

Hoping? He was hoping I'd stashed it somewhere else? Why? Did he want me to get it analyzed? "Just say you had found it in my car, what were you going to do with it? Put it back?"

"No. I was going to take it to a friend and have it analyzed. I want to know what the other lab found. Peyton said the results were inconclusive because the sample was tainted. And she said the bureau isn't going to pay for another test. We were going to have to wait until we had another victim to swab."

"Um. Oh." I looked down at my hands. They were clenched in my lap. I was petrified that JT was lying, that he was just trying to trick me into admitting I was hiding evidence. But I was more afraid of not getting the test run. "How long will it take your friend to do the analysis?"

"He can do a quick and ugly analysis in a day and a half."

"I guess that's better than nothing." I snapped on my seat belt. "Take me home."

Like a morning dream, life becomes more and more bright the longer we live, and the reason of everything appears more clear. What has puzzled us before seems less mysterious, and the crooked paths look straighter. . . .

—Jean Paul Richter

14

JT dropped me off at the office before taking the sample to his friend. I didn't need the backward-ticking clock to know we could have another victim tomorrow morning. The sense of time slipping away, not to mention my growing concern about Katie, made me jittery. When I'd gone home to get the sample, she'd been in her room, sleeping. I'd found the soup container, full, in the refrigerator.

I couldn't sit still. I couldn't concentrate. And I'd made at least ten trips to the bathroom in the last hour.

I don't know how long Chief Peyton had been watching me, but about fifteen minutes after I'd finally settled in, ready to map out our crime scenes, she pulled a chair up to my cubicle and sat down.

"How are you doing, Skye?" The chief crossed one knee over the other.

I wanted to tell her the truth, that I was frustrated, scared we wouldn't solve the case, worried that dozens—or even hundreds—of women would die because I couldn't do this job. But I couldn't say those things. "I'm doing fine." I pointed at the map on my computer screen. "I've plotted out the homes of all four victims. And where they died. There's no connection between the crime scenes. But three out of four—Richardson, Miller, and Yates—live in the same subdivision. And all three backyards are adjacent to the same school playground. It's unclear, at this point, what tie-in Hannah Grant has with the other victims. She lives close, walking distance from the others, but not in the same neighborhood. In addition, a couple of them are runners. We don't have much of a profile of the unsub yet, though."

Peyton took a closer look at the map. "That's a good start."

"We also have an eyewitness who claims she saw one of our victims, Patty Yates, being attacked. But, unfortunately, the witness's eyesight is horrible. She was a fair distance from the alleged attack, and the testimony is a little too far-fetched to believe."

"Remember, Skye, it's your job to check out the far-fetched." The chief stood. "Where is JT?"

"He . . . got a call from another potential witness."

"Why didn't you go along?"

"He wanted me to stay here and get all the details of my undercover operation hammered out. We're going to do some surveillance early tomorrow morning, since all four victims died in the morning."

"Good idea. Be sure to keep me updated. I'm counting on you and JT to handle this. Be careful, Skye. Keep your eyes open."

"Will do, Chief." I didn't take a deep breath until the chief was back in her office. Acting as nonchalantly as possible, I dug my cell phone out of my laptop case and dialed JT's number. But before he answered, somebody nudged me on the back. I swear, my butt flew at least a foot off my chair. The phone flung out of my hand. It clattered on the floor, and the battery and back cover skidded across the tile, traveling one way, the phone the other.

"Shit," I said.

"Sorry." Gabe scooped up the backless phone while I went for the rest of the parts.

"It's okay."

"Jumpy, a little?" He handed me the phone.

"Thanks. A bit." I snapped the pieces back together and crossed my fingers, hoping it would work. I don't have good luck with cell phones. It didn't power up. "Damn it. This is all I need right now. Looks like I'll be making a trip to the cell phone store once again. I wonder if they make phones that are kidproof?"

"I saw your car."

"Yeah," I said, pushing buttons and hoping for a miracle. "I don't know what to think about that. Was it an accident? Was it not? Being on a military base, I would think the parking lot would be secure."

"Yeah, you'd think. Was anything missing?" He gave me a look, the kind that said it was a certain *something* he was asking about.

"No. *Nothing* was missing."

His shoulders descended at least a couple of inches. "Good." He sprawled into the chair Peyton had abandoned. "So what's new?"

"About . . . ?" I asked.

"The case."

"Nothing yet." I sighed. "To tell you the truth, this case is making me mad. We just can't catch a break. I was hoping the witness we interviewed today would give us something."

Gabe leaned closer. "You had a witness come forward?"

"Yeah, a hundred-year-old blind woman with diabetic dementia who claims she saw a woman leap over a six-foot fence like a kangaroo to have a lesbian encounter with Patty Yates."

Gabe's eyes bugged. A wide grin spread over his face. "Sorry, I can't help myself." He laughed.

That did nothing to lighten my mood.

"By the way, I passed your mom on the way in." And that made it even worse. "She parked in a lot across from the base's entry. I think she's waiting for you or something."

I didn't even try to hide the eye roll. "She told me she's working as a private investigator. I'm not convinced someone is *actually* paying her. But at least it's keeping her busy. She hasn't shorted out her apartment building since she started."

"Who is she investigating?"

"Me."

Once again, I got to listen to Gabe have a good laugh, at my expense. But it was my fault. I was the one who'd volunteered the information.

After he'd settled down, he added, "It's too bad she can't come on base. If she could, she might've seen who busted out your window."

"Yeah, it's too bad." I decided a change of topic was a good idea. "What's your case about?"

"Missing kid."

"Oh. A kid. That explains why the chief would pull you off the other case. But why did it end up a *PBAU* case?"

"Because a witness claimed the unsub lifted a car off the ground and tossed it about twenty yards. And our witness isn't a hundred-year-old blind woman."

"That may be the case, but the witness has to be wrong."

"Tell that to the uniform who saw it."

I felt my own brows jump to the top of my forehead. "Your witness is a police officer?"

"Yep." Gabe leaned closer still. "And get this, the witness swears the unsub is a woman."

"Crazy." Maybe I had been right about that.

Gabe moved closer yet. I was really getting uncomfortable. "What's the story with the sample? Did you get it to someone?"

"Kind of," I mumbled, looking away.

"What's that mean?"

"It's in the hands of the right person." I wasn't going to tell Gabe about giving it to JT. I had a feeling he'd freak out. "Hopefully, we'll have a 'fast and dirty' analysis by tomorrow sometime."

"Cool. You'll tell me what you get?"

"Absolutely."

Gabe shifted back, thank God. "What are you doing now?"

"Trying to decide how I can make myself look like a thirty-something suburbanite with shoulder-length hair." I ran my fingers through my hair, currently cut in a no-nonsense, utilitarian chin-length bob. "And trying to convince myself that I won't die if I try to run six miles."

"So you're going undercover?"

"I guess that's what you'd call it."

"Damn!"

That was an I-wish-it-were-me damn. I could tell. "Your father can try all he wants, but there's no way you could do this one. I don't think even Mrs. Ester would buy your being a woman."

"How deep are you going?" Gabe asked.

"At this point, I'll be taking up residence in a bank-owned house for a day or two. Luckily, the people who vacated the property left all their furniture."

"Good luck." Gabe leaned forward and set a hand on mine. "And be careful." When I nodded, he stiffened, pulled his hand away, and stood. "I've got some research to do. The kid's got some crazy allergies, and the parents are worried she might have an allergy attack while she's being held hostage."

"Good luck to you too. I hope you find her."

"We will. And we'll find her alive."

That was one thing about Gabe I was coming to respect— he was always confident, positive, optimistic. Unlike me. I could work on that.

I finished planning out the details of my activities over the next few days, called a hair salon I found on the Net, and begged and pleaded for an appointment for extensions. It was only after I told the salon's receptionist it was for an important FBI investigation that she miraculously found an opening for me. I had ten minutes to make a twenty-minute drive.

I did it in twelve minutes. And, fortunately, I didn't get a speeding ticket. A beaming girl with too much makeup and too much body for the itty-bitty clothes she was wearing fired questions at me, interrogation style, as she led me to a chair in the back of the salon. Most of them I answered with the standard "It's FBI business. I can't answer that question." But I did indulge her curiosity a little by answering what questions I could.

Mom strolled in just as Carl, the stylist, was introducing himself.

Mom said, "Honey, you just got your hair cut last week. What are you doing?"

"Did you talk to Katie?" I combed my fingers through my natural-for-the-time-being hair.

"Yes, Sloan. She's fine. It was just a little anxiety. Everyone gets anxious sometimes."

"I'm worried," I confessed, staring at my reflection in the mirror.

"You're a good friend." Standing behind me, Mom smiled at me in the mirror. "Now, about your hair . . ."

"I have to get extensions. And maybe some color."

"Really? Why would you do that? Your hair is so cute the way it is. And the chemicals they use in hair dye aren't good for you." Mom made herself comfortable in the chair next to mine. A female stylist wandered up and asked Mom if she wanted anything: cut, blow-out, or set. "Oh, that sounds lovely. But I can't."

"Go ahead, Mom. My treat." I nodded at the stylist. "Give her whatever she wants."

"In that case, maybe I will get a little something done. Can you give me the same thing my daughter's getting?"

The stylist looked askance at Carl.

"Extensions," Carl volunteered. "And maybe a little color, to brighten her up." My credit card was going to be steaming tonight.

"No color!" Mom said. "Unless you have henna."

The stylist beamed and grabbed a black plastic cape. "We have henna. As well as several other herbal dyes. My name's Crystal." She pinned the cape on Mom and dug in.

"So, Mom, how's your case going?" I asked, holding my head still as Carl started working.

"Not as well as I'd hoped."

"Really? What were you hoping for? You should know by now what to expect, since it's me you're tailing."

"I was hoping you were hiding some things from me. Scandalous things. A steamy affair with a married man, something amusing. I've come to the conclusion you're a very boring person."

I swallowed a laugh. I didn't want her to think I was amused by her. She might take that as encouragement. "Me? Have an affair with a married man? Never going to happen."

"Never say never, dear."

"I totally agree," Carl said.

"I had an affair with a married man, on and off for three years," Crystal confessed.

"What about you, Mom?" I asked, not sure how to respond to Crystal's confession.

Mom's cheeks went red.

"No. Really? When?" I asked.

"It was a long time ago, before I met your father. I was young then. I'd had a sheltered childhood. Gone to an all-girls school for most of my life. Didn't know a damn thing about men."

"Me too!" Crystal said. "I went to an all-girls Catholic school."

"You were very lucky, then, to find Dad," I said.

"I was. Very lucky, indeed." Mom reached across the space between our chairs. Our fingertips barely touched. We all remained silent for a while. It was a sweet moment, the kind I have rarely shared with my mother over the years. The kind I'd craved for most of my childhood. I hated to break it, but I knew I had to.

"Mom, I'm going undercover tomorrow."

"I know." She didn't sound shocked at all.

"How?"

"I told you, I can't give up my client." This was getting a little frustrating. "That's why I'm here. I want to tell you to be careful. There are things out there, evil you can't imagine. I did all I could to prepare you. I taught you everything you need. When the time comes, I hope you'll remember."

This was the kind of nearly incomprehensible logic I was accustomed to hearing from my mother.

I responded with, "I hope so too."

"It'll be hard for me to tail you while you're under surveillance."

"Don't try, Mom. I don't want you to get hurt."

"Don't worry about me," Mom said. "I'll be fine."

"I'd feel better if you kept an eye on Katie for me. Maybe you could stay with her until I'm done with this undercover thing? I'm leaving early tomorrow morning. Five-thirty or six at the latest."

"Okay, Sloan. I'll be there."

Five hours later, I dragged myself out of the salon, flung my stiff and sleepy body into my car, and drove toward home with Mom's headlights glaring in my rearview mirror. I made a quick stop at a Burger King for some fries and a chicken sandwich. And I ran into a CVS and grabbed a cheap prepaid cell phone to get me through the next day or two. She escorted me through the drive-through and to my building's parking lot. But then she pulled a U-turn and drove home without so much as a word, or a French fry.

I was starving and exhausted, both. I dragged inside, dumped my laptop case next to the door, and set my dinner on the coffee table.

The place was quiet. No bouncy greeting from Katie. No smoke. Nothing. Right now, I was really unsure about leaving Katie to go undercover when she needed me so much. She'd been such a good friend to me all these years.

I decided it could be no coincidence that Katie was so like my mother, brilliant and seemingly mentally ill. There had probably been little clues all along. My subconscious had recognized them, drawn me to her. Kind of like some women are always attracted to men who will abuse them.

I watched the news as I ate. Before I realized it, both French fry containers were empty—I'd ordered an extra, expecting Mom to come in—and my chicken sandwich was gone too. I slurped down the last of my root beer and stumbled into my bedroom.

I didn't drift off to sleep. I plunged.

"Little mouse."

It was back again. Dread twisted in her stomach. Her skin puckered, goose bumps prickling her arms and legs. The hair on her nape stiffened.

No more. Please.

"Come out of your hole. I have a treat for you. A special treat, only for you."

The stench of death hit the back of her throat. Something

*sharp pierced through the blanket, nicking the skin of her
upper arm.*

"There you are, little mouse."

*The blanket slipped away. She tried to grasp a corner, but
she couldn't hold on. She opened her eyes and looked up,
toward the voice, and saw two glittering eyes in the shadows.
A flash of light.*

I jerked upright and blindly pawed the empty bed, looking
for my blanket. I was sweating and shivering.

"Little mouse," somebody whispered.

My heart stopped.

That was a real voice, not a dream.

Who was in my room?

My spine stiffened and a fresh coat of goose bumps covered my arms and legs. My upper arm was stinging. I wanted
to check it, but the room was dark and I was afraid to turn
on the light. I was petrified of what I'd see.

"Little mouse, it's almost time," the voice said.

I gagged. Frozen with terror, I sat curled on my bed, wishing the voice would go away. What was happening? Who was
hiding in the shadows?

Was it the unsub? Male? Female? I couldn't tell.

Silence.

Was it here? Or had it left?

Oh, God, tell me it's gone. Pleasepleaseplease.

Phone. I needed to call 911.

Damn, my cell was out in the living room.

I wasn't going out there. Not yet. Not until I was certain it
was safe.

I heard some rustling in the living room, a dragging
sound, like something hard and heavy was sliding across the
kitchen's tile floor. It wasn't safe. I hoped Katie was in her
room. Asleep.

My heart was thumping so hard in my chest, my breast-bone hurt. My ears strained, catching every minute sound, the rattle of the refrigerator's motor, the clatter of the plastic window blinds in the living room blowing in a breeze, the soft thud of heavy footsteps coming down the carpeted hall.

The intruder was coming back.

I flung myself onto the floor and scuttled like a crab into the closet.

"Little mouse, there's no reason to hide in the dark. I have a lot of surprises for you. You're going to love them. But not yet. I have to go now."

Thank God!

I heard the soft click of the front door's lock. The creak of hinges. Then the sound of the lock sliding home.

Was it gone? Had he or she left? Or was it a ruse, to coax me out of hiding?

A long time later, I crawled out of the closet. I dashed across the bedroom. At the door to the hallway, I listened for any sound that might indicate the intruder was hiding some-where in our apartment. When I didn't hear anything, I tip-toed down the hall. I checked the bathroom. Nothing there. I checked Katie's room. I checked the kitchen and living room. All clear. I checked the front door. Locked. I checked the windows. They were both open a couple of inches, but the wood pieces we'd wedged in the frame—after that note episode—were still in place, keeping the windows from opening any wider. I flipped on every light in our apartment and checked every corner and closet. There was no sign of the visitor. Nothing out of place. And no sign of forced entry.

What did he or she want? And how had he or she gotten into our apartment?

Did he or she have anything to do with my car's broken window?

Lastly I checked my arm.

There, on my forearm. A fat red droplet of blood had dried, sealing a tiny puncture wound.

Oh, my God, what the hell?

I grabbed the biggest, sharpest knife out of the wood block sitting on the kitchen counter and went back to bed. I set the knife on the nightstand, within easy reach.

Tomorrow I'd ask the property manager for a new lock.

*To him that waits all things reveal themselves,
provided that he has the courage not to deny, in the
darkness, what he has seen in the light.*

—Coventry Patmore

15

Five o'clock came very early, much too early. I flung an arm at my alarm clock, smacking the snooze button to silence Technotronic's "Pump Up the Jam," playing on my fave morning radio channel. I gradually pushed up to a sitting position and even more slowly climbed to my feet.

Mornings are *so* not my thing.

I made a beeline for the bathroom, cranked on the hot water, and filled the room with steam. The shower woke me up a little. The blast of the hair dryer woke me up a little more. The three cups of coffee I drank after that did the rest.

After checking out the newly long-haired me in the mirror, I tossed some clothes into a suitcase and added the essentials: toothbrush, makeup, hair dryer, and phone charger. I met Mom outside as I was hauling my load to the car.

"Good morning, honey." Mom tossed her newly acquired lustrous raven locks, which fell in a tumble of waves to the middle of her back, and beamed.

Sporting some running shorts, a sweatshirt, and tennis shoes, I hefted the bag into the trunk and slammed it shut. "Hi, Mom."

"You look tired again. Why aren't you getting enough rest?"

"Someone broke into my apartment last night."

"Oh, no." Mom gave me a thorough up-and-down inspection. "Are you okay?"

"I'm okay. I think. Just shaken up a little."

"I told you this complex isn't safe. You should move into mine. It's much better. The unit across the hall from mine is empty, now that Faith is in jail. She's doing hard time, I heard. Grand theft auto. Won't be getting out anytime soon. I could pull some strings to reserve it for you."

"No, Mom. I'm not ready to move. I like this place. Katie likes it. It's close to the freeway. Convenient. Cheap. . . ." And miles away from you.

"And teeming with criminals."

And her complex wasn't? Her neighbor was a car thief.

Don't get me wrong, I love my mother. We're very close. But living across from her would make us *too* close.

"I'm going to call maintenance and ask them to change the lock." I dropped my laptop case into the passenger seat. "The weird thing is, nothing's missing or damaged." *Just like my car.* "I couldn't find any sign of a break-in." *Unlike my car.* "I don't know how or why he or she got in. It's all very strange."

"I could guess. The lock on your door is crap. I could pop it with a credit card." Mom gave me a worried-Mom look. "I'm very concerned about you."

"Don't be. I'll be fine." I slid into the driver's seat, shut the door, and opened the window. "Besides, I'll be staying somewhere else for a few days. By the time I get back, the lock'll be changed. I'll make sure they put on a better one." *Maybe I should get a gun.*

"Be careful." Mom poked her head in the window to give me a kiss on the cheek. "I love you."

"I love you too, Mom. Gotta go. I'm supposed to be jogging no later than seven."

Mom shuffled to her car and together we drove to my new

temporary home, making a quick stop for donuts and more coffee on the way. Mom didn't stop at the house when I pulled into the driveway; she kept on rolling, heading back to the apartment. JT was already inside, waiting for me. I hauled my suitcase in, then went back out for my laptop and breakfast. I plopped onto a stool at the kitchen's raised counter/ snack bar.

JT helped himself to one of my donuts. "We need to show you how to wire yourself. Shirt off."

That was one surefire way to get a girl to take off her clothes.

"Shouldn't you have a female agent do this for me?" I asked, feeling my cheeks going red.

"I could call one in, but that would waste time. We don't have a female agent on the team. I'd like to get you out jogging sooner, rather than later. It's your call."

I briefly considered asking him to call in the girl agent, but I decided it wouldn't be necessary. I was wearing a sports bra, which was no more revealing than a bathing suit. I wondered if I could avoid him touching me. Probably not. "I guess it's okay." I pulled off my sweatshirt and the T-shirt underneath. JT's eyes went a little buggy for a split second. After that, he kept his reaction unreadable. That made things a little less awkward as he taped the equipment to me.

"Little less" was the operative term, though. My body had decided to respond to his every touch. My nerves tingled. My skin warmed. My blood flowed to parts that didn't get a lot of flowage very often. And my breathing went a little wonky. When I dropped my gaze, to avoid meeting JT's, I noticed JT wasn't exactly unaffected by our proximity either. His pants were fitting a little snugger than normal in the crotch area.

How tacky was it that I was staring *there*?

I jerked my gaze up to his face. His very handsome face. His very handsome scarlet face. His gaze met mine. His lips parted ever so slightly. I stopped breathing.

He leaned closer.

My heart rate kicked up to double speed.

"Sloan?" he whispered.

"Yes, JT?" I whispered back.

"I think you'd better put your shirt back on. Or you're not going jogging this morning." His teeth sank into his lower lip. I wanted to taste that lip. A whole lot more than I wanted to run six miles.

"O-okay." I grabbed my T-shirt, stuffed my head through the neck hole, and poked my arms through the sleeves. By the time I'd smoothed the shirt over the wires and transmitter, his face wasn't a deep scarlet anymore. His neck and ears, however, hadn't returned yet to their normal shade. I resisted the urge to check the other part of his anatomy that had reacted.

"Turn around," he said.

I stood and did a slow one-eighty. He stopped me when my back was facing him. "I need to switch on the transmitter. I . . . didn't do that yet because . . . well . . ."

Was he afraid one of us would say something he didn't want the crew outside to hear? Maybe. "Okay." The back of my shirt slid up, halting just above the little box strapped to my lower back.

"Done. Go ahead, say something." He switched on his radio, speaking into the little microphone attached to his shirt collar. "Ready to test."

"Testing, one, two, three," I said, feeling awkward.

He nodded. "We're good." Using pressure on my shoulders, he turned me around to face him. "Don't be afraid. We're watching you. Every minute. I won't let you out of my sight."

I tried to pretend I wasn't terrified. "I'm ready."

He headed out the side door.

I was alone. In a strange house. And someone was out there, stalking me. Someone who might have access to the military base. Who could it be? Did he or she know where I was now? Little jolts of unease pulsed through my body.

Ignoring them, I opened the back door and stepped out onto the deck. The backyard was pretty, with a large tree for shade standing smack-dab in the middle. There was a stretch of freshly mown grass, and flowering shrubs lined both sides, partially disguising the six-foot-tall wooden fences separating the yard from its neighbors'. The chain-link fence in the back created a semitransparent barrier between the playground on the outside and the lot on the inside.

At this early hour, there were no children playing in the playground, no little voices shouting, only silence. I strolled around the side of the house, unlatched the wooden gate, and jogged down the driveway, taking a left at the sidewalk. JT's plan was for me to follow the route he had mapped out. But six miles were a lot of miles for a girl who hadn't run in months. My last semester had been hell. I hadn't even tried to make time to exercise. I was pretty sure I'd end up in the hospital if I tried to make even three at this point. Instead, I opted for plan B—a more realistic plan—and took a tour around the neighborhood, concentrating on the area around the school.

The first five minutes were hell. After that, it got a little easier. The heart rate settled into a comfortable rhythm and I jog-walked at a steady pace for an hour, my eyes darting around, searching for something suspicious. A part of me wanted to see something, another didn't. I was unarmed and completely defenseless. If the killer assaulted me now, I'd be at the mercy of the men who were tailing me at a distance. Could I really count on them to get to me before the killer had injected me with some horrific disease?

That was a big *no,* I told myself. An injection took seconds.

After an hour, I rounded the corner, returning to my temporary home. "I'm done for today," I huffed into the microphone as I limped up to the front door. I shoved the key into the lock, twisted it, and let myself into the house. I pulled off the tape, removed the transmitter and microphone, set the whole shebang on the counter and headed for the shower.

While I was in there, rinsing the shampoo out of my hair, I heard a sound. Scratching. Loud. Like some kind of wild animal, or a deranged killer, was trying to dig through the door. Not even bothering with rinsing the rest of the shampoo out, I scrabbled out of the shower. There was no way in hell I was going to be caught in there, like Marion Crane in *Psycho*.

Frantic, I searched the room for a weapon. Hair dryer? Curling iron? I tried to yank the towel bar off the wall, but it was bolted on too well. As a last resort, I grabbed a can of hair spray—I knew firsthand that the stuff hurt like hell if sprayed in the eyes—and flattened myself against the wall next to the door. The scratching had stopped, so I scooped up a towel and wrapped it around myself. I tried the door.

Unlocked?

Unlocked. What killer would claw at an unlocked door?

No killer would. I inched it open and something gray leapt into the air. I screamed. It made some unearthly noise as it flew past me, landing on the counter behind me. I wheeled around, trigger finger on the hair spray nozzle.

Cat.

Big. Gray. Unhappy cat.

It made a low *mrrrrr* sound. I lunged out the door, slamming it shut behind me. There was a dull thump, a bone-chilling sound that couldn't be described by any words, and then silence. Turning, I ran smack-dab into a man's very broad chest. Stumbling, I jerked backward and lifted my hand, ready to spray whoever it was.

No spray. Where the hell was the hair spray?

The man's hands clapped around my upper arms, steadying me.

Finally I looked up.

JT.

"Oh, my God, you scared m-me," I stuttered, my hands gathering the towel, which had gone somewhat askew.

"I heard you scream."

"You're good. That was fast."

"I told you, I'm not going to let anyone hurt you."

"I'm beginning to believe you."

He glanced at the closed door and the can of hair spray lying on the floor. "We're going to bug the house today, so you won't have to be wired twenty-four–seven."

"Good idea."

A very unnatural *rrrrr* sound echoed in the bathroom.

"Vicious cat," I explained. "It tried to attack me. I think it has rabies, or maybe feline leukemia, or distemper. Whatever it is, it can't be good."

"We'll get someone in to remove it right away." His eyes traveled south. He visibly swallowed. I tightened my grip on the towel, which felt like it was sliding out of place again. "Why don't you go get dressed and we'll head up to the shooting range. I should take care of a few things at the office first."

"I think that's a great idea." Neither of us moved for a moment.

I reminded myself that there was an army of agents outside. And doing anything with JT was a bad idea. Very bad. Even if it would feel good. Very good. For one thing, JT was wearing a radio. I had to assume it was on, since he'd rushed in to check on what might have been a life-or-death situation. Everyone would hear.

But did JT ever look good today. Better than usual, and that was saying something.

I gently eased back. "I'll be just a few. Give me fifteen."

JT nodded and stiffly walked down the steps. "I'll meet you at the office," he called up from the landing. Two hard-ons in such a short time had to take a toll on a guy.

A little chuckle slipped out as I rushed to dress. Fifteen minutes later, I was sporting a pair of black pants, a knit shirt, comfy shoes, and a ponytail. I hopped into my car and drove out of the subdivision. Mom picked up my tail sometime before I reached the freeway. She waited in the lot while I ran my broken cell phone into the store for repair. Then, beyond hungry—that jog had really stirred up my appetite—I made a stop at the bagel shop just outside of the Quantico Marine Corps Base. Mom parked her car next to mine.

We strolled into the bagel shop together. I ordered my usual; Mom ordered hers. I added an extra bagel, in case JT hadn't eaten breakfast. She looked at me with worried-mother eyes as we waited for our orders to be filled.

"Mom, it's going to be okay."

"I know. I just can't help myself. I'm a mother. Mothers worry."

A stretch of silence followed as we both stared at the sign overhead.

"There isn't a client, is there?" I asked. "You're following me because you're concerned."

"Oh, no. There's a client, all right. I already got my first paycheck. Sloan, you know I couldn't afford to do this much driving if there wasn't someone footing the bill. I'm burning through a tank of gas every three days."

I could believe that. My own gas gauge seemed to be sliding toward empty much too quickly these days as well, and I wasn't doing half the driving JT was. "Will you please tell me who this mystery client is?"

"No."

I felt myself gritting my teeth. Sometimes Mom was stubborn. I don't handle stubborn people very well, probably because I could be a smidge stubborn too. "I swear, I won't tell anyone."

"I know."

"I could turn you in to the FBI for following me."

"You wouldn't do that, Sloan."

She was right. Irritated beyond what was reasonable, I

snatched my cup and bag from the girl as she handed it to me, muttered "Thanks," and stomped toward the door. I didn't wait for Mom.

As I shoved the key into my car's ignition, I told myself that I'd had a rough morning, and that was why I was overreacting. Mom was getting in her car when I sped out of the lot. She caught up to me just as I was turning onto the base, where she couldn't follow. I shoved my arm out the open window and gave her a wave as I drove out of her line of sight.

Maybe I'd make her work for her money a little.

Maybe not.

After all, she was doing something harmless, something that didn't involve illegal drugs or frying her apartment building's electrical system. She could be doing something far more dangerous than following me around town.

I found JT sitting at his desk, staring intensely at his computer screen. I dropped the white bag on his desk.

"What's new? Any word on a new victim?"

"No."

That was a surprise. A good one. "No, as in there's no new victim this morning?" My heart lightened.

"Not yet."

I felt my lungs inflate fully, and I realized I'd been stressing all morning, anticipating the moment when we'd hear about another death.

"Are you hungry?" I asked, shaking the white bag.

"A little."

"Good." I set the cup next to the bag. "Sorry, didn't get you a coffee. I've never seen you drink it, so I wasn't sure if it was your thing."

"Not a fan. Good call. You're getting better at profiling, I see."

"I hadn't thought of this as profiling, but I get it." I handed him an everything bagel, wrapped in waxed paper. "My personal favorite. I hope you like it." I stuffed my hand back in the bag and pulled out a handful of cream cheese packets, dropping them on the desk. While JT loaded his bagel up with the smooth cheese spread, I slurped coffee.

He took a bite and smiled. "Damn, that's good. Thanks."

"I figured it's the least I could do after you came to my rescue this morning."

His chuckle did some interesting things to my insides. Unwelcome at the moment, but not necessarily unpleasant things. His wide beaming smile and dimples did even more. I tried very hard to hide how much I liked his dimples as I drank some more coffee.

He pointed at my lip. "You have something, there."

I grabbed a napkin and dabbed my face. "Thanks." We stared at each other for a moment, our gazes sort of tangled up.

Someone cleared his throat. It wasn't JT. I jerked back, glancing over my shoulder.

Gabe. He was looking at me funny. "What's going on?" he asked.

"We're grabbing a quick bite before heading out. JT is taking me to the gun range to show me how to shoot. How's your case going?" I asked, shifting a little to put some distance between myself and JT.

"I need to take care of one last thing." JT stood, excusing himself as he pushed past Gabe. "Be back in a few."

Gabe leaned against JT's cubicle wall. "Not good. Outside of the one witness, we've had nobody else come forward. Get this, turns out we've met the missing kid."

"You and me? Really? Who is it?"

"Your friend with the strange taste in clothes and the weird bike."

"Tutu Girl?"

Gabe nodded. "That's the one."

My heart lurched. It was a painful sensation. And as I imagined that cute little face. "Wow. I jogged right past her house this morning. I didn't notice a thing. Such a cute little kid . . ."

Gabe shook his head. "*Kids*. I didn't expect this."

"Me either."

Gabe glanced up, in the general direction of Chief Peyton's office. We watched JT come strolling out, headed toward us. "Gotta motor. We're going to the kid's house to interview her parents."

"Good luck."

"Thanks. You too."

JT passed Gabe on his way to my cubicle. "Ready?"

"As ready as I'm going to be, I guess." I crumpled up the empty bag and tossed it and the cup, also empty, into his trash can.

"I hope I don't regret this," JT said, giving me a warning look.

"I promise, you won't regret it." I beamed.

"We'll see about that." He explained the rules of the gun range on the way there. He signed in, picked a spot, and set a weapon on the counter in front of me.

And just like that, I went from completely confident to absolutely petrified. Did I really have to pick that thing up and shoot it?

Was this a good idea?

Two hours later, after many *very* bad shots, it was decided. It hadn't been a good idea. Having me carry a gun was a serious threat to public safety. The chance that I'd hit an innocent bystander was much greater than my hitting the assailant I was aiming for. JT handed me a stun gun and showed me how to use that.

I was now armed and dangerous. God help the fool who messed with me.

God help me.

A great source of calamity lies in regret and anticipation; therefore a person is wise who thinks of the present alone, regardless of the past or future.

—Oliver Goldsmith

16

I wondered what Katie was doing right now. Was she comfy on the couch, feet kicked up on the coffee table, munching popcorn and watching TiVoed episodes of *Weird Connections*? Or was she lounging in her room, her worn and battered copy of the *CRC Handbook of Chemistry and Physics* on her lap? Whatever she was doing, I longed to be there with her right now.

I was alone. Sort of. In this strange house again. Waiting, waiting, and waiting for something to happen. I didn't even have a decent Internet connection. No Web surfing to distract me.

Talk about torture.

I checked my pocket for the umpteenth time, curled my fingers around the stun gun, tapped the switch. It was there, ready, just in case. Though I left the safety on, so I didn't zap myself. In my other pocket was my cell phone, JT's phone number already dialed. All I had to do was hit the little green button and I'd have him on the line.

Still, I felt alone and vulnerable. I didn't like either feeling. Not at all.

As I was taking my fourth tour of the house, JT's ringtone

sounded. I fumbled the phone out of my pocket and hit the button. "What's wrong?" I asked.

"Nothing," JT said. "I'm just calling to check on you. I think you've done at least thirty laps around that house."

"Have I?" Now standing in the kitchen, staring out the patio door, into the inky black night, I checked the lock. "Maybe I'm a little jittery."

"A little?"

"Okay, a lot." I sighed. "I can't help it. I feel like someone's watching me."

"We are."

"No, someone else."

"I guarantee, there's nobody else. We have eyes on every inch of that house. You'll know the minute we see anything."

I gnawed on my lip. "Okay. Maybe it's the cat. You couldn't find the cat?"

"It was gone by time Animal Control arrived." After a beat, JT asked, "Do you want me to come in for a little while?"

I wanted him to come in. And I wanted him to stay longer than a little while. But I knew that wasn't a good idea, for several reasons. "No. It's probably better if you don't."

"Okay."

Amazing how I could sense his relief in just that single word.

On my way through the kitchen, I checked the clock. It was after eleven. Six-thirty would come early if I didn't get to sleep soon. "I think I'm going to head up to bed."

"Good idea. Try to get some sleep. I'm going to try to catch a few z's myself. But I promise, I'm right down the road. I can be there in less than two minutes."

"Okay."

"You have a whole team outside, watching your back."

"I'll try to remember that."

"Sweet dreams, Sloan."

"You too."

I ended the call and tiptoed upstairs. After taking care of a few essentials in the bathroom, I headed for the master bedroom, put the cell phone and stun gun on the nightstand, and made myself comfy in the bed that the bureau had made up with brand-new pillows, sheets, and blankets. The bedding was nothing fancy, but it was cozy. I was exhausted. Must have worn myself out, walking all those laps around the house. Being horizontal felt good. But after almost an hour of trying to fall asleep, I was still awake. I resorted to reading *The Viking King and the Maiden.* I read a sexy scene between the Viking king and the maiden, where he insisted she join him in a swim, and they did things I had previously thought were impossible underwater. Needless to say, after that scene, I was ready to close my eyes and let my imagination run wild.

And wild it did run.

"Little Mouse, why do you think you can hide from me? When will you realize I know your every move? I've enjoyed playing your game. But it's growing tedious."

Trembling under her covers, she fought to breathe. It felt as if an enormous weight was sitting on her chest. Her lungs couldn't inflate. The air was stale and thick, too thick to pull into her throat.

"Little mouse."

What did he want? She was certain it wasn't something pleasant. Her skin burned. Goose bumps prickled her arms and shoulders.

Go away.

"It's time to end our game."

The familiar stink of rotted flesh filled her nose. He was close. Too close. Right above her. Her entire body tensed, even her scalp.

"I won," he whispered. "I have come for my prize."

The blanket slowly dragged down her body. Her eyes

snapped open. First she saw a shadow. And then those
strange glowing eyes.
And then the fangs.

I jerked upright, arms swinging. I struck nothing but air.
My eyes blinked, trying to make out shapes in the heavy
shadows. Where was he? Why hadn't anyone come to my
rescue? I was drenched in sweat. Breathless. Shaking.

"Little mouse."

This wasn't a dream. It was real. Someone was here, in the
house. He'd found me. Who was it? I had to know. Petrified,
I clawed at the nightstand. The lamp was the first to fall. The
clock next. *Thump, thump.*

No stun gun. No phone. I slid to the floor and searched
frantically in the dark. Where'd they go?

"There's nothing to fear," the voice said. It was a low,
scratchy voice. Although I sensed it belonged to a man, I
couldn't tell for sure. It didn't matter. Either way, it made my
skin crawl. "I want my prize." *Prize?* He was coming closer.
He couldn't be more than a few feet from me.

I looked up. Was that big shadow over there the man—the
thing—from my nightmare? Or was it just a shadow? "I don't
know what you're talking about." I needed to buy time.
Where was my backup?

"What are you looking for?"

"I . . . I knocked the lamp down. Trying to pick it up."

"You don't need it."

JT's ringtone sounded. I patted the floor, letting the sound
guide my hand. I found it, scooped it up, and hit the button.

"JT. I—I h-have a v-visitor," I stuttered.

"The team's at both doors."

"W-what're they waiting f-for?"

The sound of a dozen or more footsteps pounded through
the house. I didn't move. Sat frozen in place, arms wrapped

around my legs. The thing-person-whatever that had been in the bedroom with me must have fled the instant I answered the call. I didn't hear him leave. Next thing I knew, the room was flooded with brilliant light, and I was being gently lifted to my feet by a couple of enormous men dressed in black. JT was at the door, rushing into the room, his face almost ghostly white. He scooped me into his arms and set me on the bed. I wouldn't let go of his neck, couldn't let go. So he sat and held me, while the men in black searched the house. It was so good, having him near me—his strong, thick arms wrapped around my body. His heat warming my chilled skin.

"What happened?" he asked.

"It was the same person who'd broken into my apartment last night."

"Someone broke into your apartment? You didn't tell me. Why didn't you say something?"

"I . . . I didn't think it was a big deal." *Correction, I wasn't sure if it was real or a dream.*

"What else haven't you told me?"

"Nothing."

"Huh." He smoothed my tangled hair back from my face and I looked up into eyes dark with worry. "I wish you would trust me."

"I do."

He tapped his earpiece, letting me know he was answering a call. I nodded. A second later, he told me, "The house is clear."

I felt my whole body relax. "Thank God. I hope he's been scared off for good." JT held me tighter, cupped a hand over my head, pressing it into his chest. I closed my eyes and listened to the steady *thump-whump* of his heartbeat. Sometime later, I asked, "What are we going to do now?"

"I don't know yet. Your cover's probably blown. We should leave—"

I snuggled in deeper. "No, please. We've got an army surrounding this house. We'll be okay."

Stroking my back, JT sighed. "Okay."

I woke up, drooling on JT's chest, a rather humbling way to start the day. After glancing up to see if he was sleeping, I checked the clock. Six o'clock. I could get in a quick shower before I had to hit the road. Moving slowly, carefully, I extracted my body from JT's clutches and padded barefoot to the bathroom. I shaved, scrubbed, lathered, and loofahed myself until I was squeaky-clean. Next I blow-dried my hair and, after pulling it into a high ponytail that made me look cute, donned a little bronzer, lip gloss, and mascara. If I was going to die running six miles, I was going to look cute doing it. My only problem—lacking caffeine when I'd headed into the bathroom, I hadn't thought ahead. My clean clothes were in the bedroom.

Dressed in a towel, I tiptoed back down the hall. I met JT just outside my bedroom.

He gave me one long up-and-down look before flashing me a killer smile. He whispered, "We have got to stop meeting like this."

Clutching the towel, even though I was slightly tempted to let it fall, I gave him some faux squinty eyes. "Out of my way. I've got some jogging to do."

He stepped aside but poked his head into the door before I shut it. He whispered, "If you need some help toweling off your back, let me know."

He did *not* just say *that*.

I shoved his head out of the way and slammed the door. Then I locked it and quickly wired myself up before donning some shorts, a sports bra, a T-shirt, and running shoes. Feeling more energetic than I should, considering how little sleep

I'd had, I bounced downstairs, tracking the scent of freshly brewed coffee.

JT was dumping some bottled vitamin water down his throat when I strolled into the kitchen. I found a clean mug in the cabinet and filled it. He beamed at me as I poured, handing me a carton of vanilla-flavored creamer.

"Thank you," I said. "You seem to be in a mighty chipper mood this morning."

"So do you."

I couldn't argue with that. Since my first day with the PBAU, I'd been dragging around, exhausted, feeling like I was PMSing all the time, achy and foggy-headed. But not today, nope. I felt like I could run those six miles. And maybe six miles more. I couldn't imagine why that might be. I hadn't slept that long, and what little sleep I'd gotten had been interrupted.

The last time I'd felt this way was when Gabe and I . . . I didn't want to think about that now.

I slurped down about half my cup of coffee and headed toward the door. "It's seven. I'd better get out there."

JT's expression changed in a blink, from happy-go-lucky to life-or-death serious. "Sloan, after last night, I think you—"

I grabbed JT's hands and gave them a squeeze. "JT, I want to do this. I need to do this." When he didn't cut me off, I added, "Please. I'll be careful."

"I don't like this."

"You'll be right behind me. You and a SWAT team."

"Yes, but—"

I switched on the transmitter and zigzagged around him. "I trust you, JT." Throwing a wave over my shoulder, I race-walked out the door, squinting at the brilliant sunshiny morning. The sky was the clearest, deepest blue I'd ever seen. The trees lining both sides of the street were clothed in emerald leaves, which flashed when a breeze ruffled them; droplets of dew glittered like diamonds. The air smelled fresh and clean, like grass and flowers and nature. I pulled in a deep breath, exhaled, and jogged down the sidewalk. My heart rate kicked up a little, my breathing too; but unlike yesterday, I didn't feel like I was dying. Quite the opposite. I felt like I could run for miles.

I turned at an intersection, following the route JT had mapped out for me, which would eventually take me past Debbie Richardson's house. I was only vaguely aware of the agents tailing me, watching through binoculars from parked cars. My focus was on looking for anything out of the ordinary as I passed one vinyl-clad Colonial after another. I glanced between the houses lining the park, hoping to catch a glimpse of the unsub hurdling a fence, or a pair of lesbians sneaking a good-morning kiss before heading to work.

What I saw wasn't nearly as exciting. I saw plenty of empty yards, the occasional resident hauling a trash can to the curb or dragging the hose out to the front to douse the grass. I saw a few kids racing around on bikes and skateboards. A couple of dogs who'd escaped from their yards chased me, forcing me to up my speed from a slow but steady jog to a hard sprint. One, a poodle, almost caught me. But just as it was about to sink its little fangs into my ankle, someone whistled and it turned a one-eighty and padded back home.

As I approached Debbie Richardson's house, I saw the crime scene tape stretched across the neighbor's home, the bureau's cars parked out front. Could it be a coincidence that there'd been several major crimes in this neighborhood, two of them—a murder and a kidnapping—on this block?

"There's no such thing as coincidence," my mother's voice echoed in my head.

What if the crimes were related? What would a kidnapping have to do with the murders?

I slowed to a walk as I passed Tutu Girl's house, watching

agents come and go; crime scene investigators were combing the area for tiny bits of evidence.

In stark contrast, all was quiet at the Richardson house. I saw no signs of life. The house was dark, the windows closed, the grass slightly shaggy, ready for a cut. There were no garbage cans at the foot of the driveway. The house was abandoned.

I went on.

I thought I caught a glimpse of some movement between the Richardson house and Tutu Girl's. I twisted to get a better look. I bumped into something sitting on the ground, the rattle of glass echoed through the quiet morning. I wheeled my arms around a few times, frantically fighting to regain my balance. Losing the battle, I fell like a load of bricks onto the driveway.

Just call me graceful; I'd run smack-dab into the recycling bin.

I used it to haul myself back on my feet, noticing there were dozens of glass bottles inside, all of them palm oil bottles.

Palm oil? What the heck did someone do with palm oil? Cook with it? Clean something with it? Bathe in it? Sunbathe with it?

As I jogged across the front of Tutu Girl's house, I stared up at the front window. The drapes fell shut. I guessed Tutu Girl's mother was getting tired of nosy people snooping around. I supposed I would too.

I continued on, my eyes darting around as I ran, while thoughts of one particular FBI agent, skin gleaming, slathered in palm oil, played through my mind as I finished up the rest of the route.

I made it back home without dying. Six miles. I'd run six freaking miles. My legs felt a little wobbly. And my chest a little heavy. And, of course, I was looking a little shiny myself, thanks to the buckets of sweat that had poured out of my pores. But, otherwise, I was okay.

I found JT exactly where I'd left him: in the kitchen. But now the room was filled with the smell of garlic and onion. "I got you an everything bagel." He shook a paper bag.

"Thanks." I grabbed a paper towel and mopped my wet face.

Shoving his hand in the bag, he said, "You made good time."

"I didn't cheat," I said, feeling quite proud of myself. "I ran the full route."

"I know. You didn't tell me you were a runner." He put the bagel on a paper plate.

"I'm not. I mean, I jog a little, to keep in shape. A half hour, tops. And only when my jeans won't snap anymore. But I've been slacking recently. And I haven't run six miles since high school. My mother made me join the cross-country team. She said I spent too much time sitting on my ass, reading."

JT went to the refrigerator, pulled out a cold water bottle, and handed it to me. "At least you won't have any problems passing the FBI PFT."

I twisted off the cap and chugged half the bottle. "That's good to know." I dragged my arm across my forehead. "Whew, I'm thirsty." I polished off the water. "You have another one of those in there?"

"Sure do." He traded me a full bottle for the empty one.

After I emptied the second one, I sat down to check out the bagel.

"I bought you a few things—water, some deli meat for sandwiches, fruit."

"Thanks. That was very thoughtful."

He handed me a packet of cream cheese and a knife. "My intentions weren't all noble."

"What's that mean?" I ripped open the cheese and plunged the knife into it.

"You can't stay here alone. Not after what happened last night." He flinched. "I've decided I should stay here with you."

I couldn't say exactly how I felt about that. "Um, okay."

"I thought about it. Talked to the chief. We both agreed it's a good idea."

"Aren't you worried you'll scare away the unsub?"

After helping himself to a bottle of water, he said, "I was at first, but now . . . not so much. Your safety is more important. Besides, two of our victims were married, living with their husbands. That didn't stop the killer."

I decided I wouldn't put him on the spot right now. "So you'll be playing the part of my husband." I took a bite of the bagel. Delicious.

"Unless you would rather have another agent stay with you."

That was probably a good idea. Correction, that was probably a *great* idea.

"No, that's okay. You can stay. I know you. I trust you." The image of a shirtless JT flashed through my mind again. Skin gleaming, muscles flexing. It was a pleasant image. I took another bite of bagel, chewed, and swallowed. "But we'll sleep in separate rooms, of course."

JT didn't respond. I have a feeling he didn't like that suggestion. I didn't like it either, but I wasn't going to admit it to him.

A couple of minutes later, he asked, "So, are you going to tell me about the guy who broke into your apartment, or not?"

"There isn't much to tell. I don't know anything about him—other than he has a really creepy voice, sneaks in and out without leaving a trace of evidence, and likes to call me 'a mouse.' Do I look like a rodent to you?" I tucked my lower lip behind my front teeth.

He waggled his eyebrows. "No, I'd say you're more kitten than mouse." His expression shifted again, turning more serious. "The fact that he followed you here bothers me."

"You can bet it bothers me too." I smeared another glob of cream cheese on what was left of my bagel. I didn't want to talk about this any longer. It was making me second-guess the whole undercover thing. I didn't want to do that. "A silly question."

"Shoot." JT dumped some kind of powder from a ziplock baggy into a cup then diluted it with water.

"Why would anyone need bottles and bottles of palm oil?" I asked.

"I don't know. I'm not much of a cook. Why?"

"I sort of fell over Debbie Richardson's next-door neighbor's recycling tub and I noticed it was full of palm oil bottles. I was curious."

"Hmm . . ." He sipped.

"What, 'hmm'?"

"Was there a reason why you tripped over a recycling tub? They are a little difficult to miss."

Now I felt like a total clumsy clod. Of course, I was a total clumsy clod. I munched on my bagel before answering. "I was looking between the houses."

"Why?"

"No reason, really. I guess I thought I saw something in my peripheral vision."

"That's a reason."

"There wasn't anyone there." I took another bite of bagel and washed it down with a swig of water.

"Did you check the backyard?"

"No."

"Then you can't say it was nothing."

"I see your point." Feeling like I'd screwed up, I polished off my bagel. "Do you think it's a coincidence the kid down the street is missing?"

"What are you thinking?" JT asked, looking at me over the rim of his cup.

"I don't know. It seems a little odd that there would be such a string of major crimes in such a concentrated area without them being related in some way."

"As a general rule, I'd say you're right. But the nature of the crimes is so different, it's hard to imagine a connection. Are you thinking the unsub has moved from attacking grown women to kidnapping children?"

"It is a *female* child." I plunged my hand in the paper bag, searching for another bagel. Nothing.

"But that's where the similarity ends. Kidnapping children doesn't fit our profile."

"We have a profile?" I asked, wadding up the bag and lobbing it toward the garbage can. I missed. I shuffled over, snatched it up, and dropped it into the can. Then I made a beeline for the refrigerator.

"We have the beginning of a profile. I'd have to take a look, but I don't believe, in the history of the FBI, there's been a case of an unsub starting with homicide and moving into kidnapping minors. We're looking at two very different minds, motivations, and drives."

"I suppose you're right." I poked my head into the fridge. Grapes sounded good. I plucked a few out of the plastic bag sitting on the shelf. I stuffed one in my mouth.

"And as far as the sudden increase in crime in the area, who knows? Maybe there's been some kind of change in the demographics affecting the crime rate. We don't know enough yet to figure it out."

"I'll trust you know more about this than I do and concede. So what's next?"

"You change your clothes." Grinning evilly, he set his cup on the counter and mouthed, "I'll help."

"Help?" I echoed, my cheeks burning.

"Yeah, help figure out what to do next, of course." His eyes narrowed. He whispered, "What did you think I meant?"

I squinted at him and turned my lips into a snarly frown. "Be back in a few. I think I need a quick shower." Much, much quieter, I said, "And before you ask, no, I don't need help soaping my back."

His laughter followed me up the stairs.

Genius is more often found in a cracked pot than in a whole one.

—E. B. White

17

JT and I spent the rest of the day following Patty Yates's every last movement from the day she died, talking to everyone and anyone we could—people on the street, the employees of the hair salon she'd been about to enter before she'd collapsed, her friends, family, the people at the gym she visited irregularly. What we had: Patty hadn't complained of any illness before she'd died; she hadn't appeared sick; she was, in fact, in great health. She and her husband were trying to conceive a baby—thus the need for the Cialis. Unlike the other victims, Patty Yates didn't work outside the home. She was a stay-at-home wife who kept to herself, had no close friends, preferred to stay inside her house, and didn't seem to have any enemies.

In other words, we had nothing.

Both agreeing that we were spinning our wheels, we decided to call it a day and head back to the house to review our case and decide our next step. JT drove, as always. I rode shotgun. For the first half of the ride, we were both quiet, lost in our thoughts.

I broke the silence with a question that had been weighing heavily on my mind. "You are going to behave yourself tonight, aren't you?"

JT looked slightly wounded by my question. "Of course, I am. I always behave myself. What are you trying to say?"

Uncomfortable with the conversation—I am so bad at confrontation—I shifted nervously in my seat. "I'm trying to say the house is wired. You told me that yourself. And there will be—how many, dozens?—of people listening in on our conversations."

"I guess you'd better keep that in mind then. No dirty talk." He winked.

I smacked him. I think he liked it. So I smacked him again, harder. "I'm being serious here. You're an agent. I'm an intern. There are rules about that kind of thing."

The car rolled to a stop as we hit a wall of rush-hour traffic. He gave me what could probably pass for a reassuring look. The slightly evil gleam in his eye was the only thing that spoiled the effect. "I told you, the chief said she doesn't care what we do in our personal relationships, as long as we don't bring it into the office."

"And you think having our personal conversations taped isn't 'bringing it into the office'?"

The car in front of us moved a foot. JT inched the car forward. "There are ways to avoid having any condemning conversations being taped. Even though we stepped up the security, we didn't bug *every* room." JT and the lady in the Mercedes on our right exchanged impolite gestures. Evidently, she thought our lane belonged to her, and she didn't appreciate the fact that we were in her way. "Oh, and by the way, we didn't just wire the house with microphones. We also planted cameras."

"Of course, you did." I was suddenly feeling a little exposed. I imagined a dozen people gawking at me as I shaved my legs this morning. My stomach twisted into a knot. "Please tell me there's no camera in the bathroom."

JT blocked the Mercedes from moving into our lane again. "There's no camera in the bathroom." He gunned the engine, closing the distance between our bumper and the van in front of us.

"Thank God." I braced my hands against the dash, preparing for impact.

JT stomped on the brake just as we were about to slam into the van. I exhaled for the first time in minutes. He said, "The equipment's mostly set around doors and windows, access points to the interior. There are also some in the main living area and the bedroom, where you were sleeping last night."

"You said, 'mostly.'"

"Yeah. We also put a camera in the basement and around the exterior. Nobody's getting in without being caught on camera." He checked his rearview mirror, jerked the steering wheel, and then hit the gas, sending us lurching into the left lane, which was moving a little faster. Our speed bumped up to ten miles per hour instead of five.

Despite JT's aggressive driving, my gut untwisted. There was no way I'd be surprised by a nighttime visitor again. "That part is reassuring."

"So, you see, that leaves plenty of other rooms where we can have a conversation without having to worry about eyes and ears."

My gut twisted back into the knot. "That may be, but . . ."

The car rolled to a stop once again, and JT looked at me. "What are you worried about, Sloan?"

I met his gaze and my heart did a little flip-flop. What was I worrying about? JT was incredibly good-looking, and he seemed to like me. No, he seemed to do more than that. He'd held me so tightly last night, like a man who was worried. He comforted me. He protected me. He was the perfect man. And yet, I had a very good reason for being cautious. Not only was I worried about what a relationship with JT might do to my professional reputation, but I was bothered about something else, something I couldn't quite put my finger on.

"This wouldn't be the first time an agent and an intern

hooked up." The car in front of us surged forward, and JT hit the gas. The car smoothly accelerated as the traffic cleared at last.

I turned to stare out the window. "I'm sure it's not the first time." Maybe that was what I was worried about. JT was so flirtatious, charming, and handsome—surely, he'd had this opportunity before. Probably he had a new intern every summer. A new plaything. "Would it be the first time for you?" I asked, hoping he'd say yes; and hoping, if he did say yes, that he was telling me the truth.

"No."

I felt like I'd been kicked in the gut. "I was afraid of that," I mumbled.

"What do you think of me?"

I didn't answer. I didn't want to tell him, partly because it seemed so easy to think a certain way about him, but it wouldn't be easy to say the words. We were getting closer to the house, and soon we'd be under the watchful eye of a team of FBI agents and their little techy whatchamacallits.

JT poked my knee. "Let me guess, you think I chase all the interns, drag them into my bed, use them mercilessly, and break their hearts." It wasn't a question. It was a statement. One said with absolutely no hint of malice.

"Well . . ."

"It's not like that. There was one. Only one. It was my first month out of the academy. And it almost got me fired."

"And you think it's a good idea goofing around with me? The way I see it, that's one for one. 100%. You've only been an agent for a year."

JT checked the traffic in the right rearview mirror and cut across two lanes to catch our exit ramp. At the stop sign at the end of the ramp, he said, "That just goes to show you. . . . This isn't something I jump into lightly. I care about you."

He cared about me? He *cared*.

A part of me knew that. It was the way he held me when I

was scared. But hearing the words did something to my insides. I didn't know how to respond. Men didn't say those words very often. Especially to me. They might flirt. They might tease. They might marvel at my math skills or compliment my knowledge of comparative biology. But they didn't say they *cared* about me. "I . . . uh . . ." Did he really mean it? I looked at him.

He was driving now, eyes on the road, but he slanted them my way for a moment. Our gazes snagged. I saw no hint of deception. In fact, I could swear I spied something else— vulnerability? His gaze snapped back to the road before I could figure it out.

Neither of us said anything for the rest of the drive.

He parked the car in the attached garage. I shuffled around the car, brushing past him as he pulled the door leading into the house open for me. I mumbled, "Thanks"; then I headed for the kitchen. My cell phone rang.

"Hi, Mom," I said, looking at the caller ID.

"Hi, honey." That voice wasn't Mom's. She was a female. The voice definitely belonged to a male. The hairs on my arms stood on end.

"Who is this?" I snapped. I glanced around, looking for JT. Where'd he go?

"It's okay. It's just me, Gabe."

"You?" I sagged against the kitchen counter. "How did you get my mom's phone number to show up on my caller ID?"

"Shush. Just listen. Are there ears listening in?"

"Uh, maybe."

"Okay, just keep talking like I'm your mother."

"Sure, Mom," I said, wondering if his cover wasn't already blown.

He continued, "I didn't want my phone number showing

on your phone. In case . . . well, in case something comes up. I used a spoofing service. Any word on the sample?"

"No, Mom." I checked the clock. I'd forgotten all about it. JT had said it would be done by now, but he hadn't mentioned it today. I wondered if that whole thing had been a lie, a way to get the sample back for the chief. "I'll have to check into that for you."

"I think someone's hiding something."

"It's possible." I dug out a diet cola from the back of the refrigerator.

"Be careful. I'm not sure we can trust any of them. Something's fishy about this whole thing."

"Please don't worry about me, Mom. I'll be fine." Suddenly I wasn't so sure about that. I wanted to know what was making Gabe think the way he did, but I didn't want to ask when I was standing in the kitchen, where there were cameras and microphones to catch my every word. I headed toward the nearest bathroom, around the corner, off the narrow hallway leading to the front foyer. "There's someone staying with me in the house now."

"Who?"

"A nice agent. He's . . . being a gentleman. Don't worry."

"Let me guess. It's *JT*?"

What was that I heard in Gabe's voice? "Yes, that's the one." I closed myself in the bathroom—smaller than the coat closet in the foyer—and turned on the water.

"What's that noise?"

"Running water. I don't want anyone to overhear me." I cupped my hand around my phone and spoke softly.

"Good idea."

"Why did you say this looks fishy? Is something going on that I'm not seeing? Everyone seems to be working hard, trying to solve the cases."

"Yeah, they do."

"And they have a lot to prove, because the PBAU is sort of a joke to the people who know about it."

"Sure."

"So what's wrong? Are they keeping you at a distance, withholding evidence?"

"Not that I know of."

"Then what is it?"

"I don't know. I can't say exactly."

"I think you've been hanging around my mother too much."

"I haven't seen your mother in years."

I heard something outside the bathroom, footsteps, a thump. "I need to go."

"Be careful, Sloan. You and I have had our issues, but I've always respected you. Hell, I've admired you for years, if you want to know the truth. I would hate to see something happen to you."

Was this the day for men to make surprising confessions, or what? "Thanks. That's very touching."

"I don't trust JT. There's something about him."

"Yeah, well, I don't either. Not 100%. But I also know there are cameras all over this place, and a team of men outside watching the feed. Nobody's doing anything to me without them knowing about it."

"Okay."

JT knocked. "Sloan, are you okay?"

"I'm fine. Just talking to my mother."

"Call me if you need anything."

"Will do." I cut off the call. Then, because I was in the bathroom, I checked myself in the mirror. I decided I looked good, which was probably a bad thing, and stuffed my cell phone in my pocket.

JT was leaning against the wall when I exited. "Everything okay?"

"Yes. That was my mom. She's not used to me being away from her like this."

"She relies upon you."

"Maybe a little."

He gave me a knowing look.

"How much do you know about my family?" I asked.

"Enough to appreciate the fact that you're not telling the whole truth."

I felt my cheeks heating and tried to hide my embarrassment and discomfort with a little dose of sarcasm. "Sheesh. What happened to confidentiality?"

"What I know I didn't get from a bureau file."

"Oh."

He moved toward the bathroom. "Come here."

I watched as he filled the diminutive space with his bulk. I didn't follow him into the bathroom. There wasn't room. "Um . . . I don't think we're both going to fit."

He pulled, and I stumbled inside. He shut the door behind my back, closing us in. The pedestal sink was on my left. I steadied myself by gripping the lip of the basin. The toilet was on my right, the edge of the seat grinding into the side of my leg. JT was in front of me, his body brushing against mine. The scent of JT's tangy cologne mixed with the odor of the soap's fruity fragrance. It wasn't an altogether bad combination.

I backed up as much as I could, smooshing my butt against the closed door. "What are you doing?"

He leaned close, closer. I was sure he was going to kiss me. Here we were, in this cozy spot, outside of the range of the cameras and microphones. Just like he wanted. I didn't want him to kiss me. No, I did. Didn't. Did. Oh, hell, I didn't know what I wanted. I pressed hard against the door, closed my eyes, and waited. . . .

"I got the results," he whispered in my ear.

He wanted to talk. And here I'd thought . . . I felt so stupid. I snapped my eyelids up. "Results?"

"The DNA analysis. I just got a call from my friend. The analysis took longer than he thought."

"Yeah? And?"

"They're strange. The unsub's DNA isn't human. Or rather, it's not *just* human. There are a few extra genes."

"A few extra?" I echoed, recalling what Gabe had said about the initial results. "How is that possible?"

"I don't know. But there are quite a few extra. Either the sample was tainted with foreign DNA or our unsub is part insect."

I tried to imagine what a human being with insect DNA might look like. The results weren't pretty. "It must be tainted, then. Because I'm sure we'd notice somebody walking around with big compound bug eyes, antennae protruding out of his head, wings, or an extra set of arms."

"Unless she can change from one form to the other."

"You said, 'she'?"

"You were right. The unsub's a female. Good call. The overall results might be a little shaky, but the gender isn't in question."

I couldn't help grinning. Maybe I was a better FBI agent than I thought. Maybe I could solve this case. "Okay, so we know we're looking for a female. What do you think about the insect thing?"

"I think we need to do some reading tonight. So, if you had any thoughts about . . . you know"—he winked—"that'll have to wait. We have work to do." Before I realized what he was doing, his mouth was hovering over mine. Our lips touched, briefly, too briefly. A surge of electricity buzzed through my whole body. And the next thing I knew, I was staggering out of the bathroom, my fingertips pressed to my tingling lips. That was the shortest, softest kiss I'd ever had.

It probably didn't even qualify as a kiss. And yet my whole body was on fire.

God help me if JT ever *really* kissed me.

JT, who seemed totally unfazed, strode toward the kitchen. He said nothing about our research as he made each of us a sandwich. He carted our food into the family room, plopped onto the couch, and turned on the TV. "I had the cable turned on. Thought it might come in handy while we're here."

I followed him after helping myself to another diet cola from the fridge. "The bureau's sure going to a lot of expense."

"No, *I* paid for the cable, not the bureau." He took a bite of his sandwich and channel surfed.

I wasn't a big TV watcher, but I sat beside him. My plate rested in my lap.

"If nothing else, the noise will let anyone out there know the house is occupied. Last night, you had most of the lights off—no radio, no TV. It looked abandoned."

"That didn't stop whoever, or whatever, that was from paying me a visit."

"Hmm." He stuffed his mouth full of sandwich again.

"We haven't had any new victims since Saturday. That's the longest gap we've seen. Do you think the unsub has moved on to a new hunting ground?" I picked at my sandwich.

"No. I don't think she's left the area."

"Do you think she's stopped? How will we catch her if she's not hunting?"

"First, I don't believe she's stopped. I don't think she can. And second, it's not our job to catch her. Only to profile her and help the police identify suspects." He pointed at my plate. It was full. His was almost empty. "Aren't you going to eat?"

I lifted my sandwich. "Sure, I'm eating. At a normal pace. Didn't your mother ever tell you it isn't good to cram your mouth full of food?"

He grinned. "Nope."

I took a normal-sized bite to illustrate. Chewed. Swallowed. "That is the proper way to eat."

"If I ate like that, I'd have starved to death as a kid."

"Really? Why?"

"My older brother ate everything in sight. My mother would bring home the groceries, and Steve would have half the food gone by that night. She only shopped once a week. I learned at an early age to eat when the eating was good. Because the dry spells were easier to weather if I had a little extra meat on my bones. It's nature's way. Survival of the fittest, right?"

"Wow, JT. That sounds rough."

"We all have our stories, don't we?" He smiled and winked. "I'm going to head up and do some reading." He left me with the remote, the television tuned to a baseball game, and practically a whole sandwich yet to eat.

A little while later, I found him in an empty spare bedroom, sitting on the floor, his back resting against the wall, his laptop on his legs. "So far, I've found one possibility. The Philippine *mandurugo*. But I'm not done looking. It wouldn't be common to this area, or this climate. But it has insect-like qualities."

I stepped into the room, but I didn't stray far from the entry. "What are you talking about?"

"A vampire."

"So we're back to vampires?"

"Do you have another explanation for the DNA findings?"

"Sure. The sample was tainted. Maybe the victim had swatted a mosquito and some of its DNA was left on her neck? This is summertime. Mosquitoes are everywhere. And, when you think about it, living out here, by woods and parks, would mean the likelihood of being bitten would be pretty high."

"Hmm. You make a good argument. Maybe my friend

needs to do some more work on the sample. See if he can isolate the insect DNA and identify what species it is."

"That would be a good idea."

"I'll give him a call tomorrow." He scrolled down on the screen. He was reading a Wikipedia page on vampire legend. "Listen to this, 'The *mandurugo* . . . takes the form of an attractive girl by day, and develops wings and a long, hollow, thread-like tongue by night. The tongue is used to suck up blood from a sleeping victim.'" He turned narrowed eyes toward me. "Hmm."

"What?"

"Maybe I won't sleep in the same room with you tonight."

"Are you suggesting . . . ?" I smacked him. He laughed. So I smacked him again. And again. And again. The fifth time, he caught my wrist as I was lifting it and did a tricky maneuver. I found myself flat on my back, with my hand pinned to the floor over my head. JT was on his knees, straddling my body. My other hand was free, so I made a show of fighting him off. It didn't work. In fact, my struggling seemed to make things worse. Eventually he had both my wrists caught in one fist and was resting much of his weight upon me. It was no easy feat getting a good lungful of air, and that wasn't entirely due to the pressure of his body on my rib cage.

"Uncle," I mumbled.

He gently smoothed my hair out of my face. "If you really want to have a career in the bureau, you need to take some self-defense classes."

"I'll be sure to sign up for one first thing tomorrow morning."

He narrowed his eyes at me. "You promise?"

"Absolutely."

He climbed off. I wasn't 100 percent happy about that. But it was, without a doubt, the best thing he could have done.

"Time for bed." I beat a hasty retreat, waving over my shoulder as he hurried toward the door after me.

"Good night," he called to my back.

"Good night," I echoed, wondering what kind of dreams I would have tonight.

All of us failed to match our dreams of perfection. So I rate us on the basis of our splendid failure to do the impossible.

—William Faulkner

18

Something was in bed with me.

Something warm.

Something furry and soft.

Something with sharp claws.

I used the blanket to shield myself as I moved at a sloth's pace to the opposite side of the bed. I stretched out an arm, reaching into the shadows for the lamp on the nightstand. I bumped it. The furry thing made a noise that sent a shudder up my spine. I found the little twisty knob and the light flicked on just as the gray thing sailed at me, claws fully extended.

It was the psycho kitty.

I screeched and swatted the beast away. It flew to the floor. The door to the bedroom swung open. The cat darted past a worried-looking JT.

I pointed. "Cat."

He looked back down the hall. "Where?"

"It's probably hiding somewhere." I jumped up and dashed past him. "We need to get that animal out of here before it tears me up. It hates me."

Still standing at the door, JT watched me as I peered into the empty bedroom down the hall. "I didn't see a cat."

"It ran right past you. How could you not see it?" Where'd that evil cat go? I tiptoed down to the next open door and peered into another empty room. No cat. "Damn it. It must have gone downstairs." I decided it would be better if I shut the cat out of my bedroom, rather than go on a wild-cat chase. I headed back to the master bedroom, shoved JT inside, and shut the door behind him.

"Are you trying to tell me something?" He glanced at the bed, then at me, then at the bed again. His eyebrows climbed to the top of his forehead.

"No." I stomped to the bed, fluffed the sheet and blanket back in place, and climbed in. "I just didn't want that animal to sneak back in here."

"Who's to say it hasn't already?"

Good point. I peered over the edge of the bed.

I heard a scratching sound. I gathered the blanket to my chest and curled my legs, wrapping my arms and the blanket around my knees. I pointed. "I think it's under there."

JT didn't look scared. He sauntered over, bent. Yelled "Holy shit!" and fell on his ass.

I hopped up on my feet and danced around the bed, shouting, "Where is it? Where is it?"

JT stood up, face a brilliant red. Tears streaming from his eyes. I realized, too late, that he was laughing his ass off.

At me.

"You bastard!" I grabbed the first thing I could find and threw it at him.

He ducked and the pillow hit the wall, rebounded, and sent a framed photograph crashing to the floor. Still laughing, JT turned to survey the damage before tsk-tsking me. "Didn't your mother teach you it's bad to throw things?"

I leapt to the floor and headed for the broken frame. "It was a pillow." I carefully picked up the frame and inspected the photograph. It was a picture of a man, smiling, maybe in his midthirties, wearing a military uniform. "Besides, this is just a stock photograph, isn't it?"

"No, it was left here by the former homeowner."

"Why wouldn't they take a picture like this with them?"

"I'm guessing it was accidentally left behind."

I gently pulled the shattered glass away from the photograph, trying to keep the sharp edges from slicing into the print. "How sad. Maybe we should find out where the homeowner went and give it back? After we get a new frame."

"Maybe we should."

I put the picture back on the dresser and dumped the shards of glass into the plastic trash can next to the nightstand. JT helped me pick up the rest of the glass.

"We'll run a damp cloth over the wood floor tomorrow to get the smaller pieces. You should get some sleep." He nudged me toward the bed. I climbed in, waiting for him to leave and shut the door before I cut off the light. I fell asleep the instant my head hit the pillow.

It was back. The cat. How? I felt its claws pricking my skin through the blanket.

"Little mouse."

That isn't a cat. Cats don't talk.

My heart started drumming against my breastbone. An instant coating of sweat slicked my skin. I tried to scream; but when I opened my mouth, no sound came out. I couldn't inhale. My lungs wouldn't inflate. I couldn't move a muscle. It was as if I'd been drugged, given a paralytic.

Could this be the unsub? The timing was interesting. *There's no such thing as a coincidence.* The voice. Was it male or female? I still couldn't tell. Maybe it was female.

"Little mouse. I won't wait any longer. You lost our game."

What game? I had no clue what that meant.

JT, I screamed inside my head, *help me!*

I tried to move. A finger. A toe. I couldn't. Oh, God, I couldn't. JT was close by, but he had no clue what was happening.

"Little mouse. I'm losing patience."

The microphones.

Why weren't the agents stampeding into the room? Couldn't they hear that awful voice? It made my skin burn. My hairs stand on end. It was like nails scratching on a chalkboard, only a hundred times worse.

"Little mouse. You promised. You agreed to the rules of our game."

I didn't promise anything to anyone, but I couldn't say that. I couldn't say anything. I felt like I was suffocating. I wanted air. So badly. Desperately. I fought for a breath. Only one.

Someone help. Please.

I felt it come closer. Felt the chill grow colder, colder until it stung, burned. My neck. It hurt. The pain. Still, I couldn't move. Not an eyelash. Nothing. More pain. Blindingly sharp. I screamed in my head. Darkness crashed down upon me, and then I was thrashing, kicking, screaming so hard my throat felt like it was tearing up inside. The door smashed open, the overhead light snapped on, and JT raced into the room.

"What?" he shouted, his eyes wild.

"It was back. It was here." I bound from the bed.

"What? The cat?"

"No. Something else. Bigger. My neck." I fingered the place where it still burned slightly. "I think it bit me. Or injected me with something. I think I might be the next victim."

My stomach lurched. I gagged. I heaved. But I didn't throw up.

JT ran around the bed and turned on the lamp. He sat on the edge and pulled me to him. "Let me see."

I tipped my head to one side and pointed to the spot, which wasn't hurting so badly now. "Here, I think."

JT studied my neck for several moments, swept my hair

aside to look at it from every angle. "I don't see any marks, but we should take you to the hospital and have you checked out, just in case." He scooped me into his arms. "Why didn't you call me sooner?"

"I couldn't. I tried." I dragged my arm over my face, smearing tears across my cheeks. "I couldn't move at all. Not a finger. Couldn't breathe. Couldn't speak."

JT carted me down the stairs as if I weighed nothing. "Maybe you were drugged."

"That's what we thought the unsub was doing to her victims."

"We figured she was giving them an amnesic. Not a paralytic." His hold on me tightened slightly. He met a crowd of armed agents at the front door.

"Ambulance is on the way," one of them said as he barked orders into a handheld radio. JT refused to set me down while we waited for the ambulance, saying he was worried I might be dizzy from the drugs. Armed men stood around us in a circle. There were armed men guarding me. It was crazy. I felt like I was a president or something, being protected from an assassin. The instant the ambulance stopped in front of the house, JT and our circle of armed guards took me to the vehicle. He set me on the bed, and one EMT started asking me questions while the other one talked to JT. Minutes later, I had an IV in my arm and was strapped to the gurney.

JT poked his head inside the back door. "I'll be at the hospital when you get there."

"That's okay. You don't—"

"Yes, I do." He slammed the door, and off we went to the hospital. No lights. No sirens.

The EMT sitting next to me asked if I was feeling okay, if I was in any pain, or if there was anything he could do for me. I wasn't in pain anymore. The burning on my neck was gone. And I wasn't feeling bad at all. In fact, I was feeling fairly perky. It was as if I'd dreamed the whole thing. I could see now why the victims might not have told anyone about their attacks, if this was how they felt.

Despite feeling okay, I knew there could potentially be something very wrong with me. So I lay back and relaxed during the ride. When I finally arrived at the hospital, I was immediately wheeled into a room and greeted by not one nurse but two, plus a doctor. I was given a little privacy while I traded my clothes for one of those lovely hospital gowns. I produced a urine sample upon request, gave up some blood and saliva for analysis, and pointed to the spot on my neck where I'd been poked or bitten or whatever. I must have explained our case a dozen times to a handful of different people. Finally silence. They all left me to await the results of the tests.

JT strolled in then. He smiled, but I could tell he was hiding a very genuine concern under the expression. "How are you feeling?"

"Fine. Better than fine, actually."

"Does your neck still hurt?"

I checked, poking at it with my fingers. "Nope."

"Do you hurt anywhere else?"

"No."

"Good." He plopped his butt on the edge of my bed and patted my knee. "Now it's my turn to sit by your side, like you did for me."

"You don't have to—"

"I want to."

Once again, an awkward silence fell between us. Our gazes tangled. My breathing sped up. I had a feeling, if I looked up at the monitor I was hooked to, I'd see my heart rate was double its normal speed.

"We're going to get to the bottom of this," JT said.

"JT, why didn't anyone come in and help me when I was being attacked?"

"I can't answer that yet. I'm looking into it."

"Has anyone reviewed the tapes?"

JT shook his head. "I didn't have time. I'll look at them after you're settled in."

"Settled in? Am I being admitted?"

"I'm guessing you will be." Looking down at the bed, he set one of his hands on mine. "It's going to take a while to get back all the test results. If there's any chance you've been infected with a contagion, they won't want you running around, exposing other people."

"You're not scared." With a tip of my head, I motioned to his hand, still sitting on top of mine.

"No, I'm not." He leaned closer and smoothed my hair. I liked the way he did that. Then he reached for the little remote clipped to the bedsheet and turned on the TV. My mother, looking like she'd just rolled out of bed—which I'm sure she had—came rushing into the room. Katie was on her heels. They both were sporting white faces and bugged eyes. Did they think I was near death?

"I'm okay. I'm okay," I said before one of them collapsed.

Mom raced to my side, grabbed my hand, and cradled it to her chest. "Sloan, when I got the call, I was absolutely terrified. I was much too upset to drive. Thank goodness, Katie was awake. She drove me."

I smiled at Katie. "Thanks." Katie probably hadn't been awake before my mother had called.

"No problem." Katie was standing closer to the exit, probably hanging back because the small space was already very crowded. She looked at the monitors. "What's going on?"

"I was attacked. I'm feeling better now. I think they just want to keep an eye on me for a little while, make sure I'm all right."

Katie nodded. "Okay." To my mother, she said, "I need to get going. I have to get up early tomorrow."

Mom looked at me, at JT, and then at Katie. "Umm." She looked at JT again.

JT nodded and smiled. "Of course, I'll give you a ride home, Beverly."

Mom grinned. Katie waved and left.

Mom turned worry-filled eyes toward me again. "Now, what exactly happened? Tell me everything."

"I don't know if I can tell you everything. It might be related to our case and we're not allowed to discuss our cases with anyone, outside of police and medical personnel."

JT said, "She was sleeping in a monitored room. We'll find out what happened very soon."

Mom clearly wasn't happy with JT's nonexplanation. "I'm your mother, for God's sake. You can't tell your mother what happened?" This was not good. Mom was getting herself wound up. That always ended in disaster.

"Mom. Please. If I could tell you, I would. Don't get upset."

Mom flung her hands in the air. "My only daughter is in the hospital after being attacked, and I'm told I shouldn't get upset? What kind of shit is that?" She stomped toward the exit. "I'll be back in a little while. I need some fresh . . . air."

I knew what kind of "air" she was going for. I didn't try to stop her, hoping it would help her calm down. It could go either way. She might return, telling me she was seeing pink talking elephants everywhere and end up being escorted upstairs to the psych ward. Or she might return in a mellow *whatever* mood. Naturally, I was hoping for the latter. It was the most frequent result. But the former had happened, more often than I wished. For whatever reason, pink animals of all varieties were a common hallucination for poor Mom when she was stressed.

After Mom headed out to self-medicate, JT gave my leg another pat. "It's tough handling these situations with family. They don't understand in the beginning."

"Yours didn't come to the hospital," I said, just realizing it for the first time.

"No. They learned already they aren't going to get any

information. Anyway, my life wasn't on the line. They would've been there if there had been any chance I was checking out of the hospital in a hearse."

"I'm not sure my mother will ever get to that point."

"She will. In time."

The doctor strolled in. Asked me how I was feeling and informed me I was being moved upstairs to a room shortly. Mom wandered in just as I was thanking the doctor. She plopped into a chair, turning red eyes toward me.

"Sloan, I'm feeling better now," she said.

"Good," I said.

JT slid off my bed. "I guess I should be getting back to the house. I'd like to get a look at those tapes. Mrs. Skye, are you ready to go?"

She smiled. "Sure." She gave me a hug and a bunch of kisses. "I'll call you later, baby."

"Okay, Mom." To JT, I said, "Thanks again."

"No problem."

I settled back to watch a *Seinfeld* rerun. But just as I got comfortable, a woman's shout, followed by a huge crash, had me bolting upright in bed.

Mom?

I looked at what seemed to be a flurry of frenzied activity at the nurses' station. I looked at the wires and tubes sticking out of my arm and chest. I looked out at the nurses' station again. At the monitors behind me.

"Shit, shit, shit," I grumbled.

"Damn it, listen to me!" Mom yelled. "Those fucking monkeys are going to hurt my daughter!"

Another crash.

I slid off the bed and walked as close to the door as I could. The tubes stretched. The wires attached to the little pads glued to my chest tugged. I unplugged them, and the monitor started shrieking. I grabbed the bag of water off the IV pole and headed into the melee. Mom was swinging arms and legs, fighting off invisible monkeys and visible security guards. JT was standing nearby, trying to get her attention.

I stomped toward them, but someone grabbed my arm. I turned. My nurse. "You need to be in bed. We can't have you out here."

"That's my mother."

The nurse didn't care. "Yes, but we can't have you out here—"

"I can calm her down."

"No. Absolutely not. You must get back in bed now."

Mom screamed as a huge man tackled her to the ground. "You fucking bastard! This is a free country. I have rights." She kneed the security guard in the groin and rolled out from under him as he fought for breath.

A pair of guards dove at her. It was two on one now. Mom didn't stand a chance.

I was desperate. This wasn't the way to handle her. She was terrified. And they were making it worse. "Please." I broke away from the nurse and headed to Mom's aid; the clear bag was cradled in my arms and a plastic tube dragged on the floor. "Mom, I'm right here. It's okay."

Mom clawed past one of the men, crippling him with another well-placed shot to the groin. "Sloan? Where'd the monkeys go?"

"JT caught them." I pointed at JT.

JT gave me a what-the-hell look, then nodded. "Sure. They're all locked up now."

Mom grabbed me, hugged me. "Thank God." Next she hugged a bewildered JT. "Thank you, thank you, thank you for taking care of my baby girl. She needs a man like you. Brave and strong. You two will have a wonderful—life together. You can be married where I married her father."

Fabulous. Mom was already planning our wedding.

"Yes. I'm sure we will have a wonderful l-life," JT stammered, looking a little stiff.

I swallowed a sigh.

A pair of large male nurses strolled up, talking to Mom in soothing voices, offering her a chance to rest for a while. Mom let them guide her to a wheelchair. As they wheeled her toward the service elevator, the sound of her raves about her future son-in-law echoed down the halls, barely reaching the now eerily silent nurses' station.

The nurse, who looked absolutely livid, grabbed the sloshy bag of water out of my arms and gathered the plastic tubing, lifting it off the floor. "One of your rapid diagnostic tests came back positive. You must be quarantined. Now we may have to quarantine everyone here as well, at least until the rest of your test results are back."

I looked at JT.

He visibly sighed.

I looked at the nurses, at the doctors.

They weren't happy. In fact, they looked like they wouldn't mind doing a few uncomfortable medical procedures on me, just to make me suffer a little.

"I'm sorry." Feeling like shit, I shuffled back to my room.

A thousand fearful images and dire suggestions glance along the mind when it is moody and discontented with itself. Command them to stand and show themselves, and you presently assert the power of reason over imagination.

—Sir Walter Scott

19

The hospital wasted no time getting me admitted and moved to a room. A private room. At the far end of a very quiet hall.

Clearly, they didn't want to risk me running around, exposing any more people with whatever I'd been infected with. Made me wonder what the hell I'd tested positive for.

Something airborne?

Nobody had bothered to share my test results with me yet. That made me feel a little twitchy and uneasy. Whatever it was, it had to be a very virulent bug, extremely contagious. To test positive for anything mere hours after exposure seemed impossible. But clearly the hospital staff was taking no risk. Everyone who came into my room from that point on wore full protective gear.

By morning, I was feeling isolated. Trapped. Alone. And scared.

When would somebody tell me what was going on?

I tried to rest, but I couldn't. Every time I closed my eyes, the strangest images played through my mind—my cells being invaded by millions of little twisted bits of RNA, viruses.

I tried to distract myself by watching television, but there was absolutely nothing interesting to watch. I had no computer. That was killing me. The first thing I would do if I got my hands on one was look up tropical diseases and see which produced such rapid positive tests for infection.

Why wasn't anyone telling me what I had?

I stared at the people rushing past my glass door and tried not to cry. I failed. I had a good, long cry and then started pacing the floor, trying to convince myself that I would walk out of this hospital soon. If I couldn't, if this was going to be the end for me, I prayed I would see my mother once more, and Katie. I would tell them both how much they meant to me. How much I loved them. And I would see JT again, and I would tell him how crazy I was for him too. How I wished we could have had the chance to see where this thing between us was going.

I even made a few promises to "The Big Guy," if he'd pull a miracle out of his hat. I had little hope he'd come through for me. After all, up to this point, I hadn't done much praying. How serious could he take me when I didn't come to him until I needed something? But it was worth a shot.

Just as I was making yet another promise to God, the door to my room opened, and JT, gowned up like a doctor about to perform surgery, strolled in. I swallowed a sob as he opened his arms and flung myself at him. He caught me, of course. He sat on the bed and held me. Stroked my hair.

"Do you know what's going on?" I asked, my face buried in the crook of his neck. "Am I going to . . . ?"

He lifted my chin until I looked into his eyes. "The nurse misspoke. You did have a blood test come back abnormal. Your white cell count is elevated. Your initial ELISA screen came back positive for VHF, but that test has been known to produce false positive results in as many as three percent of patients tested."

VHF. I knew that abbreviation. Viral hemorrhagic fever. Those bugs were nothing to play around with. Ebola. Marburg, Lassa virus, Rift Valley fever, Crimean-Congo hemorrhagic fever, Hantaan, Seoul, yellow fever, and Kyasanur Forest disease. There was no known cure for any of them. And the mortality rates were very high. Chances were, even with the best medical care, if I had been exposed to one of those diseases, I had, at best, a few weeks to live. And the last week or so of my life would be hell on earth.

"Oh, God," I mumbled. "They didn't tell me."

"That's because they have nothing to tell you yet. They're running some more tests."

"How much longer will I have to wait?"

"Not much."

"What about you? Are you being quarantined?"

"No. I've been cleared. So has everyone else who was in the lobby. VHFs aren't known to be airborne contagions"

That news helped me breathe a little easier. "Well, at least that's something to be glad for."

"You're going to have plenty of other reasons to be happy soon."

"How can you be so sure?"

He shrugged. "I just am."

"Could you do me a favor?" I asked.

"Sure. Anything."

"Could you check on my mom?"

"Already done. I had a feeling you'd want to know how she was doing. She's been admitted. They're making some adjustments to her medications. No word yet on when she will be released."

"Thanks." A tear slipped from the corner of my eye.

JT thumbed it away and smiled. "Is there anything else?"

"Yes." I dragged my hand over my eyes, determined I

wouldn't cry anymore. At least, not until I had something to really cry about. "Could you bring in my go bag? And my computer? It's the only thing at this point that's going to distract me from worrying about my test results, my mother . . . everything."

"Will do." He gave me one last snuggle. Kissed my head through the surgical mask and left. A little while later, a nurse carried in my laptop case, handed it to me, and took half a gallon of blood—or so it seemed—for tests. I spent the rest of the day avoiding reading medical articles on Ebola or any other viral hemorrhagic diseases. Instead, I spent my time brainstorming our case.

Many hours later, I was no closer to figuring out who the killer was or understanding her motives. I did a lot of staring at my computer screen, and not a lot of reading. I saw very little of my nurse. Heard nothing from the doctor. At about eleven that night, I succumbed at last to exhaustion and fell into a shallow sleep that was broken and plagued by strange, disturbing dreams.

Early the next morning, before I'd paid a visit to a shower, or even had a chance to get rid of my morning breath, a doctor I hadn't met before moseyed into my room; a younger man, probably an intern or med student, trailed behind him. Neither the doctor nor the intern was wearing plague gear. I hoped that was significant.

He walked right up to me and offered a hand. "Dr. Patel. How are you feeling this morning?"

I didn't take his hand right away. "Tell me I don't have Ebola and I'll be doing great."

"You don't have Ebola or any other communicable disease."

I have never felt so relieved. I almost started to cry again. "Oh, my God. Thank you!" I kicked my feet over the side of the bed. I was so ready to get my things together and get out of this place. "I'll call my roommate for a ride home. What time should I tell her to come get me?"

"We're not ready to release you yet," Dr. Patel said.

"What? Really? Why?"

"I've referred you to another doctor."

"For what?" I asked, thoroughly confused.

"I think it's better if she told you. She'll be in shortly." Before I could ask for more details, which he was clearly unwilling to share, he led his little underling out of my room.

I padded to the door and peered out. Right away, a nurse hustled up to me, introducing herself as my nurse for the day shift. She wore a bright smile as she informed me I had to stay in my room. I wore an equally bright one as I asked if I could take a shower.

"Not quite yet. Your doctor will be in soon." She removed my IV and the stickums on my chest. I was grateful to be free of all the tubes and wires.

"Can I at least brush my teeth and use a toilet, instead of the bedpan?"

"Certainly." She watched me gather some things from my overnight bag. "I'm sorry," she said, eyeballing my mouthwash. "You can't use that here. I'll have to keep it for you."

Since when was mouthwash a public hazard? "Okay." I handed it to her and locked myself in the bathroom, enjoying the privacy. When I came out, a woman in a white coat was waiting for me.

"Dr. Doyle." She extended a hand, shaking mine. "How are you this morning?"

"Much better now that I know I'm not going to die from a hemorrhagic fever." I gave her a what's-up look.

"Dr. Patel had some concerns," she told me, "and after looking at your medical history, he felt it was best to recommend this consultation."

"What were his concerns? I gotta admit, you've got me wondering what this is all about."

"Can you tell me if you've ever been attacked before, like last night?"

"No. What exactly are you looking for?"

"I'm not looking for anything." She gave me a reassuring smile, the kind that my mother's doctor used to calm her down when she was on the verge of an episode.

Oh, God.

"You're a psychiatrist," I said.

"Yes, I am."

"Are you here to talk to me about my mother?"

"No."

"What exactly were Dr. Patel's concerns?" I asked.

"We have reason to believe the attack you experienced—which I am sure seemed very real to you—was, in fact, a hallucination."

I swear to God, I didn't see that coming. "What?"

"You do know schizophrenia has a significant genetic component."

"Of course." It had been a hallucination? "Are you sure about this?" *There is no way I could have hallucinated the broken window. The window might not have anything to do with the attack, though.*

"Because of your work with the FBI, we were able to gather some information about the episode. This information has led us to the conclusion that you have experienced at least one hallucination. I suspect you've experienced more."

I didn't know what to say. Yes, all along I'd known about the studies linking genetic factors to schizophrenia. I'd lived under the shadow of the disease all my life, waiting, watching, wondering if someday I'd see pink monkeys bouncing around the room, or end up huddled in a closet, thinking an alien was trying to control my mind. But the years had passed, and with each day that I didn't see anything out of the ordinary, I grew more confident that I'd been spared.

"Miss Skye, what are you thinking?" the doctor asked.

"I've been having these awful nightmares, but they started after I took the job with the FBI. And the case I've been working is a little strange, so I thought they were just my mind's way of coping with the stress."

"If this is the case, and you just recently started having hallucinations, I'm confident we'll be able to control your symptoms with medication. . . ."

I nodded and tried to concentrate on what the doctor was saying, but it was so hard. She was trying to tell me, nicely, that I was mentally ill. That the things I'd seen and felt and smelled weren't real. It was so hard to accept. I fingered the spot on my neck where I thought I'd been bitten.

That horrible pain hadn't been real?

For the first time in my life, I understood—really understood—my mother. I'd never imagined what a shock it would be to hear that what was plain in your eyes, what was more vivid and terrifying than anything you'd ever seen, was no more real than Santa Claus or the Easter Bunny.

". . . moved to another bed for a day or two until we're sure your condition is stabilized."

"Can I use a phone?" I asked.

"You will have limited use of the telephone. We'd like to give the medication a chance to work and need to keep your stress level as low as possible."

"Okay."

"Very good, Miss Skye. We'll get you moved into your new room very soon. If you have any questions, you can let your nurse know and she'll page me. I'll be in the building until this afternoon." After giving me another of those smiles, Dr. Doyle headed out. My nurse wandered in shortly afterward and handed me a small plastic cup with a couple of tablets in it. She waited until I'd swallowed them, then headed out.

The next thing I knew, I was handed my clothes and told to dress. I was vaguely aware that time had passed. I felt like my head was in a fog, or I was standing on the outside of my body, watching the world through a blurred window. I nodded as the nurse read my discharge instructions, and I was wheeled to the front door. Katie's car was parked outside. I shuffled to it, tossed my bag into the back and sank into the front seat.

"How are you feeling, Sloan?" Katie asked as she pulled the car away from the curb.

"I don't know. Okay, I guess."

"Are you hungry?"

"No, not really."

"Maybe you'd like to rest for a while?" Katie suggested.

It seemed as if I'd just woken up. Could it be time to sleep already? "What time is it?" I asked as I stared out the window.

"Almost noon."

"What day is it?"

"Thursday."

"What's the date?"

"June seventeenth."

"June seventeenth?" I echoed. Somehow I'd lost three whole days. How? "What's on your agenda today?"

"Nothing. Why?"

"Would you mind driving me over to the FBI Academy?"

"Um, I guess that would be okay. But . . ."

"What?" I looked at Katie.

Katie stopped the car at an intersection. She glanced at me. "Don't you remember? You're on medical leave?"

"Medical leave?" Had I been told that? I couldn't remember. Already I was hating how my medication was making me feel—stupid and slow and clumsy. The doctor had assured me the side effects would ease up over time. I was starting to have some doubts about that. "Oh, yeah," I said, trying to pretend like I'd just forgotten. "I forgot for a minute. I guess we can skip the trip to the office, then."

"Sorry about that, Sloan." After a beat, Katie added, "Hey, at least the FBI is paying you while you're off. You already collected two days of sick pay. If you're unable to return to work after a week, you'll get disability for the rest of the summer."

She didn't say the obvious—that come September 1, I would be forever off the FBI's payroll. Any chance of my landing a full-time gig with the bureau was gone. I knew I should be devastated by that realization, but instead I felt just . . . numb. Empty. Hollow.

Katie took me back to our apartment and I staggered inside, my bag banging against my leg as I walked. I dropped it on the floor just inside the door and slumped onto the couch. I turned on the TV and just sat and stared.

Was this the life I had to look forward to? Sitting in my living room, while life was a blur outside, time ticking by without my noticing?

God, I hoped not!

Nobody called. Nobody visited. Katie made herself busy in the kitchen, cooking up some experiment, like always. Eventually she told me she was going to bed. It was three in the morning. Where had the time gone? I headed to my room, changed into pajamas, brushed my teeth, and settled in, hoping the world of my dreams would be more exciting than the real world. I closed my eyes. I listened to myself breathing and tried to fall asleep.

But then I heard it.

The voice.

It was back.

"Little mouse," it whispered.

A man's errors are his portals of discovery.

—James Joyce

20

"Little mouse," the voice said again.

I'd like to say it was the knowledge that the voice wasn't real that made it so easy not to be afraid. But in reality, I was almost 100 percent sure it was the medication. Either way, my heart wasn't trying to shove its way through my rib cage, and my lungs weren't deflating, and my skin wasn't prickling with goose bumps. I was groggy but calm as I opened my eyes.

"Who are you?" I asked.

Its laugh could best be described as oily. "You don't remember?"

"No." Even though I knew the voice was a hallucination, I stared into the shadows, expecting to see a face. "I don't remember anything. Why are you here?"

"To give you what you deserve."

"What's that? I hope it's good. Like a pot of gold or something."

More of that slimy laughter echoed through the room. "I'm not a leprechaun."

"Of course you're not. You're . . . what? The tooth fairy?"

It was as if the shadows peeled back, and a gruesome face appeared before me. "Do I look like the tooth fairy to you?" it asked. The eyes shined silver, like the reflection of the flash in an animal's eyes. The nose was broad and nearly flat. The skin pearly white. The thin lips curled back to reveal pointed teeth. It was not a pretty sight.

"I don't know what the tooth fairy looks like. I've never met her . . . or is it him? Since we're talking about your 'looks,' can I just say, you could use a little help from the Queer Guys? I am not a fashionista, but even I can tell your hair is a train wreck, and your clothing. . . . That shirt is a nightmare. The color's all wrong for your complexion. And as for the rest of you—well, I pride myself in not holding what one cannot help against him. You've clearly inherited more than your share of ugly genes."

The face took on a pink tint. I think I was annoying it, whatever it was. I wished I didn't feel so numb. I might have enjoyed this. "You thought you'd escaped from me, from your obligation, but you didn't. And now I've come back to claim what is mine." The shadows folded back over the face, like a cloak.

I had to marvel at my creativity. This was truly bizarre.

"Are you sure you've got the right girl?" I scooted up, letting my headboard support my upper body. "I don't remember trying to escape from anyone—let alone someone as memorable as you."

"It was a long time ago."

"Hmm. Hasn't anyone ever told you it's bad to hold grudges? Maybe that's why I didn't recognize you. . . ." I didn't finish that sentence. Imaginary or not, this thing didn't deserve to be insulted for being ugly. After all, nobody deserved to be blamed for their appearance. There was only so much that plastic surgery could do, especially in this case.

"My time is almost up," the thing said, snarling. "But I will return tomorrow. And you will soon reap your just rewards."

"Okay. Till tomorrow, then." I waved.

The thing stuck its face in mine, and the stench of rotten meat burned my nostrils. "You should be afraid of me. Why aren't you scared anymore?"

"Because I know the truth."

"What truth?"

"That you're a figment of my imagination. You're an illusion. A hallucination."

"A hallucination? Is that what you think?" The thing turned and lurched across the room, halting in front of the wall. With its claws, it etched the words *I'll be back* in the drywall. "Is that a hallucination?"

"Okay, who do you think you are? The Terminator?" I stumbled over and traced the scrawled letters with a fingertip. My fingernail dipped into the grooves. Those jagged edges sure felt real. But maybe I had dug those letters into the wall myself? I didn't know how to judge anymore what was real and what wasn't. "I can't say for sure if it's a hallucination or not."

"What?" the monster said, clearly incredulous.

"Well, who's to say I didn't do this myself? I could, you know. With a screwdriver or something."

The monster gritted its teeth and took a look around. "You're making this difficult."

"I'm not trying to." I shrugged. "Lately it's been a bit of a challenge discerning what's real and what's not. According to my doctor, you're not real. Prove her wrong, and I'll be adequately scared."

The monster slitted its eyes at me. "Fine. But I'm out of time." Then it sort of melted into the shadows and vanished.

I slid back under the covers and fell asleep.

Sunlight cutting through the slats of the window blinds woke me up the next day. Despite having no place to go, I dove into the shower, put on some makeup, and fixed my hair. Instead of donning work clothes, however, I jumped into a pair of sweatpants and a T-shirt. I headed into the kitchen and flipped on the coffeemaker. I was feeling a little more energetic today, less doped up. Maybe there was hope I'd be able to function while taking the medication. One thing was for certain—I wasn't going to tell the doctor I was still having hallucinations. She'd increase my dose, and I'd be back to being a zombie. No thanks. I would rather live with the nocturnal visits by my ugly friend, whom I'd deemed "Mr. Stinky," than walk around in a stupor.

As it turned out, he wasn't all that scary, after all.

Coffee done, I poured myself a big mug, dumped my pills in my mouth, and downed half of it while watching the morning news. There was no sign of Katie, so I kept the volume low. After the news ended, I powered up my computer and checked my e-mail. Outside of the usual spam, I had only one message. From Gabe. It was brief. Two words. Call me. Dated yesterday.

The medication was kicking in, so I decided I needed to rest for a while before calling him. I sat on the couch. Next thing I knew, my cell phone was ringing. The display said it was four o'clock. In the afternoon. That made no sense. I couldn't have been sitting on the couch, staring at the walls, for six hours . . . could I?

The caller was Gabe.

I hit the button, answering the call, "Hello?"

"Skye! Where the hell have you been?"

"I've been feeling a little under the weather," I slurred.

"Are you okay? I heard about the attack only yesterday. Rumor was, you'd been taken to the hospital."

"Yeah. I'm all right. Thanks."

"What happened?" he asked.

I padded into the kitchen. I was kind of hungry. "Long story. I don't want to get into it right now. It had nothing to do with the case."

"You sound strange. Are you sure you're okay? Why didn't you call me?"

I opened the refrigerator. Olives. Some milk, which had expired two days ago. A block of green cheese. Maybe I wasn't so hungry, after all. "I'm on some . . . pain . . . medication. It's making me a little groggy." Understatement of the century. "But you've got me now. Was there something else?"

"I was wondering if you'd received those test results back yet."

I returned to the couch. "Oh, those. I heard something."

"I'll come over."

"O-okay."

"Can I bring you anything? Some dinner?" he asked.

"No, that's not necessary."

"Yes, it is. What are you in the mood for? Chinese? Mexican? Burgers? Pizza?"

"Nothing."

"Pizza it is, then. I'll bring enough for your roommate too. She's still living with you, isn't she?"

"Yeah." Speaking of Katie, I wondered what she'd been doing all this time. Had she strolled right past me without my noticing? I really wasn't liking what that medication was doing to my brain. Not one little bit. "That's very thoughtful, but I'm not hungry, and I'm not sure if Katie's home."

"See you in an hour," he said, and hung up before I could argue with him.

I shoved my phone under a pillow, deciding it was better if I didn't answer it anymore, and went in search of Katie. I already knew the kitchen was abandoned. She wasn't in the bathroom. Her bedroom door was shut. I opened it a tiny bit and peered into her room.

What the hell?

My first reaction was confusion. Katie was a neat freak. She was absolutely anal about keeping her stuff organized and tidy. This room looked like it had been ransacked by felons.

Had it been?

I tried to push the door open wider, but something behind it was blocking the movement. I shoved. I heaved. I turned around and used my back to push. It gave a little, just enough for me to squeeze through the opening. I stepped inside, searching the floor for a pathway to the bed. There wasn't one.

The floor, from wall to wall, was covered by clothes, papers, books, trash. I'd never seen anything like it. The bed looked like a mountain, the peak almost reached the ceiling.

What was with Katie now?

Something moved near Mt. Katie's base. I tugged at a blanket and found Katie, sleeping.

She blinked her eyes open. "What are you doing?" she mumbled.

"I . . . uh . . . just checking on you. Are you feeling okay?"

"Yes," she snapped, grabbing the blanket out of my hand and flopping it over her head. "It's a headache. No big deal."

"Okay. Sorry for disturbing you." I picked my way through the mess to the doorway, wormed through the opening, and shut the door.

Now, that was weird.

First there were the so-called anxiety attacks. Now this. *Could be stress. Could be something else. Depression?*

Before I could decide what to do, or not do, about it, a knock sent me shuffling toward the front door. I peered through the peephole. JT. I opened the door. "Hi." I stepped to the side, welcoming him in.

He flashed a brilliant smile at me and gave me an assessing look as he sauntered past. He pushed a box into my hands. "How are you feeling?" He made himself comfy on my couch.

I looked down at the box. It was wrapped in pink paper and had a big silver bow on it. "What's this?"

"A get-well present."

"That was nice of you. Thanks." I started pulling the tape off, but a second knock signaled the arrival of another guest. I checked the peephole. "Mom." I opened the door and hurried her inside. "You've been discharged?"

"Yes." She glanced at me, then at JT, then at me again.

"How did you get home?" I asked her.

"I called your cell first, but you didn't answer. So I took a taxi." She back-stepped toward the exit. "Um, Sloan, if this is a bad time—"

"No." JT was on his feet in a blink, rushing to my mother's side. "I'm not staying long."

"Don't hurry out on my account." Mom grabbed JT's hand and dragged him back toward the couch. "I'm very happy to see you again. Please make yourself comfortable. What I came for won't take but a minute." She waited until JT was sitting, and then she turned back to me. "Sloan, if I could speak to you in private for a moment."

"Sure, Mom. We can talk in my room." I closed us in my bedroom. "What is it?"

"It's about your father." She motioned toward the door. Pressed her finger to her pursed lips. Tiptoed to the door and flattened one side of her head against it. Several seconds passed as she stood there, listening. Finally she headed toward the opposite side of the room, eyeballing the new artwork chiseled into the drywall as she walked past it. "What's this?"

"It's nothing. I was . . . dreaming."

"That doesn't look like a dream." Mom traced the letters with her fingertip.

"I guess I was sleepwalking and dreaming. What were you saying about Dad?"

She jerked her hand away from the wall. "I think he's still alive."

"What?" Someone knocked on the bedroom door. We both looked at it. I sighed, stomped to the door, and pulled it open.

JT pointed toward the living room. "Someone's at your door."

"My house is a regular circus tonight." Distracted by what my mother had just said, I headed to the front door.

Gabe rushed in, ramming a hot pizza box into my hands. "So what's the story?"

I motioned behind me. "I hope you brought a large pizza. This gathering's a little bigger than I'd expected."

Gabe's eyes widened. "Oh. Uh. Yeah, it's a large. Sausage, onion, and black olives."

"I love black olives." Mom yanked the box out of my hands and carted it into the kitchen.

JT moseyed up behind me, and the two men had what looked like a stare-down. They reminded me of two snarling dogs.

"Sloan, where are your napkins?" Mom called from the kitchen.

I sidestepped out from between the two men and went to her aid, figuring they'd work out their differences better without me being in the middle of things. It seemed I was right. By the time I'd located a few rumpled napkins, they were strolling toward us, looking a little friendlier. At least they weren't about to rip each other to shreds. *For now.*

I dished out the pizza and we all found a spot in the living room to eat. I sat on the couch, wedged between JT and Gabe, my ass pinned between theirs. It might've been cozy if it hadn't been so awkward.

Mom sat in the chair, happily munching away, as if she hadn't a care in the world. "How have you been, Gabe? I haven't seen you in ages, since you dumped Sloan. . . . Gosh, how long ago was that?"

"We were in high school," Gabe said. "But I didn't dump her. Sloan broke up with me."

Liar.

"It's ancient history, Mom," I said. "Doesn't matter anymore who broke up with whom."

"Yes, that's true. Especially now that you're dating JT." Mom beamed at JT.

I felt Gabe's leg stiffen against mine.

"I'm not dating JT, Mom. It's against bureau policy. And

even if it wasn't, I'm only an intern. It wouldn't look good for me to be sleeping with one of my superiors." I didn't bother telling my mother that I'd been put on medical leave and wouldn't be returning to the bureau, anyway. That was a conversation for later.

Gabe's leg relaxed.

Mom frowned. "Oh, that's too bad. I really like JT. He reminds me of your father. Intelligent. Good-looking."

I glanced at JT. His face was the shade of a beet. The color looked good on him. Was there anything that didn't?

"Thank you, Mrs. Skye," JT said. "I like your daughter very much. But I also respect her. And I wouldn't wish to harm her career. She's an intelligent, capable woman, brave and committed, and the bureau would be fortunate to have her as a permanent member someday."

I wondered how much he knew about my diagnosis and its effect on my career. I set my plate on the coffee table, next to my cup.

"You're not eating," JT murmured.

"My appetite isn't quite normal yet."

"So, Gabe, what have you been up to since you dumped my daughter?" Mom asked.

Gabe set his empty plate next to my full one. He swiped my untouched slice of pizza and took a bite. "Well, I've been going to school. . . ."

"I need to talk to you," JT whispered in my ear as Gabe and Mom chatted. "Alone."

I motioned to Mom and Gabe. "That's going to be a bit tough right now. Can't it wait?"

"No."

My gaze ping-ponged back and forth between Mom and Gabe. They seemed to be fairly involved at the moment, engaged in a discussion of quantum gravity.

"Okay," I whispered. "But let's try not to make it too obvious." I stood, scooped my plate, and headed toward the kitchen. "Excuse me for just a minute. My stomach's been acting up." I winked at JT. "I need to go lie down for a few."

Mom gave me a look, then went right back to her conversation with Gabe. I headed into my room and flung myself onto the bed. A few minutes later, I heard JT excuse himself to use the bathroom. Seconds afterward, we were in my room, the door closed.

"So . . . ?" I said, sitting up and hanging my feet over the edge of the bed.

"First, I need to ask you not to share our conversation with anyone, not even your mother."

"Okay." Why did I feel like I was about to be blindsided? I mentally braced myself.

JT sat beside me. "You need to stop taking the medication you were prescribed immediately."

Oh, thank God. "I do? Why?"

"Because you don't need it."

Thank God . . . wait. Does that mean . . . ? "What do you mean, I 'don't need it'?"

JT put a hand on my knee. "Sloan, you're not schizophrenic."

At this point, I would have rather believed I was. The alternative was much too ugly to face. "But—"

JT nodded. "I know what the doctor told you. She based her diagnosis on the information the bureau gave her."

The bureau? "And . . . ?"

"It wasn't exactly accurate."

"I'm not schizophrenic." I hiccupped or sobbed. Or something. *Not schizophrenic.* "Oh, God."

"No, you're not."

I was happy and terrified, both. "That means the attack wasn't a hallucination." My gaze sailed across the room, landing on the marked wall. I swallowed a lump in my throat the size of Mt. Everest.

"No, it wasn't." JT's gaze followed mine.

"I'm confused. Why did you tell my doctor it was, then?"

JT went to inspect the wall closer. "I didn't. Chief Peyton did. Actually, what she did was show the doctor a section of the surveillance tape. She couldn't risk our case getting out. She'd rather see you temporarily misdiagnosed than have people panicking, running around telling the media that vampires are real."

I wanted to stand up and march over to him, but I didn't trust my legs at the moment. They were a little mushy. "I don't understand. If the doctor saw the tape, why wouldn't she know I wasn't hallucinating?"

"Because the being that attacked you doesn't record with standard video equipment." JT traced the *b* with his index finger. "Neither its image nor its voice was captured on the tape. We picked it up with infrared, which is why we know you weren't hallucinating."

I was stunned. Relieved. And terrified. I wasn't insane. At least, not yet. That was the best news I'd heard in ages.

But something was out there, something I didn't understand. And it wanted something from me.

JT turned his back to the wall, facing me. "The chief thought, after all of this, you'd like to take a couple of days for yourself."

"But what about our case? Have there been any more deaths? And what about my blood tests? Was I injected with some kind of infectious agent? And the thing that attacked me—"

JT chuckled. "One at a time." He strolled over to me and laid his hands on mine. "You tested negative for all tropical infectious diseases known to exist. No worries there. And as far as your attacker, we don't believe it's the unsub. You will be under surveillance, twenty-four–seven, until it's caught."

"It came back. Last night." I pointed at the wall. "It did that." We both went over to it this time. I stood behind him, almost afraid to get too close, now that I knew for certain it had been made by a monster. "It said I did something, tried to escape from my obligation. I thought it was a hallucination, so I didn't take it seriously. But now . . . you see what that says."

"We'll be ready for it."

I shivered. "How can you be ready for something you can't see? Or hear?" I wrapped my arms around myself. An icy draft caressed my nape. I whirled around. Nothing was behind me. "I'm going to be chasing shadows," I mumbled.

"I won't let anything happen to you." JT gathered me into his arms, and I relaxed against him. I closed my eyes and enjoyed the scent of him as it teased my nostrils. His heat seemed to seep into my pores and radiate through my body.

This felt so right, so good, being held by JT. He made me feel safe, even from invisible creatures. Safe and cherished and special. A big part of me wanted to say to hell with the stupid FBI and all its rules, and let this thing between us take its natural course. There were a million other things I could do with my life than chase bad guys and play with guns.

But then the image of Tutu Girl played through my mind.

I'm no quitter. I've been preparing for this job my entire life. The good I might do is far more important than some silly romance that probably won't last.

"What's happened with our case the past few days?" I asked.

Recognizing the tone of my voice, JT released me, backing up a step. "There's been another death. The unsub is back to killing. We don't know why she stopped for a while, but we're going to figure it out."

"I want to get back to work."

"I don't think it's safe, not now." JT grabbed my shoulders. His grip was tight. His gaze was dark, full of desperation.

"The thing chasing me isn't going to stop, whether I'm working or not."

My bedroom door swung open.

JT and I jerked away from each other; then we looked to see who had caught us.

Gabe's expression was as dark as JT's had been moments ago. "You asshole," Gabe grumbled.

JT visibly tensed. "We're having a private conversation. Get lost."

"Like hell I will." Gabe marched into my bedroom, grabbed my arm, and practically dragged me away from JT.

I wound up and smacked Gabe. "Get your hands off me."

"You don't want to know what people are saying." Gabe jabbed a finger at JT. "And it's his fault."

"What are they saying?" I asked JT.

JT fumed for a moment, then charged out of the room.

I wound up to smack Gabe again, but I didn't follow through.

"I'm telling the truth," Gabe said, softer this time.

"What are you talking about?"

"JT told some of the guys down in the BAU that he's sleeping with you."

I plopped on my bed. "What? He wouldn't."

"He did."

"But we're not."

"I guessed as much." Gabe sat beside me. *"Not yet."*

"Why would he lie?" I asked him.

"Why do a lot of guys lie? To make himself look good."

I don't know if it was hopeful thinking, or being stupid and gullible, but I didn't believe JT had told anyone we were sleeping together. I stared down at the floor and did some soul-searching. "I don't know. . . ."

Gabe set his hand upon mine. "You gotta watch these people. They aren't all that they appear."

"What's that mean?"

Mom stormed into the room. "What's going on in here? That friend of yours, JT, just ran out of the apartment like his ass was on fire. And I think there's something wrong with your roommate, Sloan. She's in the kitchen. Come and see."

Knowledge is of no value unless you put it into practice.

—Anton Chekhov

21

Mom was right. There was something wrong with Katie. She was covered in something red and wet and slimy. Katie stood in the kitchen, dripping. A pool of red ooze was collecting under her.

But that wasn't the weird part.

It was her eyes. They were locked on the far wall, the pupils pinpoints. She was trembling, her lips almost pure white. And she didn't respond when I called her name, poked her arm, or shook her.

This isn't depression.

It was time to get her to a hospital.

I tried pulling her toward the door. She didn't budge.

I looked at Gabe. Gabe glanced down at his designer sweater and jeans, scooped the dripping, shaking Katie into his arms, and hauled her to my car. He drove—I was still a little groggy from those stupid pills. I tried to get Katie to say something.

She didn't.

I soon found myself in familiar territory, in the hospital emergency room. I could tell some of the staff recognized me. They gave me a wide berth. Fortunately, it didn't impact Katie's care. She had a nurse and doctor at her bedside within minutes. The nurse checked her blood pressure and heart rate, while the doctor asked Gabe what had happened. I took care of the business end of things, giving Katie's insurance information to the lady from registration.

Mom dashed in just as we were finishing up. "How is she?"

I shoved Katie's insurance card and driver's license into my purse. "We don't know yet. They took her back to a room. Gabe went with her to answer questions. What happened?"

Mom shrugged. "One minute, I was alone, and the next, she was standing there, just like you found her."

I motioned toward some nearby chairs in the waiting room. "My life has turned into an episode of *Lost*." At Mom's nod, I claimed a seat facing the registration desk. "It's going from weird to weirder."

Mom sat next to me. "I'm sure she'll be okay."

"She hasn't been herself for a while. I've been a little worried about her. But things have been so crazy, I haven't had any time to think about what it could be."

"You've had a lot to deal with lately."

I hugged my purse to my chest. "She either sleeps day and night, or wanders around, sleepless. And then there's her room. She's always been such a neat freak, and now it looks like a feature on *Hoarders*. She's been super irritable too. I thought it might be depression. I didn't do anything. I just left her alone and pretended nothing was wrong." I dropped my face into my hands. "I feel like I've let her down."

Mom wrapped an arm around my shoulders and gave them a gentle squeeze. "You haven't. You're here now."

"But maybe if I'd done something sooner, we wouldn't be here now. It wouldn't have gotten this bad."

"Do *what*, Sloan?" Mom asked.

"I don't know. Get her to see another doctor?"

"You can't make someone do something they don't want to do."

"I know."

Mom gave me another motherly squeeze. "You've had a rough few days. I think you need some rest."

That statement only reminded me that I could have an unwelcome nocturnal visitor tonight. And now that JT had stormed off, I had no idea who, if anyone, would be keeping a watch out for it.

"Sleep is highly overrated." I turned to Mom. "Anyway, we didn't get to finish our conversation. About Dad? What makes you think he's still alive?"

"This." Mom dug into her purse and pulled out a daisy, dried between two sheets of acid-free paper.

"Mom . . ." It was hardly proof that a man who'd been believed to be dead for decades was still alive.

"I know what you're thinking. Daisies are everywhere. But here's the thing. Your father and I met at a park, and I made him a daisy crown. I wore one in my hair on my wedding day."

So far, I wasn't seeing the significance. "Yes, and . . . ?"

"Nobody knew this about us, but we made a promise to each other on our wedding night that we would always be together. Actually, your father made this promise to me. I thought it was strange at the time, but it was important to him, so I listened."

Still, nothing. "Okay."

"He said, if we were ever separated, by anything or anyone, he'd find a way to let me know he was okay. He'd send me . . . a dried daisy."

Now I got it. "You swear nobody else knew?" I asked.

"No one."

"Okay." I sat back and took stock of the situation. It was an odd coincidence. And there was a sense of believability to the story. And yet, I had my doubts. "Where did you find the flower?"

"On my nightstand. It wasn't there when I went to bed."

I inspected the flower closer. It was fragile. I couldn't tell how long it had been preserved. "Did you save any of the flowers from your wedding?"

"Yes, of course, I did. I saved every single one from my bouquet. They're safe and sound in my old copy of *The Catcher in the Rye.*"

"Maybe you'd better check and see if one's missing."

"Do you suppose someone broke into my apartment, took one of my flowers out of the book, and put it on my nightstand? Why would anyone do such a thing?"

"I don't know, Mom. But before you start believing Dad's alive, it's a good idea to double-check."

She shrugged. "I guess you're right."

"You'll tell me what you find?"

"You'll be the first to know." Mom stood. "If there's nothing else I can do, I think I'd like to go home."

"It's okay. Go home. Get some rest. I'll let you know when we get out of here."

Mom and I exchanged a hug—which used to be very rare. I don't know if it was the mental illness or something else, but Mom had never tolerated people touching her. It was a wonder she'd ever conceived a child. Lately that seemed to be changing.

Minutes after Mom left, Gabe ambled into the waiting room and flopped into a chair next to me.

"How's Katie?" I asked.

"The red stuff was some kind of paint. Evidently, she bathed in it."

"Bathed in paint? That's not something a girl does on a regular basis."

"Yeah. She couldn't say why either." Gabe snatched a copy of *Good Housekeeping* off the table next to him and started thumbing through the pages. "I left when the doctor came in, so I don't know what's going on. Before I came down here, though, I checked with the nurses' station. The doctor ordered some tests. She'll be here awhile, at least a few hours. Are you going to wait?"

"I don't know. I guess I will."

"I'll stay with you."

"That isn't necessary."

"It's okay. I don't mind." He leaned closer. "Maybe now you can tell me what's up with the DNA analysis?"

"Oh. Sure," I whispered. I glanced around. A pair of elderly men sat huddled in one corner of the room. And a woman was cradling a small sleeping child in another. None of the people seemed interested in what we were talking about. "The sample contains insect DNA. They're running further tests to try to identify which species. JT thought the unsub might—"

"JT knows about the sample?" Gabe said a little too loudly.

I stiffened and checked the men. They were still doing their own thing, but the woman was looking our way now. I held an index finger to my lips, warning him to keep his voice low. "JT was the one who found someone to run the test."

A little muscle along Gabe's jaw pulsed. "Did you tell him where you got the sample?"

"No. What's your problem with him, anyway? I've never seen you treat anyone so harshly—except for me, of course."

"I told you, I don't trust him. I haven't trusted him since I joined the PBAU. And I trust him even less now, after what he did to you. By the way, you don't seem to be very upset about that."

"I'm upset. Especially since what he told them isn't true. We haven't slept together. Hell, we haven't even kissed." *Hardly kissed.* "But I'm having a hard time believing he's going around telling people lies. I don't see him being that kind of guy, for one. And secondly, that would put his job in jeopardy too."

Gabe didn't look convinced. "You haven't known him for long. Maybe you don't know him at all."

"True, but it's obvious he cares about his job. I can tell that already."

Gabe's mouth thinned. "Whatever. Anyway, what do you think the test means?"

"I'm guessing the sample was tainted with insect DNA. Maybe the victim swatted a mosquito?"

"Yeah, maybe." Gabe looked doubtful.

"You disagree?"

Gabe shrugged. "I don't know. I've been doing some reading, and . . . you're going to think I'm crazy. . . ."

"*I'm* going to think *you're* crazy? Gabe, did you know I was prescribed antipsychotic drugs for hallucinations?"

Gabe's eyes widened. "What?"

"Yeah. The doctor decided I was hallucinating, diagnosed schizophrenia, and drugged me up."

"No shit." He gave me an appraising look, like he half expected to see something had changed since I'd been diagnosed. "I'd heard you were attacked, not that you'd had some kind of breakdown."

"I *was* attacked. The problem is, when the doctor saw the video recording of the attack, there was no attacker."

"Huh?"

"I'm not schizophrenic."

"Yeah."

"I was attacked by something . . . unnatural. Something that isn't captured with regular video-recording equipment."

Gabe didn't respond right away. "So the doctor saw you freaking out about something that wasn't there?"

"Exactly."

"Then it's true," Gabe whispered.

"What?"

"Monsters really do exist."

"Are you making fun of me?"

"Hell no." He *was* serious.

"I can't say if 'monsters' exist, but I can tell you this.

There are things out there that we don't understand. Strange, dangerous things."

"Maybe you should dig out your dad's old papers?" Gabe suggested.

"Yeah, maybe I should." I leaned back in my chair, stretching my legs out in front of me, and let my head rest against the wall.

Sometime later, Gabe nudged me awake. I opened my eyes to find I'd flopped over and was using his shoulder as a pillow. I apologized and straightened up, blinking bleary eyes to try to clear them.

"Katie's being discharged. Are you ready to go?"

"Yeah." I pushed to my feet and shuffled after Gabe, who was leading the way. Katie met us at the door. She still had red paint in her hair, and in her eyebrows. All around her fingernails were stained crimson. "How are you feeling?"

"No better. I told the doctors something is wrong with me, but they didn't find anything." She visibly sighed. "I feel like my brain is short-circuiting. My hands and feet are numb. And sometimes I have this awful itchy-crawly sensation under my skin." A tear slipped from the corner of Katie's eye. She dragged her hand across her face, smearing it. The slightest tint of red stained her cheek.

I was petrified for her.

Numbness. Itching. Now, those were physical symptoms. Vague and unspecific, but still physical. "We'll take you to a doctor," I promised. "We'll find one that can figure it out. The numb sensation in your hands and feet . . . I wonder about that." I put my arm around Katie's shoulder and walked her out to the car. Gabe drove us home and parked my car. After making sure we got into our building safely, he headed home.

Katie went straight to bed.

Now I was alone. I was scared. All I could think about was Mr. Stinky's awful face. And that terrible voice. When I closed my eyes, I could almost hear him. A little scratch, the soft pad of footsteps, the creak of a door.

There was no way I was going to sleep tonight.

Recalling the conversation I'd had with Gabe, I snatched my keys and headed down to our building's basement. Each apartment had a small storage locker down there. Somewhere, in the mountain of boxes I'd shoved into the six-by-six-by-seven space, was a small box with my dad's notes and papers. I unlocked the metal gate and opened the locker. My eyes traveled up, up, and up the stack of tightly packed boxes. This was going to take a while. And I was tired. But it was better than going upstairs, falling asleep, and being woken by that . . . *thing.*

I pulled the top box off the stack and dragged it out of the way. A quick inspection told me that wasn't the box I needed, so I repeated the process with the next one, and the next, and the next. After intense labor, I had half of the contents of the locker crammed against the coin-operated washer and dryer, which nobody used. It took me more hours spent searching to find the right carton. Of course, it was one of the last ones, jammed into a small nook at the rear of the locker. I hastily rammed all the boxes back in place, locked the gate, and carted my find upstairs. I sat up into the early morning, reading and munching on nacho chips and cheese dip.

Just after daybreak, a knock on the front door interrupted my reading.

JT.

I stepped aside. "Hi."

"I saw lights on. Did I wake you?" He took a look at me and grimaced. His gaze settled on the top of my head.

Out of instinct, my hand went to my head. My hair, I realized, was a mess. "It's okay. I wasn't sleeping." I motioned toward the couch. "Have a seat. I was just about to make some coffee."

JT didn't move. He was staring at the couch.

"Sorry. I guess I got a little carried away with the research." I rushed to the sofa and gathered up the papers and folders strewn all over. Dividing them into stacks, I set these on the floor.

"It's okay." JT caught my arm, coaxing me to stop what I was doing and turn toward him. "I won't stay long. I just wanted to talk about what Gabe said yesterday."

"Okay." I pleaded silently, *Please tell me it wasn't true.* I crossed my arms over my chest.

"I . . . um . . ." JT glanced down at his hands, and I got a sick feeling in my stomach.

"It's true?" I asked.

"Not exactly."

What did that mean? "Okay."

"You know I wouldn't do anything to risk your job, or your reputation."

"I *thought* I knew that." I took a little step back, suddenly feeling like he was standing too close. "But . . . well . . ."

"I made the mistake of trusting someone I shouldn't have."
Shit!

My heart started thumping so hard, I could hear each beat in my head. "First, why would you tell anyone anything at all? And second, why would you lie? We're not sleeping together."

"I wanted to arrange a surprise for you. And I needed this other person's help."

I shoved my fingers through my matted hair. "And now, thanks to this 'other person,' I'm viewed as the bureau's ho."

"No." JT reached for me, but when I flinched, he dropped his arms to his sides. "Nobody sees you that way. Your friend is exaggerating."

I wanted to believe JT—I really did. But why would I? Here I was, the new girl, allegedly already doing the nasty with one of her superiors. Even if people didn't say it, they were thinking I was the office whore, trying to sleep my way up the ranks.

I guess that left me with two options.

I could leave the bureau, letting people believe what they wanted.

Or I could prove them wrong. And the first step in proving them wrong would be to solve our case.

Which would it be? Option A or B?

Option B, of course.

Now I didn't just have something to prove to myself. But I had something to prove to a lot of people. And by God, I was going to do it, creepy monster stalker or not.

My decision made, I cleared my throat. "There are a lot of things about you I really like." His butt, for one. And his dimples. And his smile. And the way he held me and made me feel safe. "But if I'm going to have any hope of getting past this and having a career in the FBI, I need to work hard and prove myself. I don't need distractions or rumors or innuendo. I need a partner I can trust."

"That, you will always have."

I took another step back. "I'm sorry it has to be this way." That was no lie. Looking at him now, I felt my heart ache a little. The truth was, those little moments we'd shared were some of the most thrilling I'd ever had, with any man. To think I'd never again see that naughty glimmer in his eye, or that slightly lopsided evil smile. . . .

Making me feel even worse, I imagined him giving another woman that lopsided smile.

My heart hurt.

But at this stage in my life, my career was much more important. And so was his. This thing wasn't doing him any favors either, I was guessing. If I had to remind myself of that from now until the day I retired from the bureau, then that was what I'd do.

I forced myself to lift my chin and stand a little straighter.

"Now I think I'm going to get dressed and go for a jog. Is the team still set up over at the bank-owned house in Clarksville?"

"No."

"That's okay. You can follow me from a distance. I wasn't crazy about that stupid wire, anyway. You're welcome to help yourself to some water. I'll be out in a few."

"Thanks." JT headed for the kitchen.

I hurried to my room, wriggled myself into a sports bra, and threw on a pair of shorts and a T-shirt. Before heading out to the kitchen for some much-needed caffeine, I scraped my hair into a ponytail, brushed my teeth, and smeared some concealer over the huge purple circles under my eyes. It didn't help much. I fluffed on a little blush and glossed up my lips in an attempt to look somewhat presentable. I carried a fresh pair of socks and my running shoes out to the kitchen.

JT handed me a full mug of coffee. I thanked him, trying to pretend I hadn't felt a little something when our fingertips grazed as he handed me the cup. I dumped a lot of powdered creamer in the cup and guzzled it.

JT refilled mine and his. He picked a file off the counter. "I hope you don't mind. I looked at this while you were dressing."

"Oh. Um, no." I dug in the cabinet for something to eat and scored a box of Pop-Tarts. I offered a package to him.

He ripped open the foil wrapper. "This is very interesting stuff." He motioned toward the file, which he'd set back on the counter.

"It's my father's research. I'd never read any of it. But after what's happened to me, I thought it was time to take a look."

"Do you mind if I read a little too?"

"No. Not at all."

"Thanks." He headed to the living room, while I put on my shoes. He had gathered one stack of folders in his arms. "I'll return these as soon as I get a chance to read through them."

"Take your time. As you see, there's plenty left for me to go through." I motioned toward the door. "Ready to head out?"

"Yep."

We met Mom out in the parking lot. Evidently, she was still on the job. She waved at us from her car. I went over and poked my head in the window.

"Hey, there," I said. "We're heading up to the Clarksville house. Are you hungry?"

"Maybe a little."

"It's not your favorite, but I supposed it's better than nothing." I handed her a package of S'Mores Pop-Tarts.

"Thanks, honey." Wrinkling her nose, she ripped the wrapper and pulled one of the pastries out. "I had a feeling you'd go to work today."

"Yeah, I can't sit around."

"You never could. Just like your father." Mom filled her mouth with pastry and smiled. "Not bad. Not bad at all."

"Okay, I'm going to head out now."

Mom's expression turned serious. "Be careful."

"Will do."

"Love you!" she called to me as I hurried toward my car.

JT met me in the middle of the parking lot. He insisted on driving, so we took his car. During the short drive, I skimmed some of the files he'd taken. He parked in the driveway; Mom parked farther down the street, where she'd be less conspicuous. He and I went into the house.

There was a dead mouse lying on the foyer floor. Probably the attack cat's latest victim. JT took the stiff rodent to the garage, while I reluctantly investigated the rest of the house. No sign of a cat. No sign of any other visitors either.

"I'd love to find out where that beast is hiding," I told JT when he came back in from the garage. He looked a little pale. "What's wrong?"

"I called 911. Come here!" He turned around and ran back into the garage.

"Why? What is it?" Bracing myself for what had to be a gruesome sight, to make JT look so sickly, I followed. Inside the garage, the air was hot, and it smelled like gasoline and warm rubber. Sprawled on the concrete floor was a child. A little girl. I recognized the clothes. "Oh, my God! It's Tutu Girl." I rushed to her side and dropped to my knees. "Is she breathing?"

"Yes." JT gently rolled her over. "And she has a steady pulse."

"I know this little girl. She lives down the street. She's the missing child Gabe's team has been searching for."

"Call the chief. And open the garage door. It's hotter than hell in here."

I shot to my feet and went in search of the button to start the automatic garage door opener. Moments later, the door lifted, and a cool breeze blew through the growing gap between the floor and the bottom of the door. Then I went in search of my purse, which I'd left in JT's car. I called the chief's cell phone. She answered on the second ring, and I told her what had happened. Meanwhile, Mom came jogging up to me and tried to tell me something, while I tried to give chief the rundown. As I shushed Mom and blurted out the few sketchy details I had for the chief, the ambulance rolled up in front of the house, lights flashing. I pointed the EMT toward the garage and ended the call with the chief, following him. A second EMT followed me, pulling a gurney. Mom hung back, down at the end of the driveway.

JT and I answered questions as the two men checked the little girl's pulse, respiration, and heart rate. A marked police car rolled up as they were putting in an IV. The officer asked me questions, and I answered them, telling him where the little girl lived. He headed down to the house to see if anyone was home. Feeling helpless, I stood there and watched as the EMTs lifted the child onto the bed.

"Is she going to be okay?" I asked as they rolled her down the driveway, toward the waiting ambulance.

"Yeah, I think so. She's dehydrated. Other than that, she looks okay."

I sucked in a lungful of air. "Thank you." I felt JT behind me. He didn't touch me, but it was still reassuring having him there. I looked around for Mom, but I didn't see her. Probably headed back to her car. I glanced down at my hands. They were shaking. My insides twisted into a knot.

I had no idea I could be so upset about seeing someone else's child sick or hurt. Made me wonder if I could handle a case involving a kid, if my emotions would get to me.

"It's never easy when it's a kid," JT said, as if he could read my mind. "They get to guys who've been on the job for decades."

"That's not reassuring."

"The important thing is how you handle it. If you can keep doing the job, you'll be okay."

If I could keep doing the job.

"How about we head to the office and take a look at those files?" JT offered.

"No." I mentally pulled up my bootstraps.

JT's eyebrows rose. "No?"

I hitched up my chin. "I'm going for my run. And you're going to follow me."

"Are you sure? You look like you didn't sleep at all last night and—"

"I didn't. And you know why. But, like you said, I have to keep doing my job. If I do, I might save somebody's life."

"Okay." He gave me a pat on the shoulder. "You're tougher than you realize. I respect that about you."

I tried to pretend I wasn't blushing. I gave him a little push and started walking. "Ah, six miles is nothing." I started at a walk, swinging my arms to get my heart pumping a little. My eyes bounced back and forth, from one side of the street to the other, one house to another, among houses and trees and parked cars. Everything looked normal. Ordinary. One vinyl-sided house after another. One manicured lawn after another. Nothing stood out as I jogged down the winding

street, heading toward the wooded main road. Every now and
then, I'd peer over my shoulder, catching a glimpse of JT's
car. He would drive a little, then park; drive, then park. I
didn't see Mom's car following me. I wondered if she'd given
up and gone home.

Falling into a comfortable pace, I jogged out of the subdivision, turning onto the main street. It was cooler there, the
trees shading the road. My skin, now slick with sweat, prickled as goose bumps erupted over my arms and legs. It felt
good. I inhaled deeply through my nose, enjoying the scent of
trees and freshly mown grass. I rounded the bend, approaching the school on my left. There were no cars in the lot, no kids
or buses. By the time I turned back into the subdivision, nearly
completing the full circle, I had started to feel a little tired. I
slowed my pace to a walk as I turned the final corner.

Mom's car was still parked where it had been. I peered in
the window as I walked past.

No Mom.

Where'd she go?

Mom, not again. Not now.

Knowing others is intelligence; knowing yourself is true wisdom. Mastering others is strength; mastering yourself is true power.

—Lao Tzu

22

A million possibilities flew through my mind as I searched the area around my mother's abandoned car—none of them good. Her car was exactly where she'd parked it, but she was nowhere to be seen. She could have wandered off somewhere and gotten lost. She could have tried to follow me on foot and collapse somewhere.

She could have been attacked by the killer, who liked brunettes in their midthirties. Mom was in her forties; and her hair was black but at a distance she could pass for thirty-five–ish. Had I led her right into the path of a serial killer?

My stomach did a flip-flop, and I bent at the waist, wrapping my arm around myself, squeezing my eyes shut and willing the nausea to ease up so I could keep looking. Now was not the time to get all queasy.

"Are you okay?" JT was behind me.

I turned to face him. "Mom's not here. I don't know where she's gone."

JT glanced at the car, then at my face, which was probably as white as a nearby delivery van. "Maybe she had to go to the bathroom."

"Oh. God. I hope you're right." Able to breathe a little better, I dashed down to our borrowed house. There were still several police officers standing outside the garage. I described my mother to one of them, asking if he'd seen her. He hadn't. I raced inside, making a beeline for the half bath on the main floor. The door was hanging open. "Mom?" I called out. "Are you here? Mom?"

No answer.

I headed into the kitchen, thinking maybe she got thirsty and came in for a glass of water.

No Mom.

"Mom!" I shouted, unable to keep the panic from my voice. "Are you here? Please answer." I ran from room to room, growing more desperate with every second that passed. She wasn't on the first floor. I stomped up the stairs, clinging to the railing, breathless, dizzy. "Mom!" I checked my bedroom, the spare, the master bath, the main bathroom.

No Mom.

"Sloan," JT called from downstairs.

Hoping he'd found my mother, I flew down the steps. I met him in the foyer. "Did you find her?" I asked between heavy gasps.

"Not yet."

"We have to find her. What if the unsub has her?"

"It's a little too soon to be jumping to those kinds of conclusions, Sloan. She could have just gone for a walk. Or . . . something." He gave me a you-know-what-I-mean look.

I knew exactly what he meant. "JT, we have to find her."

"We will. It shouldn't be too difficult. She's probably somewhere nearby. . . ." He gave my shoulder a rub. It was a well-meant gesture, but for some reason, it irritated me. "Tell me what you want me to do. You can't file a missing persons report until after she's been gone twenty-four hours."

"I know." I stared at the door, wishing she'd come wandering through. "But there's a killer out there somewhere, and even if she's just meandering around the neighborhood, chasing pink monkeys or elephants or rhinoceroses, she could be in danger."

"We can search faster by car." JT steered me toward the front door. "I'll drive."

We cruised up and down the subdivision's streets. I practically hung out the window, trying to peer between houses, behind fences, and around shrubs and trees. When we didn't find her, JT turned out onto the main road, following the route I'd jogged. Just as I was about to give up, I caught sight of some movement at the rear of the school.

"Stop!" I shouted.

JT turned into the school's parking lot and threw the car into park. We clambered out. "Where?" he asked.

"This way." I sprinted along the west side of the school, my feet pounding on the paved drive, which circled the building. By the time I reached the rear of the building, I was in dire need of oxygen. I stopped, my gaze sweeping back and forth across the playground. Blue-and red play structure. Steel swing sets. Trees. No Mom. No people. "I swear I saw someone."

JT, who wasn't breathing hard at all, wrapped an arm around my shoulders. "She's not here. Let's go back to the car. I want you to sit down before you pass out. And I think you need some water. You've run close to seven miles by now."

My knees felt a little Jell-O–ish, but I wasn't going to let that stop me from looking for Mom. That was what I always did. I took care of her—no matter what. She didn't have anyone else. "I'm okay." I stepped out of his hold, heading toward the closest door, painted cherry red. Identical doors lined the face of the building at regular intervals, entries to each classroom, I guessed. "Maybe she went inside the building."

"I'm sure the doors are all locked."

"But suppose one wasn't? I think it's wise to check, just in case." The first one was locked. I cussed silently and headed for the second one, vaguely aware of JT tailing me. That one was locked too, but that didn't stop me from trying door number three.

"I'll go check the doors around the other side!" JT called.

"Thanks!"

Doors five, six, and seven were also locked. I circled around the north and then east sides of the school, finally turning toward the front, searching the area for a sign of people. Still, nothing. Not Mom. Not anyone. I followed the curved sidewalk, which wrapped around the front of the school, approaching the west side again.

No JT.

Where'd he go?

I jog-walked down the west side of the building again; my gaze lurched from one red door to another as I passed them. The last one, I noticed, was wedged open slightly. Either it hadn't been open earlier when we'd run this way, or I had been too distracted to notice it. I pulled it open and peered inside. Whiteboard. Little tables with chairs stacked on top. Lights off. No voices, no people, no JT.

I gently eased the door shut behind me and moved deeper into the classroom, senses alert, muscles tense. My ears caught every tiny sound, the hum of a fly buzzing around the room, the whirr of the air conditioner, the drip of a leaky faucet.

The echo of footsteps.

Someone was coming.

I flattened myself against the wall, hiding behind a file cabinet. The footsteps came closer. Closer. The person was right on the other side of the steel cabinet. I held my breath.

"Sloan?" the person whispered.

"JT?"

"Yeah, it's me. I checked the building. There's a janitor polishing the cafeteria floor. Nobody else."

"Okay."

We headed back outside, squinting against the glaring sunlight. The sun was hanging high overhead. I guessed it was getting close to noon.

"Wow, where'd the morning go?" I muttered.

"Are you hungry?"

"No. I'm too worried to be hungry."

JT gave me what I guessed was meant to be a reassuring look. "We'll find her." We started back to the car. Too desperate to give up, I kept looking, everywhere, at everything, hoping I'd see some clue. Not far from the front sidewalk, something caught my eye, a flash of metal in the grass. "Where are you going?" JT asked as I dashed toward the reflection.

"Checking something." The grass hadn't been mown in a week or two; it was a little on the thick and tall side. I combed my fingers through the blades, searching in the area where I thought I'd seen the glittery thing. "Found it." I plucked the silver chain from the long grass. At the end dangled one of those silver medical-alert badges. My mother wore one. I'd purchased it for her years ago, after she almost died. An ER doctor had given her a medication that interacted with her prescription drugs after an accident, causing an almost fatal heart arrhythmia.

What was the likelihood of this medical alert being hers?

Letting it fall into my palm, I checked the engraving. It wasn't Mom's. But the name was familiar. Deborah Richardson. A series of letters with pluses and minuses follow. Her blood type was very rare. I handed it to JT.

He read it, then met my gaze. "Damn, you're good!"

"It was a lucky find. What do you think it means?"

"It means we need to call the Baltimore PD so they can get a CSI team over here pronto and get this area cordoned off. I think we're standing in the middle of a crime scene." He patted his pockets. "Damn, I left my cell in the car."

"Me too."

We ran back to the car and dove for our phones. Mine

was playing "The Entertainer," indicating I'd just received a message. Hoping it was from my mother, I dialed voice mail to retrieve it. Meanwhile, JT called the Baltimore PD to tell them what we'd found.

The message, I discovered, wasn't from Mom. It was from Gabe, and it sounded urgent. "Sloan, you need to get down here to the hospital now. It's about your case."

Our case. My case. Damn.

What to do? Keep looking for Mom? Or head to the hospital?

If there was ever a test for an agent's commitment to her job, this was it. I didn't want to go. I wasn't ready to give up looking for my mother yet.

This was an impossible choice.

I tried calling Gabe back, hoping he'd give me the information over the phone. No answer. JT ended his call as I shoved my cell into my purse and muttered a few expletives.

"Detectives are on the way." JT took a step closer. "What's wrong?"

"Gabe left me a message. He's at the hospital. Said I need to get down there. It's about the case. . . ."

"But you'd rather stay here and keep searching for your mother."

I shoved my fingers through my hair, practically yanking it out of what was probably the world's messiest ponytail by now. "What would you do?" I could feel my eyes tearing up, a sob choking me. I inhaled slowly, then exhaled.

"If your mother's disappearance has anything to do with the unsub, then you need to find her."

"Exactly."

"But maybe driving around isn't the best way to do that. Maybe going to the hospital will give you the lead that'll crack this case."

"Good point." Also, in my current state, I trusted JT to be sharper and more capable than me.

JT waved toward the road. "Go. Take my car. Once I'm done here, I'll go back to searching on foot."

"Okay. Thanks." I thought about giving him a hug, just because he was being such a good friend. But with the thing going on between us, I figured that wasn't the best idea.

He handed me the keys. "I'll keep you posted."

"Thanks." I jumped into the car, made some adjustments to the seat and mirror, cranked the engine over, and bounced and sputtered away. During the herky-jerky drive, I tried to guess what Gabe had found out about our case. He'd followed the missing girl to the hospital. Had her disappearance been linked to the murders, after all?

Fifteen minutes later, I pulled JT's car into a parking spot and cut off the engine. I snatched up my laptop bag, double-checking to make sure I had my cell phone, and headed inside.

Lucky me. The emergency room lobby was in chaos. I tried to get the attention of a couple of security officers, but they were both busy talking on radios. One snapped, "If you're not a patient, you must go to the waiting room"; then he went back to his radio conversation.

This was one of those times where I wished I had a badge. I tapped on his shoulder. "I'm an intern with the FBI. I'm here about a case."

"Do you have any ID?"

"Just my driver's license. I'm an intern. Not an agent."

Wearing a totally believable security guy's stern face, he said, "Sorry, then, I can't let you back."

"Okay." I checked my cell. No bars. I headed outside, waited for my phone to connect, and tried Gabe's phone again. No answer. "Damn it."

"Sloan!" Gabe called out.

Relieved, I whirled around. "What's going on?"

"I've been waiting for you. Come on." He rushed me back inside.

Following him, I explained, "I tried to get into the ER to look for you. Without a badge, I couldn't get past the security guards."

"Yeah, I know. The hospital had to step up the security. There was a problem with some drunk asshole brought in by the police." Gabe paused at the registration desk and flashed a badge, pointing at me. "We're with the FBI."

The woman at the desk waved us back.

"Where'd you get that badge?"

"It's the chief's. She wanted to make sure we'd be able to get back in."

"What if they'd looked at the name on the ID? Or the picture?"

"Good thing they didn't." Gabe pointed at a long corridor, lined with empty gurneys. "This way. She's been isolated in an area where we can protect her."

"Who?"

"Your witness." He turned down a narrower, quiet corridor, lined with doors. The man had long legs and was using them to full advantage, which left me to jog to keep up.

"Who is she?"

"Her name is Eden Eckert." He stopped at a door, which was guarded by a federal agent. "This is Sloan Skye, the other intern SSA Peyton told you about."

The agent nodded, and in we went. I whispered, "Why the guard?" as we stepped through the door.

"I'll tell you later."

Our little friend looked even smaller lying in that big hospital bed, monitors blinking, tangled tubes dangling over the side of the bed. But she looked a lot better than she had in the garage. A woman, whom I hadn't noticed right away, was sitting in a chair on the opposite side of the bed. She stood as Gabe and I moved closer.

Gabe motioned to me. "This is Sloan Skye. She was the

one who found your daughter this morning. Sloan, this is Mrs. Eckert, Eden's mother."

"Thank you for finding my baby. I can't . . ." The woman sniffled. "I was so worried."

"It wasn't technically me who found her, but I'm glad she was found, and I'm relieved to hear she'll be okay." I glanced at the little girl, who was eagerly shoveling vanilla ice cream into her mouth. "I see she's hungry. That's always a good sign."

Mrs. Eckert did a little half sob, half laugh. "Yes, it is."

Biting back a sarcastic comment, I said, "If it's okay, we need to ask Eden some questions." We needed the mother's cooperation. Now was not the time to talk about any suspicions of neglect.

Mrs. Eckert thumbed a tear from her eye. "Sure. Anything that'll help you catch the woman who did this. If you don't, I won't be able to let her play outside without being terrified she'll vanish again."

"The woman?" I echoed.

Gabe nodded. He looked at little Eden, who had just polished off the last drop of ice cream in the bowl and was licking her lips. "Okay, Eden. Now that you've had your treat, can we talk about what happened?"

"Sure." Eden beamed at Gabe.

Gabe returned her smile. "Go ahead and tell Ms. Skye what you told me and the other agents today."

"It was Mrs. Bishop," the little girl said.

"Who is Mrs. Bishop?" I asked.

"Veronica's mama. Remember? I told you Veronica is my best friend. But she was gone away at camp. And I missed her really, really bad. So I rode my bike to her house. I wanted to ask her mommy when she'd be back. Julia came back early, after her mommy died. I thought maybe Veronica would come back with her. Mrs. Bishop asked if I wanted some ice cream." She slid a glance at her own mother and tipped her head down. "Mommy always told me not to go into other people's houses without telling her first. I should've gone home and asked, but I didn't. Because it was Mrs. Bishop. Mommy knows Mrs. Bishop."

"What happened next?" I asked.

"I ate the ice cream. It tasted kinda funny. Then I got real sleepy, even though it wasn't nap time. Mrs. Bishop told me I could sleep in Veronica's room. So I went up and took a nap. When I woke up, the door was locked, and Mrs. Bishop wouldn't let me out. The window was covered too. With boards. I couldn't get out. I was really scared. She came back later, to give me something to eat and drink. She also brought in a baby toilet. I told her I wanted to go home, but she said I couldn't. I asked her why not, and she said it was because she missed Veronica so much. That I was helping her not feel so sad."

This was a terrible story, but I still didn't see the connection to our case yet. I glanced at Gabe.

He nodded to Eden. "Tell her what happened later that night, Eden."

The little girl's expression changed. She suddenly looked small and vulnerable and horribly frightened. "Do I hafta?"

"I know it's scary, but we need to hear. We need to stop Mrs. Bishop from hurting you, and other children. This is the only way we can stop her."

The little girl didn't speak for a full minute. She just stared down at her hands, now clasped in her lap, fingers tightly curled into fists. "It's hard to say."

"It's okay." Gabe took the child's hand into his. "There are a lot of people here to protect you. She won't get near you again."

Eden eventually gave a little nod. "Later I fell asleep. Something woke me up. It felt like someone was dragging something hard and cold over my skin, like a knife. And it smelled awful, like our garage in the summertime, when we leave the garbage in there too long. I opened my eyes, and she was standing there, looking at me, but it wasn't her. She was different. Her face. Her . . . teeth. And then . . ." Eden fingered her neck. "And then she bit me." Tears streamed down the little girl's face. "It hurt. So bad. She did it again. And again. And again."

Gabe and I exchanged a glance.

An image flashed in my mind. A shocking, horrifying one. Fangs flashing in the dim light. The agony of the bite. Instantly I felt sick. Dizzy. My stomach surged up my throat. I wrapped my fingers around the bed's side rail. With my other hand, I rubbed my neck, recalling all too clearly how horrific the pain had been.

It had happened to me. Not just recently. No, years ago. When I was this little girl's age. How many times had I cowered in the dark, feeling those icy fingers of dread curl around my stomach, waiting for the beast to return?

Sounds grew distant. The world narrowed to a dark, oppressive tunnel.

"I need to step outside. For just a minute." My legs felt like half-cooked noodles, my feet heavy, as if they were encased in concrete shoes. I tried to give Eden a reassuring smile. "I'll be right back." Then, without looking at Gabe, I turned and walked out the door. In the hallway, I leaned back against the cool wall, closed my eyes, and tried to wish away the awful feeling spreading through my body like a cancer.

"Are you okay?" Gabe asked a few moments later.

I inhaled. Exhaled. "Sorry about that. Did I scare her worse? I hope not."

"She'll be okay. I'm more worried about you. What's wrong?"

"What she said brought back some unpleasant memories. That's all." I fought a shudder that was quaking up my spine.

"Oh, the attack. I didn't think—"

"No, it's not that. I understand now why my dad started researching vampires, risking his career, his reputation, everything. I finally get it." I swallowed the bile surging up my throat. "I think a vampire was attacking me. My father threw everything away to try to stop it."

Wisdom is knowing what to do next, skill is knowing how to do it, and virtue is doing it.

—David Starr Jordan

23

Fortunately, it took me only a few minutes to pull myself together. While Gabe went back into the room to talk to Eden, I channeled all the horror and confusion that lay deep inside me into a fierce determination to solve this case.

As much as I wanted to run out of there, call JT, and tell him to head over to the Bishop house to take Mrs. Bishop into custody, I wasn't ready to do that yet. I hadn't figured out how the two cases were linked.

What did the kidnapping have to do with the killer?

I took a deep breath and went back into the room. Eden looked a little wary as her gaze found mine. I smiled. "It's okay."

She smiled back.

"I'm sorry I left you like that. I'd like to explain why."

Eden dug a stuffed kitten out from under the blankets and hugged it. "Okay."

I sat on the edge of her bed. "When I was little, I had a very similar experience. And your description brought back all the terrible memories I'd pushed out of my mind. I got a little overwhelmed, but only for a minute."

She looked at me with wide eyes, full of innocence, and petted her kitten. "Were you scared when it happened to you?"

"I was. Very."

She blinked. Her eyes reddened. "Me too. I'm afraid she'll come back and hurt me again."

"That's why we need to catch her. And we need you to help us do that, and make sure she'll never hurt another little girl again. You need to tell us everything you remember."

"Okay."

"After she bit you, what happened?" I asked.

"I got very tired. I fell asleep."

"And when you woke up?"

"I was hungry. Really, really hungry. She brought me cereal and a banana for breakfast. And a sandwich and some chips and a cookie for lunch. I ate everything, and she was nice again, just like normal. And I asked her if I could go home, over and over."

"What did she say?"

"She said I couldn't go home until Veronica came back from camp."

I leaned forward. "Did she say why?"

"She said she missed Veronica a lot. And I made her feel better. That's all."

"Okay. Did she say anything else? Anything about hurting some women?"

"No. But I told Mr. Thomas that I got away from Mrs. Bishop when she was giving me a bath. I hid in the garage next door. I didn't know where else to go. And I knew you were staying there. I thought you could help me. I heard Mrs. Bishop talking to Mrs. Quinley outside. And then Mrs. Quinley screamed. I peeked out and saw Mrs. Bishop biting her, just like she did me."

Gabe and I exchanged a look.

Kimberly Quinley had been the last victim. She had died from leishmaniasis, considered by some to be the deadliest tropical disease on the planet. But what I didn't understand was how the timing could fit. The average incubation period for leishmaniasis was ten days to several years. "How long did you stay with Mrs. Bishop? And how long were you hiding in the garage?"

"I was with Mrs. Bishop for a long time. I don't know how long. I only spent four nights in the garage. But you didn't come back. I was afraid to go home because I knew Mrs. Bishop would find me there. I didn't know where else to go."

"So you heard Mrs. Quinley scream the first day after you escaped?"

Eden shook her head and clutched her toy tighter. "No, I heard her scream on the last day."

"And how long were you hiding in the garage?" I asked again.

"Four whole nights. I got real hungry, but I was afraid to go home. I could hear Mrs. Bishop outside, working in her yard, talking to people, asking if anyone had seen me. She even talked to my mommy once. I was afraid she'd hurt her too."

"Okay. I think I need to make a call." I motioned for Gabe to join me outside. We headed out of the building together. "Have they run screens for tropical infectious diseases?"

"Everything's come back negative."

I gnawed on my lip and touched my neck. "I wonder why. If the vampire's bite is toxic to adults, why isn't it toxic to children too?"

Gabe crossed his arms over his chest and shrugged. "I don't know. You're the one with the father who researched this stuff. Maybe it's in his work somewhere."

"It probably is. I haven't gotten through all of it yet. Things have been a little crazy."

Gabe leaned back against a brick column. "What are you going to do?"

"Does the chief know about this?"

"Yes."

"Okay. I'm going to call her and JT. I don't know if he's aware of what's going on. We need to profile this unsub before the BPD tries to take her into custody. But before we do that, I need to get home and dig through my dad's research, see if I can figure out exactly what we're dealing with. I hope my mother's disappearance has nothing to do with this. It sounds like Bishop is a spree attacker, preying upon any brunette woman who happens to cross her path at the wrong time. And somehow, Eden and Veronica play into Bishop's hunting pattern. Now I'm wondering if Veronica is really at camp, or somewhere else. We need to find out."

Gabe shoved his hand into his pants pocket and dug out his phone. "Okay. I'll probably see you back at the academy later."

"Thanks for calling me."

"That's what friends are for."

I dialed JT's number as I scrabbled into his car.

He answered on the first ring. "What's the story?"

"Our unsub is the neighbor Mrs. Bishop. We have her on kidnapping, but we don't have enough evidence to charge her with murder yet. Nor do we have a motive."

"Did you say, Mrs. Bishop?" he whispered.

"Yes. Why? Let me guess, she's there with you?"

"She was. She left a few minutes ago, after telling me she saw someone chasing the last victim through the park last week."

"She's lying. But how are we going to prove it?"

"DNA would be handy."

"That's for sure. Her DNA is definitely unique. But I doubt you'll get her to agree to a swab."

"There are other ways to get an unsub's DNA."

"Legal?"

"Sure."

"Well, okay. I'll leave it to you, then."

"No problem."

"You'll be careful, right?" Sitting in the running car, I stared out the windshield. The sky had darkened to a threatening gray and the first fat droplets of rain were smacking the glass. "I mean, the woman's brutally murdered several women, and she's kidnapped a child."

"If I didn't know better, I'd say you're worried about me."

I heard the laughter in his voice. "Maybe a little," I admitted.

"Well, I'll take that as a compliment."

"Take it any way you like."

"Any way?" His voice had that flirtatious lilt I so enjoyed . . . and dreaded.

"Don't get too carried away," I warned.

He laughed. Even on the phone, the sound made me all warm and soft and gooey. I was glad I was alone. He couldn't see how it affected me. After a slightly awkward moment, he said, "About your mother . . ."

"No news, right?"

"Actually, I did get something, a pretty decent lead."

My heart started pounding. I curled my fingers around the phone and smooshed it against my ear. "Yeah?"

"A woman who lives in the house nearest your mother's car saw a woman who matches your mom's description get into a late-model blue sedan, either a Chrysler or a Dodge. We have a partial plate. I got Brittany running it. Hopefully, she'll find a match."

It wasn't the best news, but it was something. "God, I hope it doesn't take too long to track down the vehicle. Thank you."

"You're welcome. Now, about your dad's research, I think we need to go over some of it. If we can figure out exactly what Mrs. Bishop is, we might be able to find a vulnerability, and a way to connect her to the crime, outside of DNA. I'm going to call my connection at the BPD and let them know who we're looking at. They can keep an eye on her until we come up with something more solid for them."

"Sounds good."

"How about we meet over at your place?" he suggested. "You have the majority of the notes there."

I glanced at the clock on the dash. "I can be there in a half hour."

"Have you eaten lunch yet?" He asked.

"No."

"Good. I'll bring food. What are you in the mood for?"

I smiled. "Surprise me. And, JT?"

"Yeah?" he responded.

"How're you going to get there? I have your car."

"Don't worry about it. I'll catch a ride from someone."

My roommate was playing with chemicals again. Could it be that my out-of-control life was finally returning to normal? *Oh, please say it's so!*

A cloud of gray smoke rolled through the doorway as I opened the door. It was a beautiful sight. Crazy, I'd never thought I'd be so happy to be standing in a thick, noxious haze. "Katie? What are you cooking up now?"

"Lunch." Katie, whom I expected to find in a rubber apron, thick gloves, and a gas mask, came bouncing to the door in a bright yellow dress, covered by a white apron printed with red cherries. The colors nearly blinded me. So did her smile. "It was supposed to be a surprise."

"A surprise? For what?"

Katie flung her arms around me and gave me an exuberant hug. "A thank-you gift. From me to you."

"Well . . . okay. Uh, you're welcome?" I followed my energetic roommate into the kitchen, eyes watering, not because I was overwhelmed with joy and gratitude, but because the smoke was burning my corneas. On the top of the stove sat a cookie sheet with some little black blobs on it. I didn't ask. "What, exactly, did I do to deserve this?"

Katie gave me another violently happy hug. "I'm feeling so much better, thanks to you."

"You are? That's great!"

"I got a call from that doctor's office you recommended."

I didn't recommend any doctor, but I didn't want to tell her that. She looked so healthy and happy and alive, it was hard to believe this was the same Katie I'd been living with the past week or so. "And?"

"I'm not going crazy!" She jumped up and down like a five-year-old who'd been set loose in a toy store.

Not crazy. I knew how it felt to hear that news. It was no wonder she was so happy. I threw my arms around her and gave her a hug. "That's great! For what it's worth, I never believed it was anxiety either. So what was it? You look like you're feeling so much better."

"You're going to laugh your ass off when I tell you."

"No, I promise I won't." I had my own suspicions about what might have been wrong.

"Okay . . . I"—she giggled—"poisoned myself."

"Of course you did. Look at what you play with." I motioned to the burned blobs.

"No, that's just it. Here I am, working in a lab day and night, and that wasn't what made me sick. The damn bug bomb did."

"The what?"

"Remember when we had all those fireflies in the apartment?"

"Sure."

"Well, the doctor told me I used too many bombs, and the chemicals are toxic to humans, if we're exposed to a high enough concentration of them. Which I was."

"And I wasn't?"

"You didn't stay in the apartment that first night. I did."

Head smack. "Of course. Your symptoms were classic signs of neurotoxicity. Shit. I should've figured that out."

"I don't blame you. You've been dealing with enough stuff." She dumped the crispy contents of the pan into the trash. "It doesn't matter now. The doctor is treating me for the exposure."

"I'm so glad you'll be okay. I was really worried about you."

"I'm just thankful you didn't get tired of me being such a bitch, and a slob." Katie tossed the pan into the sink and cranked on the faucet. "So much for the chicken Cordon Bleu. I am a pathetic cook. Can't even warm frozen chicken without turning it to charcoal."

"That's okay. JT's on his way over with some lunch. I'll split mine with you."

Katie's smile was genuine. "You are a true friend, Sloan." There was a knock at the door. "Is that your mom or JT, I wonder?"

"It probably isn't my mom. I need to tell you something." I held up an index finger; and at Katie's nod, I headed for the door. Sure enough, it was JT. And he was carrying a big paper bag printed with the name of one of my all-time favorite restaurants on its side. "You are a god."

"You've finally figured that out?" JT strolled in, wrinkling his nose. "What the hell is that smell?"

"Katie was doing some cooking."

JT cringed. "I'm guessing she's hungry too?" He set the bag on the kitchen counter. "There's plenty for all of us."

"So what's the deal with your mom?" Katie asked as she pulled three plates out of the cupboard.

"She's sort of . . . missing."

"Oh, no. Again?" Katie donned her sad face.

"It's a little different this time. She didn't just run off to hide from a hallucination. She got into someone's car and drove off."

"Oh, my God." Katie clapped her hands over her mouth.

"Really?" Her gaze bounced back and forth between me and JT, who was now digging into the pile of my dad's stuff sitting on the floor. "What can I do to help?"

"The FBI is trying to track down the car Mom was seen getting into. Until they do that, I don't know if there's anything you can do. I don't know if there's anything any of us can do." I flipped open a carton. My appetite was hardly what it normally would be, but I knew I needed to eat something. The pasta dish inside was one of my favorites—a cheese tortellini in uber fattening, garlicky Alfredo sauce. I spooned some onto my plate, took a piece of toasted garlic bread, and headed for the living room. Katie followed, her plate full of the tortellini and some of the lasagna we'd found in one of the other cartons.

I sat next to JT. "Would you mind handing me a file?" I asked him.

"Take your pick." He fanned three thick folders out on the table.

I flipped open the thickest. While I shoveled cheese tortellini into my mouth, I started skimming the reports.

About fifteen minutes later, my fork hit the plate with a *thunk*. I glanced down, expecting to find at least half the food on it. The dish was empty.

"Looks like you were hungrier than you thought," JT said, eyes twinkling with mischief.

I squinted at him. "Did you have anything to do with the magically disappearing pasta?"

"No, not me."

I didn't believe him. Not for a minute. I shoved the empty plate out of my way, dabbed my mouth with my napkin, and stared at the page I'd been trying to read for several minutes. "How long does it take for Brittany to run a license plate?"

JT wiped what looked like Alfredo sauce off his lower lip with the napkin I'd wadded up on the table. "No time at all— if she has the full number."

If. Urgh.

I needed to do something besides just sit and read. I grabbed my empty dish and carried it to the kitchen. In there, I tidied up a little, tossing the empty cartons and putting the ones with food in the refrigerator. As I turned around, I smacked into JT.

He didn't say a word. He just hauled me into his arms and held me. I closed my eyes and relaxed against him, appreciating the strength of the arms embracing me, the warmth of his body, and the scent of his skin.

A minute or so later, I stepped back. "Thanks, I needed that," I said, feeling my cheeks getting warm.

"I'm here for you. Whatever you need."

I wrapped my arms around myself and tried to look like I wasn't about to go a little crazy with worry. "Maybe you could call her? Brittany? See how it's going?"

"Sure." He dialed Brittany as I stood there, my breath in my throat. When she answered, he asked for a status update. Then he did a lot of nodding and uh-huh–ing, and asked her to call the minute she had something more. He thanked her and ended the call.

"Well?"

"The car is a rental. She's tracked it to the company that owns the vehicle. Now she's in the process of finding out who rented it. She'll have something solid soon."

"Oh, that's great!" Katie, who'd been listening in from the dining room, gave me a reassuring smile. "We'll find her, Sloan."

"Thanks, you guys." My nose was starting to burn, a sure sign I was going to cry. I blinked a few times, snuffled, grabbed a napkin off the counter, and wiped my watery eyes. "I can't imagine going through this without you."

"After all you've done for me, I wish there were more I could do." Katie sighed and looked at JT. "Give me something to do."

JT pointed at the stack of files. "You could help us dig through Sloan's father's stuff."

"Sure!" Katie bounced over to the folders. "What're you looking for?"

"Anything that mentions insects," he said.

"Got it." Katie settled on the floor, her back resting against the wall, a folder sitting open on her bent knees. JT, sitting on the couch, flipped through papers. I sat next to him, trying to read, but failing miserably. An eon later, Katie said, "Hey, check this out. There's a vampire that turns into a firefly. How weird is that? We had all those fireflies in here. What if they were all vampires?"

"Fireflies?" JT jerked upright. "Can I see that?"

"Sure." Katie handed over the file and selected another one.

JT read for about ten seconds and said, "This is it! We have our profile."

Scientists do not have to turn their backs to the standard methods of scientific research to investigate the existence of paranatural creatures. In truth, these creatures are as organic as the species we have dissected and labeled and collected for eons. In fact, one could argue their existence is more readily proven than some theories of astrophysics.

— James Skye, Ph.D., *Comparative Analysis of Vampiric Species*

24

JT and I worked on our profile all night long. And only when it was complete did he call the chief and tell her we were ready to present it. She arranged for everyone to meet at the Baltimore PD early that morning. Then, both of us looking like death warmed over from our all-nighter, JT turned to me, smacked my knee, grinned like the wolf that was about to eat poor old granny, and said, "I want you to do the honors."

"Me?" I shook my head. I don't like public speaking. In fact, I avoid it at all costs. I swear, it gives me hives. "No, that's okay. You do it." I gathered the dirty cups, snack bags, and crumpled napkins off my coffee table and hauled it all into the kitchen.

JT followed me, leaning against the kitchen counter, blocking my egress. "I insist."

Painfully aware of how tiny the kitchen was for the first time, I dumped the trash in the can. "No, really."

"Sloan." JT gave me a you're-not-gonna-change-my-mind look.

"JT." When he didn't respond, I added, "I'll pay any price." Unable to get around JT, or, rather, unwilling to try, I cranked on the water and dumped some soap into the sink.

JT considered my offer for a moment, and I decided, despite the fact that my hair would make a rat's nest look tidy, and my makeup had worn off hours ago, I might have made a mistake by making that offer. He sauntered closer, and I knew I'd made a mistake. Standing close enough to kiss me, he ran a fingertip along the scoop neck of my knit top. His teeth sank into his lower lip, and my heart rate kicked up to double time. "No, as tempting as that is, I think it's better this way."

"Why?" I snapped. When JT's brows rose to his forehead, I realized he'd misunderstood the question. "I mean, why are you insisting I present the profile?" I scrubbed a cup. The cup was very dirty. This was going to take some time. Lots of time. I leaned over the sink, trying to put a little distance between my body and JT's. It wasn't working.

"Because you deserve to."

Still scouring, I stared down at the soapy water. I didn't want to think about how close he was, or how good he smelled. Or how much I wanted to kiss him. "What did I do to you?"

"Nothing." JT leaned over my side and, with a hand on my chin, coaxed me to look at him. His expression was all business now. That was a huge relief. "You were concerned about your reputation at the bureau. . . ."

"And this would change things for me? Is that what you're thinking?"

"It wouldn't hurt."

I sighed, loud and hard, and dropped the cup into the sink full of bubbles. "Fine. I'll do it."

"Excellent." He scooped up a dish towel and shoved it into my hands. "Don't worry. You'll have everything you need." He stepped back, out of my personal-space bubble.

"One question."

JT nodded.

"What if they all laugh in my face?"

"They won't. I promise." Was that a little twitch I saw at one corner of his mouth? Was he holding back a guilty grin?

He wouldn't . . . he couldn't be feeding me to the wolves, could he?

"I don't know about that." I gave him some squinty eyes. "You said yourself everyone at the bureau thinks the PBAU is a joke. Who's to say whether the entire Baltimore PD could feel the same way? You could be setting me up."

"Who me?" He batted his eyelashes, which were disgustingly long and thick. "Do you really think I could be that mean?"

"I do."

"Then you don't know me as well as you think." He gave me a little nudge toward the bathroom. "They called us. Remember? Why would they do that if they thought we were a joke?"

"That doesn't mean they'll believe us. I mean, it's a little far-fetched. A bloodsucking vampire that turns into a firefly?"

"It'll be fine. Come on, they're all waiting. And you need a shower." He fanned the air.

"Trying to tell me something?"

"I'm trying to tell you, you should probably do something with your hair if you want anyone to take you seriously."

I patted my head. "Yeah, yeah. Why don't you tell me again how you're doing me a favor?"

* * *

An hour later, we were standing on Baltimore Street, behind the Baltimore Police Department. Concrete walls loomed around me. I had a bad feeling about this. Very bad. I had to make one final try at passing the buck to JT. What could I say or do to make him change his mind?

On the drive over, I'd tried discussing the situation with him, arguing every point he made in favor of my presenting the profile. Finally, when that failed, I begged him to do it.

JT couldn't be swayed.

I was back to bribery. There wasn't much time left.

We entered the building and were directed to a conference room at the end of a narrow hallway.

"Dinner?" I offered as I dragged my feet down the corridor. "With dessert? On me?"

"Sure. Thanks! You owe me a date, anyway." JT beamed.

"Damn, I'd forgotten all about that bet."

"I figured you had. I'm still not letting you off the hook. You're presenting the profile." He opened the conference room door for me, and I stepped inside to face at least thirty Baltimore "boys in blue," as well as Chief Peyton, Chad Fischer, and Gabe. Baltimore's police commissioner announced, "I think we're ready to begin." Everyone started heading for a seat. The shuffle of feet and scrape of chairs being dragged out from under tables echoed off the room's white walls.

JT shook a few hands as he strolled up to the front of the room. I followed him, trying to pretend I wasn't wishing I could become invisible. He chitchatted with Baltimore's police commissioner for a moment before introducing me. I shook Commissioner Allan's hand. He had a strong, sure grip. It matched his demeanor.

"Good to meet you, Commissioner," I said.

"I've heard good things about you, Miss Skye." The commissioner released my hand, but he held my gaze with his sharp eyes. This was a cop through and through, no doubt about it.

"Thank you." I felt my cheeks warming, a surefire sign that I was blushing. How embarrassing.

"Sloan's going to present the profile today," JT told him.

"Very good." Commissioner Allan motioned to the table at the front of the room. "At this point, we've identified three persons of interest in this case. First there's Trey Chapman, who has a motive and opportunity in the cases of Deborah Richardson and Hannah Grant. It appears they were once good friends, until they both discovered he was engaged to both of them . . . at the same time," the commissioner stated. "But we haven't been able to tie him to the other victims. Then there's Yolanda Vargas. She was also a friend of Hannah Grant's. She was the last person to see Grant alive. She has access to a wide variety of infectious agents. What we don't have is a motive. Nor do we have a connection to the other victims. Finally we have Rosemarie Bishop. Outside of living within a quarter mile of Richardson, Miller, Yates, and Quinley, we have nothing on her."

"I think you'll find you actually have more than you think," I said.

"Very good. I'll let you get to it. We want this monster off the street. I'll be glad to know who we're dealing with."

"I think you're in for a surprise, sir," JT said.

The commissioner's smile was knowing. "I've seen a lot of shit in the thirty years I've spent on the force. Nothing surprises me anymore."

I was curious to see if that statement would hold true in this case.

JT steered me toward the front of the room. "Good luck. I'll be right over here if you need me." He stepped to the side.

I cleared my throat, and in a heartbeat, everyone's eyes were fixed on me. "Good morning." A few mumbled responses followed. "My name's Sloan Skye. I'm an intern with the FBI. In this capacity, I've spent some time on this case. My colleagues and I have put together a profile we believe will lead you to the killer." There was the rustle of paper as the officers prepared to jot notes. "Beginning with the basics, based on DNA analysis, we know our unsub is a Caucasian female. And from the crime scenes and MO, we know she is what we call an organized killer. Organized killers are intelligent. They methodically plan their crimes, often use a ploy to lure their victims, and are socially adequate. They are able to conceal their crimes, hiding evidence and disposing of it to hamper a police investigation. They also follow the investigation in the media. To sum it up, they are the Ted Bundys of the world. Our unsub shares all of these traits, with some minor differences. Her crimes have been triggered by a stressor. As a result, she is gradually devolving as she loses control of her body and mind. Her crimes appear on the surface to be well planned. In reality, though, they could be classified as spree kills."

I stopped and scanned the room. So far, so good. The officers were with me. The chief gave me an encouraging nod. JT smiled. I continued: "There is one final difference between our unsub and a classic organized killer. The evidence tells us she is an *adze,* a vampiric creature most commonly found in Africa. The *adze* takes the form of an African species of firefly after sunset. Once it is captured by a child, it adopts the form of an adult family member. It then feeds upon the child every night, creating a strong physical and—on a certain level—an emotional dependence upon the child until it is discovered, dies, or is captured by another child." I paused, expecting a wave of gasps and murmurs to fill the room. But none came. *They believe me?* I glanced at Commissioner Allan. He gave me an I-told-you-nothing-surprises-me look.

Feeling more confident now, I kept going. "If the child is

taken away from him or her, or otherwise lost, an *adze* may go on a killing frenzy, becoming an extremely dangerous killer. Fortunately, this is, as far as I can tell, only the second incidence of an *adze* being discovered in the United States. Somehow, it was transported here, most likely in its insect form."

A patrol officer in the second row raised his hand. At my nod, he asked, "Does this creature have any identifiable features?"

"No," I answered. "When it is in its human form, he or she will appear to everyone around him or her as a normal Homo sapien."

"What about an MO?" another officer asked.

"This is one of the most reliable ways to identify the creature. Its weapon is its bite. To a child, the bite is painful, but not lethal. But to an adult, it is a deadly weapon. The moment its fangs pierce the skin, one of any number of infectious agents are injected into the victim. Ebola, dengue hemorrhagic fever, malaria, typhoid fever. The strains delivered by the *adze* incubate in an accelerated time frame, producing symptoms within hours. Victims die within twenty-four hours. That concludes our profile."

I'd done it. I'd presented the PBAU's first profile. It was over.

JT stepped up. "We would be glad to answer any questions at this time."

One officer raised his hand. At JT's nod, he asked, "What is the safest way to take an *adze* into custody?"

"Good question." JT looked at me.

He wanted me to answer all the questions too? "According to Professor James Skye's research on vampiric beings, the safest way is to apprehend her after she has shifted into insect form. She will change into *Luciola discollis* at sunset and will remain in that form for exactly sixty minutes. Therefore, you may be able to capture her easily enough, but you must transport her quickly to a tightly sealed container large enough to accommodate her human form while safeguarding against escape in insect form." After waiting for a moment, I asked, "Are there any more questions?"

A moment later, Chief Peyton joined me at the front of the room. "If there are no further questions, I'd like to add that my team is available, should your department need any additional support or information. Thank you."

Commissioner Allan stood and thanked us, and that was it. My first profile—our first profile—was done.

Once again, the room filled with the scrape of chairs and the shuffle of feet.

Chief Peyton gave me a smile. "Well done, Skye."

I slanted a look toward JT. "I didn't do it all by myself. I had plenty of help. From JT and"— my gaze swept the room, but I didn't see the person I was looking for—"Gabe too. He was the one who put the two together." The room was pretty much empty now, with the exception of the three of us. I lowered my voice. "I was totally shocked by their reaction when I said it was a vampire. Am I the only one who thought they'd laugh their asses off when I told them that their killer was a paranormal creature?"

JT and Chief Peyton glanced at each other. JT shrugged. "Not really." He laughed. "Okay, I had a small concern that they would have some doubts."

The chief motioned toward the door. "The thing is, whether they believe Rosemarie Bishop can turn into a firefly or not doesn't really matter right now. They'll find out soon enough that it's true."

I grabbed my purse, which was sitting on the table, and checked my cell phone. No call from Mom. No call from Katie either. "Hopefully, they'll take the precautions I suggested. If they don't, they're in for an unpleasant surprise."

"I have a feeling they will. I'm hoping they'll call us in when they're ready to make the apprehension. I'm going to recommend it to Commissioner Allan." Chief Peyton led me toward the exit. "You did great, Skye. But I knew you would."

"Thanks."

Outside, the chief added, "Now, about your mother. . . . Brittany asked me to give you this." She pulled a small envelope out of her pocket and handed it to me. "Take JT with you."

"Thanks." I opened the envelope and unfolded the paper.

The chief said, "She was able to track down that license plate. The car your mother was seen getting into was rented by a James Irvine. He has an out-of-state address. I suggest you check the local hotels. I have a feeling he will be a registered guest. Call in the local PD, once you have his location nailed down."

"Will do."

JT moseyed up to us. "I'm ready for that dinner now, if you are."

I laughed. "It isn't even lunchtime yet."

"That's okay. We'll call it an early dinner." He glanced at the paper in my hands. "What's that?"

"The info you've been waiting for." I handed it to JT and watched him read it.

"I guess dinner can wait till dinnertime. Let's go make some phone calls. To the office?"

"Sure."

We headed toward the car.

Gabe popped out of the vehicle parked next to JT's. "You did good, Sloan," he said, beaming. "I'm jealous as hell, but I'm happy for you."

"Jealous of what?"

"'Jealous of what?'" Gabe echoed. "You got to present our first profile."

"Sorry, maybe next time." I leaned closer. "Frankly, I think they made me do it, just in case we were laughed out of there.

Better if the new girl, with the schizophrenic mother, looks like a fruitcake than the whole team. Right?"

"No doubt." Gabe's jaw twitched ever so slightly as he glanced at JT, who was standing on the opposite side of his car, waiting for me. "The chief has me on paper duty. I'd do anything to get out of it. Where are you headed now? Got anything for me to do?"

I hooked my fingers under the door latch and pulled. "Not bureau business, sorry."

"Damn."

"But I owe you one . . . or two, after all the help you gave me on this case. If I can come up with something, I'll call you."

"Thanks." Gabe elbowed me in the side and whispered, "Watch it with that guy. Coming into the office together might look . . . you know."

"Yeah, I see your point." I pulled open JT's passenger door. "Thanks." I sat, turned to JT, who was just folding his bulky body into place behind the steering wheel, and said, "Maybe we should go back to my place before we head to the office, so I can pick up my car?"

"Sure, whatever you want."

Several hours after a trip home, a drive to the office, and a bagged lunch, we'd found Mr. Irvine. He was a registered guest at a hotel on the Baltimore waterfront. JT called his buddy at the BPD to inform him of what we were about to do. We had no search warrant, so there was no need for police backup. But he wanted to inform them that we were making a visit to a person of interest—just in case something went wrong.

JT asked, "Do you have the stun gun I gave you?" At my guilty headshake, JT took a small gun out of his desk drawer and handed it to me. "Just in case."

I stared down at it, afraid to move my hand. "I think we've already established you're safer if I don't have this. Did you forget what happened at the shooting range?"

JT thought about it for a moment; then he took the gun from me and put it back in the drawer. "I guess you're right." From another drawer, he produced a Taser and slapped that into my hand. "At least if you hit me with this, you won't kill me—though for a minute or two, I might wish you had."

I shoved the Taser into my pocket and headed out to my car. JT pulled up just as I was getting settled in. "Don't you think it would be better if we drove to Baltimore together? Nobody's going to know."

"I guess that would be okay." I made myself comfy in his passenger seat. "Thanks for helping me with this."

"No problem." He zoomed out of the lot.

A half hour later, we pulled into the hotel's parking lot. It was a pretty swanky place, hardly the kind where you'd expect to find a fugitive holed up with a kidnapping victim. As JT drove to the rear of the lot, I craned my neck, looking up, up, up. That was one nice-looking hotel. "I don't know about this."

"What's wrong?" JT parked the car and we climbed out.

"Nothing's wrong. This guy couldn't have kidnapped my mother. Or else . . ." I didn't want to think of the *or else* part. As we walked into the building, I noticed all of the people coming and going. "For one thing, how would he sneak a hostage in here without being noticed?"

"He couldn't." We stopped at the front desk. JT said, "Maybe he gave her a ride somewhere? Let's call him down and ask if he'll talk to us."

"Okay." Hoping Mr. Irvine would know something, and would be willing to cooperate, JT flashed his badge. We asked the woman at the registration desk to call Irvine's room. A few seconds later, she asked for my name. And I repeated it for her. She ended the call, gave us the room number, and directed us to the elevators.

My hands shaking, we strolled across the lobby to the elevators and stepped into the one dedicated to the concierge-level rooms. JT gave me a slightly pitying look as the elevator climbed up, up, up, but he didn't say anything. Neither did I.

When the car stopped at Irvine's floor, we stepped out and headed down a silent hall. My eyes scanned the room numbers displayed on little plaques next to dozens of identical doors. The one we were looking for was at the end.

JT didn't knock right away. He listened. I listened too. I didn't hear anything. I guess JT didn't either. He shrugged and whispered, "I guess we should knock." He rapped his knuckles on the door. A few seconds later, the lock *clacked,* the door swung open, and I got the shock of my life.

The man standing in front of me was the spitting image of my father, twenty-some years ago. Same breathtaking face, with those brilliant blue eyes that seemed too clear and bright to be real. Same perfectly carved cheekbones and angled jaw. Same wavy blond hair that skimmed his thickly muscled shoulders. Same heavily muscled body. The resemblance was so striking, it took my breath away.

JT keyed into my reaction right away. He grabbed my elbow, steadying me, and turned worried eyes my way.

"It's okay." I pulled my arm out of his grasp. "He looks like someone I knew a long time ago." I offered my hand to Irvine. "I'm Sloan Skye, and this is Special Agent Jordan Thomas. We're with the FBI. If it's okay, we'd like to ask you a few questions regarding a recent disappearance."

"Absolutely." The man stepped aside, welcoming us into a well-appointed suite with a to-die-for view of the harbor. Still feeling a little woozy after the shock of seeing a man who could easily pass for my long-dead father, I made a beeline for the closest chair. Just as my butt hit the cushion, my mother came strolling into the room, wearing a man's white shirt and boxer shorts.

"Mom!" I charged at her like a little kid who'd become lost in a packed mall on Black Friday and threw my arms around her neck. "I'm so glad you're all right!"

Mom shrugged out of my hold. "Of course I'm okay. Whatever made you think I wasn't?"

"I've been searching for you for days." I didn't bother mentioning the part about freaking out with worry.

"Searching? Why? I told you where I was going. And then, just in case you forgot, I left a note."

"I don't remember you telling me anything. And I didn't find any note. Where'd you leave it?"

"In the car. On the seat. Didn't you see it?"

"No."

"Oh, dear." Mom pressed a hand to her mouth and glanced at her new male friend. "I'm sorry, honey. I never expected you to worry about me." She motioned to the man. "I have something to tell you." She walked me back to the chair I'd abandoned and waited for me to sit. She dragged an identical one across from mine and sat, leaning forward. "This"—she waited for Irvine to step closer—"is your father."

I glanced at James Irvine, then at my mom, then at him again. "Okay, I can see why you'd think that's him, because he looks exactly like Dad did years ago, but he can't be—"

"Yes, he can. I thought he was dead, but there was never a body. He wasn't buried."

I looked at Irvine again, and I decided I didn't trust him. Who was this guy? Was he related to my father somehow— a nephew, perhaps?—or was he someone trying to pull off pretending to be him? Why? What did he want? "If this is Dad, why'd he wait so long to come back?" I glared at Irvine, letting him know I wasn't a fool. Then I stood and grabbed my mom's hand. "Maybe we should go talk about this some-where else, somewhere private?"

Mom wasn't budging. "No, Sloan. There's a reason why he stayed away. Please give him a chance to explain." When I didn't respond, she repeated, "Please."

I peeked at JT. He had nothing to say. I narrowed my eyes at the man who wanted me to think he was my father. Under closer scrutiny, I could see some faint signs of aging: a few lines at the corners of his eyes, a slight thinning of his hair at the hairline, a few gray hairs sprinkled in with the blond. Then I peered at Mom, who looked like she'd just enjoyed a tumble in the hay with her long-dead husband.

Was Irvine really her husband? My father?

If so, could he have a valid reason to have stayed away for so many years?

There was one way to know if this man was my father or not. "So, if you're my dad, what was my favorite book when I was two?" Only a parent would know such a thing. Unless, Mom had told him. "No hints from you, Mom," I warned her.

Mom nodded.

The man smiled—and damn, if my heart didn't flutter just a little at the sight. That expression brought back so many memories—genuinely happy ones—from before Mom got sick, and things got hard, and I had to become the parent.

"Your favorite book when you were two was *The Meaning of Relativity,* by Albert Einstein. You said you were going to make a time travel machine when you grew up."

"Damn," I muttered. I glanced at Mom. "You didn't tell him?"

She was teary-eyed. "I swear I didn't. We haven't done a lot of talking. . . ." She blushed.

The man, who might be my father, sat on the arm of Mom's chair. "I had to disappear for a while. To protect you and your mother."

"From what?"

"From some very dangerous . . . people." The man—my dad?—put his arm on Mom's shoulder. "The problem is, they've found you, and my staying away wasn't going to protect you any longer." Immediately my thoughts turned to my nocturnal visitor. "I can't explain everything right now." His gaze slid to JT. "We'll talk later."

JT took the hint. He moseyed toward the door. "I guess I'll head back to the office. If you're okay, Sloan?"

I glanced at my mom and dad. They both nodded. "Yeah. I'm okay." I wobbled on somewhat shaky legs to him. "Thanks for everything, JT." I gave him a little kiss on the cheek and locked the door after he left. Then I turned toward the man who'd walked out of my life over twenty years ago, and said, "We're alone now. I'm ready to hear the whole truth."

Who in the world am I? Ah, that's the great puzzle.

—Lewis Carroll

25

Before he would say another word, my father insisted I sit. He didn't have to work too hard at convincing me. I took the nearest seat, curled my fingers around the cushion's edge, and braced myself for another shock.

What could possibly keep a man away from the wife and child he supposedly loved?

My mother was gazing at him with love in her eyes and a girlish flush to her cheeks. I had to admit, she looked younger and more alive than I'd ever seen her. It was as if she'd taken a dip in the Fountain of Youth. Seeing her like this—so happy, so radiant—stirred up my emotions even more.

But I wasn't feeling all gushy and mushy and happy.

I was feeling furious. Bitter and distrusting.

Just look at her! Look at that twinkle in her eye. How could he have stolen all those years of happiness from that woman? All those minutes, hours, days, weeks, and months of this kind of joy? She'd suffered and struggled for so long.

It was wrong. So, so wrong.

". . . after I'd published that article, everything changed," he said.

I realized I'd been completely lost in thought and hadn't heard what he'd been saying. I decided it was better if I cut to the chase. Why sit through a long, drawn-out explanation about published articles and supposed danger? The bottom line was he'd abandoned us, left us to fend for ourselves, and let us believe all of this time that he was dead. Nobody did that to people they loved.

"You couldn't have loved us," I said, my voice a low growl, sounding foreign to my own ears. "You stayed away for over twenty years. Nothing could keep me away from the people I love for that long. Especially if they were in danger."

He pulled up a chair, positioning it across from me, and sat. "I understand how you feel—"

I leapt to my feet and yelled, "How could you?" My nose was burning, damn it. I didn't want to cry. I wouldn't let myself bawl. I sniffled. "Have you ever been abandoned?"

"Yes, I have, Sloan."

My gaze snapped to his eyes and I saw the emotions churning in their depth, but that didn't stop me from lashing out at him. The emotions were too powerful to hold back, like a storm surge pouring over a break wall. "If you were abandoned, how could you do that to someone else? To someone who needed you? Loved you? With all her heart!" I stabbed my index finger at my mother, who was standing at his side, like the obedient, loving wife she would have loved to be for him. "Look at her. Look at her face, her eyes. Do you have any idea how much she's suffered?"

My father looked at my mother. "Yes, I do. You can't imagine how many times I wanted to come back to her. It nearly killed me."

"Don't even try to gain my sympathy," I spat through gritted teeth.

"I'm not." Looking at me now, he said, "I don't want your sympathy."

I crossed my arms over my chest and circled around the chair, putting it between him and me. I set my hands on the chair's back, using it to steady myself. "Then what do you want?"

"I want . . . I need . . . your trust."

I laughed. It was a hollow, bitter sound, which echoed through the room.

"Sloan," my mother said.

My gaze snapped to Mom, and for a moment, the rage eased a little. But then it welled even higher. "This is bullshit, Mom. I can see you love him. But he's going to hurt you again." To him, that man, I said, "It would've been better if you'd never come back."

"You're right. I would've stayed away if I could have, after all this time." He visibly sighed. "But they've found you. Nobody else can protect you like I can."

I didn't want to know—I really didn't. But I asked anyway: "Who's *they*?"

"The *Sluagh*." He reached for Mom's hand and pulled her closer to him.

"'*Sluagh*'?" I echoed. Sounded like the bad guys in a low-budget sci-fi movie. "Seriously?"

"I know what you're thinking," he dared to say.

"Stop saying that. You couldn't know what I'm thinking, because you don't know me."

"I'm sorry, Sloan. You're right. I don't know you well enough."

"You don't know me *at all*."

"But I do. I know your favorite book. I know you like custard-filled donuts, and hate jelly-filled ones. I know you've always dreamed of being an FBI agent. And now that you have the job you've been wishing for, you're afraid you aren't capable of handling it. And I know about the creature who has been visiting you at night."

He did?

How?

Feeling a little off balance, I decided to sit again. "What do you know about that? Do you know what it is? And what does it want?"

"He's the reason why I left twenty years ago. And why I came back." James Irvine pointed at me. "He wants you, Sloan."

"I kinda got that. But for what?"

"For his bride."

Now, this was really sounding like a low-budget film. That wasn't what I was expecting. Not at all. "This is a joke."

Then again, why hadn't I been expecting such an off-the-wall explanation? All of my life, I'd been telling people my father was delusional. Enough said.

The man who called himself my father sighed. He stood, circled the room, then stopped next to my mother. "The reason why I published that article so long ago, the one that got me fired, was because I was trying to put an end to all of humanity's fears."

"I don't understand. I thought you started researching vampires because . . ." I didn't finish the sentence. For some reason, I felt stupid saying what I'd thought.

". . . because you were being attacked?" he finished for me.

"Well, maybe," I admitted, feeling foolish.

"Not exactly. You were young then. I could see why you'd think that. The truth is, I have known all my life that vampires exist." He sat again, then leaned forward. "Your mother begged me not to tell anyone, not even you. But I thought I should do the opposite, drag the proverbial skeletons out of the closet. If only mankind could accept that certain beings were real—could see them for what they are, and aren't—then maybe things could change."

"Change? How?"

He didn't answer right away. He glanced at my mother. They exchanged a look. "We could stop hiding in the shadows."

"We?" I echoed.

My father nodded. "We. As in, the Mythics. There are many of us. Some dark. Some light."

Mythics. I assumed it was a broad term, used by all kinds of mythical beings.

If this conversation had taken place a few weeks ago, I would have been convinced by now that my father was genuinely delusional. "Which are you?"

"Light. I'm the high commander of Her Majesty's armies."

"What queen is that?"

"Queen of the elves. I'm not human, and neither are you."

"Elves, you say?" An image of little happy men in red-and-green suits, singing Christmas carols while building toy trucks, played through my mind.

"I've also held a position with the FBI, consulting on cases involving Mythics when needed—though not many people know about that. Though now that the PBAU has been formed, I doubt I'll be doing much more work for the FBI."

"I see." I didn't know what to say. Then a question popped into my head. "Did you have anything to do with the formation of the PBAU?"

"Maybe a little."

That explained the chief's questions during my first day on the job.

Which led to my next question: "Did I get the job because of you?"

"No. You were selected for the job because you were the best candidate. I'm very proud of you, Sloan."

"I see." My brain was churning. I needed time to sort this all out. Elves. Mythics. My father, alive, working for the FBI. "That explains a lot." I stood. "Okay, I think I'm ready to go home now."

"No, Sloan." My father shook his head. "It isn't safe for you to go anywhere until I've explained some things."

"Your father was the one who was paying me to follow you," Mom interjected, setting a hand on his shoulder. "Of course, I didn't know it at first. He used a false name, to hide his identity. He was worried about you. About us. All of our correspondence was done through e-mail. The payments were sent electronically."

Before I could summon up a response to Mom's news, my phone rang. I checked it. Gabe. "If you don't mind, I think I'll take this call."

"Not at all." My mother turned to my dad and smiled. "We'll just head to the bedroom to . . . talk."

At the bedroom door, my dad, the elf, said, "Sloan, I must warn you, you can't tell anyone about me. You don't know who you can trust and who you can't yet."

"Warning heeded." A couple of questions popped into my head. "You didn't happen to break into my car, did you? Or clobber my partner over the head at a coffee shop?"

"No. I've kept my distance to protect you." So much for solving those mysteries. "One more thing," my father said, his expression serious. "If you absolutely must leave this suite, which I strongly suggest you avoid, be sure to return by twilight. Not a minute later."

"Will do." I waved him off, then answered the call. "Gabe, what's up?"

"Sloan, it's about Chief Peyton. The chief is missing. The team needs your help."

I glanced at the closed bedroom door. "Where are you?"

"At the Bishop house."

I checked the time. Twilight was hours away. "I'll be there in a half hour."

When I turned the corner onto Summer Sky Path, something struck me like a brick.

Twilight.

That was a major problem if I was going to help in the apprehension of Rosemarie Bishop, the *adze*. To be safe, we needed to wait until she shifted into her insect form, at twilight.

Driving my father's rental, I called Gabe, to talk about

maybe waiting one night. Gabe told me that wasn't an option. Bishop was holding the chief hostage somewhere, and she had bitten her. If we didn't locate the chief within the next few hours, and get her to a hospital for treatment, she would most likely die.

It came down to a choice. Between my personal safety and the chief's life. That was no easy decision to make.

If only I could think of a way to apprehend the *adze* before sunset safely. If only . . .

"Here's what we've got," Gabe said, rushing toward me as I scrambled out of the rental car a short time later. "The chief's been missing for a couple of hours now. Bishop says she has her hidden and has bitten her, infecting her with a strain of West Nile that replicates every ten minutes. If the chief doesn't get treatment by sunset, she'll die."

"Damn," I muttered. "What does Bishop want in return for the chief?"

"Her daughter, Veronica." He hurried me toward the high-tech mobile station, which was set up by the Clarksville and Baltimore Police Departments. "She's still at camp."

"Knowing what I do about the *adze,* I can't figure out why Bishop let Veronica go in the first place. Has anyone gone to get her?"

"JT's taking care of that. He's in a bureau helicopter, en route."

"Okay."

Gabe leaned against one of the many police cars parked in front of the Bishop house. "Of course, we aren't going to turn the kid over."

"Of course."

"JT seems to think you'll figure out a way to capture the creature without making the exchange."

My heart stopped for a moment. Luckily, it started up again. "He has a lot of faith in me." More than I had, that was for sure.

"We all do."

I dug in my pocket and pulled out my phone, dialing the hotel I'd just left. My parents' room phone rang and rang, and rang, while I chanted, "Pick it up, pick it up, pick it up." No luck there. I ended the call and stuffed my phone in my pocket again.

What now?

"Do we have communication with Bishop?" I asked as we watched officers in riot gear stream out of a black Hummer.

"We have a phone number." Gabe opened the mobile command center's door for me, and I stomped up the steps. He introduced me to the officer in charge, then directed me toward a phone that was wired to recording equipment.

"I can try to talk to Bishop, I guess," I offered, pretty much convinced it wasn't going to do a damn thing. In my mind's eye, I could see pages and pages of my father's research. I'd read everything he'd written on the *adze*. I *knew* how it metamorphosed. I *knew* what it ate. I *knew* where it lived. I *didn't know* how to capture it in human form. It wouldn't be as simple as one might think. Despite the fact that this *adze* had possessed the body of a middle-aged woman, the creature would possess sharper senses, faster reflexes, and greater strength than its host.

Did it have a vulnerability?

The lieutenant dialed the number and handed me the phone. Bishop answered on the second ring.

"Do you have what I want?" she asked.

"We're working on it." I mouthed a thank-you to Gabe as he slid a pad of paper and pen across the table for me.

"Who is this?" she snapped.

"My name is Sloan Skye. I'm with the FBI."

"I know you. This is your fault."

"My fault? Why's that?" I asked, doodling on the paper.

"Because you wouldn't leave me alone. You just had to keep digging and digging. Why can't you see?"

"See what?"

"That needing that child's blood doesn't make me evil."

"I understand," I said, not 100 percent agreeing with her, but sort of understanding where she was coming from. Maybe, I thought, as she rattled on—justifying her actions, and explaining how painful her condition was—all of those years of dealing with Mom and her delusions would help me handle this situation? Was it possible I could talk Bishop out of a standoff? "That kind of pain would make anyone desperate."

"Exactly." Bishop sighed. "I tried the palm oil. It barely took the edge off. The longer Veronica was gone, the more it burned. Until the palm oil did nothing anymore. That's when I took Eden. I took very good care of her, though. I was going to give her back as soon as Veronica came home."

"Yes, of course you were. You couldn't help yourself," I said, trying to present a sympathetic ear. "You needed a child's blood."

"I couldn't. I tried." There was silence. I wondered if she'd hung up.

"Are you still there?" I asked.

"Yes. It's hurting. Very bad."

I scribbled some notes, then slid the paper toward Gabe. "Veronica is on the way. She'll be here. But not before sunset."

More silence.

Bishop said, "The other agent said she'd be here before that."

"They sent a helicopter to pick her up." I glanced at a clock. "It's almost seven. Sunset is at eight forty-nine tonight. There's no chance they'll make it."

"They lied. Or you're lying." Anger. I heard anger. But also desperation.

"No, I'm telling the truth. Now you need to tell me where you've hidden Peyton."

"If I tell you, I won't get Veronica. You'll wait until I change and throw me in a concrete cell. Do you know what hell that would be for me? To be denied blood for so long? It hurts, Sloan Skye. Every cell in this body burns."

I skimmed my notes. "Isn't there another way? What about blood from cadavers?" I said, thinking aloud.

"Dead blood is useless."

"And adults?" I asked.

"Toxic."

"Animals?" I suggested.

"Hell no."

I scribbled some more notes. "You're not making this easy."

"Believe me, I wish I could. Do you think I chose to be this way? Do you think I like being this dependent upon anything? Anyone? Let alone an innocent child? Would you want to depend upon something for sustenance that everyone, including yourself, felt compelled to protect and cherish?"

That would be rough. "No, I wouldn't."

"Bring me the child," she demanded.

"I'll see what I can do."

The call ended. I turned to Gabe.

"Now what?" he asked. "Did you get anything else from her?"

"No, outside of the fact that she does feel a little guilty about having to feed from a child."

"Hmm." Gabe chewed his lower lip. "It has to be a kid's blood?"

"Yes."

"Why? I wonder."

"Not sure." I dug out my phone again and called Katie, asking her if she knew anyone who might be able to shed some light on the difference between the blood of adults and children. She gave me the phone number of a friend who was in medical school. I called her.

"There wouldn't be any significant difference," the medical student told me a couple of minutes later. "Blood is blood is blood, taking into account the differences between blood types, of course. There are varying levels of sugars, protein, and iron in each person's blood, but all human beings share the same components—whether they're adults or children."

So much for that. I thanked her and ended the call. "Strike one," I told Gabe.

"Maybe it isn't biological?" Gabe offered as he drummed his hands on the table between us.

"If it isn't biological, what would it be? Environmental?" Now, that made sense. "Bishop did say adult blood was 'toxic.'"

"Toxic, huh?" Gabe gnawed on his lower lip. "Here's a thought. Adults have been exposed to more pollutants than children—in food, in the air, through their skin. Some of those pollutants might appear in trace amounts in their blood."

"Okay. I could see that. So where could we find pollutant-free blood?"

Gabe shrugged. "From a donor who lives out in the middle of nowhere, eats only organic food, and doesn't touch anything that's been dyed, treated, or dusted with chemicals?"

"That pretty much rules out anyone in the U.S."

We sat and thought for a few minutes.

"What about cord blood?" I wondered. "Would that contain toxins?"

"Maybe some. There are substances that cross over the placenta, to the fetus. But the cord blood shouldn't contain as many contaminants as an adult's blood."

"It's worth a shot. Do you know anyone who's banked some?"

Gabe thought for a minute. He slapped his flattened hands on the table. "My sister just had a kid. Maybe she had some collected? She told me she was looking into it."

"If she did, do you think she'd be willing to give a little of it up, in the name of science?"

"I don't know." Gabe checked the clock. "This is a long

shot. Say she did have some collected, and she agrees to give up a little. Now would we get it now? It's late."

"I don't know. Maybe someone in the FBI can pull some strings."

"Okay. I'll see what I can do." He made a phone call and took down some information. Minutes later, we were flying down the freeway, on our way to the cord blood bank, with Fischer in the backseat. It was no small feat, getting our hands on the little plastic bag of harvested blood, but a call from some high-ranking agent I hadn't met, along with Fischer's badge, made the impossible possible. Within a half hour, we were speeding back toward Clarksville, a cooler protecting the frozen blood. As we rolled up in front of the house, I called Bishop on my cell and told her I had something that might work, but I'd only give it to her if she first told me where Chief Peyton had been hidden. As proof, I stood outside her house, in front of a window. I pulled the still-frozen bag from the cooler and held it up for her to see. "Harvested cord blood from a newborn infant," I explained.

Bishop licked her lips. "Your FBI agent is in the school, locked in the janitor's closet."

I waited on the porch while Gabe and Fischer went to the school. With the freezer clutched to my chest, I felt one very hungry *adze* staring at me with fierce eyes. My phone rang. Gabe told me they had Chief Peyton, and I handed the desperate *adze* what I hoped would be her salvation.

She didn't wait; she slammed the screen door, locked it, and sank her fangs into the plastic bag. Her eyelids fell closed, and an expression of pure bliss spread over her face. Still, I took a step back, just in case that bliss was short-lived.

"Thank you," Bishop said through her screen. "Can you get me more?"

I tried not to stare at the smudge of blood on the side of her mouth. "I can't. But maybe the government can. If you turn yourself in."

She looked down at the drained medical bag in her hand, then at me. "If there's any chance I wouldn't have to hurt a child again, I'm willing to do it." She stepped out onto the porch, extended her arms in front of herself, and I put on the handcuffs and led her down the front walk. The police took it from there.

When she reached the car, she turned to me. "You want to know about the women."

I nodded. "I do."

"Veronica was more than a source of sustenance to me. She was my . . . everything. Life lifeline. When I lost her, I tried to hold it together. I swear I did. But the hunger was excruciating, a relentless, crippling, gnawing pain. Have you ever been in such horrible agnoy that you need to lash out at someone? At the one who caused it? I'd lost everything. And all I could think about was getting Veronica back and making that bitch pay."

"What bitch?"

"My sister, the one who kidnapped Veronica and wouldn't tell me where she'd hidden her. I knew I couldn't kill her. She was the only one who knew where Veronica was. But when I saw that woman . . . those women . . . they were her. And when I bit . . ." She closed her eyes. Her expression softened. "There was peace. For a little while. Until I saw her again."

"In your mind, you were killing your sister, then? Killing a surrogate because you couldn't kill the real person?" I asked. "Those women died only because they looked like someone else."

When Bishop opened her eyes, they were dead. Cold. "Yes. It's what I had to do. I had no choice."

The officer holding her wrists gave her a nudge. "That's enough. Let's go."

I stepped back and watched as the car pulled away, my heart heavy for all the innocent lives that confused, desperate, twisted . . . monster . . . had destroyed.

A couple of minutes later, Gabe clapped me on the back. "That was fucking brilliant, Skye. Who would've thought of cord blood?"

"Thanks." Squinting against the glare of the setting sun, hovering but heavy over the western horizon, I smiled. I'd done it. I'd talked a dangerous creature into turning herself in. "How's Chief Peyton?"

"She's getting treatment. Fischer went with her to the hospital."

"I hope she'll be okay."

"If it wasn't for you, she wouldn't have any chance at all."

Turning my back on the activity still humming around us, I headed for the rental car.

"Where are you going now?" Gabe asked, following me. "I thought we could go have a celebratory drink."

As I opened the car door, I glanced at the western sky. "I'll have to take a rain check. Thanks, anyway." I climbed in, strapped myself up, and roared toward the freeway.

The final streaks of sunlight faded just as the car was rolling down the freeway exit ramp.

"The master's waiting," a voice hissed behind me.

A single event can awaken within us a stranger totally unknown to us. To live is to be slowly born.

—Antoine de Saint-Exupéry

26

I jerked the steering wheel, and the car hit the curb and bounced over it, tearing up someone's front yard as I slammed on the brakes. I flung open the door; but before I could launch myself out of the vehicle, a pair of hands, very strong ones, clapped around my neck like a collar. I flopped and fought in a panic, but I didn't break free. The world dimmed, darkened. I needed air. I needed . . .

Next thing I knew, I was gasping, lurching upright. The room was dark. I was lying on something soft. A bed, maybe. Straining to see around me, I pawed my way across what seemed to be a very wide mattress until I found the edge. I set a foot on a carpeted floor and fumbled across the room, hands in front of me, sweeping back and forth in the shadows. They struck something big, something cold, and icy dread trickled up my arms, my spine, to my nape. I shivered.

"You're awake," he said.

No shit, Sherlock. "Does that come as a surprise?" I asked, stumbling backward. This guy was the epitome of creepy. There wasn't a thing about him that didn't make my skin crawl. His voice. His smell. His touch. His face.

"Yes and no. I didn't think you'd wake so soon. It's a pleasant surprise."

"A pleasant surprise for you, maybe." I groped my way across the room, heading in the opposite direction, away from that awful voice. Within a short distance, I smacked my shin .on something, and slammed my elbow on something else. Why was this room so freaking dark? "Damn it, I'm going to break my neck. Would you mind turning on a light?"

"I suppose I could do that." A lamp snapped on, filling what I soon realized was a large space with dim light. Even so, I had to squint against the glare as I took a look around. Within seconds, I'd surveyed the situation, and my eyes had adjusted.

I was in a very large bedroom, an extremely opulent one, with Mr. Stinky, my unwelcome nocturnal visitor.

"Make yourself comfortable. Please," my host said, motioning toward the bed.

"No thanks. I'd be more comfortable in another room." *A hundred miles away from you.*

"Yes, I suppose you would."

I moved as far from the bed as I could get, without backing myself into a corner. "Do you mind telling me why you brought me here?"

"I told you I was tired of waiting. It took us three tries. I was beginning to think we'd never get you in time."

Three tries? I wondered what he'd meant by that. I took a few side steps, figuring I'd slowly work my way toward the door. I needed to keep him talking, distracted, if I was going to escape. "Waiting for what? Why'd you want to 'get' me, anyway?"

"For you to come to here." He moved toward me. I didn't like that.

Keeping my back to the wall, I bypassed a pair of closet doors. "You said you'd tried three times. When?"

"At the coffee shop. And once in the parking lot at Quantico. It's hell getting onto that base."

"At the coffee shop? Was it you who clobbered my partner on the head and tossed him in the trash?"

"Not technically."

"And you broke my car window?"

"Again, not exactly."

"Would you care to explain it, then?"

Mr. Stinky shrugged. "It was all part of the game."

"Oh, yes. 'The game.'" I started shuffling a little faster. My hands were shaking as they skimmed along the wall. My heart was pounding against my breastbone so heavily, it ached. This guy was a big question mark. I had no idea how to handle him yet. "I don't understand. What game did you think we were playing?"

"Cat and mouse. How did you know how much I enjoy a good chase?"

"I swear, I didn't know."

"There you go again." He prowled closer, and I stepped back, heading in the opposite direction now, having no choice. I had to keep as much distance between us as I could. End of story. There was no saying what this man would do to me if he got his hands on me now. "You're so clever, playing me like this. Drives me crazy." His expression turned feral. That was not a look I wanted. Not now. Not ever. At least, not from him.

Oh, shit. I started moving away from him faster. "I swear to God, it isn't an act."

He grimaced. "Don't speak that name. Not ever."

"What name? *God?*"

His expression darkened even more. "Stop it."

"What's wrong?" I scrutinized his body language. "You act as if it hurts." Had I stumbled upon a vulnerability?

"It doesn't hurt. It just isn't a pleasant sound," he said through gritted teeth.

"What about *Jesus*? Can I say *Jesus*?" I asked, noting his reaction, which looked like a kid who'd just watched a friend eat a live bug. "Is *Jesus* a bad word too? Oh, dear. *Jesus. Sweet Jesus.* My *God,* what's wrong?" He literally doubled over and clapped his hands over his ears. I shouted, *"Good God! Sweet Jesus! Jesus, Jesus, Jesus!"* I sprinted toward the door, hoping he'd move a little slower than normal, and praying that the door would be unlocked.

It wasn't.

Damn.

I whirled around to find he was standing much too close for my comfort. He thrust his arms out, caging my head between them. The back of my skull ground against the door. "That wasn't nice."

"Oh God. Sorry," I blurted, trying not to inhale through my nose. The man really did need a shower. And some superstrength deodorant. Not to mention mouthwash.

"Hmm." He grimaced, his nostrils flaring. "The scent of fear is so intoxicating."

So much for the holy words. I let my knees buckle, sliding down the door, and scuttled across the floor. "What do you want from me?"

"You know what I want."

I did, but I was trying to keep him talking, to buy time. Until I could . . . do what? How the hell was I going to get out of this? I glanced at the clock. It was a little after ten. Was anyone wondering where I'd gone? Did anyone realize I was missing?

"I've waited a long time for this, when you will be my bride."

"I can't marry you," I jabbered. "I . . . uh, don't know your name."

"It's . . . Elmer," he mumbled, his ghostly white face turning pinkish purple.

"Did you say, 'Elmer'?"

"Yes," he snapped. "Now you know my name. We can get married."

"No, we can't."

His lips, barely there as it was, thinned. "You said—"

"I . . . don't have a dress. Or anything. What kind of wedding would it be if I didn't have a dress? Or flowers? Or witnesses?"

"I took care of the witness part. The rest—"

"And isn't the father of the bride supposed to give his daughter away at the wedding?"

"That's impossible."

"But the dress." I turned on my best sad-eyed expression. "I have to have a dress."

He sighed. "I suppose I could do something about the dress. The wedding's not until tomorrow."

"Tomorrow? That's great! That gives me time to plan. How about a maid of honor? Couldn't I have a maid of honor? She could come tonight. She could help me get everything ready."

He thought about it a moment and heaved another sigh. "I'll probably regret this, but okay. I'll let you have one friend attend. But I will call her. Not you. Can't risk you warning her."

"Okay. I want my roommate, Katie. Her cell number's programmed in my phone, wherever that is. She's very discreet, if you get my drift." I hoped Katie would call my mom when she heard I was about to elope. It was my only hope.

Elmer, my soon-to-be husband, nodded, gave me a leer, which made me shiver, and left the room.

Of course, the minute he was out of my sight, I checked for an escape route. The window was boarded up, and I tore every fingernail off my hands trying to pry the wood away. The door was locked, from the outside. The adjacent bathroom had no window. I was trapped. And there was nothing I could do but wait.

I did a lot of thinking and pacing for the next couple of hours. I had a plan. I prayed it would work, but I knew I'd need some impossibly good luck to pull it off. The door's lock finally rattled at a few minutes before midnight. I cut off the lights and took my position—back flat against the wall, armed with the lamp, the only weapon I could find. The door creaked open, and a slice of light pierced the thick darkness. I jumped out from my hiding spot, swung my weapon, and clobbered the person standing in my way. A woman screamed and stumbled to the side, clearing my escape route. I charged out into a bright hallway. Somewhat blind, I raced toward the end of the hall. I made it as far as the last doorway. But then a very large man put his huge body directly in my path, and I crashed into him. He hauled me off my feet.

I kicked. I screamed. I shouted "God" and "Jesus" at the top of my lungs. Nothing worked. I was soon sitting in my dungeon again, being stared down by a woman with a pack of ice held to her nose.

She'd been the unfortunate person who'd tried to enter my room.

A few minutes later, an enormous man dragged a rolling rack full of white wedding gowns into the room and left.

"Pick wub," the woman with the ice snapped.

"'Wub'?" I echoed.

She glared.

"Oh, one. Got it." I went to the rack, flipped through them. "Sorry, there's nothing here that'll fit me. I'm a size six."

"Ib your dreabs," the ice woman said.

I gave her a serious I'm-sorry face. "I guess I deserve that for breaking your nose. Are you okay? I didn't mean to hurt you." I looked for any hint of forgiveness, but I didn't find any. I decided I'd try to get her to help me, anyway. "You see, I've been kidnapped and am being forced to marry Elmer—"

"Dot by probleb." The woman jabbed a finger at the rack. "Pick wub. Or I'll pick for you."

"Fine." I grabbed the first dress I touched and threw it on the bed. "I picked *wub*. You know, aiding in a kidnapping is a crime."

"So is breakig subwub's dose." She grabbed the rack and

started wheeling it toward the door. "This is the last tibe I'll ever bake a house call."

I followed her. "I'm very sorry. I was trying to escape. I'm not lying. I'm being held here against my will, and I'm scared."

The woman turned toward me, made a point of looking around the room, and shrugged her shoulders. "Could be worse." She knocked; the door opened; she left.

That was it. I'd lost all faith in basic human kindness. Sheesh. *Could be worse?* What kind of thing was that to say to someone who had been kidnapped? I slumped on the bed.

I was back to praying Katie would come through for me. It was looking like she was my only hope. I nibbled at a ragged fingernail and waited to see who would pay me a visit next, and hoping it wouldn't be my future husband.

A half hour later, the door opened, and Katie, hauling an overnight bag, dashed in. "Sloan? Why didn't you tell me you were engaged?" The door slammed shut behind her. "I brought everything I could think of. Makeup, curling iron, hair spray, razors. Oh, my God, was it because I was sick? Is that why you didn't say anything? You've got to tell me everything. Leave nothing out. Who is he?"

I pointed at the locked door. "Before tonight, I hadn't realized I was engaged."

Clearly perplexed, Katie glanced at the door. "What do you mean?"

"I'm being held hostage. And now you are too. Please tell me you called my mother."

Katie shook her head. "No, I didn't. I figured it was a big secret and you'd tell her if you wanted her to know."

"Damn." For the hell of it, I checked the door. Locked. "Do you have your phone?"

Katie grinned. "Sure!" She shoved her hand into the bag's front pocket. She grimaced. "Well, I could have sworn it was here a minute ago. Oh, that's right. I loaned it to the guy who drove me here. Now that I think of it, I don't remember him giving it back. You know, I thought it was strange a limo driver didn't have a cell phone." She headed toward the window. "No problem, we can just"—she yanked open the drapes—"oh."

"Yeah."

"Okay." Katie plopped on the bed next to me. "What's going on?"

I summed up the last twelve hours or so in as few words as I could; then Katie and I sat there, staring at each other, wondering what to do next.

"You might as well try on the dress," she offered, checking out the gown. "Wow, is this gorgeous! I bet it cost a small fortune." Standing, she held it up to herself and sighed. "Don't take this wrong, but I was a little jealous when I first heard. I'm beginning to think it's never going to happen for me."

"What are you talking about? Jesse adores you."

"Jesse and I broke up." She smoothed the beaded material against her body.

Now, that was a shocker. "You did? When? Why didn't I know about this?"

"It happened before the bug thing."

"Oh, hon." I scrabbled to my feet and flung my arms around Katie. "Why didn't you tell me?"

"Because you were so busy with your new job. And then I got sick, and I didn't really care . . . but I do now." She snuffled, her nose buried in the crook of my neck. "I miss him, damn it."

"What happened?" I rubbed her back.

"I don't know. He just called me one day and said it was over. And that was it, the last I've heard from him."

"Bastard. He broke up with you over the phone?"

Katie wriggled out of my embrace and smeared away the tears dribbling down her face. "I guess it's better than a text, right?"

"I'm sorry, hon. That's shitty."

She wrapped her arms around herself and the dress, hugging it to her torso. I recognized the gesture's significance. She was feeling defensive. "You never liked him, anyway. I know that. Although you tried to pretend otherwise."

"I am the world's worst actress. Not much of a liar either." I rubbed Katie's back again. "I just always had a bad feeling about him."

"Turns out you were right."

"I'm *sorry* I was right." I took the dress from Katie and set it on the bed.

"Enough about that." Katie started digging through the contents of her bag. She produced a handheld computer. "Look what I found. I forgot I had this in here." She started poking buttons. "I hope the battery's not dead. If I get it powered up, can you e-mail someone for help? How about JT?"

"I can try. He's probably asleep. But I think he forwards his e-mail to his phone." I typed up a quick e-mail, giving him as many details as I could, which wasn't much. As I typed, I said, "One particular bit of information would be very handy—our location. I don't suppose they let you see where they were taking you?"

"Not exactly. I rode in the back of a limousine. With very darkly tinted windows. I didn't see a thing, and I wasn't really trying to keep track because I didn't realize I should be." Katie's shoulders sagged. "I suck at this secret-agent stuff, don't I?"

"No, you don't suck." I patted her knee. "You didn't even know you needed to be a secret agent. We'll think of something."

Katie started pacing. "Maybe the FBI can track your cell phone? It has GPS, doesn't it?"

"Sure, but I'm guessing it's been shut off to guard against just that."

"Probably. Shit." Katie walked another lap around the

room. "The ride wasn't long. Fifteen or twenty minutes, tops. That should narrow down the search area."

"Sure. If you traveled fifteen miles, that means the search area is over seven hundred square miles. Can you give me anything?"

"Uhn." Katie took another lap, halting in front of me. I was glad she stopped. She was making me dizzy. "Okay, I *think* we got on the JFK. And I'm pretty sure we went north."

"That's a start." I added the info and shot the e-mail over to JT. Then I checked my e-mail once, twice, ten times. No response. "No answer. Damn. I bet he crashed early tonight. Our case is closed. And he thinks I'm with my mom." I checked my mailbox again. Nothing. "Maybe I can Google *'Sluagh'* while we wait. No sense sitting here, wasting time." I opened another browser window. The little machine *chug-chug-chugged.* "This Internet browser sucks. It's so slow."

"Yeah, that's why I barely used the stupid thing. Doesn't help that it has less memory than a cheap MP3 player. Did you say 'slew'?" Katie asked.

"No, I said, *'Sloo-ah.'* That's what my soon-to-be husband is."

"And what exactly is a *Sluagh*? Is he the member of some kind of international Mob or something?"

"Good guess. But not exactly." I started pecking at the tiny keys. Eventually I scored a Wiki article. "It's a paranormal creature. Comes from Scottish folklore. 'The *Sluagh* were the spirits of the restless dead,'" I read aloud.

"Uhn, sounds romantic . . . not."

I grimaced. "Believe me, it isn't romantic. Or sexy. I never figured I'd marry a Johnny Depp, but I'd always figured I'd at least end up with a human being, if I married at all."

"Is he a zombie?"

"Kind of. How do I stop this guy?" I skimmed the rest of the article, then clicked back to the search results for something better.

"We've got to find out how to slay a *Sluagh*," Katie joked

as she read over my shoulder. "Wait, if he's already dead, can you even kill him?"

"I don't know. I'm looking." I read through a few more articles, one on Wikipedia, a few on gaming sites. "I'm coming up with a great big nothing." I dropped the palm computer on the bed. "Damn it, what am I going to do?" After indulging in a brief pity party, I muttered a few curses and joined Katie in racewalking a few laps around the room.

Katie stopped. "How about you . . . bargain with him? Offer something else in exchange for your freedom?"

"Great idea, but what would I give him? Hmm. How about another bride?" I gave her a look. "I don't suppose you'd like to volunteer."

"Uh, that would be . . . hell no."

I slung an arm over her shoulder. "I was just playing."

Katie squinted at me. I don't think she believed me.

"So much for that idea." We took another turn around the room, stopping in front of the fancy dressing table positioned under the window. Looked like a genuine antique. A genuine, expensive antique. "Just look at this place, at the dress. . . . I'm guessing Elmer has a shitload of money. I can't bribe him. I'm broke." I checked out a cut-glass perfume bottle, then set it back where I'd found it. "Okay, I can't bribe him. And I can't offer him another bride. What else can I do?"

"I dunno." Katie plopped on the bed. "I've always believed there are only two things that men want—sex and power. Give them one or the other, and they'll be putty in your hands."

"Power? Hmm . . ." I scooped up Katie's palm computer and started Googling again. I needed to figure out exactly why a *Sluagh* would want to marry a girl who was half elf. I had a sneaking suspicion it had to do with both: sex and power.

Hours later, I had a headache from trying to read the tiny font on the computer's three-inch screen. And I was no closer to an answer than I'd been hours ago.

Stiff from sitting for so long, I got up and stretched. Katie was sprawled on the bed, snoring quietly. I checked the clock. It was almost three. In the morning. My eyelids wouldn't stay open anymore, and I couldn't focus my eyes. It was time for sleep.

When I woke up, my stomach was rumbly and I felt gross. I checked the clock. Nine o'clock. I took a quick shower. When I came out of the bathroom, wearing the same clothes as last night, Katie was awake, lounging on the bed, stuffing what looked like a donut into her mouth.

She waved me over, sputtering around a mouthful, "Sugar. Caffeine."

"Excellent." I claimed the last custard-filled pastry before Katie ate it. It disappeared within seconds.

"How'd the research go last night? I'm sorry I didn't stay awake to help. I haven't been sleeping well. I guess I just crashed." Katie sipped from a Styrofoam cup of coffee, grimacing. "Black. Ick. Where's the whipped cream? Chocolate? At least they could've given us a little vanilla-flavored creamer."

"The research went nowhere. I'm thinking he's marrying me to gain some kind of power. Don't know, though, if it's political or magical."

"Huh." Katie licked her fingers. "What are you going to do? Are you going to marry him?"

I shivered. "I can't. I just . . . can't."

Katie scooted over to me. She flung an arm over my shoulder. "I wish I could think of something."

"So do I." I choked down some of the black coffee and gobbled another donut. Then, flying high on a sugar and caffeine rush, I went back to the palm computer.

I had an e-mail. From JT!

The whole team's searching for you. Can you give us anything?

I responded:

Wish I could. Window's boarded. Big house. Newish
construction. I was unconscious when they brought
me in. Didn't see anything. Katie's with me. She didn't
see much either. Have one name, Elmer. That's it. No
last name.

I hit send and waited for his response. Ten minutes later, I
stopped refreshing the screen. I opened a new message and
started typing.

Need to research "Sluagh." Being held by the prince,
who's decided he must marry me. Wedding's tonight.
Time is running out. PS. Please tell my mom. And dad.
Maybe they'll know what to do.

I hit send.
Twenty minutes later, still no response from JT.
I forwarded the second message I'd written to JT to everyone in my contacts list, then went back to Googling. This
time, I looked up the word "clf."
There was lots of information on elves.
I made myself comfy and started reading. Katie took a
shower, then periodically asked me if I'd found anything
good. Each time, I responded with a grunt and a sigh and kept
reading.
Lunch was delivered by the big man from last night. He
lumbered in, set the tray on the bed, and, ignoring my pleas
and questions, plodded out again.
Katie and I ate. I refreshed my e-mail in-box a zillion
times and checked the clock every twenty minutes for the
next few hours. Time was ticking away, and I had no clue how
I was going to get myself out of this mess.
By five o'clock, Katie and I had concluded helping the

prince of the *Sluagh* gain power—regardless of what type—sounded like a bad thing for everyone. We had to stop him, and not just because the idea of being married to him made me throw up.

But how?

By seven o'clock, we'd come up with two options, both of them pathetic. Plan A—I would pretend to be sick and beg for another day. That would buy the PBAU a little more time. Or plan B—if plan A failed, which I was pretty sure it would, I would try to convince my future husband that being married to me would be worse than any hell he'd ever seen.

Not much of a plan, I know. But I'd challenge anyone in my position to do better.

I was ready to put plan A into effect the minute "Lurch," as we'd nicknamed him, trudged into our room with our dinner tray at seven-thirty. I dove into bed the second I heard the door lock rattle. Katie took her position next to me. She grinned as I jerked the covers over myself. I produced what was hopefully a believable moan as the door swung open.

Wasn't it ironic that my future rested upon my pathetic acting skills? Ironic. And very scary.

Lurch shambled to the bed and handed Katie the tray.

"My friend's sick. She needs a doctor," I heard Katie say.

"Huhn," Lurch said, and left.

I threw the covers off and stared at the locked door. "That's it? 'Huhn'? What kind of host is he?"

"I guess we shouldn't have expected better from a man named Lurch." Katie sighed. "Guess we're on to plan B."

"I guess so."

We clapped our hands together and exchanged evil grins, even though I wasn't exactly feeling like smiling.

"Let's see what kind of hell we can stir up," I said. To myself, I added, *This has to work. Or else.*

Nonviolence is the greatest force at the disposal of mankind. It is mightier than the mightiest weapon of destruction devised by the ingenuity of man.

—Mahatma Gandhi

27

It had been ages since Katie and I had teamed up to cause chaos. If I say so myself, we're pretty good at it. That gave me some hope. But only a little.

Our usual victims weren't anything like Elmer, prince of the *Sluagh*. They were snobby, self-important sorority girls who'd gone out of their way to make our lives living hell. They not only deserved what they had coming to them, but they'd been easy targets.

Not so, Elmer.

For one thing, outside of scaring me a little during his nocturnal visits, and kidnapping me to force me to marry him, Elmer hadn't done anything bad to me. He hadn't humiliated me. He hadn't hurt me. He hadn't raped me. Quite the opposite, he'd made sure Katie and I had every comfort of home, including some pretty decent meals and a wedding dress that would probably make the average fashionista green with envy.

The bottom line: my inner "nice girl" wanted to convince him not to marry me, rather than to try to scare him out of it.

Nice Sloan wasn't going to allow me to do anything over-the-top cruel.

That left me with very mixed feelings about plan B.

"What can we do to annoy an *un*dead guy?" Katie asked, standing behind me, in the bathroom. The back lace of my corset was in her fist.

Wearing fresh underwear and a corset, a wedding gift from Elmer, I twirled a strand of hair around the curling iron I held in my hand. "I have no idea. I mean, I know saying the words 'God' and 'Jesus' do something to him. But they don't cripple him. And he seems very determined to go through with this wedding. Even if I were to spend the entire night yelling, 'GodGodGod,' I don't think it would make him miserable enough to run from the altar."

"Hmm. Maybe we're overcomplicating this. Men get cold feet. All kinds of men. What makes one run?" Katie yanked on the lace, and the corset squeezed my chest like an overly friendly boa constrictor, forcing a puff of air out of my lungs.

"Yikes," I muttered. After I managed to reinflate my lungs, I mumbled, "What are you trying to do? Tie that thing so tight, I pass out? Then again, maybe that wouldn't be such a bad idea. He can't marry me if I'm unconscious." I inhaled, exhaled, to shrink my chest, and blurted, "Pull now." The corset jerked tighter, squishing my boobs and compressing my rib cage so I couldn't take a deep breath. I inflated my lungs as best I could. "Holy shit. Thank God, we don't have to wear these things every day. It's no wonder women were fainting all the time." I cooked another strand of hair, then released it. The coil bounced as it unwound from the iron.

Katie gave the lace one last yank, then tied it. "You need to watch an episode or two of *Bridezillas*. It's a show about bitchy brides. I swear, it's a miracle any of them make it to the altar."

"Sounds good, but there's no time, and we don't have a TV. Can you give me the Twitter version?"

"Sure." Katie finger-combed the corkscrews on the back of my head. "It's easy. Be a bitch. About everything. Complain bitterly about the flowers, the dress, the ring, the shoes, the venue, the food, the limo—everything and anything."

I curled another strand, accidentally singeing my earlobe as I unwound it. "Ouch. I guess I can do that." The door to the bedroom swung open. I waved at Katie. "Go, see who that is. I have to pee again."

"Watch and learn." She dove out of the bathroom, swinging the door shut behind her. After I took care of business, I inched it open just a crack, watching from the safety of my tile-and-porcelain cocoon.

"We have some problems, Lurch," Katie said.

I couldn't make out his answer. His voice was very low, and he didn't enunciate clearly.

Katie began her verbal onslaught. "First, the bride hasn't seen the groom since last night. What's up with that? And second, the bride's shoes don't match the dress. *At all.* And the veil is much too short. She has always wanted a long veil. You can't expect her to wear a short veil when she's always dreamed of a long one. This is, after all, the wedding of her dreams. And where are her flowers? How can she get married without seeing her flowers? Plus, she needs to see the menu for the reception. She's lactose intolerant, and gluten sensitive. Plus, she's a vegan. She won't touch anything that has a face or feelings."

I was laughing so hard, I almost peed my pants. And my bladder had been drained dry at least ten times in the past hour.

Katie continued, "And she needs to assign seating for her side of the family. God help us all if you put Grandma Skye next to Aunt Spencer. You don't want to know what happened the last time they were in a room together. Let's just say, the family isn't welcome in certain venues. Plus, nobody's told us where the ceremony is going to be held. What kind of wedding is this?"

I held my breath and listened, but I still couldn't make out Lurch's response. The door to the hall slammed. The door to the bathroom swung all the way open, and Katie stumbled in, holding her stomach, tears streaming down her face.

"Oh, my God, I haven't had that much fun in ages," she said.

"What did he say?"

"He said, 'Huhn,' and left."

"'Huhn,'" I echoed as I gathered my curled hair into a pile on the top of my head. "Lurch is definitely a man of few words. What do you think? Up? Or down?"

"Up. Your dress is too formal to wear it down."

"It is up then." As I fiddled with my hair, I met Katie's gaze in the mirror. "Do you think the *Bridezilla* thing is working?"

"I dunno."

"What time is it?"

Katie poked her head out of the bathroom. "It's almost eight-thirty."

"You know, the only time I've seen Elmer is after dark."

"It'll be dark in a few minutes."

My stomach twisted. "Yeah." I finished putting my hair up, slapped on a little makeup, for my benefit, not my groom's, and headed out to the bedroom. I checked my e-mail first. Finally there was a message from JT! It was short. Clearly, I couldn't count on the cavalry coming to my rescue.

Contacted parents. Father says to keep your head and
delay as long as possible. Time is on your side. Still
unable to locate you by tracing your e-mails. It's slow,
but we're getting there.

Delay as long as possible. Wasn't there anything else I could do?

Katie helped me into the dress. And at eight forty-five, the door to our room opened and my groom strolled in, decked out in head-to-toe black. The well-cut clothes were clearly expensive, but even so, he was still the same ugly, stinky, scary man I knew and *didn't* love. Just goes to show you, expensive clothes don't make the man. The man makes the clothes.

"It's time," he announced, leering at me. He grabbed my arm, hauling me toward the door.

I shuddered. "Wait a minute." I truly felt ill.

He stopped. "What is it *now*?"

"I feel sick."

"Angus told me you were pretending to be ill."

Angus? Who was that? I swallowed a mouthful of bile. "I'm not pretending. And I have to pee. I have this bladder control problem—"

"I don't have time for this. Let's go." He pulled.

I bent over and threw up. Mostly on the floor. A little splattered up the leg of his expensive pants.

He jumped backward, releasing my arm.

I looked at the open door, then at the bathroom. Pee? Or escape? If it wasn't for Katie, it would be a no-brainer. I dove through the door. My bladder could wait. I'd get help and rescue Katie. I hoped she'd forgive me for abandoning her.

Lurch, who I surmised was Angus, caught me before I'd made it to the end of the hall. *Again.*

He lifted me off the floor.

My stomach imploded, and I gagged but didn't throw up. He grumbled something under his breath as he tossed me over his shoulder like a sack of potatoes and hauled me down the stairs. We headed through the first floor of an enormous house, and finally out to a smallish limousine, parked in an attached garage. Of course, the garage door was shut. I was dumped into the back of the vehicle. I flung myself at the door on the opposite side. Before I could scrabble out, Elmer pushed his way inside.

He glared at me and shoved a bucket into my hands.

"Hey, it isn't my fault you didn't listen to me. I warned you." I glanced out the window. It was darkly tinted—so dark, I couldn't make out anything in the garage. Just for kicks, I tried the other door. Locked. It could only be opened from the outside.

"I couldn't risk you diving out of a moving vehicle. That might hurt," he said.

"Isn't that thoughtful? You're worried about my safety." Irritated, I yanked on the door handle a few more times. I can be stubborn sometimes. Nobody's perfect.

"I'm trying. You've got to give me some credit."

My bladder contracted. "I have to go to the bathroom. I'd hate to ruin this dress."

"Go in the bucket."

I looked at the bucket. "Seriously?"

"Yes, seriously. I'm not letting you out of this car. So it's the bucket or your pants."

"You know, I'm a female. It isn't easy for us to pee in a container." He shrugged. I decided I could wait. A little while. "Where's Katie?"

"She'll be riding in a separate car."

"Oh. I was really hoping she'd ride with me."

"No."

"I think I have food poisoning. I'm not feeling good. At all."

"Huhn," he said. Now I knew where Lurch got that charming expression.

The car started rolling. We were on the road.

My heart started banging against my rib cage again. I had a feeling that things were getting awfully bruised in there.

I was going to get sick again. "How about I make you a deal?" I asked, my voice an octave higher than normal. Panic does very ugly things to me.

"What kind of deal?"

"I'll do anything—pay *any* price if you don't marry me."

He thought about it for about ten seconds. "No."

Damn. "That was quick. You didn't really give it much thought. Isn't there anything you want more than me?"

"There is, but it doesn't matter."

"What? Tell me. You'll never know if you don't ask."

He sighed. His expression turned wistful. "Before I became undead, I used to live on the shore. And every night, I would sit on the deck with a beer and a steak and watch the sunset. I would do anything to be able to do that again. *Even marry you.*" His shoulders slumped. "The truth is, I know you weren't playing hard to get. You don't want to marry me, never have. Never will. I was trying to convince myself."

"So that's what this is all about?"

"You have no idea what my life is like. I can't eat. I can't drink. Not even water. And I am only able to materialize between the hours of twilight and midnight. During the rest of the time, I'm stuck in total nothingness. Imagine life without beer, without popcorn, without steak and burgers. It's hell."

"How does this marriage thing come into play?"

"You're elf. Elves are magical creatures. Very powerful. Once we're married, you'll have the power to give me a new body. To make me alive again."

"What if I agreed to do that, anyway?" I offered.

"There's no way you can, not without marrying me."

"Are you sure about that?"

"Positive."

It was my turn to say, "Huhn." I thought the situation through. Was there any way out of this quandary? There had to be. "I'm only half elf. Maybe the magic won't work."

"Maybe," he agreed. "I've considered that possibility."

"Then where will that leave you?"

"Stuck in this hell forever."

That was my out—my only chance. "You know, this sounds like a no-brainer to me. Why would you marry me knowing there is a good chance—"

"A small chance," he corrected.

"Some chance," I said, "that you might be worse off than you were before? You need a full-blooded elf bride."

A month ago, if you'd told me I'd be having this conversation with the prince of the restless undead, I'd have laughed until I'd wet my pants. What a bizarre twist my life had taken.

"I've tried finding a full-blooded elf bride." He slumped back against the seat. "There was one. She was beautiful. Sweet. Kind. She said she loved me. But then she dumped me for a fucking bogle."

"Oh, that is harsh." I had no idea what a "bogle" was. However, I figured playing the sympathy card was working, so I might as well keep at it.

"After Genevieve, I decided love was overrated. Marriage for convenience worked for my father—not so well for my mother, though. But we don't have to talk about her."

All the more reason why I needed to get out of this marriage.

"How about we make a pact?" I suggested.

His eyes, which were already squinty, narrowed to slits. "What kind of pact? I trusted you once, and look where it got me."

The car rolled to a stop. It didn't start moving again. This was it. I'd run out of time. The engine cut off.

"Give me a month to find you a bride. If I fail, I'll marry you." *God help me.*

"You don't understand. If I don't marry you tonight, on the eve of the summer solstice, I'll have to wait a whole year."

"Even better! I am sure I can find you 'Miss Right' in a year. You will marry your soul mate. The elf of your dreams. Not irritating old me. What do you say? Are you willing to wait just one more year for true love?"

He didn't answer right away. I figured I had maybe a fifty-fifty chance of him agreeing to my crazy scheme.

"I'm not saying yes or no yet. But let's just say I do

agree—I'm still going to have Angus keep an eye on you. And your friend."

"Why?"

"Because you are the world's worst FBI agent. I even warned you about the *adze*."

"You . . . did?"

"Sure. I left the note, and when you didn't figure it out, I filled your apartment with fireflies. You didn't even get that hint." He shook his head. "If you don't learn to see what's in front of your eyes, you're going to get hurt. Or worse. As it turns out, I need you alive. At least for now."

"T-that was you?" I stammered.

"Sure. And I gave your friend the name of that doctor—" The car door opened.

And before my brain registered what was happening, the groom was being yanked out by JT and Gabe. I scrambled out of the vehicle just in time to see JT knocking him to the ground and clapping on a pair of handcuffs.

Gabe grabbed me and gave me a shake, and I realized I had been standing there, yelling, not responding to his questions.

"I'm fine," I said, fighting to get away from him. "JT! Wait!"

Holding Elmer on the ground with his knee, JT jerked around. "What's wrong?"

"There's been a misunderstanding."

He looked totally mystified. I would too, if I were him. "Huh?"

"Please let him up. We worked it all out. In the car."

"No." JT stood and dragged his prisoner up to his feet. "This asshole kidnapped you. There's no misunderstanding that."

"JT, please. Can we talk for a moment?" I asked, stepping closer and giving him my sad-puppy eyes.

He gritted his teeth, shoved the prisoner toward Gabe, and

snapped, "Whatever you do, don't let this asshole out of your sight."

"You can trust me." Gabe escorted Elmer toward the police car, which had just pulled up.

JT turned his full focus on me, crossing his arms, which told me he wasn't exactly eager to hear what I was about to tell him. "So what's this all about?"

I decided I needed to embellish the truth, just a little. "Well, it started a long time ago, I guess. Evidently, when I was a little girl, I told him I'd marry him someday. But I didn't exactly remember it." At his bewildered look, I shrugged. "What can I say? I had terrible taste in men back then. Anyway, this is where it gets funny. He didn't realize I'd forgotten. He thought I was playing hard to get. And so he played along, by kidnapping me."

"Uhn."

"Not buying it?" I asked.

He gave me a would-anyone? look.

Determined to clear Elmer, I continued talking. "He bought me a fancy dress. He fed me. He even sent someone over to pick up Katie so she could be my maid of honor. Plus, he tried to help me with our case. And he helped Katie find out what was wrong with her. He's not a bad guy. He never hurt me—well, except for that one time when he bit me. I guess he's into some kinky stuff. Anyway, other than that, he's been a perfect gentleman." At JT's raised-brow, oh-really look, I amended that. "Okay, a *decent* gentleman. Nobody's perfect. But none of that matters anymore. We've come to an agreement. He won't hold me to my promise as long as I can find him a new bride within one year."

JT looked at me. He looked over at Elmer. He looked at me again. "I don't know about this."

"Please trust me. He isn't going to hurt me. Like I said,

he tried to help me. Help *us*. If I'd listened, we might've stopped Rosemarie Bishop before she'd killed Patty Yates."

"Swear to me, you're telling the truth."

"I swear."

JT's expression softened, finally. He lifted one index finger and left me standing there, outside of the parked limo, wondering what was going to happen next.

While JT sorted the matter out with Elmer and the police, Gabe strolled over, looking a little more amused than worried or angry.

"Sloan, I gotta say, with you, there's never a dull moment." Gabe leaned back against the limo. "What's going on?"

"You know, 'same ole, same ole.' Another man's fallen madly in love with me and thinks he can't live another minute without me," I joked.

Gabe's expression darkened. "Poor bastard. You've crushed yet another man's heart."

"'Another man's heart'?" I echoed. "If you mean *yours,* I think you've forgotten. It was the other way around."

Gabe cupped my cheek and his gaze dropped to my mouth. He leaned close, closer, and whispered, "What am I going to have to do to make you see the truth?" Then he let go of me.

Gabe, brokenhearted? Because of me? Nah.

"You were the one who slept with Lisa Flemming," I said, sounding more emotionally invested than I wanted.

"I *never* slept with Lisa Flemming."

"Oh, come on, Gabe. Everyone slept with her. In guy speak, she was drilled more than the Alaskan coastline." When he continued to shake his head no, I added, "You don't have to protect her reputation, Gabe. She was proud of her conquests."

Something flashed in his eyes. "And you believed her? Over me? Think about it, Sloan." He walked away.

Shit, had I been wrong about Gabe all of these years?

In the last few days, I've faced at least a dozen shocking moments. Discovering my dead father was still alive had topped the list—still did. However, learning that I might have broken Gabe's heart came in a close second.

Feeling a little off balance, I opened the limo door and slid into a seat, appreciating the cool comfort.

Katie ran up to the car a minute later, bouncing around like a rabbit. "What's going on?"

"I don't know. JT wants Elmer to go to prison. But I told JT that it was all a misunderstanding. Oh, and Gabe informed me that I'd broken his heart."

"First, I knew about Gabe. Who wouldn't? I mean, really." She literally rolled her eyes at me. "The man has taken every class with you since your freshman year. And he's been following you around like a lost puppy."

"Well, I just thought that was so he could cheat off me. Or annoy me. Or both."

Katie shook her head and heaved an exaggerated sigh. "Sloan, you are the smartest person I've ever met, but when are you going to learn to see what's smack-dab in front of your face?"

That was the third time I'd heard that in the last five minutes. "Soon, I hope."

"I hope so too!" Katie turned, her gaze fixed in the general direction of the group of police cars that had gathered in the corner of the parking lot. She stepped to one side, and I followed her gaze. Elmer was heading for the empty limo, parked about twenty feet away. "Looks like Elmer's been cleared."

"I'm glad." I closed my eyes and let my head fall back. "What a two weeks this has been! In the last seventeen days, I've made three trips to the emergency room, been diagnosed a schizophrenic, had a major infestation of fireflies, took down an *adze,* learned . . . something shocking about my father—"

"What's that?" Katie asked.

Remembering his warning, I told her, "He used to work with the FBI."

"Wow. That is a shock." Katie ducked into the limo, sitting across from me.

"Plus, I was kidnapped. And my mother went missing again. And that's on top of the usual, like her shorting out the electricity in our buildings and being admitted after having a breakdown."

Laughing, Katie said, "Just think, you still have nine and a half more weeks of summer to go."

"I don't know if I'll live through it."

Katie flopped on the seat next to me and flung an arm over my shoulder. "I have a feeling you will."

JT ducked into the limo and took a good, long look at my dress. "Hey, Sloan. Now, that's a nice look for you. Although the jogging outfit was pretty hot too. Ready?"

"For what?" I asked.

Katie scooted toward the exit. "I think I'll just catch a ride with Gabe," she said, giving me a wink.

The car door slammed shut, closing us inside.

Once again, my heart rate went out of control, but for an entirely different reason. I'd just shared a moment with Gabe. We had a history together. And who knew what kind of future? I wasn't all that clear anymore how I felt about him. Now here I was with JT. Alone. In a dark car.

"Ready to go on our date?" JT leaned toward me, cupped my cheeks, gently pressing on my head to angle it. He softly brushed his lips over mine.

I saw stars.

I heard angels.

Then he really kissed me, his mouth not only touching mine, but possessing it. And little tingling zaps of electricity buzzed through my body. I'd been kissed before, and I'd liked it just fine. But I'd never felt anything like that. I felt like the nerve cells from my scalp to my toes were electrified.

JT stopped kissing me, and I sucked in a lungful of air. He grinned, and several parts of my anatomy decided to celebrate. "Now, that was worth waiting for."

I couldn't agree more. So we did it again as the limo drove through quiet streets, heading for destinations unknown.